Ana Huang is an author of primarily steamy New Adult and contemporary romance. Her books contain diverse characters and emotional, sometimes twisty roads toward HEAs (with plenty of banter and spice sprinkled in). Besides reading and writing, Ana loves traveling, is obsessed with hot chocolate, and has multiple relationships with fictional boyfriends.

Also by Ana Huang

TWISTED SERIES

A series of interconnected standalones

Twisted Love
Twisted Games
Twisted Hate
Twisted Lies

IF LOVE SERIES

If We Ever Meet Again (Duet Book 1)
If the Sun Never Sets (Duet Book 2)
If Love Had a Price (Standalone)
If We Were Perfect (Standalone)

STANDALONES

All I've Never Wanted

TWISTED LIES

TWISTED BOOK FOUR

ANA HUANG

PIATKUS

PIATKUS

First published in 2022 by Ana Huang
Published in Great Britain in 2022 by Piatkus
This paperback edition published in 2022

11

Copyright © 2022 by Ana Huang

Editor: Becca Hensley Mysoor, Amy Briggs

The moral right of the author has been asserted

A CIP catalogue record for this book
is available from the British Library.

ISBN 978-0-349-43428-5

Printed and bound in Great Britain by Clays Ltd, Elcograf S.p.A.

Papers used by Piatkus are from well-managed forests
and other responsible sources.

Piatkus
An imprint of
Little, Brown Book Group
Carmelite House
50 Victoria Embankment
London EC4Y 0DZ

An Hachette UK Company

www.hachette.co.uk

www.littlebrown.co.uk

To everyone whose favorite color is morally gray.

Playlist

Tears of Gold (Slowed)
Faouzia
Made to Love
John Legend
God is a Woman
Ariana Grande
Infinity
Jaymes Young
Style
Taylor Swift
Crazy in Love
Sofia Karlberg
Coffee
Miguel
Heat Waves
Glass Animals
I Know You
Skylar Grey
Earned It
The Weeknd
Beautiful
Bazzi
Die for You
The Weeknd
Harleys in Hawaii
Katy Perry
Said I Loved You But I Lied
Michael Bolton

CONTENT NOTES

This story contains a morally gray alpha hero, explicit sexual content, profanity, graphic violence, and topics that may be sensitive to some readers.

For a detailed list, please visit *anahuang.com/twisted-lies-content-warnings*.

1

STELLA

"STELLA!"

My heart rate sped up. Nothing triggered my fight or flight like the sound of Meredith's voice.

"Yes?" I hid my trepidation behind a neutral expression.

"I trust you can bring all the items back to the office yourself." She slipped on her coat and tossed her handbag over her shoulder. "I have a dinner reservation I simply can't miss."

"Of—"

She disappeared out the door.

"Course I can," I finished.

The photographer shot me a sympathetic look, which I answered with a tired shrug. I wasn't the first magazine assistant who'd suffered under a tyrannical boss, and I wouldn't be the last.

Once upon a time, working at a fashion magazine would've been a dream. Now, after four years at *D.C. Style,* the reality of the job had dulled any shine the position once held.

By the time I packed up the photoshoot, dropped the items off at the office, and started my walk home, my forehead was slick with sweat and my muscles were well on their way to becoming Jell-O.

The sun had set half an hour ago, and the streetlights cast a hazy orange glow over the snow-packed sidewalks.

The city was under a blizzard warning, but the bad weather wouldn't kick in until later in the evening. It was also faster for me to walk home than take the Metro, which freaked out whenever there was so much as an inch of snow.

One would think the city would be better prepared considering it snowed every year, but nope. Not D.C.

I shouldn't have been looking at my phone while walking, especially given the weather, but I couldn't help myself.

I pulled up the email I'd received that afternoon and stared at it, waiting for the words to rearrange themselves into something less upsetting, but they never did.

Effective April 1, the cost for a private room at Greenfield Senior Living will increase to $6,500 per month. We apologize in advance for any inconvenience this may cause, but we are confident the changes will result in even higher-quality care for our residents…

The green smoothie I'd downed during lunch sloshed in my stomach.

Inconvenience, they said. Like they weren't hiking the prices of an assisted living facility by more than twenty percent. Like living, breathing, *vulnerable* human beings wouldn't suffer as a result of the new management's greed.

In, one, two, three. Out, one, two, three.

I tried to let the deep breaths wash away my rising anxiety.

Maura had practically raised me. She was the one person who'd always been there for me, even if she didn't know who I was now. I *couldn't* move her to another assisted living facility. Greenfield was the best in the area, and it'd become her home.

None of my friends and family knew I'd been paying for

her care. I didn't want the inevitable questions telling them would raise.

I would just have to find a way to cover the higher costs. Maybe I could take on more partnerships or negotiate higher rates for my blog and Instagram. I had an upcoming dinner with Delamonte in New York, which my manager said was an audition for their brand ambassador position. If I—

"Ms. Alonso."

The deep, rich voice brushed my skin like black velvet and stopped me in my tracks. A shiver chased its wake, born of equal parts pleasure and warning.

I recognized that voice.

I'd heard it only three times in my life, but that was enough. Like the man who owned it, it was unforgettable.

Wariness flickered in my chest before I doused it. I turned my head, my gaze traveling over powerful winter tires and the sleek, distinctive lines of the black McLaren pulled up beside me before it reached the rolled-down passenger window and the owner in question.

My heart slowed a fraction of a beat.

Dark hair. Whiskey eyes. A face so exquisitely chiseled it could've been sculpted by Michelangelo himself.

Christian Harper.

CEO of an elite security company, owner of the Mirage, the building where I lived, and quite possibly the most beautiful, most dangerous man I'd ever met.

I had nothing except instinct to back up the *dangerous* part of my assessment, but my gut had never steered me wrong.

I inhaled a small breath. Released. And smiled.

"Mr. Harper." My polite reply was met with dry amusement.

Apparently, only he was allowed to address people by their last names like we all lived in a giant, stuffy boardroom.

Christian's eyes grazed the snowflakes drifting onto my shoulder before they met mine again.

My heart slowed another fraction of a beat.

Tiny crackles of electricity hummed to life beneath the weight of his gaze, and it took every ounce of willpower not to step back and shake off the strange sensation.

"Gorgeous weather for a walk." His observation was even drier than his stare.

Heat rushed over the back of my neck. "It's not that bad."

It was only then that I noticed the alarming rate at which the snow was thickening. Perhaps the blizzard forecast had been a *little* off on its estimate.

"My apartment is only twenty minutes away," I added to...I didn't know. Prove that I wasn't stupid by trekking through the city in a snowstorm, I guess.

In hindsight, perhaps I should've taken the Metro.

"The blizzard's already rolling in, and there are ice patches all over the sidewalks." Christian rested his forearm on the steering wheel—an action that had no right being as attractive as it was. "I'll give you a ride."

He also lived at the Mirage, so it made sense. In fact, his apartment was only a floor above mine.

Still, I shook my head.

The thought of sitting in a confined space with Christian, even for a few minutes, filled me with a strange sense of panic.

"I'm okay. I'm sure you have better things to do than chauffeur me around, and walking clears my head." The words spilled out in a rush. I didn't ramble often, but when I did, nothing short of a nuclear blast could stop me. "It's good exercise, and I need to test out my new snow boots anyway. This is the first time I've worn them all season." *Stop talking.* "So, as much as I appreciate your offer, I have to politely decline."

I finished my near incoherent mini speech on a note of

breathlessness.

I was getting better at saying no, but I still over-explained myself every time.

"Does that make sense?" I added when Christian remained silent.

An icy gust of wind chose that moment to whip past. It tossed the hood of my coat off my head and burrowed past my layers into my bones, sparking a burst of involuntary shivers.

I'd been sweating bullets in the studio, but now, I was so cold even the memory of warmth was frosted with blue.

"It does." Christian finally spoke, his tone and expression unreadable.

"Good." The word shook through my chattering teeth. "Then I'll let you—"

The soft *click* of a door unlocking interrupted me.

"Get in the car, Stella."

I got in the car.

I told myself it was because the temperature had somehow dropped twenty degrees in the space of five minutes, but I knew that was a lie.

It was the sound of my name, in that voice, delivered with such calm authority my body obeyed before I could protest.

For a man I barely knew, he had more power over me than almost anyone else.

Christian pulled away from the curb and turned a dial on the dashboard. A second later, heat blasted from the vents and warmed my frigid skin.

The car smelled like rich leather and expensive spices, and it was eerily clean. No wrappers, no half-empty coffee cups, not even a speck of lint.

I sank deeper into my seat and glanced at the man next to me.

"You always get your way, don't you?" I asked lightly, trying to dissolve the inexplicable tension blanketing the air.

He slid a brief glance in my direction before refocusing on the road. "Not always."

Instead of dissolving, the tension thickened and slipped into my veins. Hot and restless, like an ember waiting for a breath of oxygen to fan it to life.

Mission failed.

I turned my head and stared out the windshield, too thrown off by the day's events to attempt more conversation.

The nerves scaling their way up my chest and into my throat didn't help.

I was supposed to be the cool, calm one, the one who saw the silver lining in every cloud and remained levelheaded no matter the situation. That was the image I'd projected most of my life because that was what was expected of me as an Alonso.

An Alonso didn't suffer from anxiety attacks or spend their nights worrying about every little thing that could go wrong the next day.

An Alonso didn't seek therapy or air their dirty laundry to a stranger.

An Alonso was supposed to be perfect.

I twisted my necklace around my finger until it cut off the circulation.

My parents would probably *love* Christian. On paper, he was as perfect as they came.

Rich. Good-looking. Well-mannered.

I resented it almost as much as I resented the way he dominated the space around us, his presence pouring into every nook and crevice until it was the only thing I could concentrate on.

I fixed my eyes on the road ahead, but my lungs were filled with the scent of his cologne and my skin thrummed with awareness at the way his muscles flexed with each turn of the wheel.

I shouldn't have gotten in the car.

Besides the warmth, the only upside was that I would get home to my shower and bed sooner. I couldn't wait—

"The plants are doing well."

The statement was thrown out so casually and unexpectedly it took me several seconds to realize that 1) someone had broken the silence, and 2) that someone was, in fact, Christian and not a figment of my imagination.

"Excuse me?"

"The plants in my apartment." He stopped at a red light. "They're doing well."

What did that...*oh.*

Comprehension dawned, followed by a tiny flicker of pride.

"I'm glad." I gave him a tentative smile now that the conversation was in safe, neutral territory. "They just need a little love and attention to thrive."

"And water."

I blinked at his obvious, deadpan statement. "And water."

The words hung between us for a moment before a laugh broke free from my throat and Christian's mouth curved into the tiniest of smiles.

The air finally lightened, and the knot in my chest loosened a smidge.

When the light turned green, the powerful rumble of the engine nearly drowned out his next words. "You have a magic touch."

My cheeks warmed, but I responded with a small shrug. "I like plants."

"Perfect person for the job, then."

His plants had been on life support when I took over their care in exchange for keeping my current rent.

After my friend and ex-roommate Jules moved out last month to live with her boyfriend, my options were either get another roommate or move out of the Mirage, since I couldn't afford to cover both portions of our rent. I'd grown attached to the Mirage, but I would rather downgrade my home than live with a stranger. My anxiety couldn't handle that.

Christian had already lowered the monthly rent for us when we first toured the apartment and mentioned the regular price was out of our budget, so I'd been shocked when he'd proposed our current arrangement after I brought up the possibility of moving out.

It was a little suspicious, but he was friends with my other friend, Bridget's husband which made accepting his offer easier. I'd been taking care of his plants for five weeks and nothing terrible had happened. I never even saw him when I went upstairs. I just let myself in, watered the plants, and left.

"How did you know I could do it?" He could've proposed any number of tasks—run his errands, do his laundry, clean his house (though he already had a full-time housekeeper). The plant thing was oddly specific.

"I didn't." Disinterest and a thread of something imperceptible twined through his voice. "It was a lucky coincidence."

"You don't seem like someone who believes in coincidence."

Christian's lack of sentimentality bled through in everything he did and wore—the sharp lines of his suit, the calm precision of his words, the cool detachment of his gaze.

They were the traits of someone who worshipped logic, power, and cold, hard pragmatism. Not something as nebulous as coincidence.

For some reason, Christian found that funny. "I believe in it more than you think."

Intrigue kindled at his self-deprecating tone.

Despite having access to his apartment, I knew maddeningly little about him. His penthouse was a study in flawless design and luxury, but it contained little to no personal effects.

"Care to share?" I tried.

Christian pulled into the Mirage's private garage and parked in his reserved spot near the back entrance.

No answer.

Then again, I hadn't expected one.

Christian Harper was a man cloaked in rumors and shadows. Even Bridget didn't know much about him, only his reputation.

We didn't speak again as we passed through the entrance and into the lobby.

At six foot three, Christian had a good five inches on me, but I was still tall enough to match his long strides.

Our steps fell into perfect sync against the marble floors.

I'd always been a bit self-conscious about my height, but Christian's powerful presence wrapped around like me a security blanket, drawing attention away from my Amazonian frame.

"No more walking in a blizzard, Ms. Alonso." We stopped by the bank of elevators and faced each other. His shadow of a smile returned, all lazy charm and confidence. "I can't have one of my tenants dying of hypothermia. It would be bad for business."

Another unexpected laugh rustled my throat. "I'm sure you'll find someone to replace me in no time."

I wasn't sure whether I owed my slight breathlessness to the cold lingering in my lungs or the full impact of standing so close to him.

I wasn't interested in Christian romantically. I wasn't interested in *anyone* romantically; between the magazine and my blog, I didn't have time to even think about dating.

But that didn't mean I was immune to his presence.

Something flared bright in those whiskey eyes before it cooled. "Likely not."

The mild breathlessness transformed into something heavier that strangled my voice.

Every sentence out of his mouth was a code I couldn't crack, imbued with a hidden meaning only he was privy to while I was left to scramble in the dark.

I'd talked to Christian three times in my life: once when I signed my lease, once in passing at Bridget's wedding, and once when we discussed my sans-Jules rent situation.

All three times, I'd left more unsettled than before.

What were we talking about again?

It'd been less than a minute since Christian's response, but that minute had stretched so slow it might as well have been an eternity.

"Christian."

A deep, slightly accented voice slashed the thread holding our suspended moment aloft.

Time snapped back to its usual cadence, and my breath expelled in one sharp rush before I turned my head.

Tall. Dark hair. Olive skin.

The newcomer wasn't as classically good-looking as Christian, but he filled out the lines of his Delamonte suit with so much raw masculinity it was difficult to look away.

"I hope I'm not interrupting." Delamonte Suit flicked a glance in my direction.

I'd never been super attracted to older men, and he had to be in his mid to late thirties, but *wow*.

"Not at all. You're right on time." A hint of irritation hardened Christian's otherwise smooth reply. He stepped in front of me, blocking me from Delamonte Suit's view and vice versa.

The other man raised an eyebrow before his mask of indifference fell away to reveal a smirk.

He stepped around Christian, so deliberately it was almost like he was taunting him, and held out his hand. "Dante Russo."

"Stella Alonso."

I expected him to shake my hand, but to my surprise, he raised it and brushed his mouth across my knuckles instead.

Coming from anyone else, it would've been cheesy, but a tingle of pleasure erupted instead.

Maybe it was the accent. I had a weakness for all things Italian.

"Dante." Beneath the calm surface of Christian's voice lay a razored edge that was sharp enough to cut through bone. "We're late for our meeting."

Dante appeared unfazed. His hand lingered on mine for an extra second before he released it.

"It was lovely to meet you, Stella. I'm sure I'll see you around again." His rich drawl contained a hint of laughter.

I suspected his amusement was directed not at me but toward the man watching us with ice in his eyes.

"Thank you. It was nice meeting you too." I almost smiled at Dante, but something told me that wouldn't be a smart move right now. "Have a good night."

I glanced at Christian. "Good night, Mr. Harper. Thank you for the ride."

I injected a playful lilt into my voice, hoping the callback to our absurd formality earlier would crack his granite expression.

But it didn't so much as flicker as he inclined his head. "Good night, Ms. Alonso."

Okay, then.

I left Christian and Dante in the lobby, the subjects of more than a few admiring stares from passersby, and took the elevator up to my apartment.

I didn't know what had caused Christian's sudden mood shift, but I had enough worries of my own without adding his to the mix.

I rifled through the bag, trying to locate my keys among the jumble of makeup, receipts, and hair ties.

I really needed a better way of organizing my bag.

After several minutes of searching, my hand closed around the metal key.

I'd just inserted it into the lock when a familiar chill swept over my skin and raised the hairs on the back of my neck.

My head jerked up.

There was no other sign of life in the hall, but the quiet hum of the heating system suddenly took on an ominous tone.

Memories of typed notes and candid photos turned my breaths shallow before I blinked them away.

Stop being paranoid.

I wasn't living in an old, unsecured house near campus anymore. I was at the Mirage, one of the most well-guarded residential buildings in D.C., and I hadn't heard from *him* in two years.

The chances of him showing up here, of all places, were slim to none.

Nevertheless, urgency broke the spell freezing my limbs in place. I quickly unlocked the front door and shut it behind me. The lights blazed on as I slid the deadbolt in place.

It was only after I checked every room in my apartment and confirmed there was no intruder lurking in my closet or underneath my bed that I was able to relax.

Everything was fine. *He* wasn't back, and I was safe.

But despite my self-reassurance, a small part of me couldn't shake the sense that my gut had been right and that someone *had* been watching me in the hall.

2

CHRISTIAN

The library door shut with a quiet click behind me.

I crossed the room, my steps slow and deliberate, until I reached the sitting area where Dante had made himself comfortable with a glass of scotch.

A muscle pulsed in my jaw.

If we didn't have such a long history together, and if I didn't owe him for the favor he did me, his head would already be shattered on the bar cart near him.

Not only for helping himself to my liquor, but for his less than amusing show in the lobby.

I didn't like people touching what was mine.

"Lighten that scowl, Harper." Dante took a lazy sip of his drink. "Otherwise, it'll freeze that way, and women won't like your face as much anymore."

My cold smile told him how little I cared. "Perhaps if you took your own advice, you wouldn't be sleeping in a different room than your fiancée."

Satisfaction filled my chest at his narrowed eyes. If Stella was my weakness, Vivian was his.

I wasn't interested in the ins and outs of their relationship, but it amused me to see him snarl every time I brought up the fiancée he claimed to hate.

I thought I had problems. Dante had two billion dollars worth of them.

"Point taken," he said in a clipped voice. All humor vanished, bringing back the unsmiling asshole I was used to dealing with. "But I didn't come here to discuss Vivian or Stella, so let's get to the real issue at hand. When the *fuck* can I get rid of the painting? The thing's an eyesore."

I forced thoughts of dark curls and green eyes aside at the mention of the other enigmatic woman in my life.

Magda, the painting that had been the bane of my existence for decades. Not because of what it was but because of what it represented.

"No one told you to hang it in your gallery." I walked to the bar and poured myself a drink. Dante, that bastard, hadn't recapped the bottle of my finest scotch. "You can shove it in the back of your closet for all I care."

"I pay all that money for *Magda* only to shove it in the back of my closet? That wouldn't be suspicious at all." Sarcasm weighed heavy on his voice.

"You have a problem; I provided a solution." I gave a careless shrug. "Not my fault you don't want to take it. And for the record..." I settled on the seat opposite his. "*I* paid for the painting."

Secretly, anyway. As far as the public knew, Dante Russo was the proud owner of one of the ugliest pieces of artwork in existence. Then again, people also thought said hideous piece was a priceless painting worth killing and stealing over thanks to a simple set of forged documents.

I hadn't wanted people going after it, but I'd needed an excuse for why I'd spent so many resources guarding it.

It didn't contain earth-shattering business secrets like everyone thought. But it *had* contained something personal that I'd never share.

He examined me over the top of his glass. "Why do you still care so much about it? You got what you needed from it, and you found your traitor. Just burn the damn thing. *After* I sell it back to you," he added. "For appearances' sake."

"I have my reasons."

One, to be exact, but he wouldn't believe me if I told him.

I couldn't bear to destroy the painting. It was too embedded in the jagged pieces of my past.

I wasn't a sentimental person, but there were two areas of my life where my usual pragmatism didn't apply: Stella and *Magda*.

Unfortunately for Axel, the ex-employee who'd stolen *Magda* and pawned it off to Sentinel, my biggest fucking competitor, he hadn't fallen into the exceptions category.

He'd thought the painting contained highly classified, and therefore highly lucrative, business secrets because that was what I told the few people I'd entrusted to guard it.

Little had they known the painting's value stemmed from something far more personal and far less useful to them.

I'd dispatched of Axel, waited an appropriate length of time for Sentinel to relax, then fucked with their cyber system enough that it'd wiped millions off their value. Not enough to destroy them, since something of that magnitude could be traced back to me, but enough to send a message.

The idiots running Sentinel were so dense they tried to steal the painting *back* after they sold it because they thought they could use it as retaliation against me.

They hadn't found any business secrets in *Magda*, but they knew it was important to me. They were on the right track; I'd give them that. But they should've hired someone other than a second-rate Ohio gang member to do the job.

Sentinel's attempt to cover up their tracks was so shoddy it was almost insulting.

Now the painting was in Dante's care, which served a double purpose: I didn't have to look at it, and no one, not even Sentinel, would dare try and steal from him.

The last person who'd tried ended up in a three-month coma with two missing fingers, a mangled face, and crushed ribs.

Dante made an impatient noise, but he was smart enough not to press further.

"Fine, but I'm not keeping it forever. It's ruining my reputation as a collector," he grumbled.

"Everyone thinks it's a rare piece of eighteenth-century art. You're fine," I said dryly.

In reality, the painting had existed for less than two decades.

It was amazing how easy it was to forge "priceless" art and documentation attesting to its authenticity.

"I'll go blind from looking at that monstrosity every day." Dante rubbed a thumb across his bottom lip. "Speaking of monstrosities, Madigan was officially booted from Valhalla this morning."

The atmosphere shifted with the weight of the new topic.

"Good riddance."

I had no love lost for the oil tycoon currently being sued by half a dozen ex-employees for sexual harassment and assault.

Madigan had always been a slimeball. This was just the first time he'd been held accountable.

The Valhalla Club prided itself on its exclusive, invite-only memberships for the world's wealthiest and most powerful. A good number of those members, including myself, engaged in less than legal activities.

But even the club had its limits, and it certainly didn't want to get dragged into the media circus surrounding Madigan's trial.

I was only surprised they hadn't exiled him earlier.

Dante and I discussed the trial and business for a while until he excused himself to take a call.

As the CEO of the Russo Group, a luxury goods conglomerate that encompassed over three dozen fashion, beauty, and lifestyle brands, he spent half his waking hours on business calls.

In the absence of conversation, my mind drifted toward a certain brunette.

If my thoughts were chaos, she was my anchor.

They always went back to her.

The memory of her walking down the snow-covered street, her hair tossed wild by the wind and her eyes shining like jade, lingered in my brain. The warmth of her, like a ray of sunshine peeking out after a storm, lingered everywhere else.

I shouldn't have lowered her rent when she came to see the building, and I damn well shouldn't have let her *keep* the rent after Jules moved out. In exchange for taking care of my fucking plants, no less, because a selfless concession on my part would've been too suspicious.

I didn't give a shit about those plants. They were only there because my interior designer insisted they "rounded out the apartment." But I knew Stella loved plants, and it was better than asking her to file my papers.

Living in the same building as her was the worst kind of distraction, and I had no one except myself to blame.

Twin flames of resentment and frustration burned in my chest. I was weak for Stella Alonso, and I hated it.

I pulled out my phone and almost tapped into a certain social media app before I caught myself. I entered the code for my encrypted mobile network instead.

It wasn't as powerful as the one that resided on my laptop, but it got the job done in a pinch.

My frustration needed an outlet, and today, John Madigan was the lucky target. I couldn't think of anyone more deserving.

I pulled up a list of his devices. Phones, computers, even his smart fridge and Bluetooth-enabled alarm clock, plus all their associated accounts.

It took me less than five minutes to find what I was looking for—a video he'd stupidly taken of himself forcing a blowjob on his assistant, and a series of disgusting messages he sent one of his golf buddies after the fact.

I forwarded those to the prosecution using the golf buddy's email. If they were halfway decent at their job, they could convince the judge it was admissible evidence.

The messages also went to key media outlets, because why not?

Then, just because Madigan's face annoyed me, I swapped his most valuable stocks for junk ones and donated a significant chunk of his cash to anti-sexual violence organizations.

Tension released from my muscles with each tap of a button.

Cyber sabotage was better than a deep tissue massage.

I pocketed my phone right as Dante reentered the library.

"I have to go back to New York." He grabbed his jacket from the back of the couch, his face stamped with irritation. "There's a...personal matter I need to deal with."

"Sorry to hear that," I said mildly. "I'll walk you out."

I waited until he was halfway out the door before I added, "The personal matter wouldn't happen to be Vivian's ex-boyfriend showing up at your house, would it?"

Surprise coasted through his eyes, followed by fury. "What the fuck did you do, Harper?"

"I merely facilitated a reunion between your fiancée and an old friend." One little text from "Vivian," and the ex came running. Pathetic, yet useful. "Since you enjoyed fucking with me so much, I figured I'd return the favor. Oh, and Dante?" I paused with my hand on the knob. Dante's anger was a pulsing force in the hall, but he'd get over it. He should've known better than to put on that little show in the lobby. "Touch Stella again, and you'll no longer *have* a fiancée."

I slammed the door in his face.

Dante was my first client and an old friend. I didn't provoke him often.

But like I said, I didn't like people touching what was mine.

I straightened my shirtsleeves and returned to the library, where my gaze traveled the length of the room until it rested on the giant framed puzzle hanging over the fireplace mantel.

Ten thousand tiny pieces formed a breathtaking rainbow gradient whose lines created a three-dimensional spherical effect.

It had taken me four months to complete it, but it'd been worth it.

Crosswords, jigsaws, ciphers, they all fed my insatiable need for a challenge. Stimulation. *Something* to brighten up the ennui of a world that was always five steps behind.

The harder the puzzle, the more I craved and dreaded its solution.

There was only one puzzle I hadn't solved. Yet.

I ran my thumb over the small turquoise ring nestled in my pocket.

Once I did, I could put my disturbing obsession with Stella Alonso behind me once and for all.

3

STELLA

FEBRUARY 25

It's been three days since I learned Greenfield is raising its prices, and I still haven't come up with a good solution.

I've been searching for another job, but my biggest hope right now is the Delamonte dinner coming up. Brady is convinced it's an audition for their brand ambassador position and that the deal will be in the mid-six figures...IF I get it.

I don't think I've ever wanted a deal as badly as I do this one. Not only would it solve my Greenfield problem—at least for the next calendar year—but Delamonte is a brand I've wanted to work with forever. They're the first designer brand I ever bought for myself.

Okay, it was a perfume that I bought in high school, but still. I loved that perfume, and I would honestly give up every other partnership I have to work with them.

I just wish I knew what they were looking for so I can plan

*accordingly. I don't even know how many other bloggers will be
at the dinner or who they invited.*

I guess I'll find out when I get there.

In the meantime...wish me luck. I'll need it.

DAILY GRATITUDE:

1. *Croissants*
2. *DC-NYC trains*
3. *Brady (don't tell him I said this though, or he'll
   never stop bragging)*

———

MY TRIP TO NEW YORK WAS A SERIES OF DISASTERS.

I took a train up that Saturday, and when I arrived at the
townhouse where the Delamonte dinner was being held, I
knew Brady was right. It was an audition.

Besides Delamonte staff, the only people in attendance
were bloggers.

But even though there were six of us at the dinner, Luisa
spent the entire cocktail hour gushing over Raya and Adam, the
latest darlings of the influencer world and the only couple
present.

I could barely get a word in edgewise between her excitement over Raya hitting the one point four *million* follower
mark last week and the pair's upcoming trip to Paris.

The one time I tried to interject by asking a question about
the brand's new line, Luisa answered with a three-word
response before turning back to Raya.

If my parents were here, they would disown me out of

sheer disappointment for not living up to the Alonso name and capturing everyone's attention at the event.

That was disaster number one.

Disaster number two entered after everyone had been seated and appetizers were served.

"Sorry I'm late." The lazy drawl sent shock fluttering to life in my chest. "Traffic."

No. There's no way.

I had a better chance of getting hit by a meteorite than I did running into Christian Harper twice in the same week outside the Mirage. In *New York,* no less.

But when I looked up, there he was.

Chiseled cheekbones and whiskey eyes, sin and danger all wrapped up in a flawless suit.

My food turned to ash on my tongue. Of all the people I didn't want to witness me crash and burn, he ranked at the top of the list.

Not because I thought he'd judge me, but because I was afraid he *wouldn't.* A near-stranger who treated me better than those who were supposed to love me unconditionally.

I wouldn't be able to bear it.

Luisa stood and greeted him with an effusive hug, but I couldn't hear much of her introduction over the roar of blood in my ears.

"...CEO of Harper Security...old friend..."

Christian's expression remained polite, almost disinterested, while Luisa talked, but there was nothing disinterested about the way his eyes held mine.

Dark and knowing, like they could strip away every mask I showed the world and find the broken pieces of the girl hiding underneath.

Like they thought the brokenness was beautiful anyway.

Unease burned through me, and I severed the connection with a blink.

He couldn't have been thinking any of those things.

He didn't even know me.

Luisa finished what had to be the longest introduction in the history of introductions, but it was only after Christian started walking toward me that I realized there was only one empty seat at the table.

It was next to mine.

Luisa had mentioned it was reserved for another guest. I hadn't known it would be *him*.

"Stella." The deep, smooth timbre of his voice sent a warm shiver down my spine. "This is a pleasant surprise."

I tightened and released the hold on my fork in tandem with my exhales.

"Christian." I couldn't very well call him Mr. Harper when he used my first name.

It was my first time saying his given name, and the syllables lingered longer on my tongue than expected. Not unpleasant, but far too intimate for my liking.

I resisted the urge to shift in my seat while he stared down at me, his face relaxed but his eyes like hot molten amber as they moved from the top of my head to the dip of my dress.

The scrutiny lasted less than five seconds, yet a trail of fire erupted in its wake.

Cool, calm, collected.

"I didn't realize you were..." I searched for the right term. "Affiliated with Delamonte."

That wasn't the right term, but I didn't know how else to word it. Everyone at the table was a fashion blogger or a member of the Delamonte team. Christian was noticeably neither of those things.

"I'm not," he said wryly.

"Secret fashion blogger, then?" I widened my eyes and made my voice intentionally breathless with surprise. "Don't tell me. Your blog is called...Suits and Whiskey. No? Guns and Roses. Wait, that's a band." I tapped my finger against the table. "Ties and—"

"If you're done..." I didn't think it was possible, but Christian's voice turned even drier. "Switch seats with me."

My tapping stopped. "Why?"

He had a prime seat next to Luisa, who was too busy talking to—who else—Raya on her other side to notice Christian hadn't taken his seat yet.

"I dislike the corner of the table."

My stare was one of disbelief. "What do you do if it's a four-seater?" Then *every* seat would be at the corner of the table.

Impatience greeted my question.

I sighed and switched seats with him. We were starting to attract attention from the rest of the table, and I didn't want to make a scene.

I was nervous Luisa would be upset I took her special guest's seat, but as the night wore on, Christian's weird quirk turned out to be quite advantageous for me.

I now had direct access to Luisa, who didn't seem upset at all and who finally turned to me after Raya excused herself to use the restroom.

"Thank you for coming up to New York. I know it's a bigger ask of you than the other girls." Luisa's cocktail ring glittered beneath the lights as she sipped her drink.

"Of course." Like *anyone* would turn down an invite to a private Delamonte dinner. "I wouldn't have missed it for the world."

"I'm curious why you don't move to the city. There are more opportunities here than in D.C. if you want to get into fashion." She sounded equal parts curious and disapproving, like I was intentionally being obtuse by not seeking greener grass elsewhere.

A cotton ball formed in my throat at the indirect reminder of Maura and what was at stake.

"I want to be close to family." Maura was like family, so I wasn't *completely* lying. "But I'm considering a move soon."

Also not lying. I *was* considering a move. I just knew it couldn't happen anytime soon.

"By the way, congratulations on a wonderful Fashion Week." I switched subjects to something more relevant. I wasn't here to talk about my personal life; I was here to land a deal. "I especially loved the pastel dusters."

Luisa lit up at the mention of the brand's latest fall/winter collection, and soon, we were deep in conversation about the trends we'd spotted at last week's New York Fashion Week.

I couldn't attend in person because of work—only senior editors at *D.C. Style,* like Meredith, were budgeted to attend NYFW—but I'd caught up on my anticipated shows online.

When Raya returned from the bathroom, her face soured at the sight of me and Luisa chatting animatedly.

I tried my best to ignore her.

Once upon a time, Raya and I had been friends. She'd started her account two years ago and reached out to me for advice. I'd been happy to share what I knew, but after she surpassed me in followers a few months ago, she'd stopped answering my messages. The only contact we had these days was the occasional hello at an event.

Her meteoric rise could be traced directly to her relationship with Adam, who was a big influencer himself in the travel space. When they started dating last year, their content went viral and both their accounts exploded.

There was nothing like cross-promotion and feeding the public's voyeuristic desire to follow the love lives of strangers.

Meanwhile, I'd been blogging for almost a decade, and my account had been stuck at just shy of nine hundred thousand followers for over a year. It was still a huge audience, and I was grateful for each and every one of them (except the bots and creepy men who treated Instagram like it was a hookup app), but I couldn't deny the truth.

My social media was stagnating, and I had no clue how to revive it.

I faltered and lost my train of thought in the middle of a sentence.

Raya swooped into the lull like a vulture after prey. "Luisa, I'd love to hear about Delamonte's fabric archive in Milan," she said, pulling the CEO's attention back to her. "Adam and I are visiting Italy this spring, and..."

Frustration bit at my veins as Raya successfully hijacked the conversation.

I opened my mouth to interrupt them. I could *see* myself doing it in my head, but in real life, the words couldn't make it past the filter of my upbringing and lifelong social anxiety.

Disaster number three.

To anyone else, Raya's interruption wouldn't rise to the level of a disaster, but my brain couldn't always untangle the difference between a setback and a catastrophe.

"You did well."

My heart skipped a beat at Christian's voice before it returned to its normal rhythm. "With?"

"Luisa." He tilted his head toward the other woman. I hadn't realized he'd been paying attention to our conversation; he'd been conversing with the guest on his other side the entire time. "She likes you."

I gave him a doubtful stare. "We talked for five minutes."

"It only takes one to make an impression."

"One minute isn't enough to get to know someone."

"I didn't say get to know someone." Christian brought his wine to his lips, his words relaxed yet perceptive. "I said make an impression."

"What impression did I make on you?"

The question sparked and hissed like a live wire between us, swallowing enough oxygen to make every breath a struggle.

Christian set his glass down with a precision that pulsed in my veins. "Don't ask questions you don't want the answer to."

Surprise tinged with hurt bloomed in my chest. "That bad?"

From what I remembered, our first meeting had been fairly standard. I'd said a total of two words to him.

"No." The word was a rough caress against my skin. "That good."

Warmth suffused my skin.

"Oh." I swallowed the breathless note in my voice. "Well, in case you were wondering, my first impression of you was that you were very well-dressed."

That'd been my second impression. My first impression had actually been that *face*. So perfectly chiseled and symmetrical it should be stamped inside textbooks as a prime example of the golden ratio.

But I wouldn't admit that even if Christian put a gun to my head.

If I did, he might think I was flirting with him, and that would open a can of worms I didn't want to deal with.

"Good to know." His dry tone returned.

The servers brought out dessert, which he declined with a shake of his head.

I took a bite of layered chocolate cake before I asked, as casually as I could, "How do you know Luisa likes me?"

"I know."

If this was the way Christian conducted all his conversations, I was surprised no one had tried to stab him in a boardroom yet. Or maybe they'd tried and failed.

"That doesn't answer my question."

"Lu, are you coming down to D.C. anytime soon?" he asked, ignoring my pointed response and cutting into Luisa's conversation with Raya like the other blogger wasn't even there.

"No plans yet." Luisa gave him a curious stare. "Why?"

"Stella was telling me about this spot that would be perfect for your menswear shoot."

I almost choked on a mouthful of cake.

"Really?" Luisa eyed me with renewed interest. "That would be perfect timing. Our location scout has been having the hardest time finding a spot that's on theme and not overdone. Where is it?"

"It's..." I scrambled to come up with an answer while silently cursing Christian for putting me on the spot like this.

What place in D.C. makes sense for a menswear shoot?

"You said it was an old warehouse somewhere," Christian prompted.

Clarity dawned in an instant.

There was an old industrial building on the fringes of the city that I've shot at a few times. It was a bustling factory until the 1980s, when the owner moved his headquarters to Philadelphia. In the absence of new owners, the building fell into disrepair and became overgrown with weeds and ivy.

It was a trek to get there, but the contrast of green against old steel provided a striking backdrop for photoshoots, especially luxury ones.

How does Christian know about that?

"Right." I released a small breath and smiled at Luisa. "It

doesn't have an actual address, but I'm happy to show you or a team member how to get there if that's something you're interested in."

She tapped her nails against the table in thought. "It's very possible. Do you have sample photos?"

I pulled up some of my old photos and showed them to Luisa, whose eyebrows popped up with approval.

"Oh, those are *gorgeous*. Can you send them to me? I have to show them to our scout..."

My heart skipped when Luisa gave me her cell number so I could text her the link, but when I looked up, the thrill evaporated at the sight of Raya and Adam whispering furiously to each other while casting side glances in my direction.

Anxiety buzzed beneath my skin like a swarm of bees.

Those whispers brought me back to my middle school days when everyone giggled and talked behind their hands when I walked into a room. I'd hit my growth spurt early, and at age thirteen, I'd been tall, skinny, and awkward enough to be an easy target for bullies.

I've since grown into my own skin, but the anxiety had never gone away.

"Why don't you let us in on your joke?" Christian's casual request masked a dark undertone that wiped the smiles off Raya's and Adam's faces. "It must be a good one."

"We were talking about something personal." Raya rolled her eyes, but her expression contained a hint of nerves.

"I see. Next time, refrain from doing so at a public event. It's disrespectful." The content of Christian's rebuke was mild, but he delivered it with such vicious contempt Raya's face flushed crimson.

Instead of defending his girlfriend, Adam stared down at his plate, his own face pale.

The exchange had been so short and held in such low tones

the rest of the table was oblivious. Even Luisa didn't notice; she was too busy texting someone (probably her location scout).

"Thank you," I said quietly, wishing I was bold enough to call out Raya myself.

"They were annoying me," was Christian's detached answer.

Nevertheless, warmth settled in my stomach and stayed with me through the rest of dinner and the end-of-night goodbyes.

By the time I exited the townhouse half an hour later, I felt marginally better about my ambassadorship chances, but it was far from a sure thing. I was still convinced Luisa favored Raya, no matter what Christian said.

Speaking of whom...

I slid a side glance at him as he fell into step with me. I was staying at a boutique hotel not far from Luisa's place, but I doubted Christian was staying there as well. He probably had a place in the city; at the very least, he'd stay somewhere like The Carlyle or The Four Seasons, not an eight-room hotel with no designer amenities.

"Are you following me?" I asked lightly as we turned the corner onto a side street.

Christian's presence dominated the sidewalk, soaking into the shadows and rendering the air around us invincible. So quiet and lethal even the darkness didn't dare touch him.

"Merely making sure you return to your hotel safe and sound," he drawled.

"First the car ride the other day, now this. Do you always provide your tenants with such hands-on service?"

A smoky gleam passed through those whiskey eyes and sent heat rushing to my cheeks, but Christian refrained from making the obvious joke.

"No." Short and simple, delivered with the self-assurance of someone who never had to explain himself.

We walked in silence for another minute before he said, "To answer your earlier question, I know she likes you because I know Luisa. It sounds counterintuitive, but whenever she's impressed with someone, she puts them on the back burner. She's more interested in grilling those she's not sure about."

I was already so used to his abrupt topic changes I didn't skip a beat.

"Maybe." I'll believe it when I see it, a.k.a. get the deal. "How do you know her so well?"

Luisa was twenty years older than Christian, but that didn't mean anything. Older women slept with younger men every day. It would explain the way she lit up when she saw him.

A tiny frown creased my forehead for a reason I couldn't name.

"I'm friends with her nephew. And no, I never slept with her." A hint of laughter threaded through his voice.

My cheeks blazed hotter, but thankfully, my voice came out cool and even. "Thank you for the information, but I'm not interested in your love life," I said with a regal tilt of my chin.

"Never said anything about love, Ms. Alonso."

"Fine, I'm not interested in your *sex* life."

"Hmm. That's a shame." The hint of laughter intensified.

If he was trying to get a rise out of me, he wouldn't succeed.

"Only for you," I said sweetly.

We stopped in front of my hotel. The light from the windows slashed across Christian's face, casting half of it in shadow. Light and dark.

Two halves of the same coin.

"One more thing." My breaths formed tiny white puffs in the air. "Why did you show up at dinner tonight?"

It wasn't to catch up with Luisa; he'd barely spoken to her all night.

A shadow passed through his eyes before it sank beneath the cool amber surface. "I wanted to see someone."

The words soaked into the pocket of air separating us. I hadn't realized how close we'd gotten until now.

Leather, spice, and winter. That was all that existed before Christian stepped back and tipped his head toward the hotel entrance. A clear dismissal.

I opened my mouth then closed it before I brushed past him.

It wasn't until I reached the revolving glass doors that my curiosity overpowered my hesitance.

I turned, half expecting to see Christian already gone, but he remained at the base of the stairs. Dark hair, dark coat, and a face that was somehow even more devastating when partially cloaked in shadow.

"Who did you want to see?"

It was so cold my lungs burned, but still I waited for his answer.

Something amused and dangerous surfaced in his eyes before he turned away. "Good night, Stella."

The words drifted into my ears after the night had already swallowed him whole.

I exhaled a rough breath and shook off the pinpricks of electricity dotting my skin.

However, thoughts of Christian, Luisa, and even Delamonte vanished when I entered my room, checked my phone, and disaster number four struck.

I'd kept my cell in my purse the entire night because I didn't want to be *that* person texting at the dinner table. Luisa had been doing it, but she was the host; she could do whatever she wanted.

Now, I realized my attempt at appearing professional might have backfired, because my screen was littered with missed calls and texts from Meredith. The last one was from twenty minutes ago.

Oh God.

What was wrong? How long had she been trying to reach me?

A dozen possibilities raced through my head as I called her back, my heart in my throat and my palms clammy with sweat.

Maybe the office was on fire, or I'd forgotten to send the Prada bag back to—

"Stella. How nice to finally hear from you." Her frosty greeting slithered down my spine like the cool skin of a reptile.

"I'm so sorry. I put my phone on silent and just saw—"

"I know where you were at. I saw you in the background of Raya's Instagram Stories."

Despite her contempt for bloggers, Meredith followed their social media religiously. Something about competition and staying on top of trends.

I seemed to be the only one who saw the irony in that.

I swallowed hard. "Is something wrong? How can I help?"

Never mind that it was near midnight on a Saturday night. Work-life balance didn't exist for junior magazine employees.

"There was an issue with next week's photoshoot, but we figured it out while you were partying," Meredith said coolly. "We'll discuss this on Monday. Be in my office at seven-thirty a.m. sharp."

The line went dead, as did any hope she would let the night's transgression slide.

I had a sinking feeling that come eight o'clock on Monday morning, I would no longer have a job.

4

STELLA

"You're fired."

Two words. Three syllables. I'd mentally prepared myself for them since Saturday night's fiasco, but they still hit me like a punch in the gut.

Breathe. In, one, two, three. Out, one, two, three.

It didn't work. Oxygen couldn't bypass the knot in my throat, and tiny pinpricks of black swam across my vision as I stared at Meredith's seated figure.

She sipped her coffee and paged through the latest *Women's Wear Daily* like she hadn't reduced my life to rubble in the space of ten seconds.

"Meredith, if I—"

"Don't." She raised a manicured hand, her expression bored. "I already know what you're going to say, and it won't change my mind. I've been watching you and your lack of enthusiasm for a while, Stella, and Saturday night was the last straw."

The coppery taste of blood filled my mouth from how hard I bit my tongue.

Lack of enthusiasm? *Lack of enthusiasm?*

I was the first person in and the last person out of the office. I did eighty percent of the work on shoots for a fraction of the credit. I never complained even when she threw the most outrageous requests at me, like getting Chanel to ship a limited-edition couture gown to us from *Paris* with less than twenty-four hours' notice.

If that was a lack of enthusiasm, I shuddered to think what she considered an appropriate level of dedication.

"Yes, I noticed," Meredith said, mistaking my silence for agreement. "I admit, you have a good eye for style, but so do a thousand other girls who would kill to be in your position. You clearly don't want to be here. I see it in your eyes every time I talk to you. Honestly, we shouldn't have hired you in the first place. Your blog generates enough traffic to be considered a competitor, and our contract forbids our employees from engaging in competitive business practices. The only reason we didn't fire you earlier was because your side job didn't interfere with your work."

Meredith took another sip of coffee. "On Saturday night, it did. You'll receive an email and official termination paperwork by the end of the day."

Panic squeezed my lungs at the prospect of losing my job, but I also detected a kernel of something else.

Anger.

Meredith could make all the excuses she wanted, but we both know she'd been dying to fire me for years. She was part of the old guard who didn't like the changes bloggers were bringing to the industry, and she took out her resentment on me.

Maybe if you treated your employees better, I'd be more enthusiastic. Maybe if you weren't so insecure, you'd see how my blog could help the magazine, not hurt it. On that note, you should check out the skin tone guide I posted last week because the color of your top does nothing for your complexion.

The uncharacteristic slew of insults rushed to the tip of my tongue, but I swallowed them before they spilled out and got me blacklisted in the industry.

All I wanted was to work in fashion and be close to Maura. That was why I'd stayed in the city and got a job at *D.C. Style* despite my parents' insistence that I find a job "more befitting an Alonso."

I gave up a lot of things for other people, but my dream wouldn't be one of them...unless it was out of my hands, and I got fired.

"I understand." I forced a smile that matched the vise wrapped around my chest in tightness.

"Have your things cleared out by this afternoon," Meredith added without looking up from her computer. "There are boxes waiting for you at your desk."

Humiliation washed over my skin as I exited her office and walked to my desk. Everyone knew I'd been fired. Some of them shot me pitying glances; others didn't hide their smirks.

But none of their reactions compared to what my family's would be once I told them what happened. They already disapproved of me "wasting" my Thayer University degree on a fashion career. If they found out I'd been fired...

My hands shook before I caught myself and steadied them. I refused to give my coworkers the joy of seeing me sweat as I picked up my boxes and swept out of the office with as much dignity as I could muster.

*Everything will be fine. Everything **is** fine.*

My Uber ride home was a blur. I couldn't stop picturing my parents' faces when they find out what happened. The disappointment, judgment, and, worse, the silent *I told you so's* that would undoubtedly make up half our conversation.

I told you working at a fashion magazine isn't sustainable.

I told you to stop spending so much time on your blog. It's a hobby, not a job.

I told you to do something more meaningful with your degree. Become an environmental lawyer like your mom, or at least work for a respectable newspaper.

And that was only one consequence of my firing.

I hadn't even thought about the impact on my finances or my ability to find another job.

Pressure ballooned in my chest, but I managed to make it back to my apartment before I collapsed.

The cardboard boxes containing my office desk items landed next to me with a thud as I sank onto the living room floor and closed my eyes.

Everything is fine.

Everything is fine.

Everything is fine.

The silent mantra succeeded in calming my shallow breaths.

It wasn't the end of the world. People got fired every day, and I still had money coming in from my blog and brand collaborations.

Plus, I could sell some of my wardrobe for extra cash. The money I'd receive from that would be pitiful, even for designer items, but it was better than nothing.

Worst came to worst, I could agree to some high-paying partnerships I'd turned down in the past.

I refused to collaborate with brands whose products I didn't genuinely love, which drove Brady nuts because I was so picky about the clothes I wore and the products I used. It significantly hindered my earning potential, but I would rather earn less and be genuine than shill something I didn't believe in for a quick check.

Of course, that'd been when I had a full-time salary to supplement my side business.

Everything is fine.

Everything is fine.

Everything is—

The familiar sound of my ringtone dragged me out of my thoughts before I slipped too far down my spiral.

I forced my eyes open and checked the screen.

Brady.

I was tempted to let it go to voicemail, but maybe he had an update on one of my pending collaborations. I would agree to anything paid right now.

Well, almost anything.

"Hello?" My voice came out scratchy and hoarse, but at least I wasn't crying.

"How'd it go?" A car honked in the background, nearly drowning out Brady's voice. "You ignored all my calls! Give me the deets, ASAP."

A migraine blossomed behind my temple. "How did what go?"

"*Delamonte.*" The *duh* was implied. "A little birdie confirmed the dinner *was* an audition, so tell me. Do they love you or do they love you?"

The reminder of Delamonte did nothing to improve my mood. "They love me. Just not as much as Raya."

No matter what Christian said, I was convinced the Delamonte deal was a lost cause. If I couldn't keep my job at a small-market magazine, how could I be the ambassador for one of the world's leading fashion brands?

It technically wasn't a direct correlation, but in my shock-numbed, panicked mind it was.

A short pause followed my statement before Brady exploded. "Are you shitting me? Did you see the boots Raya wore in her latest post? Talk about tacky. That's not Delamonte's style at all. *You* are Delamonte! Your aesthetic is so fucking perfect for them, it's like they...it's like they created you in their super-secret lab. Or something."

"Yes, well, Raya has more followers than me, *and* she has Adam. It's like a two-in-one deal."

I hated wallowing in self-pity, but once I got started, I couldn't stop.

I'd been trying to reach a million followers for *years*, and Raya got it done in less than two posting about her new boyfriend and using the tips *I* gave her.

I didn't mind sharing what I knew. Life, for the most part, wasn't a competition. But I would be lying if I said that knowledge didn't sting a bit.

"She's only growing so fast because of Adam and vice versa," Brady grumbled. "I hate to say it, but influencer couples are what's hot right now. You rarely see individual influencers skyrocket like that. People love following other people's love lives. It's sick."

I mustered a dry laugh. "Too bad I'm not part of a couple."

D.C.'s dating pool was, for lack of a better word, dismal.

Then again, I no longer had a job taking up my time, so there was that.

I'd tell Brady about *D.C. Style* after I had time to process it myself. Talking about it would make it real, and I could use a little fantasy right now.

He was so quiet I thought the line cut off because Brady was *never* quiet. A quick check told me that wasn't the case. I was about to prompt him again when he finally spoke.

"No, but you *could* be..." he said slowly.

My migraine intensified. "What are you talking about?"

"I'm talking about you getting a boyfriend. Think about it." His voice pitched higher with excitement. "Your followers have *never* seen you date someone. You don't date, right? Imagine if you did. They'd go *crazy!* And look at all the couple content that's going viral. People eat that shit up. You'll be at a million followers in no time! If you hit that milestone, Delamonte will notice. Rumor has it they won't make a final decision for another few weeks. Trust me. They already love you—I *know* they do. You just gotta give them a little extra push."

My jaw unhinged.

"Are you joking? I'm not going to string someone along and date them just so I can get more followers and a brand campaign!"

"Then be honest. Tell them the truth up front. Find a *fake* boyfriend. Someone who'll also have something to gain from this."

"Another influencer?" I winced at the prospect.

Not that it mattered because there was *no way* I would do what Brady was suggesting. The idea that I had to get a boyfriend to be deemed "interesting" made my skin crawl.

We'd progressed from the days when women couldn't go anywhere or do anything without their husband's approval, but the sad truth was, our value was still tied to our ability to "land" a partner, at least in society's eyes.

The number of times people asked me *why* I didn't have a boyfriend yet was proof of that. Like my being single was a problem I needed to solve instead of a choice I'd made. Like my lack of a partner somehow meant *I* was lacking somehow.

I didn't have anything against dating. I was happy for my friends who'd found their One, and I'd be open to a relationship if I met the right person.

But I was pretty sure the right person wouldn't result from a ruse to get more social media followers and further my career.

"Maybe another influencer," Brady said thoughtfully. "Or

someone who'll benefit from having a beautiful woman on their arm."

My stomach turned.

"You make it sound so sleazy. No way." I shook my head. "I don't have the time or energy for a real *or* fake relationship."

"Stella, I'm telling you this as your friend *and* manager." His voice was sterner than I'd ever heard it. "You want the Delamonte deal? You want a million followers? You want to show Raya and all the girls out there dying to see you fail that you still have what it takes to stay on top? Then get a boyfriend."

Brady's words ran through my mind long after I hung up.

It was the twenty-first century. I shouldn't *have* to date someone to stay relevant.

But as much as I hated to admit it, he was right. There was a reason celebrities always magically entered relationships before a big album drop or movie premiere, and why unmarried politicians rarely won campaigns.

I rubbed my temple.

The idea of a fake boyfriend seemed absurd, but was it *that* absurd?

If movie stars could "date" someone for publicity, so could I. That I wasn't a celebrity was irrelevant; the principle was the same.

I can't believe I'm considering this.

I pulled up my Instagram and stared at the number at the top of my profile.

899K. I'd been stuck there for over a year, and it reminded me of where I was going in life—nowhere. Same city, same routine day in and day out.

The lure of a million followers and what it represented dangled in front of me like a sparkling diamond.

Validation. Opportunity. Success.

If I just reach and stretch...

The 899K stared back at me, taunting me.

I knew better than to derive value from my follower count, but that number impacted my income and livelihood.

Maybe it was ego.

Maybe I wanted to prove to everyone, including myself, that the blood, sweat, and tears I'd poured into growing the account hadn't been in vain.

Or maybe Brady was right, and I needed to shake things up.

Whatever it was, it compelled me enough to exit out of the app and into my contacts list.

I stared at the list of names, my eyes instinctively homing in on the male ones.

I can't believe I'm considering this.

But I had no job and nothing to lose...except my integrity.

Unfortunately, integrity didn't pay the bills, and it wasn't like I was murdering or stealing. It would just be a little white lie to sell the show that was my online presence.

My teeth dug into my bottom lip.

Then, before I could second guess myself, I called the first name that looked good.

"Hey Trent, it's Stella. I know, it's been a long time, but I have a question for you..."

5

STELLA

I'D OVERESTIMATED THE NUMBER OF STRAIGHT, SINGLE men in my life.

After vetting my contacts, I found three who could potentially fulfill the role of my fake boyfriend, and after two disastrous test dates, that number had dwindled to one.

My first date kept trying to sell me on crypto while the second asked me for a bathroom blowjob in between the entree and dessert.

By the time my third date rolled around, my optimism had dwindled into a dying ember, but I clung to that flickering flame like it was my last hope.

Which it was.

No one knew when Delamonte would make their decision, but it had to be soon. I had a limited time to find a fake boyfriend, throw some couple photos up, and pray it would drag my account out of its slump. When it came to landing competitive brand deals, every little bit helped.

It wasn't the world's best or most well-thought-out plan, but it was *a* plan. No matter how ludicrous it was, it made me feel like I was taking control of my life, and that knowledge—that I wasn't completely helpless and still had the power to shape my future—was the only thing keeping me afloat at the moment.

"Third time's the charm." The words rang with equal parts hope, weariness, and a touch of self-loathing.

I'd thrown myself into the Boyfriend Plan, as Brady called it, because I had no choice, but a part of me flinched every time I thought about what a successful plan would entail.

Deception. Lying. Pretending to be someone I wasn't.

I'd cultivated close relationships with my followers over the years. Some of them had been with me since I was a college freshman posting grainy photos of my campus looks online.

The thought of betraying that trust made my stomach turn.

However, I couldn't let Maura down. And, if I was being honest, I *really* wanted a million followers.

It was the big milestone. The door that would open a thousand more opportunities and prove that I wasn't the disappointment my parents thought I was.

My friends thought I had the perfect family, and I'd never told them the truth because it seemed like such a trivial problem. Judgmental families were a dime a dozen.

But that didn't mean it didn't sting.

My parents didn't always voice it, but I saw the disappointment in their eyes every time they looked at me.

I took a deep breath, smoothed a hand over the front of my dress, and checked my reflection in the hallway mirror one last time.

Hair twisted into an elegant knot, earrings that added a touch of glamour, and lipstick that brightened my winter-dulled skin.

Perfect.

I took the elevator downstairs and spent the ride checking

my emails for Delamonte updates or responses from the dozen jobs I'd applied to over the past week.

Nothing.

No news was good news, right? Maybe not for the jobs, but at least for Delamonte.

Until I received an email or a press release announcing their next brand ambassador from them, I wouldn't dwell on negativity. I didn't want to accidentally manifest losing out on the campaign.

The elevator doors pinged open. I stepped out and ran a thumb over the crystals dangling from my necklace. Rose quartz for luck in love, citrine for general good vibrations.

Here's hoping they work.

"Hi, Stella!" The eager voice pulled my attention to the front desk, where the concierge beamed at me, all shiny teeth and puppy dog eyes from behind the marble counter.

I released my necklace and smiled back. "Hi, Lance. Stuck on the graveyard shift again?"

"That's what happens when you're the youngest member on the team." He heaved an exaggerated sigh before examining me. "You're all dressed up tonight. Hot date?"

Part of me briefly entertained the idea of asking *him* to be my fake boyfriend before I dismissed it. That would be too messy for a multitude of reasons, the least of which was the fact he worked in my building.

"Hopefully." I gave a playful spin, my metallic skirt flaring around my knees. I'd paired it with a fitted black sweater and boots for an elegant but simple first date look. "How do I look?"

"You look beautiful." There was a wistful note in his voice. "You always—"

He didn't get a chance to finish before I slammed into a

brick wall. I stumbled and I instinctively reached up to steady myself.

Soft wool and masculine heat touched my fingers.

Not a wall, my dazed mind noted.

My eyes traveled up past the peaked lapels of a black suit, the open collar of a crisp white shirt, and the tanned column of a strong, masculine throat before they rested on a beautifully carved face, shadowed with disapproval.

"Ms. Alonso." Christian's cool voice sent goosebumps skittering across my skin. There was no trace of the semi-playful dinner partner from New York. "Distracting my staff from their job again?"

Again? I'd never distracted anyone from anything, except maybe the time Lance helped me carry a package to the elevators and the resident behind me in line had to wait an extra two minutes.

I removed my hand from Christian's chest. His heat seared so deep I felt it in my bones even when I stepped back and upped the wattage of my smile.

Calm, cool, collected.

"I was making conversation. I wanted Lance's opinion on something, but since you're here, I might as well ask you." I spun again. "What do you think? Is this outfit date-worthy?"

I didn't even complete my first spin before Christian's hand closed around my arm.

When I looked up, the shadow of disapproval had morphed into something darker. More dangerous.

Then I blinked and the darkness was gone, replaced by his usual polite impassiveness.

Somehow, that unsettled me even more.

"You're going on a date."

Christian had a talent for turning every question into...well, not a question.

"Yes." An uncharacteristic burst of mischief bloomed inside me. "That's where you take someone out for dinner, drinks, maybe some hand-holding. It might sound like a foreign concept, but you should try it sometime, Mr. Harper. It'll do you some good."

Maybe it would loosen him up a little.

For all his charm and wealth, he was wound tighter than the spring of his Audemars Piguet watch. It was evident in the precision of his walk, the set of his shoulders, and the unnatural flawlessness of his appearance.

Not a hair out of place, not a speck of lint on his clothes.

Christian Harper was a man who thrived on controlling everything, including his feelings.

He stared down at me, his jaw so tense I could practically hear his teeth grind. "I don't hold hands."

"Fine, no hand-holding. Cuddling then, on a bench over-looking the river, followed by some whispered sweet nothings and a goodnight kiss. Doesn't that sound nice?"

I swallowed a laugh at the way his lip curled. Judging by his expression, my suggestion sounded as nice as being thrown into a vat of bubbling acid.

"You don't usually date."

My amusement faded, replaced with a pinprick of annoyance. "You don't know that. I could've gone on a hundred dates since I moved in and you wouldn't have known."

"Have you?"

Dammit. I couldn't lie, not even when every cell in my body urged me to wipe the knowing look from his eyes.

"That's not the point," I said. "Maybe it hasn't been a hundred, but it's been a few."

Two, and they were test dates that reminded me why I hated dating. But he didn't need to know that.

"And where is your date tonight?"

It was an innocent question, but intuition told me to keep the exact location to myself. "A bar."

"How specific."

"How none of your business." I gave him a pointed stare.

Christian's smile didn't soften the smooth, bladed edge of his voice. "Have fun on your date, Stella."

The conversation was over, which was just as well. I was already running late.

But as I left for my date, I couldn't focus on the man I was about to see.

I was too busy thinking about whiskey eyes and black suits.

HALF AN HOUR LATER, I WISHED I'D STAYED IN THE LOBBY with Christian because my date was going as well as expected, which was to say, not at all.

Klaus was one of the few male fashion bloggers who lived in D.C., and I'd liked him well enough the few times we chatted at events.

Unfortunately, those chats had been too short for me to realize what became obvious after an extended conversation.

Klaus was a massive, raging douchebag.

"I told them I don't work for free. I understand it's a charity, but I am a *luxury* blogger." Klaus adjusted his secondhand Rolex. "What part of me screams *free posts for cancer awareness?* Of course, it's a great cause," he added hastily. "But it takes time for me to shoot and post, you know? I even gave them a ten percent discount off my usual fee, but they said no."

"There's a reason it's called charity." I finished my drink. Two glasses of wine in twenty minutes. A record for me, and a testament to how much I *didn't* want to be here. But Klaus was my last hope, and I gave him more leeway than usual. Maybe he meant well but couldn't express it in the right manner. "They can't afford to pay thousands of dollars for every post."

"I didn't ask them to pay for every post. I asked them to pay *me*."

Dear Lord, give me strength.

"I did that campaign for free. It took me less than an hour, and I didn't die," I pointed out.

I had a soft spot for charities, and I accepted almost all of those collaborations if the organization was legit. Brady hated it, mainly because they were always unpaid, and he earned nothing from those deals.

Klaus laughed. "Yes, well, that's the difference between men and women, isn't it?"

My spine stiffened. "What's that supposed to mean?"

"It means most men ask for what they're worth and most women don't." Klaus's casual shrug made my eye twitch. "It's not an insult, merely an observation. But someone's gotta make less money, right?"

My fingers tightened around the stem of my wineglass.

I suddenly wished it weren't empty. I'd never been more tempted to throw a drink in someone's face.

He wasn't *wrong* about the whole *ask for what they're worth* thing, but his tone was so condescending it overshadowed everything else. Plus, he'd nickel and dimed a cancer charity, of all things.

"Klaus." My even voice betrayed none of the anger simmering in my blood. "Thank you for the drinks, but we've reached the end of our date."

He stopped fiddling with a stray lock of hair to stare at me. "Excuse me?"

"We're not compatible, and I don't want to waste either of our times."

I would also rather stab my eye out with a Christian

Louboutin heel than spend another minute with you, I added silently.

Klaus's face flushed an angry, mottled red.

"Whatever." He stood and yanked his coat off the back of his chair. "I only stayed out of pity, anyway. You're nowhere *near* as hot as everyone says you are."

Says the guy who buys followers and uses a fake account to comment how hot he is under his own posts. The retort tingled on the tip of my tongue until my aversion to confrontation squashed it.

If I had a penny for every comeback I kept to myself, I wouldn't *need* the Delamonte deal. I would already be a millionaire.

I waited until Klaus stormed out in a cloud of overpowering cologne and indignation before I groaned and buried my face in my hands.

Now that Klaus was off the table, I officially had zero prospects for a decent fake boyfriend.

No fake boyfriend, no follower growth, no Delamonte deal, no money, no care for Maura...

My thoughts ran together in a jumbled stream.

Was there another way to grow my account besides getting a fake boyfriend? Maybe.

Would growing my account fast enough guarantee I get the Delamonte deal? No.

But once my brain latched onto an idea, trying to pry it off was like trying to crack a vault with a toothpick. Plus, with no job and no bites on my resume, I was getting desperate.

The boyfriend idea might've made me uneasy, but it'd also offered a glimmer of hope. Now, that glimmer had dulled into an ugly, tarnished brown.

I drained my water, hoping it would alleviate the dryness in my throat. All it did was send me into a small coughing fit when it went down the wrong pipe.

"I assume the whispered sweet nothings and goodnight kiss are off the table."

My skin grew hot at the familiar drawl behind me.

Cool, calm, collected.

I waited for my lungs to fill with air before I responded.

"Once is a coincidence, twice is a pattern." I turned my head. "What's three times, Mr. Harper?"

First, the car ride home. Second, the Delamonte dinner. I didn't count our lobby run-in earlier that night since we lived in the same building, but overall, I'd bumped into Christian a suspicious number of times over the past two weeks.

"Fate." He slid onto the stool next to mine and nodded at the bartender, who greeted him with a deferential nod of his own and returned less than a minute later with a glass of rich amber liquid. "Or that D.C. is a small city and we have overlapping social circles."

"You might be able to convince me you believe in coincidence, but you'll never convince me you believe in fate."

It was a notion for romantics and dreamers. Christian was neither.

Romantics didn't look at someone like they wanted to devour them until there was nothing left except ashes and ecstasy. Darkness and submission.

Something hot and unfamiliar coiled in my stomach before the bells above the front door jangled and broke the spell.

"How long have you been here?" I hadn't noticed his arrival.

"Long enough to see you eyeing those cocktail picks with longing while your date was talking."

"It wasn't a bad date. He just had to leave early for...an

emergency." It was a blatant lie, but I didn't want to admit it'd failed. Not to Christian.

"Yes, it looked positively scintillating." His voice was drier than a gin martini. "I could tell by the way your eyes glazed over and strayed to your phone every five seconds. The true signs of a woman infatuated."

Annoyance squeezed my lungs.

Between Klaus and Christian, the nunnery was looking better by the second.

"People say sarcasm is the lowest form of wit."

"But it's the highest form of intelligence." Christian's mouth tugged up at my raised eyebrows. "Oscar Wilde. I know the *full* quote well."

Why was I not surprised?

"Don't let me keep you," I said pointedly. "I'm sure you have better things to do with your Friday night than drink with the girl who takes care of your plants."

"I'll leave after you explain why you looked so unhappy after he left." Christian settled onto his stool, the picture of relaxed elegance, but his eyes were sharp as he waited for my response. "Somehow, I doubt you were disappointed by his exit."

I rubbed my thumb over the condensation on my water glass, debating how much to tell him.

"I needed his help with something." Shame crept into my chest.

"With what?" He was a cobra in a king's suit, with no patience in sight.

Just say it. "I need a fake boyfriend."

There. I said it and didn't die, though embarrassment warmed my neck.

But to his credit, Christian didn't laugh or chastise me. "Explain."

Alcohol and desperation had loosened my tongue, so I did. I explained everything—Maura, Delamonte, *D.C. Style*. I even told him I got fired.

A part of me worried he'd evict me since I no longer had a steady income, but I couldn't stop the words from pouring out.

The pressure inside me had found a temporary release valve, and I was taking full advantage.

Although my friends knew I'd been fired, they didn't know I was paying for Maura's care. No one did except for the Greenfield staff...and now, Christian.

For some reason, telling him felt natural, almost easy. Perhaps because it was easier to share secrets with someone who didn't know me well and, therefore, would hold less judgment.

When I finished, Christian stared at me with a long, assessing gaze.

The silence stretched so long I worried I'd broken him with the sheer absurdity of my idea.

I tucked a loose curl that had fallen out of my updo behind my ear. "I know it sounds ridiculous, but it could work. Potentially?" Doubt turned my statement into a question.

"It doesn't sound ridiculous." Christian set his now-empty glass down. The bartender reappeared in a flash and refilled it. After a weighted glance from Christian, he topped off my drink as well. "In fact, I have a mutually beneficial proposal."

"I'm not interested in sleeping with you."

I was desperate, but I wasn't *that* desperate. It was one thing to get a fake boyfriend. It was another to sleep with someone for money, even if that *someone* was rich and gorgeous.

Annoyance passed through Christian's eyes. "That's not my proposal," he said, his voice edged with irritation. "You need money, and I need a...companion who can accompany me to functions. They're a necessary and, unfortunately, frequent part of my business."

"So you want arm candy." Something akin to disappointment settled in my stomach. "I'm sure you could find a date with a snap of your fingers. You don't need me for that."

Even now, all the women in the bar were staring at Christian with dazed, dreamy expressions.

"Not just a date, Stella. I want someone who I can have an actual conversation with. Who puts people at ease and who can work a room with me. Someone who doesn't want more after the date is over."

I tapped my fingers on the table. "And if I do that..."

Christian smiled. "Let's make a deal, Ms. Alonso. You agree to be my companion when needed, and I'll pay for the entirety of Maura's care."

My tapping stopped.

Pay for the entirety of Maura's care?

My first instinct was an enthusiastic, resounding *yes*. Not having to worry about Greenfield's bills would take a load off my shoulders.

But the exhilaration lasted only a minute before warning bells clanged between my ears.

If something sounded too good to be true, it probably was.

"Thank you, but I can't." The words were painful to say, but they were for the best. "Paying all of Maura's fees...it's too much."

Was it stupid of me to turn down his payment offer when I so desperately needed it? Maybe. Especially when I knew paying for her care wouldn't put a dent in his wallet? Probably.

If he were anyone else, I might've accepted, considering my circumstances. But between the initial lowered rent and our laughable deal for even *lower* rent after Jules moved out—

taking care of his plants did not equate to the thousands of dollars he let slide every month—I already owed him too much.

And my gut told me that when it came to men like Christian Harper, the less one owed them, the better.

Because eventually, the payment would come due, and it would cost more than all the money in the world.

Christian took the refusal in stride. "I understand. Then let's amend the deal. If you act as my companion, I'll act as your boyfriend."

My heart leapt. Now *that* was a more balanced arrangement.

Still, I shouldn't.

It was wild and absurd and utterly ridiculous if I thought too hard about it, but...*Christian Harper* as my (fake) boyfriend. If that didn't explode my follower count, nothing would.

"With a stipulation, of course," he added.

Of course.

"What stipulation?"

"You are not, under any circumstances, to show my face on social media."

My excitement fizzled faster than a firework in water. "That defeats the whole purpose of what I'm trying to do."

Christian's face could sell out stadiums and theaters. Not showing it off online would be a monumental waste.

"Based on what you told me, it's the perceived relationship that matters, not who the other person is." He tapped a finger on my phone. "Social media is a form of voyeurism, and couples are more interesting than individuals. It's the unfortunate truth. But people also love a little mystery. You can show my hand, my back, any part of me except my face. It won't diminish what you're trying to do. It might even help."

"But..." *Your face is so pretty.* "People will know it's you if we attend events together, so what's the point of not showing your face?"

"I have no problem with people knowing we're together." The smoothness of his words wrapped around me like a silken scarf. "However, I keep the details of my personal life private and my digital footprint as clean as possible."

I shouldn't be surprised. Christian was a cybersecurity expert, so his aversion to social media and sharing data online made sense.

Still, I found it hard to believe anyone in this day and age could keep *all* photos of themselves off the internet.

"Huh." It was too late for me. My digital footprint was so large it could qualify for its own zip code. "Can't relate."

A smile flickered over his mouth. "Do we have a deal, then?"

"As long as you agree to my conditions as well." This time, I was the one who smiled at his flash of surprise. "You didn't think you were the only one who got to make the rules, did you?"

"Of course not." Lazy amusement surfaced in his eyes. "What are your terms?"

I ticked them off on my fingers. The bartender was serving customers at the other end of the bar and no one was sitting near us, so I wasn't worried about eavesdroppers.

"One, we engage in physical contact only when necessary. Handholding is okay. Kissing is permitted on a case-by-case status. No sex." I peeked at Christian to see if that would be a dealbreaker. His expression remained impassive, so I continued.

"Two, we continue the arrangement as long as it's beneficial to *both* of us. If either of us wants to end it for whatever reason, we give the other two weeks' notice. And finally..." I took a deep breath. "We remember what this is. A *fake* relationship. That means no catching feelings and no falling in love with each other."

I didn't think Christian would fall in love with me, and I doubted I would fall in love with him, but it was good to set the right expectations. It kept things from getting ugly down the road.

A soft laugh rumbled from his throat. "I accept those terms. I'll draw up the contract tonight."

"A written contract seems like overkill."

"I never make a deal without one." He raised an eyebrow. "Is that a dealbreaker?"

Part of me wasn't comfortable with a formal contract for something so fluid, but another part agreed it was the smart thing to do. It would lay out the ground rules in clear terms and protect both of us.

Just in case.

"No. A contract is fine."

"Good. And don't worry, Ms. Alonso." Laughter remained in Christian's voice as he lifted his glass to his lips. "I don't believe in love."

6

STELLA

MARCH 13

I think I signed a deal with the devil.

Okay, that sounds a little dramatic, but you get the idea. Christian has been ~~super~~ nice and helpful since we met, but he didn't get to where he is today by being all warm and fuzzy.

It's been four days since we signed (I still can't believe he made me sign a formal agreement, but I guess that's why he's a CEO). And every time I think about our first couple post, I feel a little sick.

I'd come to terms with having to lie to my followers, but my friends and family will see the post too. Well, not my parents, but Natalia will see it and she'll tell Mom and Dad. And I'll have to explain the sudden appearance of a boyfriend to my friends, who KNOW I don't want a boyfriend. They're going to flip out, especially Jules. She hates not being in on all the gossip.

Then there's the matter of hiding Christian's face when I make our official post. Maybe I can put an emoji over it. It's so cheesy it could be funny...

. . .

CHRISTIAN EMOJI IDEAS:

1. *Devil (for obvious reasons)*
2. *Neutral face (basically his expression 80% of the time)*
3. *Heart face (makes sense if he's supposed to be my boyfriend, but might be too cutesy?)*

"I'M SO HAPPY WE CAN CATCH UP." JULES SIGHED AND popped a fry in her mouth. "I feel so out of the loop since I got back."

Jules and her boyfriend Josh went on a weeklong trip to New Zealand a few weeks ago, and this was my first time seeing her since she returned. Between her demanding schedule as an attorney and Ava's constant travels as a photographer for *World Geographic* magazine, it was hard for all of us to be at the same place at the same time.

We still scheduled at least one meetup every month, though, even if it had to be virtual. At least then, Bridget, who lived in Europe, could join.

Adult friendships took *work* and conscious effort to maintain, but the ones that stayed were the ones that mattered most.

That was why it was so hard to lie to Jules, Ava, and Bridget. They knew I'd been fired, but they didn't know about Christian.

At the same time, I didn't want to burden them with too many of my problems, and the longer I kept things from them, the less I wanted to explain why I hadn't said something in the first place.

The fish tacos I ate for lunch churned in my stomach.

"You haven't missed anything big." Ava brushed a strand of

hair out of her eye. "My life is just work and wedding stuff until October."

Despite her casual words, her face glowed with excitement.

Her boyfriend Alex proposed last summer, and they were planning a fall wedding in Vermont. Knowing Alex, it would be the most lavish wedding the state had ever seen. He'd already hired the top wedding planner in the country to coordinate an army of florists, caterers, photographers, videographers, and whoever else was involved in the nuptials.

"Hmm." Jules sounded disappointed that there wasn't juicier news waiting for her. "What about you, Stel? Any chance you hooked up with a celebrity at an event? Won a million dollars? Got offered a trip to Bora Bora in exchange for pictures of your feet again?"

My laugh came out strained. "Sorry to disappoint, but no."

Though I did get a fake boyfriend.

The words were on the tip of my tongue, but I swallowed them along with the rest of my water.

I needed more time to process my situation before I discussed it with anyone else.

"Oh." Jules pouted. "Well, the year's still young. And oh my God, speaking of celebrities..." Her eyes lit up again. "You won't *believe* who we saw at the airport on our way back to D.C. *Nate Reynolds!* He was with his wife..."

I relaxed into my seat as she rambled on about her favorite movie star. That was a safer topic than anything about my life.

The remnants of shame prickled my skin, but I consoled myself with the fact that I wouldn't lie to my friends *forever*.

I'd tell them about Christian soon.

Just not today.

We stayed at the restaurant for another half hour before Ava had to meet Alex for some wedding thing and Jules went to "surprise" Josh after his shift at the hospital. I was pretty sure that was code for sex, but I wisely chose not to ask.

After we said our goodbyes, I took the train to Greenfield.

It was an hour-long ride from the city, and when I'd worked at *D.C. Style*, I had to rush here after work. Sometimes I didn't make it; when I *did* make it, I usually only got ten or fifteen minutes with Maura before visiting hours ended.

That was one perk of being unemployed, I guess. I no longer had to take the train to and from the middle of nowhere at night, and I didn't have to worry about not having time to see her.

I absentmindedly toyed with my necklace as I watched the city's concrete sidewalks and European-inspired architecture give way to open fields and flatter land.

I hadn't talked to Christian in person since our agreement, though he'd texted me the following day asking me to join him at a fundraiser.

I didn't even know what the fundraiser was for, only that it was a black-tie event and would take place at the Smithsonian Museum of Natural History.

The jolt of the train as it stopped at the Greenfield station coincided with the uprising of nerves in my stomach.

It'll be fine. It's just a party. You've attended plenty of black-tie events.

I inhaled and exhaled a lungful of air.

It'll be fine.

I stood and waited for a group of tired-looking commuters to pass before I followed them off the train. I only made it halfway before a chill gripped the back of my neck and yanked my head up.

It was the same chill I'd experienced in my hallway the night Christian gave me a ride home.

My eyes darted wildly around the train car, but it was

empty save for an elderly man snoring in the corner and the attendant trying to wake him up.

Some of the tension bled out of my shoulders.

Nothing was wrong. I was on edge about the fundraiser and the fake dating arrangement, that's all.

Greenfield was a ten-minute walk from the train station, and when I arrived, I'd already shaken off my misgivings from the train. I couldn't live my life looking over my shoulder, especially when there was nothing there.

Greenfield encompassed three buildings and several acres in suburban Maryland. With its bay windows, bamboo floors, and abundance of greenery, it resembled a high-end boutique hotel more than it did a senior community, so I wasn't surprised it was rated one of the best luxury assisted living facilities in the country.

It also looked different during the day, and not just because of the light. The air was calmer, and the scents were sweeter even in the dregs of winter.

It was a brand-new day, and with every brand-new day came hope.

Optimism inflated in my chest when I stopped outside Maura's room and knocked on the door.

Today, she would remember me. I was sure of it.

I knocked again. No answer. I hadn't expected one, but I always knocked twice just in case. She may live in a care facility, but her room was her room. She deserved some say over who entered her personal space.

I waited an extra beat before I twisted the knob and stepped inside.

Maura sat in a chair by the window, staring out at the pond in the back of the facility. The water was frozen, and the trees and flowers which flourished during summer were nothing more than bare branches and withered petals during winter, but she didn't seem to mind.

She wore a small smile as she hummed a low tune. Something familiar yet indistinguishable, happy yet nostalgic.

"Hi, Maura," I said softly.

The humming stopped.

She turned, her face registering polite interest as her eyes swept over me. "Hello." She tilted her head at my expectant stare. "Do I know you?"

Disappointment pulled at my chest, followed by a sharp ache.

Alzheimer's varied greatly from person to person, even those in the middle stage, like Maura. Some forgot basic motor skills like how to hold a spoon but remembered their family; others forgot who their loved ones were but could function fairly normally in daily life.

Maura fell in the latter category.

I should be grateful she could still communicate clearly after being diagnosed with Alzheimer's four years ago, and I *was*. But it still hurt when she didn't recognize me.

She was the one who'd raised me while my parents were busy building their careers. She'd picked me up and dropped me off at school every day, attended all my school plays, and consoled me after Ricky Wheaton dumped me for Melody Renner in sixth grade. Ricky and I had only "dated" for two weeks, but eleven-year-old me had been heartbroken.

In my mind, Maura would always be vibrant and full of life. But the years and disease had taken their toll, and seeing her so frail made tears thicken in my throat.

"I'm a new volunteer." I cleared my throat and pasted on a smile, not wanting to cloud our visit with melancholy. "I brought you some tembleque. A little birdie told me it's your favorite." I reached into my bag and pulled out the chilled coconut pudding.

It was a traditional Puerto Rican dessert Maura and I used to make together during our "experimentation" nights.

Every week, we'd try a new recipe. Some of them came out amazing, others not so much. The tembleque was one of our favorites, though, and we justified making it more than once by dressing it up with different flavors each time. Cinnamon one week, orange the next, followed by lime.

Voila! A new recipe.

In my eight-year-old mind, it made sense.

Maura's eyes lit up. "Trying to butter me up with sweets on your first day." She clucked. "It's working. I like you already."

I laughed. "I'm glad to hear that."

I handed her the dessert I'd made last night and waited until she had a firm grasp on it before I took the seat opposite hers.

"What's your name?" She spooned some pudding in her mouth, and I tried not to notice how slow the movement was or how hard her hand shook.

"Stella."

What looked like recognition glinted in her eyes. Hope ballooned again, only to deflate when murkiness snuffed out the glint a second later.

"Pretty name, Stella." Maura chewed with a thoughtful expression. "I have a daughter, Phoebe. She's around your age, but I haven't seen her in a while..."

Because she died.

The ache in my chest returned with a vengeance.

Six years ago, Phoebe and Maura's husband had been on their way home from the grocery store when a truck T-boned their car. Both died on impact.

Maura sank into a deep depression after, especially since she had no living relatives to lean on.

As much as I hated Alzheimer's for robbing her of the life she'd lived, sometimes I was grateful for it. Because the absence of good memories also meant the absence of bad ones, and at least she could forget the pain of losing her loved ones.

No parent should ever have to bury their child.

Maura's chewing slowed. Her brows drew together, and I could see her struggling to remember why, exactly, she hadn't seen Phoebe in a while.

Her breathing quickened the way it always did before agitation set in.

The last time she'd remembered what happened to Phoebe, she'd gotten so aggressive the nurses had to sedate her.

I blinked back the sting in my eyes and upped the wattage of my smile. "So, I hear tonight's bingo night," I said quickly. "Are you excited?"

The distraction worked.

Maura relaxed again, and eventually, our conversation meandered from bingo to poodles to *The Days of Our Lives*.

Her memories were patchy and varied from day to day, but today was one of the better ones. She used to own a pet poodle and she'd loved watching *The Days of Our Lives*. I wasn't sure she understood the significance of those topics, but at least she knew they were important on a subconscious level.

"I have bingo tonight. What do you have?" She abruptly switched topics after a ten-minute monologue on hand washing laundry. "A beautiful girl like you must have fun plans for Friday night."

It was Saturday, but I didn't correct her.

"I have a big party," I said. "At the Smithsonian."

Though *fun* wasn't the adjective I'd use.

Nerves sloshed through my stomach, making me queasy.

Signing a contract was one thing; carrying it out was another.

What if I bombed at the event? What if I tripped or said something stupid? What if he realized I wasn't the companion he'd hoped for after all and terminated our agreement?

I instinctively reached for my crystal pendant. I'd chosen an unakite jasper today for healing, and I clutched it for dear life until the cool stone warmed and settled my nerves.

It's fine. Everything will be fine.

Maura, oblivious to my inner turmoil, brightened and leaned forward at the mention of a party. "Ooh, fancy. What are you wearing?"

In that moment, she sounded so like her old self my chest squeezed.

She used to tease me all the time about boys. Preteen me would huff and complain, but I spilled all my secret crushes to her anyway.

"I haven't decided, but I'm sure I'll find something. The real question is, what should I do with my hair?" I gestured to my curls. "Put it up or leave it down?"

Nothing animated her like the topic of hair. Hers was pin straight, but she'd had to learn how to care for my specific hair texture when I was young, and she'd become an unofficial expert over the years.

I still used the post-shower hair routine she put together for me when I was thirteen: apply curl cream, detangle with a wide-tooth comb, squeeze out excess moisture, apply argan oil, and scrunch hair upwards for definition.

It worked like a charm.

A smile curved my lips at Maura's indignant harrumph. "It's a party at the *Smithsonian.* You *must* put it up. Come here." She beckoned me over. "Have to do everything myself," she muttered.

I stifled a laugh and moved my chair next to hers while she took the pins out of her bun so she could work her magic.

I closed my eyes, letting the peaceful silence and the familiar, soothing tug and pull of her fingers wash over me.

Her movements were slow and hesitant. What took her minutes to do when I was a kid took her triple the time now. But I didn't care how long it took her or what the result looked like; I only cared about spending time with her when I still could.

"There." Satisfaction filled Maura's voice. "All done."

I opened my eyes and caught our reflections in the mirror hanging on the opposite wall. She'd twisted my hair into a high, lopsided updo. Half the curls were already falling out, and the rest would probably follow as soon as I moved.

Maura stood next to me with a proud expression, and I flashed back to the night of my first ever school dance—of us standing in our exact positions now, except we'd been thirteen years younger and a thousand years more carefree.

She'd done my hair that night, too.

"Thank you," I whispered. "It's beautiful."

I reached up to gently squeeze her hand, which rested on my shoulder. It was so thin and frail I worried it would snap.

"You're welcome, Phoebe." She patted me with her other hand, her expression softening into something hazier, more reminiscent.

The oxygen cut off halfway to my lungs.

I opened my mouth to respond, but no words made it past the tears welling in my throat.

Instead, I lowered my gaze to the floor and tried to breathe through the fist squeezing my heart.

You're welcome, Phoebe.

I knew Maura loved me even if she didn't remember me,

and she'd treated me like her own daughter when she *did* remember me.

But I *wasn't* her daughter, and I could never replace Phoebe.

I didn't want to.

But I could care for her and give her as comfortable a life as possible. That meant doing everything I could to keep her at Greenfield, including making a deal with Christian Harper.

My stomach twisted. I couldn't screw up the party tonight with him, and I couldn't stall any longer. I had to announce our relationship soon if I wanted to get the Delamonte deal.

Maura had taken care of me when I didn't have anyone else to lean on. It was time I did the same for her.

She was worth the sacrifices.

7

STELLA

I STAYED AT GREENFIELD FOR ANOTHER HOUR, TALKING and doing puzzles with Maura. We'd migrated to the community room after I got my emotions under control, and we'd spent the rest of our time together assembling a five-hundred-piece mountain landscape.

I would've stayed longer, but I needed to get ready for the fundraiser. I was already cutting it close; when I got home, I had just under two hours before Christian was supposed to pick me up.

A wave of nerves crashed against my insides and drowned out the lingering melancholy from my visit with Maura.

Tonight would be my first time spending an entire evening with Christian. The Delamonte dinner didn't count since we hadn't spoken much during the dinner itself.

I turned on the shower and stepped beneath the spray of hot water, trying not to panic too much at what lay ahead of me.

Christian Harper was just a man.

Not a king, even if he was richer than one, and not a god, even if he looked like one.

I had nothing to be nervous about.

Since I was on a time crunch, I washed my hair, showered, shaved, and exfoliated with record speed instead of lingering in the shower like I wanted.

But despite my rush, I was still doing my makeup in my bathrobe when the doorbell rang.

Christian wasn't supposed to show up for another half hour. *Unless...*

My heart rate picked up when the unsettling chill I'd experienced on the train drifted through my mind.

Stop it. It is not *him.*

I didn't know why I was worrying so much when he'd been radio silent for two years, but the last thing I needed was to manifest my stalker back into my life by focusing too much energy on him.

I jumped when the doorbell rang again.

Had it always been so *loud?*

I capped my mascara and hastened to the living room even as my pulse beat triple time.

It's not him. It's not him.

I slowed to a stop at the front door and peeked through the peephole with my heart in my throat.

A second later, relief cooled my lungs, and I opened the door.

Christian stood in the hall, looking even more devastating than usual in a black tuxedo. With his perfectly wavy hair and clean-shaven face, he could've passed for a movie star on his way to the Oscars.

A tingle of awareness spread across my skin, mixed with curiosity at the white box in his hands. Medium-sized and flat, tied with a silky gold bow that obscured the logo.

I pulled my eyes awa
Do not be distracted b

"You're early." Gettir
event. Sometimes, I liked it

I didn't appreciate bein
not leaving Greenfield earlie
left to myself.

"You're not dressed." Chr
done face to my bare, red-pai
passed through his eyes for a sp

"Because you're *early*."

He ignored the pointed reminder. "May I come in?"

I was tempted to say no and tell him to return at our arranged pickup time, but since he technically owned the apartment, I opened the door wider and stepped aside.

The air shifted the minute Christian entered. It grew heavier, more languid, like the first sultry bloom of summer after a season of spring rains.

The heat seeped through the thick terrycloth of my robe and curled low in my stomach as his eyes swept across the room, taking in the bowl of crystals by the front door, the bamboo plant on the windowsill, and the cozy, aesthetic corner I'd set up for lifestyle shoots.

He paused at the fuzzy purple unicorn propped against my couch pillows.

Amusement filled his eyes. "Cute."

"Cute?" I tried not to sound too insulted. "Mr. Unicorn isn't cute. He's *beautiful*."

At least, he had been during his heyday. Now, one of his eyes was crooked, half his hair had fallen out, and stuffing leaked from a tiny rip in his stomach, but he would always be beautiful to *me*.

I didn't care if Mr. Unicorn was a shadow of his former

my companion since I was seven, and I
until he disintegrated into dust.

"...ies," Christian said dryly. "I didn't mean to
...*eautiful* Mr. Unicorn. Good job on the original
...y the way."

Heat crawled up my neck. "I was seven. What else was I
supposed to name it? Mr. Lisa Frank in the Wild?"

A low laugh caressed my skin like velvet. "Now *that* would
be quite a name, but we can discuss alternatives for your pet
unicorn later." He held out the white box. "This is for you."

I ignored the subtle *pet unicorn* dig and eyed the box with
equal parts anticipation and wariness. "What is it?"

"Your dress for tonight."

My heart skipped a beat when I unraveled the bow and saw
the name scrawled in gold across the top. It was one of the top
couture houses in the world.

I didn't want to accept more from him than I already had,
but I couldn't resist opening the box. A *little* peek never
hurt any...

Oh my God.

My resistance crumbled the second I saw the dress nestled
against a bed of delicate white tissue paper.

I was no stranger to gorgeous clothing. I'd attended dozens
of fashion shows and received some truly amazing items from
designers, but *this*...

This dress might be the most stunning thing I've ever seen.

"Thank you. This is..." I ran a reverent hand over the green
silk. "Incredible."

"Try it on. See if it fits." Christian leaned against the wall,
his eyes glowing with soft satisfaction. "I'll be here."

He didn't have to tell me twice.

It took all my willpower not to run to my room. The second
I shut my door, I slipped out of my robe and into the gown.

Wow.

I sucked in a sharp breath. The rich green color popped against my skin and gave it an ethereal glow while the tastefully low V-neck transformed my B-cups from modest to something more luscious. The skirt draped to the floor in graceful folds and would've been almost demure had it not been for the daring slit up one side.

The dress shimmered with subtle luminescence every time I moved, and when I turned and twisted my head, I could see the delicate straps crisscrossing over my back.

There wasn't an ounce of excess fabric or a pocket of bad tailoring.

Christian had gotten my measurements exactly right. Every inch of silk clung to my body like it'd been custom made for me.

I wasn't prone to dramatics, but I didn't think I was being dramatic when I said I would die for this dress.

It was perfect.

I allowed myself an extra minute of gown appreciation before I finished getting ready.

Makeup? Check.

Heels and jewelry? Check.

Clutch large enough to hold my phone, keys, credit card, a small piece of agate, and lipstick? Check.

I added a shawl in case I got cold, checked my teeth for stray lipstick, and steadied myself with a deep breath before I returned to the living room.

Christian was still leaning against the wall, staring at a small object in his hand. I couldn't make out what it was before he straightened and slipped it into his pocket.

Our eyes connected, and a fire lit in my stomach.

He wasn't looking at the object or anything else in the room anymore.

Every ounce of his attention had redirected toward me, and I could *feel* the weight of it on my skin, like a lover's rough caress.

Liquid electricity dripped down my spine and pooled in my stomach.

With a simple look, Christian lit me up from the inside out.

"Perfect." Reverence weighed his soft assessment.

Perfect.

No matter how hard I tried, I had never been perfect, nor would I ever be.

Still, the single word set the caged butterflies in my chest free before I wrestled them back into their hold.

He's talking about the dress, you idiots. This isn't even a real date. You signed a contract stating so less than a week ago.

The butterflies fluttered, uncaring.

"You have a good eye for clothing." I forced my legs to move until I stood less than three feet from him. His delicious, masculine scent flooded my lungs and edged out the soothing notes of my favorite lavender eucalyptus candle. "I'm impressed."

"It's one of my many talents," Christian drawled.

The suggestiveness was subtle, but it was enough to send a rush of heat over my cheeks.

Laughter danced in his eyes when I lifted my chin and fixed him with what I hoped was an unimpressed stare.

Cool, calm, collected.

"Good to know." I didn't take his bait.

It was one thing for my body to freak out around him. It was another to show it.

I blew out the candle and turned off the lights before following Christian downstairs. A discreet black town car waited for us outside the entrance.

"No McLaren tonight?" I settled into the backseat.

Christian slid in next to me, the driver shut the door, and just like that, we were ensconced in a hushed, private world of Italian leather and sleek wood accents. A closed partition separated the driver's and passenger seats, keeping our conversation private.

"Parking is a pain, and I don't trust valets." Christian flicked his gaze toward the phone in my lap. "I noticed you haven't told your followers about us yet."

The word *us* mingled with the scents of my perfume and his cologne before it dissipated with a soft sigh.

I raised an eyebrow at his casual yet strangely weighted observation. "I thought you didn't have social media."

"Just because I don't use social media doesn't mean I'm not aware of what happens on there."

"You think you know everything."

"I do." The words rang with the confidence of someone who truly believed what they were saying.

No wonder his name was Christian. He had a major God complex.

"Then you would know I'll announce it. Soon." My teeth sank into my bottom lip as my nerves made an untimely reappearance.

"You should." Christian's languid reply drowned out my flickering anxiety. "You're attending tonight's event with me. You should get something out of it."

"I will. I'm just waiting for the right photo opportunity." I eased a calming breath through my lungs. "Maybe I'll post tonight."

If a fancy gala didn't make for good social media fodder, I didn't know what would.

"Good."

Awareness flushed through me at the hint of possessiveness in his voice.

A stray strand of hair slipped from my updo and wisped around my face. I'd been so thrown off by Christian's early arrival I'd forgotten to set it with more hairspray.

Luckily, it was one of those styles that looked better the messier it was, but a strange current kept my lips sealed and my body taut when Christian lifted his hand to tuck the stray hair behind my ear.

The movement was languorous, his touch whisper-light, but my nipples peaked at the soft graze of his skin against my cheek. Hard, sensitive, begging for an ounce of the same attention.

I wasn't wearing a bra.

Christian stilled. His attention honed in on my body's reaction to his simple touch, and I would've been horrified had I not been so distracted by the ache blooming in my core.

Whiskey and flames ignited in those striking eyes.

His hand remained by my cheek, but his attention touched me everywhere—my face, my breasts, my stomach and achingly sensitive clit. It left a trail of fire so scorching I half expected my dress to disintegrate.

"Careful, Stella." His low warning pulsed between my legs. "I'm not the gentleman you think I am."

Images of crumpled silk and discarded suits, rough words and rougher touches, flashed through my mind. The products of instinct, not experience.

My reply fought its way past my dry throat. "I don't think you're a gentleman at all."

A slow, lazy smile tugged at his lips. "Smart girl."

He leaned back and lowered his hand at the same time he turned his head to look out the window. The streets of D.C.

whizzed by, but all I could focus on was the warm, possessive weight on my leg.

Christian's hand rested on my thigh almost carelessly, like it was the natural home for his touch and not something he'd planned.

My dress's slit bared most of my right leg, and the sight of his strong, tanned hand against my exposed skin did nothing to alleviate the liquid pressure coiled in my stomach.

But the longer I stared, the more my lustful haze faded, replaced by aesthetic instinct.

Emerald silk. Black suit. Cufflinks and an expensive watch that glinted in the dying rays of sunlight.

The perfect, effortless photo of a couple's night out.

Before I could second guess myself, I raised my phone and snapped the picture.

I snuck a peek at Christian. He stared out the window, his profile flawless against the glass. If he knew I'd taken the photo, he didn't show it.

Then again, I hadn't captured his face, so it wasn't against our terms.

I finally summoned the courage to post when the car stopped in front of the Smithsonian.

Date night with my love <3

I hesitated at the *my love* part of the caption before I pressed the share button.

If I was doing this, I might as well go all in. *My boyfriend* didn't have the same ring as *my love*.

"You ready?" Christian asked as the driver opened the back door.

I tucked my phone into my purse. Ten seconds and my notifications were already blowing up, but I would deal with them later.

I had a gala to attend.

I took his hand and pasted on a smile.

Cool, calm, collected.

"Absolutely."

It was show time.

8

CHRISTIAN

Black had always been my favorite color.

Silent. Deadly. Impenetrable.

I felt at home in it, like shadows merging with the inky wells of night.

Yet in the span of a second, she'd upended that as she had every other thing in my life.

Heat poured through my blood as Stella walked in front of me and slowly turned, taking in the lavish decor. The museum's long-running elephant display served as a thirteen-foot-tall centerpiece while projections of marine life danced on the walls, giving the illusion that we were underwater. Black-clad servers circulated with champagne and hors d'oeuvres, and a stage sat at the far side of the room, waiting for the host to climb on and congratulate everyone on how much money they'd raised at the end of the night.

The seats for this event were eight thousand dollars a pop.

I'd spent more than that on her dress, and it'd been worth every cent.

"This is beautiful," Stella breathed, her attention resting on something behind me.

Green eyes. Green dress. Symbolic of life and nature.

Green.

Apparently, it was my new favorite fucking color.

"Yes, it is." I didn't turn to see what she was so enraptured by, nor did I pay attention to the curious stares people sent our way.

I hadn't been spotted with a woman on my arm in over a year. By tomorrow morning, the city would be abuzz about the date I'd brought, but I couldn't care less.

From the moment Stella had stepped into her living room wearing that damn dress, every other thought had crumbled into dust.

A soft flame of resentment burned in my chest. I hated the hold she had on me, but still, I couldn't stop looking at her.

A turn of my head in the car ride over.

A last-minute flight to a far-flung country to keep myself away.

Scattered weeks and months when I'd thrown myself into work to forget her.

No matter what I did, something always drew me back— the gentle lilt of her voice, the scent of fresh florals and greenery. A turquoise ring that burned a hole in my pocket long after I'd vowed to toss it in the trash.

It wasn't love. But it was maddening.

Stella's gaze slid over to meet mine. A soft exhale parted her lips at whatever she saw on my face, and the urge to push her against the wall, fist her hair, and coax her mouth open until I claimed it completely ignited in my chest.

Tension twisted between us like an invisible rope, so tangible I felt its abrasive scrape as it snaked around my chest.

The moment stretched a second into eternity before Stella averted her gaze.

Her knuckles turned white around her clutch, but her voice was calm and even when she spoke again.

"You never told me what the event is for." She avoided my eyes as she looked around the room again. "Ocean conservation?"

The stranglehold around my chest had loosened, but the release left me oddly dissatisfied.

"Close. Baby turtles."

My mouth tipped up when her head whipped around.

My answer eroded some of the earlier tension, and Stella's grip on her purse visibly loosened.

"I didn't figure you for a turtle lover, Mr. Harper. What's next? Feeding ducks? Adopting puppies?"

Her playful questions coaxed a wider smile from me. "Don't hold your breath. I watched a lot of *Franklin* growing up."

Her face glowed with laughter. "Ah, that explains it. I was an *Arthur* girl myself."

I filed that away for future reference. There were no unimportant details when it came to Stella.

"Aardvarks are underappreciated, but sadly, they're not a pet cause for Richard Wyatt's wife. No pun intended," I added.

A knowing gleam entered her eyes. "I assume Richard Wyatt is important to your business. Potential client?"

I hid another smile at how quickly she pieced it together. "Yes. Big private equity guy, big money, looking for a new security team. His wife is his weakness."

I'd lasered in on the Wyatts the minute we entered. They held court in the northeast corner of the room, surrounded by fawning admirers, including the human equivalent of a lump of coal.

Mike Kurtz, the CEO of Sentinel Security.

My good mood faded at the sight of him.

The bastard went after every account I did. There wasn't a single original thought rattling beneath that overly gelled hair.

Kurtz looked up, and an oily smile spread across his face before he broke off from the group and strode toward me.

We were both in our early thirties, but I already spotted the touches of cosmetic surgery propping up his fading looks—a chin augmentation here, some Botox there.

Beside me, Stella eyed the new arrival with curiosity, which deepened my foul mood. Kurtz didn't deserve an ounce of her attention.

"Christian! How nice to see you again." He smoothed a hand over his tie, oozing as much sincerity as a commission-starved car salesman. "I'm so glad you're not licking your wounds over the Deacon and Beatrix accounts. I hope you're not *too* upset with me about poaching your clients." His chuckle scraped against my skin like nails against chalkboard. "It's nothing personal. Just business."

Irritation flared. I'd lost two accounts to Sentinel in one week. Deacon and Beatrix were trivial compared to the VIPs topping my company's client list, but the losses pissed me off nonetheless.

I didn't like losing.

"Of course not," I said easily. I'd be damned if I showed even a smidge of weakness in Kurtz's presence. "I don't blame them for testing other services, but quality always wins in the end. Speaking of which, how's the system rebuild going? It's awful what can happen when your systems are subpar."

Kurtz's face tightened. He was a bottom feeder, but he was smart enough to recognize I'd had a hand in causing the system failure that wiped millions off Sentinel's market value last year.

He just couldn't prove it.

"It's going great," he finally said. "But the strength of a company is measured by client retention, not by freak failures. I'm sure Richard Wyatt would agree."

"I'm sure he would."

He smiled.

I smiled.

A bullet hole in his forehead would be the perfect complement to his vanity. He would die young and unravaged by old age.

Forever thirty-three.

It'd be an act of mercy, delivered with the swiftness of one silenced gunshot.

40320 Eastshore Drive. Security code 708.

So easy.

One bullet in the middle of the night, one rival snuffed out forever.

Temptation licked at the edges of my consciousness before I doused it.

Sentinel and Harper Security were well-known competitors. If foul play befell Kurtz, I would be one of the first suspects, and I didn't have time for the fucking paperwork *that* would bring.

"Speaking of quality..." Kurtz turned to Stella, who'd been watching our exchange with a bemused expression. "Who is your *stunning* date?"

She answered after several beats of hesitation. "I'm Stella." She graced him with a tentative smile.

Something dark and volatile burned in the pit of my stomach.

"I'm Mike." He oozed sleazy charm as he held out his hand.

She didn't get a chance to shake it before I cut in between them to whisk two glasses of champagne off a passing server's tray.

"I almost forgot to give my condolences," I drawled. I handed one glass to Stella and twined my free hand with hers. "I heard about the...unfortunate incident with one of your clients. It's a shame there aren't more reliable bodyguards these days, but at least the client has most of his fingers left."

Stella slid a glance in my direction.

She was the type of person who had a smile and kind words for everyone, who paid for her old nanny's care at her own expense and would give someone the shirt off her back.

The vicious undercurrent of my conversation with Kurtz was probably as foreign to her as selfless charity was to me.

I could only imagine how she'd react if she discovered some of the things I'd done.

Not that she ever would.

There were some things she could never know.

The warmth from her palm radiated up my arm and eased some of the black, restless energy churning in my chest.

It felt wrong to touch her when I was this on edge, like my darkness would seep through my touch and devour her light.

I forced myself to dial back the hostility, if only for her sake. I didn't want to taint our first "date".

Still, I couldn't resist a final dig at Kurtz.

"You might want to brush up on your employee training, though." I took a languorous sip of my drink. "Sometimes, the greatest threat to a company isn't external competition. It's internal incompetence."

Kurtz's face flushed a satisfying shade of crimson. "A pleasure as always, Harper." Sarcasm dripped from his reply. He nodded at Stella. "Stella, it was lovely meeting you. I hope to see you again soon, and with a more agreeable date."

My hand flexed around my champagne glass.

Over my dead fucking body.

"Friend of yours?" Stella asked wryly asked after Mike stormed off.

"My least favorite one. Mike Kurtz, the CEO of Sentinel Security..."

"Harper Security's biggest competitor," she finished.

A pleasant warmth chipped away at my earlier irritation. "Been Googling me, Ms. Alonso?"

She lifted her chin, her cheeks turning an adorable brick-red. "I don't enter pretend relationships without doing my research."

"Hmm." I fought a laugh at her dignified tone. "Then you'll know I attended MIT. Mike was a classmate. We competed for everything—grades, girls, internships. I was always a step ahead, and he hated it. He's made it his life's mission to one-up everything I do." A wry note entered my voice. "He's yet to succeed."

Unless he counted the Deacon and Beatrix accounts, which were nothing in the grand scheme of things.

I was competition to him. He was an annoyance to me.

Stella's brow furrowed. "That sounds like an exhausting way to live."

"Perhaps."

People like Mike were too small-minded to devise their own goals, so they looked to those who were more successful than them for a roadmap instead.

No originality. No true purpose or drive. Just a mindless need to stroke their egos for an audience of one.

It would've been sad had I given two shits about their lives.

"Well, I'm sure you'll get the account." Mischief lit Stella's eyes. "I, personally, wouldn't entrust my wellbeing to someone who wears a light blue suit to a black-tie event."

This time, I didn't hide my laugh.

Stella and I circulated the room for the next hour before we finally came face to face with Richard Wyatt.

After the obligatory small talk, I steered the conversation toward his security needs, but he seemed more interested in my relationship with Stella.

"Christian Harper with a girlfriend. I never thought I'd see the day." Richard chuckled. "How did you meet?"

"We met at Queen Bridget's wedding," I said smoothly. "I saw her across the room and asked her to dance. The rest is history."

In truth, we'd exchanged only a quick greeting at Bridget's wedding, but the story Stella and I had concocted for our meet cute served several purposes: it was simple, easy to remember, more interesting than admitting we met during an apartment tour, and close enough to the truth we wouldn't trip ourselves up if someone dug deeper.

Plus, name-dropping Bridget always impressed clients, though Richard's face remained unreadable.

"Speaking of history, I understand you've had bad experiences with protection services in the past." I steered the conversation back to the topic at hand. "But given your public profile, a bodyguard is a necessity, not a luxury."

Richard gave me a wry look. "It's always business with you, Harper."

Yeah, I didn't attend this fundraiser for my fucking health. Baby turtles? Cute, but not cute enough for me to spend a Saturday night saving them or whatever the hell the party was supposed to do.

I didn't *need* Richard as a client. Most of my money came from behind-the-scenes software and hardware development, not protection services.

But his pickiness when it came to hiring was legendary, and I thrived on a challenge.

"You should spend more time with family," he said. "Relax a little. I took my wife and kids skiing last month, and it was the best..."

I tuned him out as he yammered on about his son's natural talent at snow sports. I gave negative fucks about his family vacation, and his kids sounded annoying as shit.

Stella, on the other hand, appeared genuinely interested. She asked questions about his kids' hobbies and offered to connect him with an eco-friendly fashion brand that might be a good partner for his wife's annual charity fashion show.

It was all so cordial I wanted to shoot someone just to liven things up.

"Where was your last family vacation?" Richard drew my attention back to him.

"I don't go on family vacations." Even if my family were alive, I would rather cut off my arm than go on some group cruise through the Caribbean.

Richard's bushy brows collapsed into a frown while Stella squeezed my hand in what felt like an admonishment.

"Christian can be a workaholic, but he isn't *all* business all the time," she said quickly. "Fun fact: we danced at the wedding, but I didn't agree to date Christian until later. When I ran into him while volunteering at a senior living facility."

My smile froze. *What the fuck?*

That was *not* the story we'd agreed on.

"Christian volunteering?" Skepticism colored Richard's words.

I didn't blame him. My charity went as far as writing a big check.

"Yes." Stella's smile didn't budge. She ignored my warning glance to stay on script and continued, "He was a bit uncomfortable at first, but it's grown on him. He's a natural. The residents just adore him, especially during bingo night."

She lowered her voice. "He doesn't admit it, but he lets them win on purpose. I saw him hiding a winning card once."

Bingo night? *Letting them win? For fuck's sake.*

"Huh." Richard eyed me with newfound interest. "Didn't know you had it in you, Harper."

"Trust me." My tone matched the Sahara in dryness. "Neither did I."

We chatted for a few minutes longer before Richard's wife came up to us. She and Stella instantly struck up a rapport and drifted off on their own conversation, leaving me and Richard to discuss business.

He listened to me make the case for why he needed a professional protection team, but he interrupted me before I could make an official pitch.

"I know why you came, Harper, and it's not for the baby turtles. Not that I would tell my wife that. She was thrilled when you RSVPed yes." Richard cast an affectionate glance at his wife, who was talking to the ambassador from Eldorra.

My shoulders stiffened. *Where the hell is Stella?*

She'd been talking to Richard's wife just ten minutes ago.

My eyes scanned the room, but I didn't find her before Richard spoke again. "My phone has been ringing off the hook with security offers since I let go of my old team. And yes, I know Harper Security is the best." He held up a hand when I opened my mouth to respond. "But I like to get on well with the people I work with. I need to trust them. You've always been a cold bastard, but..." He rubbed a hand over his jaw. "Perhaps I was wrong."

The puzzle pieces for why Stella had gone off script clicked into place.

She must've picked up on Richard's baffling need for *personal connection.*

None of my business partners and current clients gave a

shit about personal connection. They only cared about getting the job done.

There was a first for everything, I suppose.

I hid a tiny smile before I closed the deal Stella had opened for me.

I'd underestimated her.

Once I had the opening, it took me less than ten minutes to extract a verbal agreement from Richard. He'd have the contract in his inbox by the end of the night.

Kurtz was out of the game before he even got in the ring.

When Richard left to greet another guest, I scanned the room again for Stella.

Richard's wife and the ambassador were still talking by the elephant display. Kurtz was hitting on some unlucky blonde at the bar.

No Stella in sight.

Even if she'd gone to the bathroom, she should be back by now.

It'd been too long.

Something's wrong.

My heartbeat slowed until it was a distant drum in my ears.

I pushed through the crowd, ignoring the protests and dirty looks as I searched for any glimpse of dark curls and green silk.

Nothing.

A fleeting image of her lying on a floor somewhere, hurt and bleeding, flashed through my mind. Panic swelled, so foreign my body fought its encroachment until the hot, frantic rush finally overpowered my resistance and flooded my veins.

Most people's reactions wouldn't have veered immediately into *she's in danger* territory, but I worked in personal security. That was my fucking job.

Plus, I'd accumulated a long list of enemies over the

years. Many wouldn't hesitate to get to me through someone I cared about, and Stella and I had debuted as a couple tonight.

Dammit. I should've been more careful, but I'd vetted the guest list. Other than Kurtz, who was as competent as a toddler operating heavy machinery, I hadn't seen anyone who was cause for concern.

Of course, someone could've easily slipped in with the servers, ushers, or dozens of other people working the party.

My jaw ticked as I entered a dimly lit hall off to the side of the main room.

If anyone touched a goddamn hair on her head...

A door swung open at the end of the hall and, like I'd conjured her through sheer force of will, Stella stepped out, looking calm and unharmed.

Surprise crossed her face when she saw me.

"Hey! Did you close the—" Her sentence cut off with a soft gasp when I closed the distance between us and backed her against the wall.

"Where were you?" My pulse beat a furious rhythm as I scanned her from head to toe, searching for injuries or signs of distress while she stared at me like I was an alien that'd crash-landed on earth.

"I was in the bathroom." She spoke slowly the way she would to a child. It was only then I noticed the bathroom signs marking the doors.

A frown creased her brow. "Is everything okay? You're acting weird."

No, they're not. Things haven't been okay since the day I first saw you.

"I thought something happened to you." The roughness of my voice startled me almost as much as the intensity of my relief.

I shouldn't care this much. Nothing good ever came from allowing other people control over my emotions.

But goddammit, I did, no matter how much I hated myself for it.

"Next time, let me know before you run off." The roughness deepened into a command.

I had no desire to experience the terror that had gripped me in the past ten minutes again.

It was ugly, foreign, and completely unacceptable.

"I didn't run off. I went to the *bathroom*." A hint of fire flickered beneath Stella's words. "I don't need to tell you every time I leave your side. That wasn't in our agreement. Besides, you were busy."

"You were in the bathroom for half an hour?"

"Someone spilled champagne on my dress. I was trying to fix it."

My eyes dropped to the small, dark stain on her skirt.

"It didn't work." Her bottom lip disappeared between her teeth. "I'm so sorry. I know how expensive it must've been. I'll find a way to pay—"

"Fuck the dress." It'd cost nearly ten thousand dollars, but I couldn't summon two shits about what happened to it.

If I had my way, I would tear it off her myself.

A hot, heady awareness replaced my panic. No one else was in the hallway, and Stella's scent—fresh, subtle, but damn intoxicating—clouded my head.

The memory of her in the car, staring at me with those big green eyes and parted lips, her hard nipples all but begging me to take them in my mouth and taste how sweet they were, flashed through my mind.

Not unlike the way she was staring at me now, only this time, defiance sharpened the edges of her softness.

And fuck, that was a turn-on.

Heat rushed to my groin until my cock ached with a painful throb.

"What I want..." I pressed a thumb against the pulse at the base of her neck. Its wild flutter told me she wasn't as indifferent to the pull between us as she pretended to be. "Is for you to be safe. There are bad people in this world, Butterfly, and some of them are in the room right outside. So next time, I don't care if I'm in the middle of a conversation with the Queen of fucking England. Interrupt me. Understand?"

Stella's eyes narrowed. "Butterfly?"

Beautiful. Elusive. Hard to catch.

When I didn't answer, she released an exhale that caressed my chest and tightened my groin to the point of pain. "Is that all you want?"

"Not even close."

A tiny shiver rippled through her. "Because you don't want to go through the trouble of finding another regular companion for events."

"Because I don't want to be jailed for murder if anyone touches a hair on your head."

A grim smile touched my lips when her eyes widened. She had no clue who I was or what I was capable of.

Meanwhile, I knew more about her than I cared to admit.

Frustration and loathing burned beneath my skin.

I pushed myself off the wall and stepped back.

Adjusted my cufflinks.

Tried to ease the relentless, pounding need in my chest.

"It's time to return to the party." Ice cooled my voice. "Shall we?"

We returned to the party in silence.

I didn't take my eyes off her the rest of the night and told myself it was because I didn't want a repeat of my earlier scare.

After all, I'd always been good at lying to myself.

9

STELLA

"Stella! I know you're in there. Open up!"

Oh no.

I buried my face in my silk pillowcase, hoping the voice would go away, but knowing its owner, they would camp out in my hall until I inevitably had to leave for fresh air and food.

My morning visitor was nothing if not persistent.

"Stella Alonso! You can't hide from me." A pause, followed by a more conciliatory, "I have matcha."

A groan escaped into my pillow.

I shouldn't have put Jules on my list of approved visitors, but I also hadn't expected her to beat down my door at...I raised my head and glanced at my digital clock...seven fifty-four in the morning.

Since she was already here and the chances of her leaving without answers were slim, I forced myself out of bed and into the living room.

I wish I'd had more time to prepare for human interaction. I hadn't even gotten the chance to wash my face yet, much less meditate or practice my morning yoga.

I stifled a yawn as I swung open the door and blinked at the fuzzy purple-clad figure in front of me.

"It's about time." Jules stood in the hall, one hand planted on her hip and the other carrying a drinks tray from a nearby coffee shop. "Five more minutes and I would've broken down your door."

"With your arm strength? Doubtful."

I cracked a smile at her offended gasp. "Who are you and what have you done to Stella? She would *never* say something so hurtful."

"The Stella you're talking about typically doesn't have people pounding down her door at eight in the morning."

I rubbed a hand over my face. My head felt like it was stuffed with cotton balls, and I couldn't concentrate on anything other than how much I'd rather crawl back into bed.

"First of all, it's eight oh-five. Second of all, *can you blame me* after the bombshell you dropped on Instagram yesterday? You—" Jules exhaled sharply and smoothed a hand over her fuzzy purple coat. "No, we're not doing this in the hallway. Let's talk inside. Can I come in?"

"Would you leave if I said no?"

Her laser stare burned through her giant sunglasses and into my skin.

Right.

I sighed and opened the door wider. "You mentioned matcha?"

I gave up on coffee years ago because it worsened my anxiety. Matcha lattes were the closest I came to espresso these days.

"Yes. Consider this my bribe for all the juicy details." Jules handed me the drink as she waltzed inside and pushed her sunglasses on top of her head. "Now..." She inhaled a long, deep breath. *"You're dating someone? You called him my love?*

How did I not know about this? How long have you been dating?"

I winced at the increasing volume of her questions while a construction crew invaded my head.

Bang. Bang. BANG!

Every swing of a hammer reverberated through my skull with bone-rattling force.

How much did I drink last night? Not *that* much, right? I usually limited my alcohol intake to three glasses per night, but I wouldn't be this hungover after three glasses.

I pinched the bridge of my nose and tried to piece the fuzzy pieces from last night together.

Baby turtles. Whiskey eyes. Champagne and gowns and...

"Is that all you want?"

"Not even close."

The memory of my encounter with Christian slammed into me with such force it knocked the breath out of my lungs.

Everything came rushing back—our agreement, the photo I posted, the delicious roughness of his hand in mine when we were talking to Mike, and the headiness of his scent when he pinned me to the wall.

Part of me was annoyed by his overprotectiveness when I'd just gone to the bathroom, for God's sake.

Another larger, more shameful part thrilled at the idea that he cared.

Pathetic? Probably.

True? Undeniably.

No one had cared that much about me since Maura, and Christian and I weren't even really dating.

"...who is it?"

"Hmm?" Was Christian at home, or had he already left for the day?

I tried to picture him eating and sleeping like a normal person and couldn't.

"Who's your boyfriend?" Jules repeated. "You didn't tag him, but that *watch*..." She wiggled her eyebrows. "I can tell just by his hand that he's hot."

Another piece from last night slotted into place.

My Instagram post. I'd been so busy at the gala I hadn't checked my notifications.

I swallowed past the sudden lump in my throat. "I—"

"Good morning!" A quick knock on the half-open door interrupted my response. Ava entered, looking far too bright-eyed and fresh-faced for this early in the morning. "Am I late? Did I miss anything good?" She set a white Crumble & Bake bag on a side table. "Breakfast pastries," she explained, following my gaze.

She opened the bag and handed out muffins.

My mouth watered at the smell.

At least my friends brought food to my interrogation. I wasn't above accepting bribery.

I almost groaned as the taste of warm, freshly baked muffin exploded on my tongue. *Definitely not above accepting bribery*.

"Stella was just about to tell me who her mystery man is." Jules ripped off a piece of blueberry muffin and popped it into her mouth.

Ava's face lit up. "I bet he's hot," she said. "You can tell by the watch."

"That's what I said!" Jules beamed. "Great minds think alike."

The banana muffin turned sour in my mouth as they stared at me expectantly.

It was one thing to lie on social media; it was another to lie to my friends' faces. I didn't tell them everything about my life —they thought I had a great relationship with my family, and they didn't know about Maura. Being the "perfect" family was so important to my parents that sharing anything that didn't align with that felt more difficult than it should have.

Ava and Jules were my best friends, yet I still kept so much of my life to myself.

But could I stand here and tell them Christian and I were dating when we weren't? Not really, anyway.

One step at a time.

They'd only asked for his name, not the details of our relationship. I'd cross that bridge when I got to it.

"He's—"

I was interrupted yet again, this time by the insistent ring of my phone.

I didn't have to check caller ID to know who was calling, and a quick glance at the incoming FaceTime proved me right.

"Hi, Bridget." I rubbed my face again. I would kill for some yoga right now. I never felt right when I started the day without it. "I assume you're calling to join the inquisition?"

"Funny." Bridget raised an elegant blonde brow. "But since you mention it, yes. This is the *second* time I've been kept out of the loop regarding your love lives. I don't appreciate it."

Last summer, Jules shocked us all when she announced she was dating Ava's brother Josh. Josh and Jules had hated each other since the day they met, and a romantic relationship between them had seemed as likely as snowfall in Miami.

However, they were still going strong after they made things official seven months ago, so I guess the old adage was true. There really was a thin line between love and hate.

Despite the nerves coiled in my stomach, I had to fight a laugh at Bridget's uncharacteristic grumbling.

"I'm sure you have more things to worry about than our love lives, *Your Majesty*," I teased.

She'd been a princess during our college days, but she

became queen after her older brother abdicated and her grandfather stepped down due to health reasons.

It still boggled my mind that I was best friends with a literal queen, but Bridget was so down to earth I forgot she was royalty half the time.

She wrinkled her nose. "More things? Yes. More *interesting* things? Debatable."

"Guys, please. Let's get things back on track," Jules said. "Who have you been hiding from us, Stel? Give us a name. Picture. Anything. *Please,* I need to know before I die from curiosity."

She flopped onto the couch in a dramatic heap.

I shook my head.

If I looked up *drama queen* in the dictionary, I'd find Jules Ambrose's face next to it, but I loved her anyway. At least she was into fun drama and not the nasty, backstabbing kind.

"Fine. I'll tell you, but don't freak out." I drew my bottom lip between my teeth. "It's Christian Harper."

Three blank stares greeted my confession.

I couldn't remember the last time my friends had been this speechless. They usually talked more than a daytime talk show host.

The taste of copper filled my mouth from how hard I was biting my lip.

"Rhys's old boss?" Bridget's brow creased with confusion.

Her husband Rhys used to work for Harper Security. That was actually how they met. He'd been assigned to her after her previous bodyguard returned home to Eldorra for paternity leave.

"Yes."

"What does he have to do with this?" Jules looked equally confused.

"He's my boyfriend."

Still nothing. I might as well be talking to the Madame Tussaud's wax versions of my friends for all the reaction they showed.

"Who's your boyfriend?" Ava asked.

Oh, for goodness' sake.

"*Christian Harper.*" I threw my hands up. "He's the guy in the photo I posted last night! We're dating. Well, fake dating, but that's another story."

Silence stretched for a long, stunned second before chaos erupted.

"*Christian Harper?*"

"What do you mean, *fake dating?*"

"He's dangerous—"

"How long has this been going on—"

"Is he forcing you into this, because I saw the way he looked at you—"

"*Stop.*" I pinched the bridge of my nose.

This was why I didn't share things about my life often. Not because I didn't want accountability, but because of other people's reactions and expectations, whatever they may be.

I forced a calming breath through my nose before I addressed my friends' points one by one.

"Yes, Christian is my fake boyfriend. Like I said, it's a long story. He is *not* dangerous—I mean, he's a little intense, but he runs a security company. His job is literally to protect people's lives. Plus, he's friends with Rhys, so he can't be that bad. Last night was our first fake date, and no, he is not forcing me into this."

The last part was definitely true. The rest was debatable, but I kept that to myself.

"I wouldn't say he's *best* friends with Rhys. They have..." Bridget paused, "an interesting relationship."

"Forget Rhys," Jules said. "No offense, Bridge. He's great

and all, but I want to know about the boyfriend part. Stel, you don't even want a real relationship. Why on earth are you in a fake one? Are you in trouble?" Concern dimmed some of the sparkle in her eyes.

Guilt flared to life in my chest.

I hated burdening people with my problems, but I should've anticipated their worry. Any romantic relationship was out of the norm for me. I wasn't opposed to dating, I just... wasn't interested.

I liked the *idea* of it. When I read a romance book, watched a romantic scene, or saw cute couples at dinner, a yearning for something similar tugged at my gut. But once the book or movie was over and I re-entered the bright light of reality, the yearning disappeared.

Romanticizing love was easy. Falling in love was harder, especially when my previous relationships had all lacked...*something*. Some sort of emotional connection that would make the risk of falling worth it.

Plus, I'd gotten used to being single, and I doubted the reality of love could live up to my fantasies of it, so I didn't even try.

"I'm not in trouble. I promise," I said when I noticed Jules's skeptical expression. "I just..." *Need more social media followers so I can make more money.* My skin heated at how shallow that sounded.

The truth was more complicated, but I couldn't dig into it without telling my friends about Maura, and *that* was a conversation I wasn't prepared to have at eight-thirty in the morning.

"I'm in the running for a huge brand deal, but I don't have as many followers as some of the other girls. I figured I could improve my chances if I hit the million mark."

Bridget's frown deepened. "How does that tie in with getting a boyfriend?"

I reluctantly explained the rest of my plan. It sounded even more ridiculous when I said it out loud to people who weren't familiar with the influencer world, but there was no point in holding back.

When I finished, the silence was a thousand times heavier than the one before.

"Wow," Ava finally said. "That's...wow."

"Is sex part of the deal? If it's not, it should be. Christian looks like he would be a *beast* in bed." As expected, Jules was the first to get over her shock and jump straight to the dirty part. "No offense, but you could use a little lovin' in your life. As much as we adore you, there are some things we can't provide."

"No, it isn't, and it never will be," I said firmly.

I'd made it clear to Christian that our arrangement wouldn't encompass any physical displays of affection unless they were necessary to sell our public image as a couple.

Sex didn't factor into the equation. *At all.* No matter how gorgeous he was or how good he *might* be in bed.

My skin heated at a mental image of a naked—

Don't go there.

This was what happened when I missed my morning routine. My brain freaked out and started picturing things it had no business picturing.

I couldn't even remember the last time I'd fantasized about sex, let alone had it.

"Are you *sure* everything's okay?" Ava's concern was palpable. "You've never cared that much about your follower count before."

I hadn't obsessed over it the way other bloggers did, but saying I didn't care was giving me too much credit.

Everyone trying to grow a platform on social media cared, and those that said they didn't were lying.

Those little numbers could wreak havoc on anyone's mental health.

"I'm not trying to be combative," Ava added softly. "If this is what you want to do, we'll support you. It just seems a little..."

"Out of character," Bridget finished.

I stared at the half-empty takeout cup in my hand. "Maybe. But maybe it's also time to try something new."

I was twenty-six. I'd had one "real" job since I graduated and no significant developments in my personal or professional lifes. I considered blogging my second job, but a lot of people didn't and I hated how I let their opinions affect the many hours of real work I poured into writing, styling, photography, and social media.

I was basically doing the same thing I'd been doing since college, only I was older and a little more jaded.

Meanwhile, Ava had moved to London (even if it'd only been temporary), got engaged, and landed her dream job traveling the world as a photographer; Bridget got married and became a freaking *queen,* and Jules passed the bar, became a high-powered attorney, and moved in with her boyfriend.

Everyone was starting new chapters of their lives while I was stuck in the prologue, waiting for my story to be told.

I swallowed the bitterness coating my tongue. If I didn't shake things up, I'd be an unfinished manuscript forever. A thousand potential words that never made it onto the page. Someone who *could've* been something instead of someone who *did* something.

"Understandable. Change is the spice of life," Jules agreed. Her face softened before she added, "Like Ava said, we're not trying to challenge you on this. We just want to make sure it's what you really want. If you're happy, we're happy."

"I know." I cracked a tiny smile. "At the risk of sounding completely cheesy...I love you guys."

"Did you hear that?" Jules placed a hand over her chest and looked at Ava. "She loves us. She really loves us!"

"You know what that means," Ava said solemnly.

"You guys—" I barely had a chance to put my drink down before they tackled me in a hug. "Stop!" I laughed, my earlier melancholy melting beneath their affection.

"Don't mind me. I'm just over here in Eldorra, not jealous at all," Bridget said.

I raised my phone so we could see her again. She wore a half-amused, half-envious expression.

"You need to visit us soon. We miss you."

We hadn't seen her in person since Ava's birthday last year, when she'd surprised us at the party.

"I will, I promise." Bridget grew serious. "In the meantime, be careful with Christian. He's not the type of man who does anything out of the goodness of his heart."

No, he wasn't. But I didn't need Bridget to tell me that.

After my friends left an hour later with promises not to tell anyone, including their significant others, about my deal with Christian, I showered and brewed myself a fresh pot of tea before I finally picked up my phone. I stared at the Instagram icon on my screen and held my breath as I tapped into my profile.

Oh. My. God.

I stared at my numbers, sure I was hallucinating.

Over one hundred thousand likes, four thousand comments, and ten thousand new followers overnight.

I pinched myself and flinched at the sharp burst of pain. *Not hallucinating.*

I'd expected good engagement on the photo with Christian, but I hadn't expected *this*.

Giddiness ballooned in my chest while my mind raced with possibilities.

Would another photo with Christian go viral in a similar manner, or was this a one-off because it was the first one?

There was only one way to find out.

Visions of a million followers, six-figure brand deals, and paying an entire year's worth of Maura's care in one go with savings left over danced in my head.

Maybe I'd signed a deal with the devil when I agreed to my arrangement with Christian...

But that didn't mean it wasn't worth it.

10

CHRISTIAN

I STARED AT STELLA'S LATEST INSTAGRAM POST FROM OUR ride to the fundraiser over the weekend. My hand on her bare thigh, the vivid green of her gown contrasting with the coal black sleeve of my suit.

Some photos were worth a thousand words. This photo said only one.

Mine.

A strange sensation sparked in my chest before I brushed it aside and tapped on the comments beneath the post. The reactions ranged from curiosity to joy to despair from hundreds of distraught men who bemoaned the loss of a chance with her.

Jayx098: How could you cheat on me like this? I already told my parents we were getting married :(

Brycefitness: ditch the bf and go on a date with me instead. I'll make it worth your while ;)

Threetriscuits: i can also wear a suit and cufflinks. just sayin'

My eyes narrowed. I tapped on brycefitness's profile and

studied it. Big muscles. Small brain. Standard gym bro who thought he was God's gift to women.

How many pounds on a barbell would it take to crush someone? *Hmm...*

A new text message popped up, disrupting my calculations.

Luisa: Christian Harper. You've been holding out on me.

Luisa: Why didn't you tell me you were dating Stella??

A frown touched my face. I eyed brycefitness's profile one last time before I closed out of the app. He'd gotten lucky.

Part of me, even the part that thrilled at the coppery scent of blood and fear, recognized my reaction wasn't normal. It'd been one comment on Instagram, for fuck's sake.

I had a business to run, yet here I was, scrolling through fucking social media on my burner account.

No profile photo, no bio, no followers. One following.

The turquoise ring burned in my pocket as I typed out a response.

Me: It was irrelevant.

Stella hadn't shown my face in the photo, but enough people saw us together at the gala for news to spread.

Apparently, the news had since escaped the confines of D.C. society and reached New York.

Luisa: You acted like you didn't know her at the dinner!

Me: I didn't want to sway your decision.

There was a long pause before she replied.

Luisa: What decision?

Me: Don't lie, Lu. I'm better at it than you are.

Luisa: You're such an ass.

Luisa: Anyway, it wouldn't have swayed my decision. I'm 95% set on who I want our next brand ambassador to be.

I stared at the text. My fingers drummed an absentminded rhythm on the armrest.

After another moment of deliberation, I replied.

Me: I'm glad. It's been a long time coming.

Neutral, semi-disinterested.

She took the bait, as I knew she would.

Luisa: You're not going to ask who it is?

Me: I was at the dinner too. The answer is obvious.

I left it at that. Luisa was smart enough to know who I meant.

A knock split the silence.

I flicked my gaze up. "Come in."

Kage entered, so tall and broad he barely fit through my office's door frame.

"I hear you got a girlfriend." He wasted no time in cutting to the chase. "How did I not know about this?" An accusatory note crept into his voice.

He was my oldest and, now that Rhys was gone, my most sought-after employee by clients. He was also the only person at Harper Security who didn't blow smoke up my ass—a liberty I granted him for saving my life in Colombia a decade ago.

"I run a security company, not a gossip magazine. My personal life is no one's business." An edge ran beneath my otherwise indifferent tone. His liberties only went so far.

Kage held my stare for a second before he looked away. "Understood. But the team is curious. You dating an influencer is...unexpected."

I leaned back in my chair and steepled my hand beneath

my chin. My phone had been blowing up all day with people expressing similar sentiments. Every new message and call chipped away at my patience, and Kage's observation was no different.

"Been looking into her, have you?" I asked coolly. Stella's social media was out there for everyone to see, but the thought of my guys poring over pictures and videos of her sent a surge of irritation through my blood.

"Uh, well..." Kage ran a sheepish hand over the back of his neck. "We looked her up during lunch."

Christ. Every employee at Harper Security was ex-military or ex-CIA, yet they gossiped like high schoolers.

"She's hot." Kage sank into the chair opposite mine. "Somehow, I'm not surprised your girlfriend looks like a goddamned supermodel. It's the charmed life of a billionaire CEO," he added dryly.

A dark flame kindled in my chest before I smothered it.

"The only thing I'm interested in discussing right now is how we lost the Deacon and Beatrix accounts," I said coldly. "*Not* my girlfriend."

The other man instantly sobered. "I dug into it, and it looks like a classic case of price undercutting. Sentinel promised them more for less. Deacon and Beatrix were always stingy bastards. It's no wonder they jumped ship."

True, but I didn't want rumors circulating that Harper Security couldn't hold on to its clients.

"You think it's a big deal?" Kage correctly assessed my silence. "Do we need to get them back?"

"No." Rule number one of surviving in a cutthroat business: never show weakness, not even to one's own team. "Let me worry about business strategy. You do what you do best."

"Kick ass and be devastatingly handsome?"

"If that's what you think, you need a new mirror, because it's lying to you."

"Not all of us can be you, Mr. Pretty Boy, but no woman has ever complained about my looks." He wiggled his eyebrows. "Speaking of, wanna wingman me later? It's been a while since we hit the bar together. I know you're a taken man now, but you can draw in the ladies while I close the deal."

"Can't." I stood and adjusted the sleeve of my suit. "Prior engagement."

"Why am I not surprised? We haven't gone out together in months." Kage unfolded himself from his chair. "You ever gonna tell me what these mysterious 'prior engagements' are?"

I responded with a sardonic stare.

"Fine. I can take a hint," he grumbled. "Have fun with your *engagement*."

After Kage left, I tidied my desk to its meticulous pre-work state before I exited the office.

Ten minutes later, I was speeding down Connecticut Avenue when my phone rang.

I no sooner accepted the call than an annoyed growl filled the interior.

"What the *hell* are you thinking?"

"Hello to you too, Larsen." I made a smooth turn onto a private, tree-lined road. "It's a shame you haven't acquired more manners now that you're royalty. The palace's etiquette lessons are severely lacking."

I stopped at the gate and flashed my membership card at the armed guard. He examined it and nodded.

The security scanners took my car's specs before the gates slid open with a smooth *whir*.

"Funny," Rhys said flatly. "Clients should pay extra for your sense of humor."

"That's rich, coming from a guy who has *no* sense of humor."

My mouth tugged up at his second, even more annoyed growl.

Rhys Larsen used to be my top bodyguard until he fell prey to the disease people called love. Now, he was the Prince Consort of Eldorra.

Sometimes, I texted him photos of him looking bored and grumpy at various diplomatic functions just to fuck with him. I didn't need to say anything for him to get the gist.

You're whipped, and it's pathetic.

My obsession with Stella might be spiraling out of control, but at least I wasn't attending ribbon-cutting ceremonies for a charity she liked and planting trees for an Earth Day photo op.

"Don't try to change the subject. What the hell are you doing dating Stella?" Rhys demanded.

I parked the car in the private garage and walked toward the entrance. The heavy double doors opened with a wave of my card over the reader.

"The same things every man does in a relationship."

"Cut the vague bullshit, Harper." A note of warning slipped into his voice. "She's Bridget's best friend. If she's upset, Bridget's upset. And if Bridget's upset…"

"You're going to knock me out with your ceremonial crown?" My shoes echoed against the polished floors, where the giant gold *V* etched into the middle glowed against the surrounding black marble. "Duly noted. Now, I believe you have an event early tomorrow morning. Better get to sleep, Your Highness. You need your beauty rest for the photo ops."

"Fuck you."

"Sadly, while I'm sure you have the women of Eldorra swooning, you're not my type." I passed by the restaurant and the entrance to the gentleman's club before I reached the library. "Give the queen my regards."

I hung up before he could respond.

I should've known he would get snippy about the Stella situation. He was fully whipped by his wife, and she was protective of Stella.

Understandable, but that wasn't my problem. I hadn't signed up to be nagged by her friends about my intentions.

I opened the doors to the library and found the person I was meeting seated at our usual table by one of the stained-glass windows. Leather-bound books soared three stories to the cathedral ceiling, and the low murmur of conversation interrupted the otherwise reverent hush.

There was no stern librarian yelling at patrons for talking, but a thirty-thousand-dollar annual fee granted club members more freedom than in any public space.

The library at Valhalla Club was where deals were made and alliances were forged. Every power player in D.C. knew that.

"You're late." Cool green eyes tracked my progress as I approached the table. A rare eighteenth-century chessboard sat on top of the thick oak next to two empty crystal tumblers and one full decanter of Glenfiddich 40 Year single malt scotch whisky.

"That eager to lose?" I removed my jacket and draped it over the back of my chair before I sat, my movements unhurried and deliberate.

I rolled my sleeves up and poured myself a glass of scotch. Nothing like a good drink to start off the evening.

Alex Volkov pinned me with a wry stare. "We're tied for wins."

"Not after tonight."

Alex and I had standing chess matches at the Valhalla Club

every month for the past five years. Our games were always hard fought and harder won.

We rarely interacted outside the hushed confines of Valhalla and the rare occasion when he needed my help with something cyber-related, but our monthly meetings were one of the few social engagements I truly enjoyed.

"Your hubris will be your downfall one day, Harper." Alex filled his glass halfway and raised it to his mouth.

"Perhaps," I agreed. "But not today."

"We'll see."

Normally, our games were silent with concentration, but Alex surprised me as he moved his pawn to e4.

"So, you and Stella."

"Yes." A non-answer for a non-question.

"What are you holding over her?"

I paused for a fraction of a second before I countered his move.

The Alex Volkov I knew wouldn't give two shits about anyone else's personal life.

"Asking for your fiancée?" Like Rhys's wife Bridget, Alex's fiancée Ava was also best friends with Stella.

"Stella has never been interested in a relationship." Alex ignored my question. "She also didn't mention a single thing about you or a boyfriend until she posted that photo. Therefore, it stands to reason that you're blackmailing her." Those sharp green eyes narrowed. "Then again, *you* aren't interested in dating, which means you either want to use her for something or the two of you have struck a mutually beneficial deal."

This was why I enjoyed Alex's company. He kept me on my toes.

"Don't let the conspiracy theories cloud your brain," I drawled. "You're losing."

Blatant lie. We were on equal footing so far in the game.

"Your diversion tactics leave something to be desired, so it's not my brain that's clouded," Alex said. "Maybe Stella will be the one who'll crack your *I don't believe in love* shell. It's always the unexpected ones."

I'd never heard him say so many words in such a short period of time. My amusement deepened. "Maybe, but doubtful."

My feelings toward Stella were...unusual, but they weren't love. It was hard to feel something I actively despised.

Love made the world go round, all right. In endless, tedious cycles that produced horrid songs, even more horrid movies, and annual abominations like Valentine's Day.

I rarely found it anything other than poisonous.

"Since when did you become so chatty?" I pushed my knight into a defensive position. "Don't tell me you've evolved into an actual human being. We should put out a bulletin in the Valhalla newsletter. The other members will be thrilled."

Valhalla Club didn't have a newsletter, but its members had their own methods for tracking their friends' and foes' lives alike.

"As thrilled as they are to learn of your new relationship status, I'm sure." Dark humor glinted in his eyes. Yet another change from the stoic Volkov I'd met years ago.

We continued the game, but now that Stella had been brought up *again*, I couldn't stop my thoughts from straying down paths they had no business traversing.

She hadn't posted on social media since the night of the fundraiser. She usually posted every day. She hadn't reached out to me for more photos despite the success of her first post.

Was she second-guessing our arrangement?

A trickle of something cold and foreign washed down my spine. It took me several beats to identify it.

Uncertainty.

Something as unfamiliar to me as rainstorms were to deserts.

We have a contract. She won't go back on her word.

Yet the urge to check in with her gripped my attention and pulled it away from the carved ebony and ivory pieces scattered strategically across the board.

"Checkmate." Alex's cool voice dragged me back to the library.

I blinked away images of green eyes and lush lips and examined the final layout.

Alex had executed a checkmate pattern I should've seen from a mile away.

"That was quick." Disappointment shadowed his face. "You're off your game today."

"We're just getting started, Volkov." I cleared the board. "Get back to me after the second round."

But he was right. I *was* off my game, all because I'd been busy thinking about someone who had no business occupying my thoughts the way she did. She thought her rent at the Mirage was low? That was nothing compared to how she lived rent-free in my fucking head.

Stella may appear sweet and gentle, but she was more dangerous to me than any weapon or rival.

———

AFTER A SECOND CHESS GAME WITH ALEX, WHERE I redeemed myself with a beautifully executed checkmate after two hours of play, I returned home at precisely a quarter to nine.

It took me less than one minute to determine that something was amiss.

The door to my office was open, and I *always* closed it before leaving.

I granted very few people access to my apartment when I wasn't here. *None* of them would come this late at night.

Adrenaline burned through the scotch-fueled murkiness in my blood.

I'd taken advantage of Valhalla's private car service to shepherd me home given how much I drank, but I had enough presence of mind to soften my footsteps as I inched toward my office.

I glimpsed dark hair through the opening before I pushed open the door, crossed the room in two long strides, and pinned the intruder to the wall with my hand wrapped around their throat.

Icy rage misted my vision with red-tinged white.

I did not appreciate people invading my personal space. Touching my things without permission. Breaking into *my* house and challenging my authority.

My fingers flexed around the soft column of their throat.

The vibrations of a fear-laced gasp trembled against my hold before it spilled into the air.

"*Christian.*" The familiarity of the soft plea tugged the haze away from my eyes until all I could see was green.

Huge, lush green eyes, framed by inky lashes and acrid with panic.

Fuck.

An arctic splash of recognition wrenched my hand from her throat.

We stared at each other, our breaths ragged in the quiet space between us—hers from fear, mine from adrenaline and regret.

A tendril of anger worked its way into the mix and

stretched my words taut. "Ms. Alonso. Care to explain *what* you're doing here?"

She was one of the few people on earth who had a key to my apartment, but I'd instructed her to visit during specific time windows. Friday night wasn't one of them.

She was lucky I wasn't the shoot first, ask questions later type like some of my men.

An image of Stella shot passed through my mind, and coldness gathered in the pit of my stomach.

She lifted her chin, clearly unimpressed with my greeting and sharp tone. "I was watering your plants like *you'd* asked me to." Despite her pointed tone, her breaths remained shallow, and tiny shivers worked their way through her body until my tendril of anger dissipated.

It was only then that I noticed the shattered watering can on the floor. The escaped water formed a small, glistening puddle against the customized wood, and the can's shiny black ceramic pieces reflected my face back at me.

A hundred different faces, broken up with jagged edges and distorted features.

I dragged my eyes back up to Stella's. "You're watering my plants at nine o'clock at night?"

"I forgot earlier because I was busy. You said only to come in on weekdays, and I didn't want to leave them all weekend. They're very sensitive to—"

"Busy doing what?"

I no longer cared about the plants.

"Personal things." Instead of collapsing beneath the weight of my heavy stare, she straightened and tilted her chin another inch higher. "We're not actually together. You're not entitled to know my every move."

Annoyance wisped through me at the reminder.

"I am when your busyness leads you to break into my apartment at nine o'clock at night."

"I didn't break in. I had a key!"

"Used outside the allotted time frames. A good lawyer could argue the case in my favor."

Stella's eyes narrowed. Her breaths had finally evened, and I suspected her flushed cheeks weren't due to embarrassment. "You're the security expert. If you're that worried, perhaps you should create a key that can *only* be used during your specified time windows. That wouldn't be difficult for a genius like you, would it, Mr. Harper?"

I allowed a soft laugh to slip free.

Stella's sass came and went like flashes of lightning. Every time it appeared, it electrified me, because that was when I glimpsed the real her. The one lying semi-dormant beneath her carefully cultivated calm and desperate desire to please. Somewhere within that cocoon of mild manners was a brilliant butterfly yearning to break free.

"It wouldn't be difficult at all." My gaze grew heavy-lidded as I perused her from head to toe. "But then I wouldn't come home and find you waiting for me."

A sliver of toned stomach peeked out from under her cropped gray sweatshirt while matching terrycloth short shorts clung to her hips and thighs. An endless expanse of smooth, golden brown legs ended with bare feet and red-polished nails.

My throat ran dry. I yearned to run my hands up her body, to hear her sigh with pleasure as I explored the sleek contours of her curves.

She was dressed for bed, with not a stitch of makeup on her face or jewelry adorning her limbs, but she glowed so brightly it reached the darkest corners of my soul.

"I thought you didn't want that." Breathless nerves surfaced in her reply.

"Don't assume what I want, Ms. Alonso." I kept my voice

placid, almost disinterested, but there was nothing placid about the current crackling in the air.

One touch, and the room would ignite.

"Noted." Stella's fingers curled around the hem of her shorts until her knuckles whitened.

My eyes dipped to her thighs, and desire flamed hotter in my veins when they clenched beneath my attention.

It was a small movement, nothing more than a subtle tensing of her muscles, but she might as well have reached down and caressed the hardness aching at my groin.

"You should leave," I said softly, the words rough with restraint.

She didn't move.

"Unless..." I raised my hand and skimmed it down the side of her neck until I reached the frantic flutter of her pulse. "You want to stay."

I should stop touching her, and I should keep my distance, but I was mesmerized.

Stella's swallow was audible in the thick, condensed silence.

"I don't." She wavered the tiniest bit on the word *don't*.

"No?" I grazed my thumb over her skin. The small point of contact seared through flesh and bone until the heat spilled into my blood. I lifted my eyes to hers again, my voice hardening. "Then why are you still here?"

Distraction. Obsession. Confoundment.

She was all those things and more.

She should've been a simple puzzle to break apart and piece back together, but she was proving more complicated than expected. She was like a jigsaw missing one piece. No matter how hard I searched, I couldn't find the missing piece, and until I did, she'd continue haunting my thoughts.

There was, of course, another explanation, but I dismissed that one the second it surfaced.

The one that told me I didn't want to solve Stella Alonso, because once I did, the thread connecting us would be severed.

And for some galling, unknown reason, I didn't want it to be severed.

She opened her mouth to respond, but I released her and stepped back, cutting her off without a word.

"It's time for you to leave." It was no longer framed as a suggestion but an order. "Don't let me find you in my apartment outside the permitted times again, or you'll discover there are limits to my generosity."

Indulging her tonight was a mistake. I'd already bent too many rules for her.

If it had been anyone else in my office, I would've punished them for the transgression, not fantasize about how their skin would feel against mine.

Fire sparked in Stella's eyes.

I expected her to snap back, *anticipated* it the way an alcoholic anticipated his next sip of liquor. But the fire cooled almost as soon as it kindled, smothered beneath a layer of newly formed ice.

"Understood." She reached into her pocket and retrieved a brass key, which she forced into my hand. "In fact, you won't find me in your apartment again, period."

I didn't realize how hard I was gripping the key until the jagged edge dug into my palm.

The slam of the front door reverberated through the ensuing silence.

I usually enjoyed the silence. It was peaceful and restorative, but now it seemed oppressive, like an invisible weight pressing against my chest.

The key sank deeper into my palm before I uncurled my

hand and shoved it in my pocket.

I stepped around the broken watering can and stalked to my room, where I yanked off my tie and tossed it on the bed.

It didn't ease the expanding tightness in my throat.

Beneath the ice, Stella had been hurt. I'd glimpsed a kernel of it before her defenses kicked in.

A strange pang hit my chest before I made an impatient noise.

For fuck's sake.

I'd had a hell of a day. Not just with work, but with all the nosy fuckers in my life who swarmed all over me now that I was finally "dating" someone. I didn't have time to analyze microexpressions.

I removed my cufflinks and my watch, which I placed parallel to each other on the nightstand.

Understood. In fact, you won't find me in your apartment again, period.

What the hell did that mean? If she reneged on our rent deal...

A muscle ticked in my jaw.

I shouldn't care. I didn't even *like* the damn plants. I only kept them because my interior designer insisted they "pulled the aesthetic together," and I refused to admit failure by letting them die.

But it was the principle of the matter. I couldn't set a precedent where people backed out of an agreement with me without consequences.

The memory of the fleeting hurt in Stella's eyes resurfaced like an annoying gnat that wouldn't go away.

"Dammit to hell."

With an annoyed growl, I abandoned my better instincts, slammed the bedroom door behind me, and made my way downstairs.

11

STELLA/CHRISTIAN

STELLA

Christian Harper had some nerve.

Anger simmered in my stomach as I unlocked my apartment and opened the door with more force than necessary.

It wasn't an emotion I felt often, and it ate away at my insides like acid.

I didn't know why I'd reacted so strongly to Christian's dismissal. I'd heard worse from Meredith and the trolls in my comment sections.

But there was something about the way he did it that clawed under my skin.

One second, I thought he would kiss me. The next, he was kicking me out of his apartment. The man flipped hot and cold more often than a broken faucet.

Worse, there'd been a moment when I'd *wanted* him to kiss me. When the curiosity over how that firm, sensual mouth would taste pulsed in rhythm to the ache between my thighs.

Frustration twined with my anger.

I didn't know how he managed to pull so many dormant emotions out of me.

Was it his looks? His wealth? Neither of those things had mattered to me before. I'd met too many rich, good-looking jerks to be suckered in by their false charm.

I set my bag on a nearby table and forced my lungs to expand past the pressure. Confrontation always set me on edge. Even when I wasn't in the wrong, I *felt* like I was.

You won't find me in your apartment again, period.

The memory of my rash declaration erased any calming effect my deep breaths may have had.

I'd "quit" in the heat of the moment. But as stupid as the deal was, I *had* promised him I would care for his plants in exchange for lower rent.

What if he raised my rent or, worse, evicted me? What if he ended our arrangement? I hadn't heard from Delamonte yet, but I'd already gained ten thousand followers since I posted the photo of us on our way to the fundraiser.

My account was growing for the first time in a year and ending our arrangement early would kill any momentum I had.

No momentum equaled no growth equaled less money.

Regret kicked my heart palpitations into overdrive.

That was why I'd trained myself to suppress emotional outbursts. The consequences always overshadowed the temporary relief.

I closed my eyes and attempted to return to my deep breathing.

It didn't work.

Dammit.

I was too tired and jittery for yoga, so I rifled through my bag for my phone. Social media wasn't the best anxiety-reducing tactic, but it was a great distraction. I just had to stick to my carefully curated YouTube feed of cute animals, styling tips, and hair and makeup tutorials.

Any other app was too much of a minefield to navigate when I was feeling like this.

Lip gloss, moisturizer, cafe receipt...

I paused when my hand brushed a plain white envelope.

I didn't remember putting that in my bag. I didn't even *own* mailing envelopes since I did everything via email these days.

I picked up the envelope and slid a finger under the flap to open it. It was unmarked—no addressee, no return address, no stamp.

A sheet of equally plain white paper was nestled inside.

Foreboding slithered down my spine when I unfolded it. At first, I thought it was blank, but then my eyes focused on the single line of black type at the top.

You were supposed to wait for me, Stella. You didn't.

No direct threat, but the message was ominous enough to send my dinner rising in my throat.

Ugly memories from two years ago swamped me in a rush.

Candid photos of me in the city—laughing with friends through the window of a restaurant, scrolling through my phone while I waited for the metro, shopping in a boutique in Georgetown. Letters that swung wildly from effusive declarations of love to graphic fantasies of what the sender wanted to do to me.

All sent to my personal home address.

That went on for weeks until I became so paranoid and stressed I couldn't shower unless Jules was sitting right outside in the living room. Even then, I'd been plagued with nightmares of my stalker storming into my house and hurting her before he came for me.

Then one day, the letters and photos just stopped, like the

sender had dropped off the face of the earth. I thought he'd either tired of me or gotten arrested.

But now...

Terror turned my blood into ice.

I was dimly aware that I hadn't moved since I read the note. I *should*. I should check the house for intruders and call the police, not that they'd been any help the last time this happened.

But I was paralyzed, frozen with disbelief and the sharp, metallic taste of fear.

It'd been two years since I'd heard from my stalker. Why was he back *now*? Had he always been there, watching and biding his time? Or had he left, then returned for whatever reason?

And if the note was in my purse...

My breaths rushed out faster. Tiny black dots danced in front of my vision as the implication crystallized.

No stamps and address meant the stalker had gotten close enough to slip the envelope into my bag. He'd been *right there*. He'd probably touched me.

Invisible spiders crawled over my skin.

I'd cleaned out my bag last night and hadn't seen the note, so it must've happened sometime that day.

My brain cycled through the list of places I'd visited that day.

Coffee shop. The Georgetown waterfront to shoot a campaign with my tripod. The grocery store. The metro. Christian's apartment.

The list wasn't long, but save for Christian's house, every place had been crowded for someone to slip the note into my bag without me noticing.

The silence of the apartment morphed into something

thick and ominous, interrupted only by my shallow, gasping breaths.

No matter how hard I tried, I couldn't get enough oxygen into my lungs, and I—

The harsh, jarring ring of the doorbell ripped through the quiet and caused every hair on my skin to stand on end.

It was the stalker. *It had to be.* No one would visit this late at night without notice.

Oh, God.

I needed to hide, call 911, do *something,* but my body refused to obey my brain's commands.

The doorbell rang again, and my fight or flight finally kicked in.

I stumbled toward the nearest hiding spot—a side table wedged between the couch and the air-conditioning unit. The phantom breath of my stalker brushed against my neck as I crawled beneath the table.

I could *feel* him behind me, a malevolent presence whose icy fingers clawed at my shirt and squeezed the oxygen from my lungs.

The floor tilted, and my head collided with one of the table legs as I attempted to sink as deep into the darkness as possible.

The pain was only a whisper of sensation compared to the chills swamping my skin.

Another ring of the doorbell, followed by knocking.

"Stella!"

I couldn't distinguish who the voice belonged to. I didn't even know if it was real.

I just wanted it to go away.

I pulled my knees to my chest and wrapped my arms around them. The A/C was off, but I couldn't stop shaking.

I wasn't ready to die. I'd barely lived.

The knocks continued, growing louder and more frequent

until they finally stopped. A pause ensued, followed by the sound of a key turning in the door.

Footsteps echoed against the hardwood floors, but they paused when a whimper clawed up my throat.

A few seconds later, a pair of black leather loafers stopped in front of me.

I squeezed my eyes shut and scooted deeper into the corner until my back hit the wall.

Pleasepleaseplease—

"Stella."

I had a taser in my bag. Why hadn't I grabbed my taser? I'd only held onto the letter, which I'd dropped onto the floor next to me. It was useless as a weapon unless I planned to paper cut the intruder to death.

Stupid, useless, disappointing...

Tears burned behind my closed lids.

Would my family care if I died? They might be sad at first, but eventually, they'd be relieved that the family's biggest disappointment was gone. They hadn't even wanted me. I'd been an accident, a disruption in their long-running plan to only have one child.

If I died, they could finally get their plan back on track. If I—

A hand grasped my chin and tilted it up.

"Stella, look at me."

I didn't want to. I wanted to stay in my well of denial forever.

If I can't see the monster, it doesn't exist.

But the voice didn't sound like it belonged to a monster. It sounded deep and velvety and too authoritative for me not to obey.

I slowly opened my eyes.

Whiskey. Fire. *Warmth.*

My chills skittered away at the banked fury glimmering beneath those dark pools of concern, but Christian's face softened when our gazes connected.

"You're okay."

Only two words, but they contained such calm reassurance that the dam inside me finally broke.

A sob tore from my throat, and moisture spilled past my eyes until his face blurred.

I heard a low curse before strong arms engulfed me, and my face pressed against something hard and solid. Immovable, like a mountain in a storm.

I curled into Christian's embrace and let out weeks of stress and anxiety until I ran dry. It wasn't just the note, though that had been the tipping point. It was *D.C. Style,* my family, Delamonte, my social media, and the deep-rooted sense that no matter how hard I tried, I would never live up to the expectations of those around me. That I would always be a disappointment.

It was my *life.*

Somewhere along the way, it'd careened so off course I couldn't even see the main path anymore.

I felt like a total failure.

Christian didn't say a word as I sobbed out my frustration on his chest. He just held me until my tears dried enough for mortification to seep into the void left behind by my expelled emotions.

"I'm sorry." I lifted my head and swiped the back of my hand against my damp cheeks. My mortification deepened when I saw the tear blotches staining his expensive-looking button-down. "I—" I hiccupped. "I ruined your shirt."

Of all the ways I'd pictured the night ending, having a mini meltdown in Christian Harper's arms wasn't one of them.

He didn't even glance down. "It's a shirt. I have plenty."

We were still on the floor, and I would've laughed at the sight of him sitting so casually on the hardwood in his designer clothes had his words not created another well of moisture behind my eyes.

An hour ago, I'd thought he was the biggest jerk in existence. Now...

I blinked the fresh tears away. I'd embarrassed myself enough already, thank you very much, and I couldn't keep up with my roller coaster of emotions.

First my argument with Christian, then finding the note.

The note.

Dread resurfaced as a slow, insidious wave that washed away my short-lived relief. Whoever sent the note was still out there. They hadn't been a physical threat so far, but...

My eyes strayed toward the deceptively innocent-looking letter.

Christian followed my gaze. His face hardened, and I didn't stop him when he picked up the paper and read the typed message.

When he lifted his eyes again, their cool amber color had darkened into obsidian.

"Who sent this?" His calm, almost pleasant tone contrasted with the danger flickering in the air.

I pulled it tight around me, taking strange solace in his quiet fury.

"I don't know. I came home, looked through my bag, and found it." I swallowed past the lump in my throat. "I've...I've received similar notes before. But it's been a while since the last one."

The flicker of danger ignited into a flame. The intensity of it soaked every molecule of air, but instead of unnerving me, it made me feel safe, like it was a titanium wall shielding me from the outside world.

I'd never told anyone except Jules about my stalker before. I *wanted* to tell Christian, if only because he was the security expert and would have ideas about how to track the creep down. But I was crashing now that the adrenaline from finding the note had worn off.

Exhaustion tugged at my eyes, and every time I opened my mouth to explain the situation, a yawn escaped instead.

Christian must've known I lacked the energy for anything except sleep because he didn't ask for details. Instead, he stood and held out his hand.

After a brief hesitation, I scooted out from under the table and took it.

Dizziness overtook me as he pulled me to my feet, but when it passed, I almost did a double take at how *normal* my apartment looked.

Same aromatherapy candle sitting on the coffee table. Same cashmere blanket draped over the back of the armchair. No trace of the wild panic that'd cycled through me less than thirty minutes ago.

We always expected our external world to reflect our internal one, but it was situations like these that reminded me the world would go on no matter what happened to us individually.

It was equal parts reassuring and depressing.

I sank onto the couch while Christian did a quick security sweep of the apartment. My legs couldn't hold my weight anymore, and I'd almost fallen asleep against the deep cream cushions when he returned to the living room.

"You can't stay here. The apartment's secure," he added when I straightened with alarm. "But the person who wrote the note is still out there and probably knows where you live. You have to move."

Anxiety tightened my stomach. "To where? This is my home."

"It's not safe."

"I thought the Mirage had the best building security in the city."

Christian's only response was a tightening of his jaw.

I took a deep breath. My fog of terror had cleared enough for rational thinking to sink in again.

"Whoever the culprit is, they got to me outside the building. There's nowhere I can move that would be safer than here. Besides..." My fingers curled tight around the edge of the couch. "I'm not letting some coward who hides behind anonymous letters drive me out of my own home."

I'd spent too many years in the passenger seat of my life, letting other people steer me to where they wanted me to go. Living in fear of their commentary about my actions and making myself small to fit into whatever box they put me in. My parents' expectations, my boss's demands, my stalker's notes, which left me so paranoid I jumped at every slam of a door and snap of a twig.

They acted, I reacted.

I was sick of it. It was time to wrestle back control, and learning how to say *no* was the first step.

"I'm not moving," I repeated.

If the stalker had broken into my apartment, it would've been a different matter, but he hadn't. Besides, I was right. There was nowhere I could move that would be safer than the Mirage.

Christian stared at me, his expression carved of granite.

I forced myself not to look away even as my body fought against the weight of his gaze.

He'd seen me vulnerable, but I refused to let him see me weak.

My breath pressed tight against my lungs, and it wasn't until Christian dipped his head in acquiescence that I released it.

Relief and a kernel of pride rushed to fill the void.

He hadn't said a word, but I had the unshakeable sense that I'd just faced off against a lion and won.

"Fine, but you're not staying here without extra protection."

I could live with that. I welcomed it, even, as long as the extra protection wasn't too intrusive.

For a second, I thought Christian would offer to stay the night with me, and I hated how my heart skipped a beat at the thought.

"Kage, I need you for an assignment...yes. Overnight." Several beats passed before he spoke again, his voice hard. "I don't give a fuck if you're dining with the Pope or having sex with Margot fucking Robbie. I want you on the tenth floor of the Mirage in twenty minutes."

Disappointment curled through me before I crushed it. Of *course* Christian wouldn't stay with me. He was the CEO. That type of work was probably beneath him.

He hung up, and something niggled at the back of my mind in the silence that followed.

"Why did you come to see me? Before you..." *Found me in the middle of a panic attack.* "Before you realized what happened."

Christian slipped his phone into his pocket. "I wanted to clear the air after our exchange."

It was a smooth, neutral reply. Almost *too* smooth.

"Why?"

"Do I need a reason?"

"You have a reason for everything, or you wouldn't do it."

The corner of his mouth lifted, but he didn't elaborate on his earlier answer.

He'd said twenty minutes, but someone knocked on the door less than ten minutes later.

That *someone* turned out to be a mountain of a man, all muscles and tattoos and good-looking in a way that must be irresistible to women with a weakness for bad boys.

Kage, I assumed.

Christian briefed him on the situation, but they were so quiet I couldn't make out what they said. Whatever it was, it brought a frown to Kage's face that softened when he finally turned to me.

"Don't worry, darlin'." His soft Southern accent eased the knots in my shoulders like magic. Next to him, Christian's jaw flexed, but it happened so quickly I might've imagined it. "I'll be right here the whole night. No one's gettin' past me. They didn't call me The Mountain in the military for nothin'."

I mustered a small smile. "Here I thought it was because you're as big as a mountain."

The corners of Kage's eyes crinkled. "That, too."

"Kage is one of my best. Like he said, no one will get past him." Christian's face remained impassive, but when he rested his gaze on Kage, the other man's smile disappeared.

Kage stepped back from me like I'd suddenly caught fire.

I yawned again, too tired to think much of their strange interaction.

Sleep tugged at the edges of my consciousness, and I didn't resist when Christian lifted me from the couch with firm but surprisingly gentle hands.

"Don't pass out on the couch. Mr. Unicorn doesn't like to share sleeping space."

"Funny. If the security thing doesn't work out, you should

be a..." Another yawn split my face as we walked toward my bedroom. "A comedian."

"I'll keep that in mind." Christian's dry response overpowered Kage's chuckle from behind us.

When we reached my room, I fell into bed more than I climbed into it. I was a lead weight, and gravity was an anchor dragging me toward my mattress.

"Good night," I mumbled. My eyes were already closed, but I felt Christian's presence in the room like a warm security blanket. "And thank you. For...."

I never finished my sentence.

The last thing I remembered was a warm hand smoothing my hair out of my face before darkness pulled me under.

CHRISTIAN

After Stella fell asleep, I returned to the living room to find Kage examining the note.

"Whoever put this in her bag knew how to cover their tracks," he said. "It's generic as hell. The paper, the type, the ink...unless he was careless enough to leave fingerprints on it, there's no way of tracking him down with this alone."

He echoed everything I'd already deduced.

If it'd been a digital message, I could've hunted the sender down in no time. Physical evidence was much harder to trace.

Whoever sent the note was smart, but they'd slip up eventually. Everyone did.

My hand flexed as the memory of Stella's wide-eyed terror surfaced. Fury crackled through me, its cold burn searing me from the inside out.

I'd tamped it down earlier so I could focus on Stella, but now, it came rushing back like a tidal wave.

I was going to find the fucker who wrote her that note.

And I was going to make them pay.

Not with a bullet—that was too good for them. They deserved something more painful. More prolonged.

But until then, I needed to keep Stella safe.

"I want you and Brock shadowing her until we find this fucker," I told Kage. "Don't let her see you."

After Kage, Brock was one of my best guards, and he'd recently returned from a three-month job in Tokyo.

Skepticism crossed Kage's face. "She's gonna be okay with that?"

"She won't find out."

If I asked Stella, she'd say no. She'd already pushed back on moving; I wasn't giving her another chance to compromise her safety. The only reason I'd acquiesced on the moving issue was because she was traumatized enough without me arguing with her right after her panic attack.

Where would she have moved to, anyway? Like she said, the Mirage is the most secure building in the city, a voice in my head taunted.

There was an obvious answer, but since she wasn't moving, the point was moot.

"Fine. You're the boss." Kage glanced at the closed door to Stella's bedroom. "Surprised you're not staying with her. She's your girlfriend, and you live right upstairs."

My jaw tightened.

I was tempted. *So fucking tempted.* That was the problem.

I didn't trust myself around Stella. I'd already broken too many rules for her, and staying with her overnight would cross the invisible line I'd drawn for myself.

It was always a dance for me, staying close enough to sate the beast inside me and staying far enough so I was never out of control. A constant war between want and preservation.

However, I'd come down to...not apologize, necessarily, since I didn't do apologies...but to set things right between us.

When she didn't answer, I thought she was in the shower, but the longer I waited with no response, the more my mind conjured all sorts of scenarios—of Stella injuring herself, of an intruder who somehow made it past the Mirage's airtight security and into her house.

I'd never felt the sort of panic that'd consumed me when I thought something had happened to her, and that was not fucking okay.

She was already a weak spot for me; I couldn't afford for that spot to grow.

"I separate my business and personal lives. This is business." I responded to Kage in a clipped tone. My stare burned the air between us. "Touch her for any reason other than to save her life, and you die."

I didn't care how long Kage and I had been friends.

No one touched her except me.

His face twisted into a scowl. "Give me more credit than that."

He hadn't been happy when I'd pulled him away from the woman he'd brought home, but he showed up as I knew he would. I didn't trust anyone else to look after Stella tonight, not even myself.

"Text me updates every hour. I don't care if it's four in the goddamn morning. I want those check-ins."

That was as close to staying with her as I would allow myself.

Kage sighed. "You got it."

I cast one last glance at Stella's bedroom door.

Every cell in my body screamed for me not to leave. I *despised* the idea that Kage was watching her instead of me.

When he'd called her *darlin'* and she'd smiled at him, I'd come close to losing my best employee at my own hands.

In a rare moment of weakness, I'd used our fake dating arrangement to get closer to her, but a part of me had secretly hoped it would shatter the mystery and end my fixation with her.

Instead, it was doing the opposite. The more time I spent with Stella, the more I wanted to be around her. To let her into places I'd never shown anyone.

It was unacceptable.

I brushed past Kage, took the elevator up to my penthouse, and went straight to the bar.

The lights of D.C. glittered like a carpet of stars outside the floor-to-ceiling windows, but I couldn't appreciate the sight. I was too wound up.

If anything had happened to Stella...

Ice spread through my veins.

I filled my glass with a heavier than usual pour.

Sat.

And waited for the first text from Kage.

12

STELLA

THERE WAS SOMETHING ABOUT THE MORNING AFTER THAT always made the previous night's events seem surreal.

Less than twelve hours ago, I'd been curled up beneath a table in my living room, convinced I was living my last moments on earth.

Now, I was drinking my daily wheatgrass smoothie and eating toast in the kitchen like it was a normal day.

If it hadn't been for Kage's presence, I would've thought last night had been a dream. Or rather, a nightmare.

"Are you sure you don't want any food?" A pang of guilt hit my chest when I noticed the purple smudges shadowing his eyes. He must've stayed awake all night, and he hadn't known he would get called to an overnight shift. When was the last time he'd slept?

"Yeah, I gotta leave soon, anyway. Christian gave me the all-clear when I told him you were up." Kage eyed me with a frown. "You gonna be alright?"

"Yep. I'll be fine." I injected extra pep into my voice. If I *acted* like everything was okay, it'd be okay.

Besides, in the glaring light of day, my panic last night seemed disproportionate to the situation.

It was just a note.

I lived in a highly secure building, I was surrounded by people when I went out, and Christian was going to run forensic analysis on the letter. He was the best at what he did; he'd find the culprit in no time. I was sure of it.

Kage didn't seem fully convinced by my response, but he didn't argue.

After he left, I went through the motions of my morning routine as best as I could. Forty-five minutes of yoga, followed by fifteen minutes of meditation, journaling, and many hours of agonizing over what to say to Christian, if I said anything at all.

I should thank him for what he did last night, but every time I pulled out my phone, self-doubt paralyzed me.

I thought him staying with me and asking Kage to look after me was a big deal, but what if he didn't? He'd worked in security for years. His clients included billionaires and royalty, for Pete's sake. What'd happened to me probably wasn't even a blip on his radar.

Plus, he hadn't reached out all day. No texts or calls, not that I should've expected anything else. Obviously, Christian had more important things to do than babysit me. He ran a multimillion-dollar company, and we weren't even really dating. He'd already gone above and beyond by asking Kage to stay with me overnight.

I didn't want to embarrass myself by making last night a bigger deal than it was, so I kept my mouth shut and busied myself preparing for an influencer event with an up-and-coming fashion designer that afternoon.

I'd been tempted to skip the event, but I needed something to take my mind off the note and its implications.

You were supposed to wait for me, Stella. You didn't.

A shiver rolled down my spine as I locked my apartment door behind me. I hadn't drunk coffee in years, but I was so jumpy I might as well have downed five shots of espresso.

It's fine. You'll be in public. Everything will be just fine.

THE EVENT TURNED OUT TO BE MORE FUN THAN I'D expected. It was an early look at the designer Lilah Amiri's new collection, and the clothes were *incredible.* The perfect mix of elegance and sexiness. Lilah herself seemed genuinely friendly, which was rare in the fashion world. We'd even exchanged contact information so we could meet up for coffee sometime.

After she excused herself to talk to her publicist, I stopped in front of a stunning, semi-sheer black gown that shimmered with subtle golden threads. The skirt draped to the floor in a lavish sweep, and the way it shone beneath the lights made it look like it was woven from the stars themselves.

The gown was a study in quality, both from the design and craftsmanship perspectives.

My mind drifted toward the stack of unfinished fashion sketches buried in the back of my drawer. Guilt pierced my gut as I tried to remember the last time I'd sketched.

Was it two, maybe three years ago?

I'd always wanted to start my own fashion brand. That was one of the reasons I started blogging and took the job at *D.C. Style.* I'd wanted to establish a name in the industry and make the right connections first.

But somewhere along the way, I'd gotten so caught up in the daily "emergencies", brand partnerships, and follower counts that I'd lost sight of my end goal.

My guilt thickened.

I told myself I didn't have the money to start my own brand anyway, but the truth was, I hadn't really tried to make something work.

Buzzing from my phone pulled me out of my thoughts.

Natalia.

Dread snuffed out every other emotion faster than a candle in a rainstorm.

I shouldn't feel that way about calls from my sister, but they were almost as stressful as the calls I used to receive from Meredith.

I eased a deep breath into my lungs.

Cool, calm, collected.

"Hi, Nat." I dipped my head and walked to a quiet corner near the exit.

"Hi. There's been a change in dinner plans," Natalia said, crisp and no-nonsense as usual. "Dad has to leave for a last-minute work trip tomorrow, so dinner's been moved to tonight. Can you be there at seven?"

My heartbeat wavered. "*Tonight?*" I checked the clock. It was just shy of five. "Nat, that's in two hours! I'm at an event right now."

It was ending soon, and it wouldn't take me long to reach my parents' house in suburban Virginia, but I wasn't ready.

I thought I had a week left to mentally prepare for our monthly family dinner.

Sweat misted my skin at the thought of walking into an Alonso dinner unprepared.

"While I'm sure your influencer commitments are life and death"—sarcasm weighted Natalia's words—"we're *all* busy. Dad is literally going to negotiate a peace deal. Can you make it tonight, or should I tell them you're busy?"

Should I tell them you're disappointing them once again?

Natalia and I weren't close, but I could still read the subtext behind her words.

"No." I gripped my phone so tightly I heard a small crack. "I'll be there."

"Good. They also want you to bring your boyfriend."

My stomach flipped. "What?"

"Your boyfriend," Natalia said slowly. "The one you've been posting pictures of on Instagram? Mom and Dad want to meet him."

Over my dead body.

There was no way in hell I'd bring Christian to something as intimate as a family dinner. That would blur the lines of our arrangement too much.

"He can't make it. He has an important business dinner tonight."

I was becoming alarmingly good at lying.

First to my followers, and now to my family.

The drink I'd downed earlier sloshed in my stomach, making me lightheaded.

"Fine," Natalia said flatly. "Just you, then. Don't be late." She hung up.

"It was lovely chatting to you too," I muttered.

I tucked my phone into my purse and whisked another cocktail off a passing server's tray.

I was still a bit queasy, but if I was going to face my family tonight, I needed all the liquid courage I could get.

AS EXPECTED, MY PARENTS WEREN'T THRILLED WHEN I showed up without Christian. They were used to getting their way, and when they didn't, it wasn't pleasant for anyone involved.

"It's a shame your boyfriend couldn't make it." Mom spooned a delicate heap of creamed corn onto her plate. "I expected him to make more of an effort to meet us. *Especially* considering we didn't know he existed until Natalia told us." Disapproval frosted her words.

Neither of my parents were active on social media, so it didn't surprise me they relied on Natalia to report my comings and goings.

I took a gulp of water, but it did nothing to ease my parched throat or racing nerves. "He couldn't cancel his dinner, and I didn't want to say anything about our relationship until it was serious."

"*Is* it serious?" My father raised his eyebrows.

Standing at a muscled six foot three, Jarvis Alonso was intimidating both in stature and presence. He'd played football at Yale, graduated top of his class, and held various positions in the private and public sectors before ascending to his current role as Chief of Staff to the Secretary of State.

Meanwhile, my mom was one of the top environmental lawyers in the city and a notorious shark in the courtroom.

Together, they ran the household like they ran their offices —with iron fists.

"I mean, we're not getting married anytime soon," I said lightly, evading the question.

"You called him *my love* in your caption." Natalia smoothed a manicured hand over her hair. "That sounds serious to me. How long have you been dating again?"

I glared at her, and she blinked back with innocence.

"Three months." Christian and I agreed that was a decent time frame for our "relationship." It was long enough for people to think we were serious but short enough that it wouldn't raise too many questions about why we hadn't told anyone we were dating until a week ago.

"He's coming to our next dinner." My mom slipped into her lawyer voice. It was a voice no one disobeyed, including my father. "One month should be adequate notice for him to clear his schedule."

I kept my tone even. "Yes, of course."

Absolutely not.

I'll come up with another excuse closer to the date. For now, it was easier to appease my parents than to argue.

"Excellent. Now that that's out of the way, let's go around the table and share our accomplishments for the past month." My mom straightened. I'd inherited her height and green eyes but not her passion for a legal career, much to her disappointment. "I'll start. I won the case against Arico Oil..."

I pushed my food around my plate as my parents and sister shared their latest professional triumphs. This was everyone's favorite part of dinner except mine. It gave them a chance to brag and gave me a severe case of stomach cramps.

After my dad finished telling us about the multi-country tour he'd organized, it was my sister's turn.

"As you know, I was up for a promotion at work. I had some *strong* competition but..." Natalia looked around the table, her face glowing with excitement. "I got it! I got the promotion! You're looking at the World Bank's newest vice president."

She beamed while my parents erupted into congratulatory cheers and my stomach dropped like an anchor to the ocean floor.

"Congrats, Nat." I swallowed the lump in my throat and forced a smile. "That's amazing."

I was happy for her, truly.

But as always, the weight of my inadequacies eroded any joy I might've gleaned from my family's accomplishments.

My mom was saving the environment, my dad was negotiating world peace, and my sister was on track to become the youngest president in World Bank history.

What was I doing?

Pinning my hopes on a campaign I might not get, pretending to date a man I wasn't sure I even liked, and lying to over nine hundred thousand people about my relationship status.

While my family was sipping daiquiris on life's luxury cruise liner, I was barely keeping my head above water.

After the hubbub over Natalia's promotion died down, all eyes turned to me.

"Stella," my father prompted. "What did you accomplish this month?"

I got fired because I didn't check my phone for a few hours on a Saturday night. But on the bright side, I gained ten thousand followers after I posted a picture of me and the man I'm dating as a publicity stunt.

"Well." I cleared my throat and scrambled for something safe to share. "My blog was featured as one of the top—"

The ring of my father's phone interrupted me.

"Excuse me." He held up one finger. "I have to take this." He stood and walked toward the living room. "Hello, sir? Yes, this is a good time..."

I glanced at my mother and Natalia, who were busy discussing how to celebrate Natalia's promotion.

I might as well be invisible.

Relief bloomed in my stomach as I stabbed a cherry tomato and brought it to my mouth.

At least I didn't have to make up some stupid accomplishment to satisfy my parents. For once, their lack of interest in my career was a blessing, not a curse.

I made it all the way to dessert without having to answer a single question when my phone lit with a new text.

Christian: How's dinner?

A quick flutter disturbed my chest.

Me: How did you know I was at dinner?

Christian: It's dinnertime. Call me psychic.

A small smile curved my mouth.

Smartass.

Me: The food is great. The company could be better.

Me: How was your day?

We texted back and forth for a while about my event and his day at the office (boring, according to him). It was our first conversation since last night and surprisingly normal.

Neither of us brought up the note until dessert was finished.

Christian: I have some updates regarding last night.

Christian: When will you be home?

I could practically hear the shift in tone over text.

My stomach pinched with nerves as I typed out my reply.

Stella: In the next hour or so.

The trains ran less often this time of night.

Christian: Give me your address and I'll send a car. Until we find the person who sent the note, you shouldn't be taking the metro by yourself this late at night.

A strange warmth glided through my veins.

Normally, I would've turned him down, but I *didn't* want to take the metro alone again. The station closest to my family's house was always creepily empty after rush hour, and taking an Uber would be too expensive.

I sent him the address as requested.

*Christian: **The car will be there in twenty minutes.***

*Christian: **I'll see you soon.***

Another flutter disrupted my heartbeat.

The simple promise in his last text shouldn't excite me so much...but, for reasons unknown to myself, it did.

13

CHRISTIAN

I'D SLEPT A TOTAL OF THREE HOURS LAST NIGHT. THE anticipation of Kage's hourly texts made anything more impossible, and I'd crashed that morning after he confirmed Stella got through the night okay.

I lived by my systems. Seven hours of sleep a night, evening workouts three times a week in my private gym, and complex work and important meetings in the morning when I was sharpest, followed by duller tasks in the afternoon.

My discipline had catapulted me to where I was today— CEO of a Fortune 500 company with a vast intelligence network and a direct line to almost every major power player in the world.

In the span of twenty-four hours, Stella had thrown those systems into complete disarray.

I'd slept until noon, rescheduled my meetings for after lunch, and skipped my workout so I could do a more thorough scan of her apartment for secret cameras or surveillance devices before she returned home.

My disrupted schedule should've pissed me off, but the

rush in my blood when her front door opened felt a lot less like anger and a lot more like anticipation.

Despite my vow to stay away from her, her absence proved more of a distraction than her presence. I'd spent all day hounding Brock for updates until I caved and texted her myself.

I leaned against the wall as Stella stepped inside, her head bent over her phone.

"Security tip number one: don't look down at your phone until you're in a secure location."

She jumped and screamed until she saw me.

"Christian!" She placed a hand over her chest, her face two shades paler than usual. "What are you *doing* here?"

"Scanning your apartment for hidden cameras. There are none," I added when she paled further.

"You can't enter my apartment without notice! That's an invasion of privacy."

"Privacy doesn't exist when it comes to security." Everyone wanted privacy until they were in trouble. Then they gave up keys and passwords like they were nothing.

I'd merely skipped the inevitable back and forth with Stella about access and jumped straight to the protection part.

"Sounds like something a tyrant would say."

"I'm glad you understand."

Her glare lit the air between us with aggravation. "Christian, let me put it in plain terms. It is *illegal* for you to enter private homes without prior permission, even if you own the building."

Hmm. I suppose it was.

Too bad I gave zero fucks about the law.

Legality did not mean right, and illegality did not mean wrong. One only had to look at the fucked-up justice system to realize the law was nothing more than a house of cards, created to give its citizens a false sense of security and weakened by doorways open only to a select few.

I had to keep up the appearance of a civil, law-abiding citizen, but as anyone knew, appearances can be deceiving.

And sometimes, we had to take justice into our own hands.

"Do you know how..." Stella's knuckles turned white around her phone. "Do you know how many nightmares I've had of coming home to find an intruder in my house? Of being attacked while I'm in the shower or sleeping? Our homes are supposed to be our safe havens, but I..." The tiny crack of her voice caused a strange twist in my chest. "How can I feel safe knowing someone could walk in here any minute and I wouldn't...I wouldn't..."

Her words gave way to shallow, panting breaths. I could see the anxiety blooming in her eyes until the black of her pupils swallowed the green of her irises.

Fuck.

I'd known she might get upset, but I also figured she'd want someone looking out for her. Take the reins and handle her security so she didn't have to worry about it. I wanted—no, *needed*—to watch over her.

It was a rare miscalculation on my part.

I rubbed a thumb over the face of my watch, strangely restless from both my error and Stella's palpable distress. Figuring her out was a constant challenge.

A tight sensation unfurled in my chest until I had to push myself off the wall and walk toward her to ease its grip.

"You *are* safe. I won't let anything happen to you." I placed my hands on her shoulders, steadying her. "Stella. It won't happen again. Now breathe for me."

I softened the edge of my voice from a command to a request.

The air was thick with recrimination, and something sharp

and foreign pierced my gut at the tiny shivers wracking her body.

What was it? Guilt? Remorse? Regret?

I couldn't tell, so I focused on Stella instead.

"That's it," I murmured when her breathing finally evened out and color returned to her face. "Just like that."

She closed her eyes and exhaled one last deep breath before she stepped back. A chill set in at the loss of warmth.

"I know you're trying to help, and I appreciate it," she said. "But you have to let me know what's happening. This is *my* life."

A brief pause before I answered. "I understand."

"Thank you."

Just like that, the tension in the air dissolved.

Stella's ability to release a grudge as quickly as she picked it up was as baffling as it was impressive.

I never forgot a slight. Ever.

"You said you had updates for me. Did you find who sent the note?" Her hopeful voice sent a pang through my chest.

"Not yet." My jaw flexed. The forensic analysis had turned up nothing. "But we'll find him. Don't worry."

I tilted my head toward the couch and waited until Stella was seated before I got down to business. "You said last night wasn't the first time you've received such a note. Tell me what happened before."

In order to track the asshole down, I needed as much intel as possible. Information was gold, and right now, I was grasping at straws.

"Don't leave anything out," I added. "Even the smallest details can be important."

Stella twisted her necklace around her finger, her expression distracted. Several beats passed before she finally spoke.

"It started two years ago," she said in a low voice. "I came home one day and found the first letter in my mailbox. It was mostly about how beautiful they thought I was and how they'd like to take me on a date. I was freaked out that they knew where I lived, but the content wasn't particularly alarming. It sounded like something a high schooler would write to his secret crush. But the letters kept coming, and he started including candid pictures of me along with them. That was when I *really* freaked out. I installed a new security system and bought a taser, but I still didn't feel like it was enough. Every time I left or entered my house, I..."

A small bob disrupted the delicate lines of her throat. "I was living with Jules at the time, which helped a bit. But I was also worried about her getting caught in the crossfire if anything happened. I told her about the notes and she insisted we go to the police, but they were dismissive of the whole thing. They basically told me to stop posting so much about my life and whereabouts on social media if I didn't want creeps reaching out to me."

Her voice grew smaller with each word, as did her posture until she was curled up in a sitting fetal position.

I didn't have to be a mind reader to read the subtext.

A part of her thought those bastards had a point.

"Did they?" My soft response belied the cold burn of anger invading my veins.

It was time I paid the Chief Superintendent a call.

"The stalker stopped soon after, so I guess it doesn't matter." Stella twisted her necklace tighter around her finger.

"It does matter. The police had a job, and they didn't do it." My muscles tightened at the uncertainty in her eyes. "What they said was bullshit. It's not your fault. Millions of people post every fucking thing they do on social media every day. It doesn't mean they're inviting people to harass them. Would you blame a woman for being assaulted if she was wearing a short skirt?"

She flinched. "Of *course* not."

"Exactly. People make their own choices. You have the right to live your life how you want without worrying about creeps who can't curb their worst impulses."

"I know. I just..." Stella faltered, then shook her head. "I know."

She was quiet for a moment before she gave me a tentative smile that thawed some of the ice in my blood. "That was the most I've heard you curse since we met."

A short laugh wound past the dimming rage in my chest and into the air.

"Sometimes, the situation calls for it." I held out my arm. "Come here, Butterfly."

I disliked comforting people almost as much as I disliked having them in my personal space, but considering everything she'd gone through, I could bend my rules this one time.

And all the previous times you've bent the rules for her, a voice inside my head taunted. *What happened to staying away from her? Hmm?*

I shoved the voice into a metal box in the darkest recesses of my mind and slammed the lid shut.

Smug bastard.

After a brief hesitation, Stella scooted closer until I could pull her into my lap. She didn't resist, and warmth glided across my skin as I ran a thumb over the elegant line of her jaw.

"Do you still have the letters from two years ago?" I asked.

The more physical evidence I had, the better.

She nodded. "They're in my bedroom. I can get them."

"Good. I'll get them later." I wasn't quite ready to let her go yet. I couldn't remember the last time someone sat in my lap, but the sensation was oddly soothing.

"I hate this." Stella's voice dropped to a whisper. "I hate feeling helpless. I wish I *knew* what he wanted. He's always talking about what he...what he'd like to do to me, but as far as I know, he's never approached me. None of the guys who've hit on me seem like they're capable of stalking and harassment, but I guess we never know." A small tremble rippled down her spine. "He was gone for years, and now he's back. Why?"

That, I had an answer to. "Because of me. Look at the timing," I said in response to her visible confusion. "You posted a photo of us on social media—your first time officially announcing a boyfriend. A few days later, he sends you a note saying you should've waited for him. I don't know where he went these past two years, but it's obvious our relationship triggered him."

The simplest explanation was usually the correct one, and the sequence of events lined up too perfectly to be a coincidence.

"Oh, God." Stella's face drained of color. "Does that mean I should stop posting about us? What if he escalates things next time?"

"No," I said firmly. "We'll ramp up your security, but we need new posts to draw him out. The sooner we find him, the sooner we can put the bastard behind bars." *Or six feet in the ground.* "Trust me." I rested a reassuring hand on her back even as my muscles coiled at the thought of *anyone* threatening her. "I won't let anything happen to you."

Not even if I had to take a bullet myself.

"Right. That makes sense." Stella drew in a deep breath before another frown touched her face. "What if..."

I waited, curiosity brewing at the rising color on her cheeks.

"What if he comes after you and you get hurt?"

A fire sparked in my chest, so suddenly and unexpectedly it would've brought me to my knees had I been standing.

My pulse drummed at the unfamiliar warmth sluicing through my veins, but I kept my face impassive as I curled a hand around the back of her neck.

"I can take care of myself, but your concern is duly noted." My words lengthened into a drawl. "I didn't realize you cared that much about my safety."

"I don't *care*. I mean, I do, but I...you know what I mean."

"I'm not sure I do."

I held back a laugh at her adorable growl of frustration. "You're *insufferable*."

"I've been called worse."

Stella sat sideways on my lap, so close I could count every lash framing those beautiful green eyes and spot the tiny mole behind her right shoulder.

Warmth, light, and grace, all wrapped up in a perfect package and sitting right there for me to take.

Desire coursed through my veins, but I forced it at bay. Despite our banter, Stella's muscles remained tense, and her lips were raw from how hard she was biting them.

She wasn't as calm as she pretended to be.

Our moral compasses pointed in different directions, but we both wore masks to shield our true natures from the world.

The only difference was our motives behind the deception and the lies we told ourselves.

Stella lifted her chin. "I'm sure you've been called all sorts of things, but you're not as scary as you want people to think you are, Christian Harper."

My eyes narrowed. "No?"

"You lowered my rent, agreed to be my fake boyfriend, and you're helping me find the stalker for free. Those aren't the actions of someone heartless."

If she only knew.

"I didn't do them out of pure selflessness."

"Maybe not the first two, but what are you getting out of helping me with the stalker?" she challenged.

"The world thinks you're my girlfriend. Can't have anything happen to you or it'd look bad for me." The lie slipped as easily from my tongue as my own name. "I'm the CEO of a security company, after all."

That, and a world without Stella in it was one that didn't deserve to exist.

My hunger to piece together her puzzle tethered me to sanity and fed the tiny part of me that still believed in goodness and humanity.

It was the order to my chaos, the flame to my ice.

Without it, I would be unmoored, and that would be the ultimate danger—both to myself and the people around me.

Doubt crept into Stella's eyes. "Is that the only reason why?" She sounded less sure than she had a minute ago.

My hand stilled on the back of her neck.

The air between us stretched so taut it vibrated against my skin, and the sudden change in atmosphere dragged us into a place where there was no threatening note, no stalker, and no fake arrangement.

There was just the weight of her on my lap, the scent of her in my lungs, and the warmth of her in my soul.

It was raw, real, and so fucking addicting.

"Do you want there to be another reason?" A question and a challenge, disguised by a cloak of softness.

Stella's lips parted with a soft, audible exhale. A dozen unspoken words consumed that single breath, and I wanted to keep every one of them for myself, to hoard them close to my chest the way a dragon guarded its treasure.

But instead of giving me the hit I so desperately craved, she gave a slow shake of her head.

"Don't lie to me, Stella." I rubbed my thumb over the back of her neck in a lazy, languid stroke.

The sound of her swallow filled the space between us.

Her teeth dug into her lush lower lip, and the desire to pull her hair back and plunder the softness of her mouth consumed me.

Just one taste.

The reasoning of an addict desperate for his next fix.

I'd never tasted her—yet—but I imagined she'd be even sweeter than in my imagination.

Our breaths thundered together in an erratic drumbeat.

One taste. Then I could sate this ceaseless hunger inside me.

One taste, and—

A sharp ring snapped the taut air in half and left me with whiplash.

Stella's eyes widened a fraction before she scrambled off my lap like I'd suddenly caught fire.

Dammit.

Irritation solidified in my chest at the interruption as I stood and picked up the call. I walked to the corner of the room and turned my back so she couldn't see the displeasure darkening my face.

"This better be important."

"It is. I've got intel that Rutledge might jump ship to Sentinel." Kage wasted no time beating around the bush. "Not fucking good, especially after the Deacon and Beatrix situation. People are going to talk."

My irritation intensified.

Unlike Deacon and Beatrix, Rutledge was one of our biggest accounts. Losing him would be unacceptable.

"Explain."

I switched gears to business mode as Kage laid out what he'd heard. The executive security world was a small one, and one could learn a lot if they had eyes and ears in the right places.

"It's not confirmed yet," he said after he finished. "But I figured you'd want to know. If he leaves..."

"He won't." Rutledge's exit wouldn't be a fatal blow, but it would make Harper Security look weak. And in my circles, showing weakness was akin to pouring blood into a shark pool. "I'll have a talk with him. In the meantime, keep an eye on Sentinel. I want to know if anyone on the team so much as fucking sneezes."

They were up to something. Once was luck and twice was coincidence, but three times? That was a pattern, and not one I particularly liked.

"You got it," Kage said.

I hung up, my mind already working through the implications of losing another account to Sentinel. I wouldn't, of course. I knew Rutledge well, including his weak spots. But I always liked to have a backup plan in case everything went south.

One of these days, I'd have to take care of Sentinel for good.

Should've wiped out their entire damn system like I'd wanted.

It'd take more work, but I could hide my tracks well enough that no one could pinpoint me as the culprit.

"Is everything okay?" Stella's voice pulled me out of my musings. "That sounded intense."

"Yes." I smoothed my expression into placidness before I turned. "Just a hiccup at work. Nothing important."

If I were alone, I would've already put the pieces for

Sentinel's demise in motion. Since I wasn't, and I was with Stella, I set those pieces aside.

For now.

"I hope you're not planning a competitor's ruin," she said solemnly. "That would be a bit heavy for a Friday night."

I almost smiled, both because she'd unerringly hit the nail on the head and because I spotted a glimmer of her usual sparkle in her eyes.

She'd regained her composure during my call. The rosiness had dissipated from her cheeks, and she was curled up on the couch next to that stupid purple unicorn with a faint curve of her lips.

"Don't worry. I keep the destruction to business hours, Monday through Friday." I raised a brow at the mischief in her growing smile. "Care to share the joke?"

The sparkle in her eyes brightened. "Check my Stories."

"I don't have social media." The lie rolled off my tongue, though technically, it wasn't a lie.

Christian Harper didn't have social media; CP612 did.

"Seriously?" Stella shook her head. "We'll have to fix that, but for now...." She typed something into her phone. "Check your texts."

I opened her message, and I had to blink twice to make sure I was seeing correctly.

She'd sent a screenshot of a Stories poll. A picture of me, back turned and phone to my ear, took up the left side of the screen; a familiar purple unicorn dominated the right side.

The question was simple: *Who would you rather cuddle with? Mr. Harper or Mr. Unicorn?*

"You're losing, by the way," Stella said. "Mr. Unicorn is beating you fifty-three to forty-seven percent."

I stared at her, sure I was hearing wrong and that she didn't have the fucking audacity to pit me against a raggedy stuffed animal with a crooked eye in some absurd social media poll.

I was also sure I couldn't be *losing* to said stuffed animal.

"The poll must be broken because that's ridiculous." I tried not to sound as insulted as I felt.

"It's not, but you have twenty-three hours and fifty-one minutes to catch up." Stella's smile dimmed, and a touch of nerves resurfaced in her eyes. "Draw him out with more posts, right?"

Her stalker.

She may not be willing to admit the attraction between us, but she trusted me enough to take my recommendation implicitly.

I blamed the fleeting ache in my chest on heartburn. My doctor was going to have his hands full during our next checkup.

"That's right. And for the record..." I tapped my phone screen. "You need followers with better taste if they're choosing a unicorn over me. I'm wearing Brioni, for fuck's sake."

Stella's laugh finally pulled a smile out of me.

Despite what happened two nights ago, her light still shone through, and she was more resilient than a lot of people, including myself, gave her credit for.

That's my girl.

14

STELLA

MARCH 25

It's been a month since my dinner with Delamonte, and I haven't heard a peep from them about the brand ambassador selection. Brady assures me they'll choose soon, but he's been saying that for weeks. At this point, I'm convinced I didn't get it.

On the bright side, I'm still gaining followers, and I've gotten two new brand deals in the past week. They don't pay as much as Delamonte would've, but every bit counts. Also, I'm almost at 930K followers, which is wild and a little depressing. It turns out all I needed to do was to get a boyfriend to be more interesting [insert sigh].

Speaking of which...I posted another photo of Christian the other day. The same one I snapped of him when he was on his call (he still hasn't gotten over losing to a unicorn in my poll. I told him he would've won had he shown his face, which went over as well as you'd expect). Not my most creative work, but I'm still nervous about my stalker seeing a photo of us together and snapping.

I know Christian said we need to draw him out, which

makes sense. And I trust him to keep me safe. I gave him the stalker's old letters and his team is...doing whatever it is security people do with creepy anonymous notes.

Still, I have a bad feeling this could all go wrong VERY quickly.

I don't want to let the stalker situation rule my life, and I WON'T.

But...I'm going to stay put in my apartment and work on my blog until I get an update from Christian. Just in case.

It's better to be safe than sorry.

DAILY GRATITUDE:

1. *Food/grocery deliveries*
2. *Cute loungewear*
3. *Building security*

"Get dressed. We're leaving in an hour."

I gaped at Christian, who stood in my doorway in a crisp black button-down and dark jeans. It was my first time seeing him in anything other than a suit, and the effect was equally devastating in a completely different way.

"Excuse me?" I tried not to stare at the way his shirt stretched over his broad shoulders and muscular arms.

"We're leaving in an hour," he repeated. "There's an art gallery opening I need to attend. Dress code is dressy casual. I presume you own an appropriate outfit."

I was wearing a crop sweatshirt and shorts. The chances of anyone dragging me out of my apartment when I'd already changed into my sleepwear were next to zero.

"This wasn't on our calendar, and I'm busy." I kept my hand on the doorknob, barring him from entering.

He couldn't just show up and demand I go somewhere with him last minute. I needed time to mentally prepare for outings that involved extensive socialization with strangers.

Christian fixed me with a dubious stare. "Yes, you look positively swamped with..." His gaze coasted over my shoulder, and my skin warmed when I remembered what he'd find. A pint of Ben & Jerry's, *The Devil Wears Prada* onscreen, and the remnants of a takeout salad. "Dairy and fashion magazine tyranny. Miss your old job already?"

"I watch it for the outfits." I squeezed the doorknob for strength. "I'm sorry, but next time you want me to accompany you to an event, give me more than an hour's notice."

Christian appeared unfazed by my pointed suggestion. "I didn't know Richard Wyatt would be at the opening until thirty minutes ago."

Wyatt. The client he'd hoped to sign at the fundraiser. "I thought you already closed the deal."

"Ninety percent. He came back with concerns after reviewing the contract, and I'd prefer to address them in person tonight." His brows dipped with approval. "When was the last time you left your apartment? You're wilting."

My mouth parted in shock at the utter rudeness of his comment. "I am not *wilting*. I am merely...hibernating."

Wilting was a word used to describe dying plants, not a healthy human being. I'd never been more insulted, though he wasn't entirely wrong.

I'd only left my apartment once in the past week, and that was to check on Christian's plants. We'd gotten over our argument in his office last week, and I had both my keys to his place and my watering responsibilities back.

I'd been subsisting on smoothies and food deliveries, which

wasn't good for my wallet *or* waistline, and my skin craved the natural warmth of sunshine.

But every time I attempted to go outside, my mind spiraled to the note and all the places my stalker could've gotten to me.

I'd depleted the burst of courage I'd gotten the morning after I found the note, and I had no idea how to replenish it.

"Call it whatever you want. The result is the same," Christian said, clearly unimpressed by my euphemism. "Fifty minutes to get ready."

"I'm not going."

"Forty-nine minutes and fifty-seven seconds."

"Nothing's changed in the past three seconds. I'm. Not. Going."

"This was our deal." His cool voice sent a rush of indignation down the back of my neck. "You accompany me to events; I pose in your photos and act as your boyfriend. You don't want to cut off the momentum when it's going so well, do you?"

He was right, but that didn't mean I appreciated Christian telling me what to do.

"Are you *blackmailing* me?"

His smile was all lazy charm and amusement. "Not blackmailing. Persuading."

Now he liked euphemisms.

"Same thing in your world."

"You're learning." Christian tapped the face of his watch. "Forty-four minutes."

Our eyes clashed in a battle of defiance versus indifference.

I had no desire to leave my apartment. I could live here for the rest of my life and be happy. It was safe, quiet, and fully equipped with movies, ice cream, and internet. What more could a girl want?

Human company. Sunshine. A life, a voice whispered.

I gritted my teeth. *Shut up.*

Make me. I could practically see the disembodied voice sticking its tongue out.

Arguing with myself and sounding like a fifth grader. That had to be a new low.

"Forty-two minutes, Stella." Christian's eyes flickered with the soft glow of rising danger. "I have a business deal to close, so if you insist on holing yourself up like a scared hermit, tell me now so I can terminate our deal."

Scared hermit. The words slithered down my spine like a taunt.

Was that how he saw me? Was that who I *was*? Someone so thrown off by *one* anonymous note that I let it rule my life?

Where was the girl from the morning after, the one who'd marched out of the house and vowed not to let fear win?

She was as ephemeral as morning rain and dreams of perfection. Always fighting to live and always dying by the blade of my anxiety.

The doorknob slipped against my hand.

"Fine." The word rushed out before I could change my mind. "I'll go."

If only to prove that I wasn't as weak as the world thought I was.

No smile, but the glow of danger dimmed until mere embers remained. "Good. Forty minutes."

My lips pressed together. "You are, without doubt, the most insufferable countdown timer that's ever existed."

Christian's laugh followed me into my room, where I flicked through my closet before settling on a silky camisole under a blazer, jeans, and velvet flats.

Apprehension tore at my nerves, but I kept my expression neutral as I reentered the living room.

Cool, calm, collected.

Christian didn't say a word when he saw me, but his stare pressed against my body in a way that warmed me from the inside out.

We rode to the gallery in silence except for the soft classical music piping from the speakers. I was grateful he didn't try to make conversation. I needed to gather all my energy for a night out when my body had already been in *home relaxation* mode.

My nerves intensified when the gallery came into sight.

I'm fine. You're fine. We're fine.

I was with Christian, and my stalker wouldn't attack me in the middle of a public party.

I'm fine. You're fine. We're fine, I repeated.

Luckily, the gallery opening was less crowded than the fundraiser. There were three dozen guests max, encompassing a mix of creative and high society types. They milled about the stark white space, talking quietly over glasses of champagne.

Christian and I circulated the room, making small talk about everything from the weather to cherry blossom season. I pitched in where I could, but unlike at the fundraiser, I let him take the lead.

I was too tired to be witty and charming, though it *did* feel nice to be in public again for the first time in a week.

I stuck by Christian's side until Wyatt arrived with his wife.

"You do what you have to do," I said. "I'm going to check out the rest of the exhibition."

There was no way I could listen to them talk business without falling asleep.

"Interrupt me if you need me." Christian leveled me with a dark stare. "I mean it, Stella."

"I will." *I won't.* The thought of interrupting someone mid-conversation gave me hives. It was awkward and rude and I would rather throw myself into an ice pool in the dead of winter.

While he spoke with Wyatt, I made my way through the exhibit one piece at a time. The artist Morten (first name only) specialized in abstract realism. His paintings were lush, sometimes haunting, and always beautiful. Bold strokes of color depicted the darkest of emotions: rage, envy, guilt, helplessness.

I stopped in front of a canvas half-hidden in the corner. In it, a gorgeous young girl stared off to the side with a wistful expression. Her face was so realistic it could've been a photograph had it not been for the streaks of color dripping down her cheeks and onto her abstract torso. The streaks coalesced into a dark pool of water at the bottom of the painting, while her black hair curled away from her face and faded into a rendition of the night sky.

The piece wasn't as big or flashy as the other paintings, but something about it tugged at my soul. Maybe it was the look in her eyes, like she was dreaming of a paradise she knew she'd never reach. Or maybe it was the melancholy of it all—the sense that despite her beauty, her life was more dark days and lonely nights than it was rainbows and sunshine.

"You like this one." Christian's voice startled me from my reverie.

I'd been staring at the painting for so long I hadn't realized he'd finished his conversation with Wyatt.

I didn't turn around, but the heat of his body enveloped mine at the same time goosebumps peppered my arms. It was a paradox, much like the man standing behind me.

"The girl. I..." *Relate to her.* "Think she's beautiful."

"She is." The soft, meaningful dip in his voice had me questioning whether he was talking about the painting or something else.

A seed of awareness blossomed at the prospect, and it only grew when he rested a hand on my hip. It was so light it was a promise more than a touch, but it thrilled me all the same.

I couldn't remember the last time I wanted a guy's touch.

"Did you close the deal?" The catch in my voice sounded painfully obvious in this quiet corner where nothing existed except for heat and electricity and anticipation.

The bright lights dimmed, then faded into blackness when my eyes fluttered shut at the slow slide of Christian's hand up the curve of my hip and onto my waist.

His soft rumble of satisfaction vibrated through my body and settled low in my core.

"Yes." He grazed the other side of my waist with his hand before that one, too, rested against my side.

I shouldn't have closed my eyes. In the absence of visual distraction, he *consumed* me. My world had narrowed to the weight of his hands on my skin, the scent of him in my lungs, and the velvety caress of his words as they worked their way down my neck, over my aching breasts, and to the pulsing need between my thighs.

My earlier annoyance toward him disappeared, replaced with a desire so fierce and unexpected it left me breathless.

"Are you still thinking about the painting, Stella?" Knowing amusement deepened into something darker, more wicked.

The brush of Christian's mouth against my neck sent another wave of goosebumps scattering across my skin.

A soft moan rose in my throat and burst, unbidden, into the thick, languid air.

Mortification flushed my skin, but that, too, evaporated when he slid his hand from my waist to my stomach. His knuckle rasped down the silk of my top, from just below my breastbone to just above my jeans.

The pulses of desire intensified, so hard and insistent my thighs clenched in an attempt to ease my need.

It only made it worse.

I was seconds away from unraveling, and Christian had barely touched me.

A shiver skated down my spine at the thought of what he could do if he actually tried.

The curve of his lips branded my neck with male satisfaction. "I'll take that as a no." He dipped his thumb, ever so briefly, in the tiny gap between my stomach and the waistband of my jeans.

"Open your eyes, Stella. The photographer's watching."

My eyes flew open right as I heard the distinctive click of a camera shutter.

The event photographer.

The sound came from my left, which meant the angle was perfect for capturing an intimate couple moment between me and Christian without showing Christian's face, which was buried in the right side of my neck.

An icy bucket of realization doused the fire in my blood.

This wasn't real. *None* of this was real, no matter how good of an actor Christian was.

This was business, and I would do well to remember that.

I shrugged him off me and finally turned to face him.

"Nice job." I smoothed a hand over my front, trying to wipe away the lingering memory of his touch. "That was the perfect setup. Do you think the photographer will let me post the picture? With credit, of course."

Christian's eyes narrowed. A faint flush colored his sculpted cheekbones, but sardonic coolness laced his reply.

"I'm sure he will."

"Perfect."

Awkward silence filled the previously charged air before

his gaze drifted back to the painting over my shoulder. "You don't like it just because it's beautiful."

It wasn't a question, but I welcomed the change in topic. It was safer than whatever had transpired between us a few minutes ago.

Already, the breathless, lust-driven woman who'd melted beneath a simple touch seemed like a fever dream gone awry.

I didn't lose my mind over men. I didn't think about their hands on me or wonder how their kisses would taste.

"It's the piece that speaks to me most," I said after a brief hesitation.

I ached too much for the woman in the painting to consider it a favorite, but it entranced me in a way few things did. It was like the artist had crawled inside my mind and splashed my fears onto canvas for all to see.

The result was equally liberating and terrifying.

"Interesting." Christian's tone was unreadable.

"What about you? What's your favorite piece?" A person's taste in art revealed a lot about them, but he hadn't shown more than a cursory interest in any of the gallery's works.

"I don't have one."

"There has to be *one* you like more than the others." I tried again.

His stare could've frosted the inside of a volcano.

"I'm not an art enthusiast, Stella. I'm here purely for business, and I have no desire to waste time assigning preferences to objects that mean nothing to me."

Okay, then. I'd struck a nerve, though I had no clue which one.

Christian wasn't an expressive person by nature, but I'd never seen him shut down so fast. All traces of emotion had disappeared from his face, leaving only practiced blankness behind.

"Sorry. I didn't realize art was such a touchy subject," I said, hoping to warm the sudden chill in the air. "Most people love it."

At the very least, they didn't hate it.

"Most people *love* a lot of things." Christian's tone said all he needed to say about his thoughts on the subject. "The word is meaningless."

Don't worry, Ms. Alonso. I don't believe in love.

His words from the night of our arrangement floated through my mind.

There was a story there, but extracting blood from stone would be easier than getting that story out of him tonight.

"Not an enthusiast of art or love. Noted."

I didn't look at another piece, and Christian didn't speak to anyone else. Instead, we walked toward the exit, bound by an unspoken agreement that it was time to call it a night.

It wasn't until we stepped outside that his shoulders relaxed.

He slanted a sideways glance at me during our walk to his car. "It feels good to leave the house, doesn't it?"

I sucked in a lungful of cold, fresh air and tilted my head up at the sky. The moon shone high and bright, bathing the world in silvery magic.

The night lurked with dangers, but those shadows seemed to disappear whenever Christian was around.

Even when he was moody and intractable, he was a source of security.

"Yes," I said. "It does."

15

STELLA

Despite my reluctance to attend last week's art gallery opening, it did break my self-imposed ban on not leaving the house.

I also hadn't heard a peep from my stalker since the first note, which helped. By the time the following Wednesday rolled around, I'd relaxed enough to venture into public on my own again.

That was the thing about humans. We were hard-wired for survival, and we took every opportunity to convince ourselves that our problems weren't as bad as we thought they were.

Hope and denial. Two sides of the same coin. They kept us from falling into a well of despair even in the darkest of times.

I visited Maura, shopped for groceries, and met Lilah for coffee, where I picked her brain about everything fashion design-related.

The only person I didn't see was Christian, who was busy with work. At least, that was what he said. Maybe he was as discomfited by our interaction at the gallery as I was.

My pencil paused at the memory. The roughness of his

voice, the heady scent of leather and spice, the way his touch seared through my clothes and into my skin...

Restlessness bloomed in my chest.

I shifted in my seat and shook my head before I channeled the ceaseless buzz into the task at hand—a stack of unfinished fashion sketches I'd dug up from the depths of my drawer after my meeting with Lilah.

I'd collected dozens of them over the years. I started each one intending to finish and make it *the* piece that would launch my brand, but inevitably, self-doubt and imposter syndrome would hit, and I'd abandon it for another photoshoot or a blog post. Things I *knew* I was good at and that had a track record of success.

But not this time.

Trying and failing is better than not trying at all.

Lilah's words from our meetup haunted me. It was the first time someone had ever told me it was *okay* to fail.

Failure hadn't been an option growing up. It was straight A's or nothing. Once, I'd been so anxious about an eighty-nine percent I got on a math test I broke out in hives and had to go to the nurse's office.

Thayer hadn't been much better; the school swarmed with Type A overachievers. As for *D.C. Style*...well, look what happened the last time I made a mistake.

But I didn't live at home anymore, I wasn't in college, and I didn't work for anyone except myself.

I could do what I wanted, especially with the partnership deals I was getting now.

I didn't *want* to fail, but the idea that I *could* without the world ending unchained my creativity.

I'd been stuck the last time I tried to sketch, tracing and retracing the same lines until I tossed the entire thing out of frustration.

Now, my pencil flew over the page as I detailed the lace patterns of a blouse and the elegant silhouette of an evening gown.

It was a different type of creative outlet than my blog and social media.

Those, I did for other people.

This, I did for me.

I'd loved fashion since I snuck a copy of my mom's *Vogue* into my room at age eight. It wasn't just the clothes themselves; it was the way they transformed the wearer into whoever they wanted to be.

An ethereal princess, a glamorous CEO, a badass rocker,f or a vintage icon. Nothing was off limits.

In a household where rules were ironclad and the path to success cut straight through the Ivy League toward any one of a dozen "acceptable" careers, the chaotic, colorful world of fashion had called to me like a siren song in the dark.

I finished my first sketch and moved on to the second.

A tiny seed of pride sprouted with each sketch I completed. To others, they were just drawings, but to me, they were proof of perseverance after years of holding myself back.

Sometimes, victory was as simple as finishing.

I was so engrossed in my work, I didn't realize how much time had passed until my stomach growled in warning.

A glance at the clock told me it was already two in the afternoon. I'd been sketching nonstop since nine.

Part of me was tempted to skip lunch and keep drawing so I didn't lose my momentum, but I forced myself to change and pick up some food at the cafe next to the Mirage.

It was past lunchtime, but the tiny shop bustled with activity.

Since I didn't feel like venturing further for tea and a sandwich, I took my spot behind a scowling woman in a gray suit and waited.

Out of habit, I pulled out my phone and tapped into my profile.

My last photo was the one the photographer took of me and Christian at the art gallery. It was doing even better than our debut picture, and my follower count was already at 950K. At this rate, I'd hit the million-follower mark by summer.

Instead of excitement at the prospect, all I could focus on was the image of Christian's arms wrapped around me.

We looked so much like a real couple. Sometimes, like when he'd comforted me the night I found the note or pulled me into his lap after I told him about my stalker, we *felt* like a real couple.

Unease squirmed through my gut.

The stalker situation had thrown a wrench into our arrangement. It connected me and Christian more than we'd originally planned, and I—

An incoming call notification replaced the photo of us on my screen.

Delamonte New York.

The breath stole from my lungs, and all thoughts of Christian fell to the wayside as I answered the call.

"Hello?" My calm greeting belied my nerves. Hope peeked out from behind the churning mass, but I forced it back into the shadows.

I didn't want to get my hopes up only to be disappointed when—*if*—Delamonte told me they were going in a different direction.

"Hi Stella, this is Luisa from Delamonte. How are you?"

"I'm good. How are you?" I wiped my free hand against the side of my thigh.

"I'm good," Luisa said. "I apologize for calling you out of

the blue like this, but I figured this would be a good follow-up to the email we sent this morning."

My stomach swooped. I'd been so busy with my sketches I hadn't checked my email since waking up.

Of course the one day I didn't check it obsessively was the day I had an important message waiting for me.

"I'm not sure if you've seen it yet. In case you haven't..." I could hear the smile in Luisa's voice. "I want to formally extend an offer for you to be Delamonte's brand ambassador in the upcoming year. We didn't officially announce the selection process because we wanted to choose our ideal candidates without getting swamped with unsolicited pitches, but after much deliberation, we think you would make a wonderful addition to the Delamonte family..."

A loud buzz drowned out the rest of her words, and I stared blindly at the chalkboard menu as the line inched forward.

Formally extend an offer...Delamonte's brand ambassador in the upcoming year...make a wonderful addition to the Delamonte family...

I wanted to pinch myself, but I wasn't ready to reenter reality in case this *was* a dream.

The campaign meant a ton of money, which meant I could easily pay for Maura's care and fund the startup costs for a fashion line, which meant...

The loud whir of the coffee machine dragged me out of my racing thoughts soon enough to catch the end of Luisa's statement.

"...look over the contract and let us know. The deadline for acceptance or refusal is next week, so take some time to think about it."

I don't need to think about it! I'll take it!

"Thank you so much. I will." The logical part of me knew I

shouldn't agree to anything without reading the fine print first, even if it was for a dream deal.

"Excellent," Luisa said warmly. "I hope we can work together. Your aesthetic is the epitome of our brand, and your account is doing amazing. Fifty thousand new followers in just a few weeks! That's incredible. And...before I say this, I want you to know this had nothing to do with our decision...but Christian has always had exquisite taste. I'm not surprised that extends to his love life. He's never had a real girlfriend before, so the fact you're dating is quite revealing."

My smile dimmed. Guilt slowed the tiny effervescent bubbles of giddiness that had been hurtling through my veins until a second ago.

I'd gained those followers because I'd been lying to my audience. Granted, it wasn't a malicious lie, and it didn't hurt anybody, but guilt ate at me all the same.

"Like I said, that had nothing to do with our decision. But it's a bonus." Luisa cleared her throat. "Anyway, I have to run to a meeting, but look over the contract and discuss it with Brady. We sent a copy to him as well, so let us know if you have any questions."

"I will, thank you." I hung up in time to place my order. I'd finally reached the front of the line, but I was so buzzed I was no longer hungry, so I just ordered a tea and a croissant.

By the time I returned to the Mirage, I'd drowned my guilt over my fake relationship with justifications and euphoria from landing the Delamonte deal.

I was going to be their new brand ambassador. Me, Stella Alonso, the face of one of the world's top luxury brands.

Not only was it a six-figure deal, but it'd open doors to more opportunities than I could dream of. I could up my base rates, network with—

The turn of my doorknob sent me crashing back to earth.

It was locked, which meant it'd been *un*locked before I put my key in.

My high evaporated, replaced with an eerie crawling sensation up the back of my neck.

I was ninety percent sure I'd locked my door on my way out. Was I remembering wrong? The Mirage had never had a break-in, but...

I glanced around the empty hallway, the eerie sensation intensifying. I grabbed my taser from my bag before I unlocked the door and inched through my apartment. Part of me felt ridiculous; the other part screamed at me in warning.

I found nothing amiss in the living room, kitchen, bathroom, or Jules's old room. The only place left to check was my bedroom.

I slowly pushed open the door.

At first, everything looked normal. Untouched bed, closed windows, no open drawers or upended furniture.

I was on the verge of relaxing when my gaze snagged on the item waiting for me on my nightstand.

And I screamed.

16

CHRISTIAN

LUISA: FYI, YOUR GIRL GOT THE DEAL.

I stared at my phone, suddenly more interested in Luisa's text than Kage's briefing on the Rutledge situation.

I'd told her to update me when she made a final decision, and she'd chosen correctly, as I'd known she would.

My only regret was not seeing Stella's face and the way her eyes must've lit up when she got the news.

We'd have to celebrate later—for appearances' sake, of course, since that was what a real couple would do. Maybe dinner in New York or a weekend in Paris...

"...could keep the Rutledge account, but we don't know if Sentinel—Christian, are you listening to me?" A hint of annoyance worked its way into Kage's voice.

"Yes. We held onto the Rutledge account, Sentinel will try to steal more of our clients, and they're allegedly working on something big, but we don't know what it is yet. Continue." I looked up, my face hardening. "And don't question me again."

Kage's mouth tightened, but he continued as ordered.

"We're still gathering intel on Sentinel's secret project, but we think..."

I dropped my eyes back to my phone and opened Stella's profile. She hadn't posted anything new in the past few days, so I settled for examining the photo of us at the art gallery.

Even from the side, she was a vision.

Lush dark curls, flawless skin, and long, lean lines that transformed even the plainest clothing into a masterpiece.

Something tugged low in my gut at the memory of how she'd felt beneath my hands. Of the way her scent filled my lungs when I buried my face in her neck and the little hitch in her voice when I'd touched her.

She'd looked so enraptured by that painting I almost hadn't wanted to interrupt her, but I couldn't help myself.

Trying to stay away from her was like the ocean trying to stay away from the shore.

Impossible.

I rubbed my thumb over the phone screen while Kage droned on.

In truth, I hadn't needed to convince Wyatt of anything at the gallery opening. He'd already agreed to hire Harper Security; we just needed to sign the contract, which I could've scheduled during business hours.

But according to Brock, Stella hadn't left her house since her family dinner, and she'd needed a push to go outside. She shone too brightly to stay cooped up out of fear.

"What's the latest update on the background checks?" I interrupted whatever Kage was saying to focus on the most important matter at hand: Stella's stalker.

As expected, he was lying low, and he'd been careful with all the notes he'd sent her. They were all infuriatingly generic with not a single shred of physical evidence to point us in the right direction.

In the absence of new evidence, I'd had Kage pull together a list of everyone in Stella's life, including old classmates, coworkers, and other influencers. A majority of stalking victims knew their stalker in some capacity, so that was the best place to start.

Kage frowned but wisely didn't complain. "Nothing suspicious yet. I'll let you know as soon as we get a hit." He hesitated, then said, "Listen, I know she's your girl, but we're using a lot of resources on—"

He was interrupted again, this time by an incoming call on my phone.

Stella.

It was like I'd conjured her with my thoughts.

I picked up, expecting her to tell me about the Delamonte deal. She dashed those expectations immediately.

"Christian." Stella's voice cracked.

Ice doused the warmth that'd flared at the sight of her name.

Something's wrong.

"Where are you?" I skipped the useless questions—*are you okay? what's wrong?*—and cut straight to the heart of the matter.

Despite my calm voice, my hand curled so tight around my phone it cracked in protest.

"Home." Her reply was barely audible.

"I'll be right there."

I didn't bother putting on a jacket before I left; the only thing I could think about was how upset Stella must be to call me.

If she could, she would keep all her problems to herself and try to handle them on her own. Always helping others and never asking for herself. The fact she hadn't...

My heart slowed to a deep, ominous thrum, and my hand flexed with the sudden need to strangle something before I forced it to relax.

Until I found out exactly what happened, I needed to keep a level head and not kill anyone—specifically Brock, who was *supposed* to be looking after Stella.

Kage gawked at me as I yanked open the door.

I never walked out of a briefing, ever. I liked to know everything that was happening in my business, even if it was boring as shit.

"Where are you—"

"Briefing's over." I slammed the door behind me, cutting him off mid-sentence.

My footsteps pounded out a cold, furious rhythm as I called Brock on my way to the garage.

Why the *fuck* hadn't he alerted me that something was wrong? What was the point of having someone shadow Stella if they couldn't do their goddamn job?

"Stella. What happened?" I bit out when he answered.

There was a short, startled pause before he answered. "Nothing, sir."

"Nothing." My voice dropped to subzero temperatures. "If *nothing* happened, why did she just call me, sounding like she was on the verge of tears?"

Another pause, this one laced with uncertainty.

"She was home all morning. She went to the coffee shop, received a call, and looked happy as hell. She was still smiling when she returned to her apartment. I don't know what happened after that." I heard an audible swallow. "You told me not to monitor her when she was inside her house."

I had, and that was a fucking mistake. *Screw boundaries.* They didn't apply when it came to her safety.

I could practically hear Brock sweating over the line. "Boss, I swear, I didn't—"

"We'll talk about this later."

I ended the call and climbed into my car. If he didn't have useful information for me, I wasn't going to waste my time talking to him.

My only focus was on getting to Stella as soon as possible.

Fury flickered in my chest, its icy burn a balm to the hot, unfamiliar panic in my lungs as I sped toward the Mirage.

Between my McLaren and the semi-empty streets, I made it there in five minutes flat.

When I arrived at Stella's apartment, I found her in the living room, staring at a sheet of paper in her hands.

I didn't have to read it to know it was another note from her stalker.

Crimson edged my vision, but I kept my expression neutral as Stella lifted her head to look at me.

"I found it in my bedroom," she whispered. "He was inside my *house*. He's never—this is the first time he's ever..." Her shallow breaths filled the ensuing silence.

I recognized their erratic rhythm and the tiny shivers wracking her body.

She was on the verge of a panic attack.

I crossed the room and eased the letter out of her frozen hands, the gentle movement at odds with the violent roar of blood in my ears.

A cursory glance revealed three typed words.

I warned you.

The roar intensified.

"He's not here anymore, but I'll check the apartment just in case." I forced a soothing note into my voice, even though I wanted to hunt down the fucker and flay him alive. "Stay here."

I pulled on a pair of gloves and swept the apartment for

other signs of disturbance. I didn't find any, but I'd have to do a more thorough check later.

For now, I needed to get Stella out of here.

I reentered the living room and snapped the gloves off my fingers. The sweep had settled some of the banked rage in my gut, but the sight of Stella curled up on the couch, her knees drawn to her chest and her face blank, brought it roaring back.

"Everything looks clear, but you're moving into my place until we sort this out." My voice was even but firm.

I should've listened to my gut and insisted she move in with me after the first note, but I hadn't wanted to push her too far, too soon.

But now that the creep had gotten into her apartment, in *my building*...

My hand flexed again.

I wanted to wrap it around the throat of the perpetrator and squeeze the life out of them while he begged for mercy. I wanted to watch the light drain from their eyes at the realization of how badly they'd fucked up.

The soothing images of their torture matched the metallic taste of blood on my tongue. I could already *taste* the vengeance.

Once I found the bastard, I was going to enjoy making them regret every second of their miserable existence.

I breathed through the coldness mounting in my chest and folded the letter into a neat square that I tucked into my pocket.

I knelt in front of Stella so we were at eye level.

"My apartment is airtight. *No one* can get in without my permission. You've seen the systems I have in place," I said, my face softening. "You'll be safe there. Do you understand?"

After a long silence, she responded with a tiny, almost imperceptible nod.

Movement. We were making progress.

When we arrived at my apartment, I took Stella to the only guest room equipped with bedroom furniture.

Since I never allowed overnight guests, I'd turned the others into something more useful: a cyber-surveillance center, a second office for videoconferences, an extra closet for my suits.

With its king-size bed, walk-in closet, and ensuite bathroom, the one real guest room could've passed for a master bedroom, but Stella sank onto the bed without examining her new surroundings.

"Get some rest," I told her. "I'll take care of moving your things."

No response.

I recognized shock when I saw it. As much as I wanted to stay with her, the best thing I could do was give her time to process while I sorted everything else out.

My first order of business after I left her room was another call to Brock, who I ordered to bring up the essentials—night clothes, toiletries, that ugly unicorn Stella loved so much.

My next call was to the Mirage's chief of security.

Charles picked up after half a ring. "Sir?"

"I want all the security footage from the past day sent to me within the hour." I dispensed with the niceties and rubbed my thumb over the turquoise ring in my pocket.

No matter how cold the temperature or how long I left it untouched, the stone was always warm.

"Of course. For which camera?"

"All of them." Stella lived on the tenth floor, but the perpetrator had to have entered and left elsewhere in the building.

"*All* of them? Sir, that's—"

"Someone broke into my girlfriend's apartment today, Charles." My easy tone didn't match the danger rising beneath its surface. "You must know that already since you're my head of security. Perhaps you even have a lead on who broke in. So tell me. Which cameras should I look at if not all of them?"

Silence thundered for a beat before he responded. "I'll have it to you in thirty."

"Good. And Charles?"

A nervous swallow rattled the line. "Yes, sir?"

"Fire every security personnel who was on duty today."

I hung up before I had to listen to his tedious protests.

The security team at the Mirage was good, but they weren't irreplaceable. There was a reason they were guarding a building and not my VIP clients.

And if they couldn't even do *that* right, then they had no business being in my employ.

I provided my staff with exceptional pay and benefits, but I expected exceptional work in return.

Brock showed up soon after my call with Charles with a duffel bag and the unicorn. He set them down in the living room before he turned and ran a hand over his buzz cut.

"Boss, I—"

"You're dismissed for the night."

My anger had cooled enough for me to recognize that it wasn't Brock's fault the stalker had snuck into Stella's apartment. His job had been to keep an eye on her, not her house.

Still, my irritation ran sharp enough to turn my words into blades.

Relief spread across Brock's face before he tensed again. "Just for the night, right? Not forever?"

My lips thinned.

"Right. Gotcha." He nodded and hoofed it out the door. "G'night."

I exhaled a long, slow breath and pinched the bridge of my nose.

Sometimes, I truly despised people.

And objects.

I glared at the raggedy stuffed animal polluting my living room. I didn't understand why Stella loved it so much, or why her followers would rather cuddle with it than *me*—I hated cuddling, but it was the principle of the matter—but since she did, I swallowed my distaste and took it to the guest room along with her luggage.

"You have a visitor." I dropped the *thing* on the bed next to her and resisted the urge to Lysol my hands.

Stella blinked down at the unicorn but didn't touch it.

"Figured you'd want its company." *Though God knows why.* "I also brought some of your clothes and toiletries."

A strange awkwardness prickled my skin at her continued silence.

Fuck, I hated this. Less than an hour in my house, and she'd already thrown me further off my equilibrium.

But the discomfort was worth knowing she was safe.

Right now, I didn't trust anyone or anything to protect her except myself.

I cleared my throat and nodded at her bathroom. "A hot shower might make you feel better. Wash off the day."

No response.

The less Stella reacted, the more the pressure in my chest expanded.

I didn't know where it came from, but I loathed it as much as I loathed polyester, incompetence, and dessert.

Since she didn't seem interested in moving on her own anytime soon, I opened the bathroom door to start the shower but immediately grimaced.

Christ.

I hadn't entered this bathroom since I moved in years ago, so I assumed the foul smell had something to do with the long-unused drain.

My housekeeper kept the marble floors and counters squeaky clean, but she hadn't said a damn thing about the smell.

Could *no one* do their job right?

My teeth clenched as I worked through my options.

Obviously, Stella couldn't use this bathroom until I fixed the smell. There were other guest baths available, but they also hadn't been used in a while.

After a minute of tortured indecision, I walked to my private bathroom and turned on the bathtub faucets. I silently cursed the universe as I opened an unused bottle of bubble bath I didn't even remember buying and slowly poured it into the water.

You really know how to fuck a guy over.

I didn't know how the hell I ended up drawing a bath for someone else like a damn nineteenth-century attendant, but at least there were no witnesses to my indignity. If anyone saw me like this, I would never live it down.

Stella didn't protest when I returned to the guest room and carried her into my bathroom along with her toiletries. I set her down on the cushioned bench near the tub and tilted my chin at the eucalyptus-scented bath.

"All yours until I fix a small issue in your bathroom," I said. "There's also a guest bath across the hall and to your left if you need to use the toilet at night."

I turned and was already halfway out of the room when she stopped me.

"Christian. I don't..." Her small voice shot an arrow straight through my ribs. "I don't want to be alone right now."

Goddammit.

My hand curled around the doorknob until the metal seared into my flesh.

"What are you suggesting?" My voice pitched low with a warning she didn't heed.

Despite my strange desire to shield Stella from danger, I wasn't a protector by nature. My version of protection always came wrapped in the pieces of a snuffed-out life and tied with a bloody bow.

Unfortunately for her, she was too innocent and trusting to recognize true danger when she saw it.

"Can you stay with me?" Embarrassment colored her request. "Just for tonight."

My muscles tightened at the suggestion. I turned, taking in her pale face and the wary way she eyed the tub, like she expected a monster to emerge from its depths and swallow her whole.

"The bathroom is clear, and I'll be right outside the door."

I wasn't immune to bad ideas, but staying in the room with her while she bathed might be the worst idea that had ever existed.

"I know. I just..." Stella faltered. "No, you're right. That was...I don't know what I was thinking."

A shiver wracked her body. She didn't move from the bench.

I closed my eyes for a brief moment while my silent curses aimed at the universe escalated.

I shouldn't. I really fucking shouldn't.

I'd already crossed a line by bringing her into my house and into my fucking *bathroom*, but the look on her face...

I turned my back again, loathing myself more with every second that passed.

"Let me know when you're ready."

Despite my curt tone, a breath of relief touched my back and made my jaw clench.

I didn't shift positions until I heard the splash of her getting into the tub.

Stella was naked in my bathroom.

Under normal circumstances, my brain would've latched onto the obvious—the rosy bloom of her cheeks, the way her skin glistened with water, the fantasy of the sweet curves that lay beneath the bubbles.

Instead, a deep ache settled in my chest at how small and vulnerable she looked in that giant tub. No longer the oasis of calm she presented to the world, but a storm on the verge of breaking.

She reached for her shampoo, but I stopped her before she made contact.

"I'll do it."

Instead of arguing like I'd expected, Stella remained quiet until I pulled the bench to the edge of the tub and uncapped her shampoo.

"Your suit will get wet," she murmured.

I didn't spare my custom Brioni a glance. "I'll survive."

I washed her hair, cleaning each strand with painstaking meticulousness and massaging her scalp with firm, deep strokes until she sank against the side of the tub with her eyes closed.

Her lashes swept against her cheeks in a dark fan, and her breaths gradually evened out into a steady rhythm.

Heat steamed up the mirrors and drenched the room in a sultry haze.

Wearing a suit in a hot bathroom was fucking hell, but I didn't bother removing my jacket.

It was my first time touching Stella for such an extended length of time, and I was going to savor every second.

It wasn't sexual, but the simple glide of her hair against my palms slowed my pulse to a torturous crawl before kicking it into overdrive.

Touching her killed me, then brought me back to life again.

The quiet roar of my heart thrummed in my ears. I rinsed out the shampoo and worked the conditioner into her strands.

The irony of me cleaning Stella wasn't lost on me. She was the purest soul I knew, and I was neck-deep in blood.

The angel and the sinner.

Two oppositional forces with nothing binding us except a sheet of paper and the unquenchable need in my soul.

I didn't deserve to touch her, but I wanted her too much to care.

After I finished washing her hair, I picked up her loofah, dipped it in the water, and lathered it up.

The gentle lap of the water against the tub tightened low in my gut.

"Lean forward." Restraint roughened the edge of my voice.

Stella obliged.

I ran the loofah over her back, my eyes tracking every inch of its slow journey down her smooth, bare skin.

The air pulsed with tangible energy as I dragged it up over her shoulder and across her front. Low enough to skim the tops of her breasts, but high enough to keep things appropriate.

Stella's body went taut when my arm brushed her neck. I paused, picking up on the renewed rapidness of her breaths.

Its rhythm was different this time—heavier, more weighted.

Heat sparked in my gut, and I stood so abruptly she jumped at the movement. "We're done."

There was something fucked up about lusting over someone who was traumatized, even for me.

I yanked a bathrobe off where it hung on the wall and held it open, my eyes averted and my jaw tight.

After a beat of hesitation, Stella climbed out of the tub and slipped into it.

I cinched the belt so tight it elicited a small gasp, but at least the oversized robe covered her from her neck to her calves.

I dried her hair briskly and was about to push her through the bedroom and into the hall when her earlier request resurfaced in my mind.

Can you stay with me? Just for tonight.

A new set of curses scorched my tongue before I swallowed them.

"Do you want to stay here for the night?" I asked gruffly.

She hugged her arms around her waist and, after another moment of hesitation, nodded.

Fuck my life.

Still, I pulled back my covers and nodded at the bed. "Get some rest. We'll deal with everything in the morning."

It was early in the evening, but exhaustion lined her face and cast shadows beneath her eyes.

I left the room to grab her nightclothes so she could change into something more sleep-friendly, but by the time I returned, Stella was already fast asleep. It was the most at peace I'd seen her in weeks.

I'd never let another person sleep in my bed before. I thought the sight of her nestled amongst the black and gray silks would be strange, but it felt right.

I placed the clothes on the nightstand next to her and tried to catch up on work, but my brain couldn't focus.

With my building security compromised, the incompetent but annoying shits at Sentinel breathing down my neck, and a thousand emails to wade through, all I could think about was the woman sleeping a few feet away.

She'd been in my house for less than two hours, and she was already wreaking havoc on my life.

I rubbed a hand over my jaw, my aggravation at war with my desire to protect her at all costs.

I'd been wrong.

Stella wasn't a distraction. She was a danger—not only to my business but to myself and the parts of me I hadn't known still existed.

17

STELLA

I woke to sunshine and the faint scent of leather and spice.

That was the first sign something was amiss since I exclusively used lavender scents in my bedroom.

The second sign was the color of the sheets. Slate gray silk, luxurious in its simplicity and rumpled with sleep, but a far cry from the soft cream ones I'd bought two years ago.

The fog of sleep lingered as I stared at the dent in the pillow next to mine and tried to piece together what happened last night.

I was clearly in a man's room. The dark colors and the watch and cufflinks on the nightstand were a dead giveaway.

Had I gone out drinking and hooked up with someone at their place? Unlikely.

Had I stayed the night at Ava's place? But her guest rooms didn't look like this, and—

"You're awake."

A scream clawed up my throat at the unexpected voice behind me.

I whipped around, my heart thundering with panic until the speaker stepping out of the bathroom came into focus.

Dark hair. Whiskey eyes. Chiseled face.

Christian.

This was his room. Why was I in—

Yesterday's memories slammed into me so fast and hard they knocked the breath from my lungs.

The note in my bedroom, calling Christian, moving into his place, him *bathing* me...

Oh God.

Dread and mortification curdled in my stomach. I would've thrown up had I eaten anything more than a croissant yesterday.

"You didn't want to be alone, so I let you stay in my room for the night." Christian straightened his sleeve. It was eight in the morning, but he was already dressed in one of his signature suits and loafers. His hair was perfectly styled, his face sharp and clean-shaven. "That was a one-time exception, given what happened, but you'll be sleeping in the guest room from now on. It's there for a reason."

I frowned, trying to reconcile the cold man in front of me with the one who'd carried me to his room and taken care of me yesterday.

A flush sluiced down my skin when I remembered the heat of his body behind me and the graze of his touch against my bare skin.

It hadn't been sexual, and I'd been too in shock to react much at the time, but the memory ignited a soft burn that warmed me from the inside out.

Christian's eyes darkened like he could see straight into my mind. "Breakfast will be served in half an hour. I'll see you then."

He walked out before I could respond.

I guess he wasn't a morning person.

A headache throbbed behind my temple as I tried to make sense of the past twenty-four hours.

Yesterday morning, I woke up in my own bed feeling fairly optimistic about the stalker situation.

Now, I was living in Christian Harper's house because the stalker broke into mine.

Whoever they were, they knew where I lived and could break into one of the most secure buildings in the city.

Fear slowed the beats of my heart.

It's fine. You're fine.

Maybe they could break into the Mirage, but they couldn't break into Christian's penthouse. Right?

I reached for my necklace, only to realize I wasn't wearing one.

Christian had brought only the essentials last night, which meant my crystals were sitting downstairs in my room.

The bite of fear intensified at the thought of returning to my old apartment. I'd loved that apartment, but I couldn't imagine going back after the break-in shattered its sanctity.

I hated my stalker for destroying that peace almost as much as I hated him for the notes.

After all these years, I still couldn't understand why he'd targeted me. Was it my social media presence? My looks? Or was I just unlucky enough to catch the attention of some creep who had too much time on his hands?

I forced a deep inhale into my lungs.

Everything's fine. You'll be fine.

It was broad daylight, and Christian was right outside. As moody as he was, he wouldn't let anything happen to me.

I didn't know why, but I felt the conviction of that in my gut.

You'll be fine.

I repeated the reassurance in my head as I went to the guest room—a.k.a. my new room for the foreseeable future—and changed out of my bathrobe into day-appropriate loungewear.

When I entered the dining room, Christian was already seated at the head of the table with a cup of coffee, a pen, and that morning's newspaper crossword.

The table itself groaned beneath the weight of a full breakfast spread. Glass pitchers of coffee, juice, water, and tea gleamed next to platters of every type of breakfast item imaginable: eggs prepared six different ways, crispy bacon, fluffy lemon ricotta pancakes and Belgian waffles and French toast.

Croissants, muffins, and scones filled two large woven baskets, while a make-it-yourself smoothie bowl section boasted every fruit and topping I could think of.

It was a buffet for twenty, not two.

"Are you hosting a brunch party?" I asked, uncertain why anyone needed *this* much food for themselves.

"No, but Nina went all out, so you may as well enjoy it."

Before I could ask who Nina was, a round-faced woman with a dark bun and cheerful smile entered the room.

"I'm Nina." She gave Christian a disapproving glance before she handed me a glass of something green and creamy. "Wheatgrass smoothie, right?"

I relaxed beneath the warmth of her friendliness. "Yes, thank you. How did you know?"

This must be Christian's housekeeper slash part-time chef. I'd never met her, though I knew she was the only person who had the keys to his house besides me.

"Mr. Harper told me it was your favorite." She winked at me while Christian glared at her.

"That'll be all for now. Thank you." His polite dismissal only half masked the razor's edge running beneath his voice.

Nina suppressed what looked like a laugh before she left.

"I see caffeine hasn't improved your mood." I loaded a plate with food and sat next to him. "I'd hoped it would bring Dr. Jekyll back. Mr. Hyde isn't doing it for me."

He'd always been on the aloof side, but I felt the distance between us vividly this morning.

"Funny. I see a night of sleep *has* improved your mood." Christian folded the crossword and set it aside before he added, "How are you feeling?"

"Hungry. I haven't eaten since yesterday morning," I admitted.

I knew that wasn't what he was really asking, but I didn't want to talk about the note right now. I just wanted to eat and pretend everything was normal.

I tore off a piece of my croissant and popped it in my mouth. A sigh of pleasure rose in my throat.

Croissants were a gift of heaven. I was sure of it.

"Good. I wasn't sure what you were in the mood for, so I had Nina make a bit of everything," he said, his tone gruff.

Warmth flickered to life in my chest.

I gave him a shy smile, touched by the gesture even though he wasn't the one who'd cooked the food.

A faint hint of pink colored his cheekbones.

Was he...*blushing?*

Before I could make sense of the staggering sight, the pink disappeared, and Christian's face turned to granite again.

"Since you're here, we should go over the rules."

My brow furrowed. "Okay..."

"You're here because you're in danger, and since you're now fully under my protection, we need to take appropriate steps to secure your safety," he said crisply. "Staying here until we catch the person who's been leaving you those notes is the first step. My team will move the rest of your belongings in today. While you're here, you will sleep in the guest room and

adhere to the house rules. No bringing friends or men over..."
His voice iced at the word *men*. "And no touching unrecognizable devices. There's a fifty-fifty chance they could kill you.
Other than that, consider this your home for the foreseeable
future."

Fifty-fifty chance they could kill me? What kind of devices
did he *own*?

"Oh." I forced a bright smile. "Well, who can resist a
welcome like that? You really know how to make a girl feel all
warm and fuzzy."

Christian ignored my sarcasm. "It's good that you're not
posting where you are in real time, but I want you to wait
twenty-four hours to post instead of your usual three to four.
Vary your schedule and keep it unpredictable, including the
routes you take home. You will also have a bodyguard. Brock
will look after you when you're not with me. He'll be unobtru-
sive; you won't even know he's there unless you need help.
Finally..."

"Oh, good. I was afraid that was it. Go on."

"You have to tell your friends the truth." Christian fixed me
with a hard stare. "If they don't know you're in danger, they can
inadvertently *put* you in danger or be in danger themselves.
Ignorance isn't always bliss."

My smile faded. A protest worked its way to the tip of my
tongue before I squashed it.

Christian was right.

As much as I hated making my friends worry and having a
bodyguard watching every move I made—similar to a stalker,
though with less nefarious intentions—I needed the protection.

Plus, I couldn't have my friends thinking everything was
okay when it *wasn't*. What if the stalker targeted them when he
couldn't get to me? I would never forgive myself if something
happened to them because I didn't give them proper warning.

My nails dug angry half-moons into my knees.

Cool, calm, collected.

Cool, calm, collected.

"Okay," I finally said. "I'll tell them. But I have a few rules of my own."

If this new living arrangement was going to work, I needed some say in it. Christian was the security expert, but this was *my* life.

"Of course you do." Dryness filled Christian's voice. No doubt he remembered my insistence on including my own set of rules in our fake dating arrangement.

"This is your house, and I'll respect your rules. But I also ask that you respect my privacy. That means no coming into my room without permission, even when—*especially* when—I'm not there. Don't go through my belongings even if they're in a common space. Don't tell me where I can go or who I can see unless it's a direct threat to my safety. And..." My teeth sank into my bottom lip as I contemplated my last request.

"And?" He raised a dark brow.

My nails dug deeper into my skin. "No bringing women home. I don't care if you sleep with them, but they can't be here while I'm here. It's not...it won't look right."

Exclusivity was implied but not explicitly stated in our contract. I had no issue maintaining celibacy, but I doubted I could say the same for someone like Christian. He probably had women flinging themselves at him every day, regardless of his relationship status.

A strange twist wrung my heart and left it out to dry when I pictured him with another woman.

I told myself it had everything to do with keeping up appearances and nothing to do with...anything else.

Christian's amusement disappeared beneath pools of amber ice. "I don't cheat, Stella."

"It's not cheating when we're not really dating."

What was I saying? It wasn't like I *wanted* him to sleep with other women. It was too risky, and…

My stomach cramped. I must've inhaled my croissant too fast.

Tick. Tick. Tick. I watched the muscle jump in his jaw with nervous fascination. Christian's anger was a rolling wave, slow and insidious as it swallowed everything in its wake. But when he spoke again, his tone was as smooth and placid as a summer lake.

"Noted."

Noted? That was the vaguest answer he could've given, but I was too apprehensive to ask for clarification.

We didn't speak again for the rest of the meal.

That afternoon, while Christian worked in his home office and the movers hauled the rest of my belongings up from my apartment, I explored the eight thousand square feet of bachelor luxury that would be my home for God knew how long.

I came here every week to take care of his plants, but I left immediately after. I never took the time to study my surroundings.

Christian's penthouse took up the entire eleventh floor of the Mirage, which was as high as buildings got in D.C. due to the city's height limit.

Light gray marble floors, black leather furniture, floor-to-ceiling windows offering a three-hundred-sixty-degree view of the city. The house reflected the man: sleek, exquisitely decorated, and beautiful in a way that was cold but impersonal.

He had the lavish touches one would expect from someone of his wealth, such as a private rooftop pool and a state-of-the-art gym down the hall from the den, but my favorite room was the library.

Piles of cushions turned the deep windowsills into sunny

reading nooks while modern orange couches added an unexpected pop of color. Hundreds of books lined the customized black shelves, and I could tell by their worn spines that Christian actually read them instead of using them as props.

That was where I chose to bite the bullet and call my friends. I'd been putting it off all day, but I couldn't stall much longer.

I called Ava first. Bridget lived in Eldorra with plenty of protection, and Jules already knew about the stalker, so it wouldn't take long to update her.

"Hey!" Despite my less-than-ideal circumstances, Ava's bright voice made me smile. "What's up?"

A lot. "Not much. Are you home?" I wanted to make sure she wasn't in transit when I dropped the bombshell.

"Yep, just got back." I heard the closing of a door and a faint masculine voice in the background. I assumed it was her fiancé Alex.

I felt better knowing Ava had Alex by her side.

Alex Volkov was a force of his own, and while he made me a bit uneasy—I was almost certain he harbored psychopathic tendencies—he would put his life on the line to protect Ava.

"Great." I twisted the bottom of my shirt. I should've scripted how I would break the news to her, but it was too late now. "How was work?"

"Fun, but *beyond* busy. We have our annual Best Of feature coming up, and..."

I half listened as she told me about her latest photography assignment, her upcoming wedding, and my Delamonte deal.

I needed to discuss the contract with Brady, but with everything that'd happened over the past twenty-four hours, it'd completely slipped my mind.

Closing the Delamonte deal had consumed me for months. Now that I finally had it, it was barely a blip on my radar.

The universe had a messed-up sense of timing.

"What else is going on besides Delamonte? How are things with Christian?" Ava asked. "You haven't posted about him since the art gallery photo. That was super cute, by the way."

There it was. The opening I'd been looking for.

My phone slipped against my palm as I forced my next words past the lump in my throat.

"About that. I, uh…" I coughed. "I moved in with him yesterday."

There was a beat of silence before a disbelieving *"What?"* boomed over the line.

I winced and held my phone away from my ear. For someone so small, Ava had a powerful voice.

"You *moved in* with him? I thought you were…" She dropped her voice to a whisper. Alex must be nearby. "Only fake dating. Why are you suddenly living with him?"

"That's the other thing." My chest expanded with a deep, fortifying breath. "I…"

I have a stalker.

The words sat on the tip of my tongue, but I couldn't get them out.

I'd been keeping my secret for so long, the idea of sharing it with my friends made my heart kick like a trapped animal against its cage.

Christian and Jules knew the truth, but only out of necessity—Christian because he found me the night I discovered the note, Jules because we'd lived together when the stalker made his first appearance. And she didn't know the stalker was back.

"I, um…" *Just say it.* I stood and paced the room, too restless to sit. "I moved in because I…I have a stalker. And he broke into my apartment yesterday."

The words finally spilled out and landed on the floor with a heavy thud. The force of it reverberated through my bones, but the ensuing silence was so thick I could taste it over the line.

"What?" Ava breathed. Softer this time, and dizzy with shock.

I stopped next to the potted fern. The earthy smells of soil and greenery worked their way into my lungs, grounding me and giving me the fortitude to explain the situation. I started with the notes from two years ago and ended with my discovery yesterday.

The more I talked, the easier it was, though a whisper of unease lingered in my stomach. I hated worrying my friends.

"So that's why I moved in with Christian," I finished. "It's the safest thing to do while the stalker is still on the loose."

I rubbed an absentminded thumb over my necklace— amethyst, for calming energies and stress relief. I'd hunted it down immediately after the movers brought my stuff up.

I needed all the stress relief I could get.

"Yes, but…" Ava blew out a sigh. "I'm sorry. I still can't get over the part where this started *three years* ago, and you didn't tell me. This isn't a secret boyfriend or…or a side gig moonlighting as a dancer, Stella. You're my best friend, and your *life* was in danger." She didn't sound angry; she sounded hurt, which was even worse. "I would've helped you."

"There was nothing you could've done. If anything had happened to you because of me, I never would've forgiven myself."

Another long pause. "Do Jules and Bridget know?"

My teeth sank into my bottom lip. "Jules knows about the first batch of letters since we were living together at the time. Bridget has no clue. The notes stopped coming after a few months," I added. "So it wasn't an issue for too long."

Until they restarted.

"God," Ava breathed. "This is bananas."

"Not more bananas than getting kidnapped by your boyfriend's psycho uncle, right?" I hid my nerves with a shaky laugh.

Despite her sunny demeanor, Ava had lived through more traumatic events than I have.

"Right. They could make soap operas out of our lives," she said dryly. "Listen, just stay with me until you catch this guy. Alex won't mind, and he'll sort things out. Actually, let me get him." She raised her voice. "Alex, can you come over here? I have—"

"No! Don't tell him." Involving Alex in something like this was a *bad* idea. He was as liable to murder someone as he was to help them. "I've got this under control. Besides, Christian is the security expert, and you have enough on your plate with the wedding."

"Screw the wedding—crap. Hold on." Ava must've covered the speaker because her words became muffled. "No, honey, of course I still want to get married! I was talking to Stella about the, um, wedding planner...no, *don't* fire her. She's great. I was just frustrated in the moment. Bridal nerves, you know. I'm fine now. Yes, I promise...why did I call for you? Uh, I'm craving those new raspberry lemon cookies from Crumble & Bake. Can you please run down and get some for me? Thank you! Love you."

Ava returned, sounding breathless. "Sorry about that. Alex has been so on edge about the wedding. He made our florist cry the other day." She sighed. "We're working on his interpersonal skills."

Usually, brides were the ones who obsessed over every detail, but Alex was type A to a fault.

"Anyway." Ava turned serious again. "Are you sure you don't need help? I know Christian probably has it handled, but Alex knows everyone."

"Yes, I'm sure. There's no need to drag more people into my mess than necessary."

The situation had already ballooned out of control, with the move and a bodyguard and God knew what else. The last thing I wanted was for it to turn into even more of a circus.

"You're not dragging us anywhere. We *want* to be there. You're our friend, Stella," Ava said gently. "If you're in danger, we want to help. That's what friends do. That's what you would do for us."

A knot of emotion formed in my throat. Natalia and I were sisters by blood, but Ava, Jules, and Bridget were my family by choice.

We'd been there for each other through the highest of highs and the lowest of lows, and even if I'd shielded them from the worst in my life, just knowing they were there helped me make it through the day.

Sometimes, all we needed was the knowledge someone somewhere cared about us.

"I know. If I need anything, I'll tell you. I promise."

"Okay." Despite her palpable reluctance, Ava didn't press the issue. "Stay safe. And I'm not just talking about the creep sending you notes."

I'm also talking about Christian.

She didn't say it, but I heard her loud and clear.

"I will." I took another deep breath. "I have to go, but I love you."

I could tell Ava wanted to say more, but she held back. "Love you too."

I hung up.

One down, two more to go.

I called Jules next. She was going to lose her shit, but she already knew about the stalker, so maybe she'll lose less of her shit?

Oh, who was I kidding? I would be lucky if she didn't show up at my door wielding a machete and a plan to scour every neighborhood in D.C. until we found them.

"Hey, J," I said when she picked up. "Are you home? You're not near any sharp objects, are you? Good, because I have something to tell you..."

18

CHRISTIAN/STELLA

I SPENT THE DAY REVIEWING THE SECURITY FOOTAGE FROM yesterday. There were hours of useless video, but I kept coming back to the same spot—a half-hour "technical glitch" which coincided with Stella's trip to the coffee shop.

The stalker had not only broken into her apartment; they'd also hacked into the Mirage's closed-circuit surveillance system. It should've been impossible, but the thirty minutes of static that'd replaced what should've been a crystal-clear view of the hallway outside Stella's apartment confirmed it.

I'd already ordered a full emergency overhaul of the building's security system. Every code changed, every nook and cranny swept for evidence of tampering. They all came back clean, which meant one thing.

It'd either been an inside job, or the stalker had inside help.

My blood iced at the prospect.

Every employee had to pass extensive screenings before I hired them, but life changed. All it took was a debt or a loved one in danger to make a person vulnerable to bribery and persuasion.

I would know; I was often the one doing the bribing and persuading.

I eased a breath through my lungs and shrugged off my fury with a subtle roll of my shoulders.

There was a time and place for business. Dinner with Stella wasn't it.

I was already running a second round of checks on everyone who worked at the Mirage and Harper Security. I would know by tomorrow whether anyone had weaknesses outsiders could exploit.

Until then, I'd keep the ugly details of the investigation to myself.

Outwardly, Stella had bounced back from the break-in, but she was good at hiding her true emotions.

Even her closest friends thought she was unflappable when the signs of her anxiety were so clear—the way her breathing changed and her eyes darkened, the way she twisted her necklace around her finger whenever she was upset.

She didn't show any of those signs now, but that didn't mean she'd put what happened behind her. It'd only been twenty-four hours, for fuck's sake.

"By the way, Luisa told me about the Delamonte deal," I said, filling the lull in our conversation. "Congratulations."

Since the meal started, she'd talked about everything except the break-in. She hadn't even mentioned how her friends took the news, not that I cared. I only cared that they didn't endanger her by doing something stupid.

But if she didn't want to talk about what happened, I wouldn't force her to.

Instead of sitting next to me like she'd had at breakfast, she occupied the chair at the other end of the eight-person table.

The distance irked me more than it should have, but a tiny

smile touched my lips when her eyes brightened at the mention of Delamonte.

"Thank you. I can't believe I got the deal. I still need to talk to my manager and sign the contract, but..." Her smile dimmed. "Well, you know what happened. Anyway." She cleared her throat and took a sip of her water. "I'm excited. The campaign can open a lot of doors for me."

"Is that what you want? To work with brands full time?"

From a logical standpoint, moving Stella into my house was one of the worst decisions I could've made.

She was my biggest distraction. My weakness.

That was why I'd tried to keep my distance that morning, but I didn't fucking appreciate her telling me she didn't care if I went out and fucked other women.

Like I'd been able to focus on any other woman since I met her.

I'd lasted less than a day trying to stay away from her.

"I think it's good for the short term," Stella said in response to my question. "I'm not sure it's sustainable for the long term. I actually..."

I waited while indecision played across her features.

It was the look of someone who had a secret they were desperate but afraid to tell.

"I *might* start my own fashion brand eventually. It's not a sure thing," she rushed out. "Just an idea I had. We'll see."

My eyebrows rose, more in intrigue than surprise.

Stella starting a fashion line made more sense than her working at a magazine.

Some people were leaders, others were followers. Stella might think she was the latter, but she was too talented and shone too brightly to be hemmed in by other people's expectations.

"I think it's a great idea."

She blinked, clearly startled by my response. "Really?" She sounded doubtful.

"You've already built one brand with your blog and social media. Building a second shouldn't be hard." My mouth tilted. "Correction. It shouldn't be *as* hard."

Stella's brow furrowed. "I never thought about it that way."

"Trust me. Even if you don't have a physical product yet, you're probably further along than you think." She had the industry and marketing knowledge, which was often the hardest part. Creating the actual product was easy. "Do you have a business plan?"

My calm question betrayed the hum in my blood.

I was dragging out the conversation, but this was the first time we were talking about something real, something other than my work, her stalker, and our arrangement.

Stella shared most of her life online, but I wanted to hear about it in her words. I wanted to understand the way she thought, felt, and saw the world.

I wanted to unravel every thread that made her *her* and lay them all bare so I could examine them. Figure out what it was about this woman, in particular, that entranced me when there were thousands who were objectively just as beautiful and who desired me more.

"Does sketch, sew, and pray for the best count?"

Another smile threatened to bloom at her hopeful tone. "Impressive, but I'm afraid you'll require something more concrete."

She sighed. "I was afraid of that. I can do the creative stuff, but I hate math. Anything more than basic accounting goes way over my head."

"When you hit a certain level of success, you can hire someone to run the business side of things for you. Until then..." I tapped my fingers on the table. Once, twice. "I'll help you."

The words hovered between us, as shocked by their existence as I was.

Between the inside leak, her stalker, and Sentinel breathing down my neck, I already had a million things on my plate. I didn't need to add a fucking fashion line to the mix.

But now that the offer was out there, I couldn't take it back.

And, if I were being honest, I didn't want to.

Stella's eyes widened. "*You'll* help me. Personally?"

"I believe that's implied by the word *I'll*, yes."

"Why?"

"Does it matter?"

She hitched a stubborn brow.

I sighed. "I'm not writing the plan *for* you, Stella. I'll send you a template and review it as you go. It won't take much time."

Depending on how her draft was, it might take a whole fucking lot of time, but I kept that to myself.

"Plus, I can say I was there from the start when you become the next big thing," I added.

"You sound so sure that'll happen."

"I *am* sure." I'd witnessed businesses come and go over the years. The ones that thrived were often led by people with the same qualities: creative, passionate, disciplined, and willing to learn.

Stella had all those qualities in spades. She just needed to discover that for herself.

Her shy, answering glance sent a strange warmth spiraling through my chest. "I, um, actually sketched out a few designs. Do you want to see?"

My smile finally blossomed in full, slow and languid. "I'd love to."

Silence ensconced our walk to her room, where she pulled a stack of papers from her desk drawer and handed them to me.

"I wanted a line that fits the types of clothes I already cover on my account. High quality with a mix of price points for different consumers. And lots of dresses," she added. "I love dresses."

Her teeth sank into her bottom lip as I examined the sketches.

"They're just drafts." She twisted her necklace around her finger. "I haven't sketched in a while, so I'm rusty—"

"They're beautiful."

Stella's sketches were lush and intricately detailed, full of rich colors and perfectly cut silhouettes. They were designs that belonged on the runways of Milan and Paris, not stuffed in the corner of a room in D.C.

She faltered. "Really?"

"Yes, and I don't lie to spare people's feelings. If they were terrible, I'd say so. They're not." I handed the sketches back to her. "You're talented. Don't let anyone, including yourself, tell you otherwise."

Stella's lips parted a fraction at my words.

It was a tiny movement, but my eyes latched onto it like a magnet to steel.

The air thickened, suffocating us with a tension that ticked like a bomb waiting to explode.

"Do you understand?" My voice was low, but it burned between us like kindling doused with gasoline.

A visible swallow disrupted the delicate lines of her throat.

"Yes." The soft exhale of her reply brushed my skin and tugged low on my groin.

She was so close.

I could end the game now, bend her to my will and stoke the embers of attraction between us until they ignited into flames. Give her a taste of what she could have if she succumbed to the inevitability of us.

Everything.

"Good."

I dipped my head and, in a subtle, almost unconscious movement, my lips touched hers.

Two seconds. One syllable. An electric instant that scorched every inch of my skin.

Somewhere in the distance, a sheaf of papers fluttered to the floor.

I inhaled Stella's soft gasp like it was my last ounce of oxygen, and a groan worked its way up my throat at her sweet taste.

It was barely a kiss. We hadn't even moved, yet our brief contact *consumed* me.

The air in my lungs, the beat in my heart.

In that moment, Stella was the only thing that existed.

I breathed her in. Exhaled. And pulled back.

We stared at each other.

Our almost kiss had lasted no more than a fraction of a minute, yet we were both flushed and panting like we'd run a marathon.

Surprise and something weightier darkened her eyes into emerald pools.

"Christian..." The sound of my name on her shallow breath poured lust straight into my veins.

My groin tightened.

I couldn't believe I had a hard-on after a few seconds of chaste contact, yet here we were.

"Our first business meeting is next week. Come prepared." I rolled up my sleeves, my cool voice at odds with the flames licking my skin. When did it get so fucking hot in here? "Good night, Stella."

I left before she could respond.

Every molecule of my body demanded I stay and finish what I'd started, but it was too soon. Someone broke into her house yesterday, for God's sake.

Still, when I stepped into my bathroom and turned the water as cold as it would go, the burn in my blood remained.

MARCH 31

I...

What. Just. Happened.

19

STELLA

A week after I moved into his house, I discovered Christian's dirty little secret.

In a dark corner of his den, tucked between DVDs of *Reservoir Dogs* and *The Godfather,* he owned a collector's edition of *Spice World.*

That was right. Christian Harper, the CEO of Harper Security and possibly the most terrifying man I'd ever met, owned a special edition of a movie featuring a nineties girl band that, coincidentally, was one of my favorites for no reason other than its pure campiness.

I didn't know people still owned DVDs, but I wasn't giving up the opportunity to rewatch one of my childhood obsessions on his state-of-the-art flatscreen.

Based on what I'd observed of his schedule, Christian wouldn't be home for another two hours, so I allowed myself to let loose.

I sang and danced along to the movie, only stopping to take a bite of the ice cream sitting on the coffee table.

I wasn't the greatest singer *or* dancer, so I probably looked ridiculous, but I was too happy to care.

It'd been a good day.

I'd officially signed the contract with Delamonte, and our first shoot was scheduled for next week in New York. It was a small shoot, hence the short notice, but I was excited to start the partnership and visit the city again.

I'd also finished another set of sketches and started filling out the business plan template Christian sent me. It wasn't as boring as I'd feared, though some parts, like the financial analysis and production plan, gave me a headache.

Neither of us mentioned our almost/sort of kiss since it happened. We'd kept our conversations strictly to small talk, work, and my fashion line, which was just fine with me.

In fact, things had been *so* normal between us I questioned whether the "kiss" really happened. Maybe it'd been a figment of my imagination, born of the same craziness that'd compelled me to show him my sketches.

I'd never shown them to anyone before.

Meanwhile, fears of my stalker had receded, locked behind the bulletproof glass and steel-reinforced walls of Christian's penthouse. If I thought too much about it, the anxiety came rushing back, but I was busy enough that I didn't *have* to think about it. I could lose myself in my bubble of self-delusion for... well, not forever, but for a while.

So, like I said, it'd been a good day.

I spun, an ice cream spoon in my mouth and feet bare against the cool marble floors.

I was so caught up in my song and dance I didn't notice anyone had entered until I glimpsed a dark figure on my next spin.

A surprised scream exploded into the air before my brain processed the lean, muscled frame and tailored suit.

The spoon clattered from my mouth to the floor and dripped melted dulce de leche ice cream down the front of my shirt.

"Not the usual greeting I receive from women, but an improvement to your prior yodeling." Despite the wry insult, amusement softened the finely chiseled lines of Christian's face.

His eyes, however, were anything but soft. They were blades swathed with black silk, their edges so cold they burned hot against my skin.

They traced the lines of my throat down my torso to my bare legs and feet before sliding back up to my face.

Slow and leisurely, like a cat toying with a mouse.

All the while I held still, afraid any movement would slice me open and bare my wild, beating heart to the electric air.

I was suddenly hyperaware of how short my shorts were, how much skin my cropped sweatshirt bared, and how ridiculous I must look with gel eye patches on my face and leave-in conditioner slicked in my hair, to say nothing of the fact that I'd been dancing and belting along to freaking Spice Girls in his living room.

Mortification chased the flames left behind by his scrutiny, but I clung to the tattered edges of my dignity with bloodied fingertips.

"I wasn't *yodeling*. I was exercising my vocal cords." I bent and retrieved the sticky spoon from the floor as gracefully as I could. "I also thought I was alone. You never come home this early."

"I didn't realize you paid that close attention to my schedule." The velvety drawl brushed against my skin like the most sensual of caresses.

Christian peeled away from the shadows and walked toward me. He wore head-to-toe designer business wear, but those bright amber eyes and the predatory grace with which he moved reminded me of a panther lazily stalking its prey. A beast drawing out the inevitable because he'd grown tired of the ease with which he captured what he wanted.

"I don't, but we've lived together for a week. I don't have to study your comings and goings to know your schedule."

Christian was an early riser. So was I, but by the time I went up to his rooftop for sunrise yoga every morning, I already heard his shower running and smelled coffee brewing in the kitchen.

He left at seven-thirty on the dot and returned twelve hours later, looking as polished as when he'd stepped out the door.

It was unnatural.

Thump. Thump. Thump.

My pulse banged against my wrist and chest and in my ears when he stopped in front of me.

Spice and leather. Crisp black lines and silver cufflinks. Intimidating in their perfection but comforting in their familiarity.

"Do you know why I came home early today?" Christian lifted his hand, and for an exhilarating, terrifying second, I expected him to cup my breast.

Instead, he rubbed his thumb over the spot of ice cream above my chest.

The light touch scorched its way through my veins and pooled between my legs.

"No." I barely heard myself over the storm brewing in the air.

The sounds from the movie had long faded, replaced by the frantic drum of my heart.

"We have an appointment." Amusement filled his eyes at my frown. "Our first business consultation."

I blinked, my brain too hazy to process his words in real time.

Business consultation...

I'll schedule a weekly meeting and add it to your calendar. Come prepared.

"Oh. *Oh.*" My business plan. The one I'd only half filled out.

Reality washed the film of pheromones off my vision and returned my breaths to normal.

"I haven't completed it yet," I admitted. "It's only half done."

Thinking through what I wanted for my business took longer than writing it down.

I braced myself for a lecture or at least a sigh of disappointment, but all Christian said was, "Let me see what you have so far."

I retrieved the papers from the coffee table and handed them to him.

The phantom of his touch lingered on my skin, but the tension from earlier dissolved into nerves as I waited for his feedback.

After an interminable silence, he handed the document back to me. "Good."

"Good?"

That's it?

"Yes, good. The executive summary is clear and succinct, and you've clearly done your market research. It could use a few tweaks, but we'll do that after the full draft is complete." His lips curved. "I didn't expect you to put together a full plan in one week, Stella, especially since you haven't done one before."

Relief loosened the knot in my chest. "You could've told me that earlier. You nearly gave me a heart attack!"

I was the student who'd *always* completed her homework on time. The thought of missing an assignment made my skin crawl.

Disappointment. Failure.

I shook off the insidious voices before they could dig their claws into me, but their echoes remained, dampening my enthusiasm.

"If I told you, would you have gotten as much done?"

I sighed at his logic. "Probably not."

"Exactly." Christian's gaze slid to the TV. "Though I'm sorry I interrupted your thrilling Spice Girls performance. You truly missed your calling as a girl band member."

I narrowed my eyes, well aware that my middle school music teacher had once compared my vocal skills to that of a dying cat.

She hadn't been a very nice teacher.

"My performance was for me, not you. You were intruding." I removed my under-eye patches as casually as possible. Between the singing, dancing, and ice cream, I'd embarrassed myself enough without having one of the patches slide off on its own.

"It's my house."

"It's still polite to announce your presence."

"I would've, but I was too fascinated by the sight of you stumbling around my living room like a drunken baby elephant." Laughter rumbled from his chest at my indignant gasp. I wasn't the best dancer, but I was a better dancer than a *drunken elephant*. Probably. Maybe. "In a charming way, of course."

My dignity would never recover from this.

"Of course. That makes me feel so much better." I lifted my chin and switched subjects before I exploded from sheer mortification. "Speaking of performances, I have my first Delamonte photoshoot next week. In New York." Christian's laughter died down, though traces of amusement lingered around his mouth. "Dates?"

I told him.

"Noted. We'll take my jet."

I stared at him, sure I'd heard wrong. "You're coming with me?"

"The word *we* does imply that, yes."

In public, he was so polite and friendly, but in private, he could be a sarcastic ass.

"Don't you have a business to run?" He must have more important things on his plate than accompanying his fake girlfriend to a photoshoot.

"If my business can't survive two days without me, then I haven't done my job as CEO. Not to mention, your not so friendly secret admirer is still on the loose. Chances are slim he'll follow you to New York, but we don't want to risk it."

"Brock can accompany me. I like him. He's nice."

Granted, I'd met him once and never saw him again, but I felt his warm, reassuring presence whenever I left the house. Having a bodyguard wasn't as bad as I'd imagined.

Plus, I wasn't tempted to have sex with him, which was a big plus.

Christian's expression didn't shift, but the temperature suddenly plunged twenty degrees.

"Brock will not be accompanying you. I will." His words contained so much frost I could've used them to carve an ice sculpture. "His job is to stay out of sight and keep you safe. Nothing else. Has he been doing his job, Stella?"

I sensed it was a trick question.

"Yes?" I ventured.

I didn't know what raised Christian's hackles, but I didn't want to get Brock fired.

"Good."

I was beginning to hate that word.

I crossed my arms, both to hide how unnerved I was and to shield myself from the arctic waves of Christian's displeasure.

"Bad day at work?" I asked. "Or is morphing into a mercurial beast part of your nighttime routine?"

His only response was the press of his gaze on my skin.

I'd been joking, but now that I looked more closely, I observed tiny signs of stress. Tension tautened the blade of his jaw, and a small furrow creased his brow. His body hummed with the dark, restless buzz of frustration.

"Bad day at work?" I repeated, softer this time.

I expected Christian to brush off my concern. To my surprise, he answered frankly. "Difficult client."

"I imagine you deal with a lot of those."

Harper Security's client list was a who's who of CEOs, celebrities, and royalty. That was a ton of ego for one company to handle.

"Not as much as you'd expect." He slid out of his jacket and draped it over the back of the couch. His shirt stretched taut over his broad shoulders, and his muscles flexed with every movement.

Stop. Now is not the time to ogle.

"If someone insists on being a pain, we show them the door, and they're never allowed back in. I run a security company, not a daycare. I don't have time to babysit inflated egos. That being said..." A wry note crept into his tone. "Some egos are attached to useful contacts. This client is pissed because I signed a contract to provide services to their competitor. He's threatening to pull his account if I don't dump the competitor."

Grown men were truly pettier than high schoolers. "I assume he's a big client?"

"One of my biggest."

"You don't want to lose the account, but you also don't want to tarnish your reputation or set a bad precedent by cutting the other loose," I surmised. I chewed my lip, thinking it over. "I mean, it's a pride issue. He doesn't want his competitor to have what he has, so why don't you offer him something extra? Upgrade him to a VVIP package and make it clear his competitor doesn't have the same level of access."

VIP was the standard for his clients, but VVIP was the next level.

"I don't have a VVIP package."

"Now you do. At least make him *think* you do," I amended. "Throw in some extra security features, take him out for drinks. Tell him to keep the package quiet because it's available only to a very select few. Kind of like a secret club. It'll soothe his ego, and he'll be thrilled because he has something over his competitor. People like that just want to feel like they're better than someone."

It was a lesson I'd learned after years of working in the fashion world.

Christian examined me with a faint smile. "Perhaps you have more business acumen than you give yourself credit for." His low murmur wrapped around my senses like a lush velvet blanket.

"More empathy than business acumen," I said, embarrassed. "I'm still terrible at negotiations and accounting."

Learn how to accept compliments, babe. "Thank you" is a perfectly adequate response.

Jules's voice echoed in my head.

I was trying, but some compliments were easier to accept than others.

"Anyway, try it and see how it goes." I cleared my throat. "In the meantime, you need to destress. Do you meditate?"

He stared at me.

"It'll help you sleep better."

Silence.

Okay, then. I guess that was a *no*.

"How about yoga?" I tried. "We can do it together. I'll coach you through it."

Christiaan looked like he would rather drown in a vat of acid. "I appreciate the offer, but I'll stick with a hot shower and sleep," he said dryly.

"Shower and sleep aren't enough." Not with how deep the frown lines were carved into his brow. Businessmen were all the same, forever chasing the next big deal with no regard for their health until it was too late.

I snapped my fingers. "Okay, I have an idea. Sit on the couch."

"I'm not meditating."

"You already said that." Not in so many words, but his silence spoke volumes. "It's not meditation. Just sit. Please?"

Suspicion lurked in his eyes, but he complied.

My heart hammered hard enough against my ribcage to bruise as I came up behind him and rested my hands on his shoulders.

His muscles immediately bunched.

"What," he said, his low voice twined with so much danger I tasted it in my throat, "are you doing?"

"Giving you a massage." I forced my stampeding nerves behind a veneer of calm. *This is to help him relax. That's it.* "Don't tell me you're opposed to those, too."

His jaw tightened.

Night had descended, draping the floor-to-ceiling window across from us in inky black. Our reflections were so sharp the window doubled as a mirror.

"You're giving me a massage." The inflection of his words was impossible to read.

"That's what I said. Now, relax." I kept my voice as low and soothing as possible as I smoothed my palms over his neck and shoulders. His muscles bunched further, which defeated the entire purpose of the exercise. "The *other* kind of relaxing."

I loved getting massages, but I enjoyed giving them almost as much. There was something so satisfying about feeling the tension melt beneath my hands and knowing that I'd helped someone feel better, if only temporarily.

It took a while for Christian to relax, but he gradually sank into the couch and tipped his head back, eyes closed.

The air hummed with awareness and the mingled sounds of our soft, even breaths.

I tried to focus on my movements and not on the powerful masculine form draped insouciantly beneath me, like a panther at rest after a long hunt.

Christian's muscles were sleek and sculpted, all sinuous lines and coiled strength.

Like everything else about him, his body was a lethal, perfectly honed machine.

My eyes drifted up to his face and the dark sweep of his lashes against bronzed cheeks.

Firm, sensual lips, chiseled cheekbones, a straight blade of a nose, and a jaw so perfectly cut Michelangelo must've sculpted it himself.

It should be illegal for anyone to possess a face like that.

A lock of thick, dark hair brushed his forehead. Unable to help myself, I smoothed it back and luxuriated in the soft strands as I gently massaged his scalp. Christian's hair was the perfect length—short enough for easy maintenance, long enough for a woman to run her hands through it while...

Stop. Focus.

I swallowed past the dryness in the throat and the renewed ache in my lower belly.

Below me, the rhythm of Christian's breathing changed to something harsher, more primal.

I slid my palms down his neck and over his shoulder—

A small gasp sliced through the silence when his hand closed over mine, halting its movements. The iron grip branded my skin with so much heat I felt it in my bones.

"Enough."

Rough restraint and whiskey glares.

He'd opened his eyes, and I was already getting consumed by them when I latched onto my tiny, remaining shred of self-survival and dragged myself out.

I pulled my hand out from underneath his and stepped back, heart in my throat, pulse racing with pure adrenaline.

"You're right. That should be enough. I hope it helped." *Cool, calm, collected.* "Anyway, I—I'll see you tomorrow. Good night."

For the second time that week, I fled to my room and locked the door behind me. I closed my eyes and leaned against the cool wood until my heartbeats slowed to a normal pace.

What was *wrong* with me? I'd never gotten so worked up over a guy before. I even visited a sex therapist once in case my low libido was cause for concern, but she'd reassured me it was normal. Not everyone experienced sexual attraction all the time or in the same way.

Unless, apparently, they lived with Christian Harper. I couldn't pinpoint what had changed.

I'd always thought he was attractive, but my reactions to him hadn't been this intense or frequent until he found me after the first note. Sure, the night of the gala had been intense, but I thought that'd been a fluke.

Maybe my brain was confused and thought our fake relationship was real? Or maybe I was mistaking gratitude for something deeper.

Whatever the reason, I wished the strange feelings would go away.

I brushed my teeth and climbed into bed, but sleep remained elusive thanks to the persistent, throbbing ache in my core.

Finally, I couldn't take it anymore.

I slipped my hand between my legs, and my mouth parted in a silent gasp at the first brush of my fingers over my clit.

I didn't need sexual release often, but that one touch ignited months of pent-up frustration until the only thing that mattered was chasing sweet, heady relief.

My back arched off the mattress as I played with my clit with one hand and my nipple with the other. I was hypersensitive after not touching myself for so long, and sparks of pleasure raced through my body, lighting every nerve ending on fire.

Small whimpers mingled with the slippery sounds of my fingers against my clit while a familiar erotic film unfolded in my mind.

Me tied up, the rough scratch of ropes abrading my skin while a faceless stranger had his way with me.

Hands collaring my throat, bites on my skin, and a hard, relentless rhythm that wrenched inhibited screams from my throat.

Dark fantasies I only indulged in beneath the cover of night.

I'd never disclosed them to previous lovers because I'd been too nervous to share them and because I didn't trust them to carry out the scenarios the way I wanted.

Ironically, in my fantasies, it was never about the man. My phantom lover had remained faceless all these years, an amorphous figure who didn't require an identity to provide me with what I wanted—the safe loss of control and an off switch for the ceaseless worries plaguing my brain. Nothing but the sharp stings of pleasure and adjacent pain.

But as wetness soaked my fingers and the pressure built between my thighs, the faceless figure came into focus for the first time since my fantasies started.

Golden brown eyes. Lethally soft smile. A heated brush of lips against mine and a ruthless grip that dug into my skin with just enough pressure to make my head swim.

The knot of pressure exploded with such force I didn't have time to scream before I tumbled over the edge, swept up in wave after wave of orgasmic bliss with nothing to hold on to except visions of whiskey, rough hands, and a man I shouldn't want but couldn't help crave.

20

STELLA

I avoided Christian with the determination of an escaped convict fleeing the FBI in the week leading up to New York.

It was surprisingly easy, given how early he left in the morning and how late he returned at night. I suspected he might be avoiding me as well, and I half expected him to back out of accompanying me to the shoot.

No such luck.

The morning of my Delamonte shoot, I found myself thirty-five thousand feet in the air, sitting across from a man who seemed as hellbent on ignoring me as I did him.

Except for a courteous exchange of *good mornings*, we hadn't spoken to each other since we left the house.

I sipped my lemon water and snuck a peek at Christian. He was working on his laptop, his brow furrowed with concentration. His jacket lay on the seat next to him, and he'd pushed his shirtsleeves up to reveal his watch and tanned, muscular forearms.

How had I not realized how sexy forearms were until now?

I stared at where his Patek Philippe glinted against his bronzed skin. Jules was right. There was something about men wearing watches...

"Something on your mind?" Christian didn't look up from his computer.

I hadn't been doing anything wrong, but my heartbeats collided like he'd caught me stealing.

"Just thinking about the shoot," I lied. I took another sip of water.

Between the tension on the plane and my Delamonte shoot that afternoon, I was surprised I could keep anything, even liquids, down.

"What are you going to do while I'm on set?" I asked. "Go into the New York office?"

Harper Security was headquartered in D.C., but it had offices around the world.

"I'm not flying with you to New York so I can hole myself up in another office." Christian typed something on his keyboard. "I'll join you on set."

Surprise ballooned in my chest, followed by a pinprick of anxiety. "But the shoot could take hours."

"I know."

I waited for an elaboration that never came.

I held back a sigh. Christian was more mercurial than a broken thermometer.

For lack of anything better to do, I settled deeper into my seat and examined the luxury surrounding us.

Christian's private jet resembled an airborne mansion. Buttery cream leather seats formed intimate seating areas, and an elegant, cloud-like navy carpet muffled the steps of the two smartly outfitted attendants who looked like they'd stepped out of the latest issue of *Vogue*.

Besides the main cabin, the jet also boasted a bedroom, a

full bathroom, a four-person screening area, and a dining table set with magnetic-bottomed plates and silverware engineered to stay still through turbulence.

It must've cost a fortune.

Christian seemed as comfortable with his opulent surroundings as someone who'd grown up with a silver spoon in his mouth, but my research told me he hailed from a normal, upper-middle-class family. According to the only public inter-view he'd ever given, his father had been a software engineer and his mother a school administrator.

"Why did you choose private security?" I asked, breaking the silence. "You could've gone into any field."

Christian had graduated summa cum laude from MIT. He could've gotten a job anywhere after graduation—NASA, Silicon Valley, the CIA. Instead, he chose to build his own company from the ground up with no guarantees of success, in a field few MIT grads touched.

"I enjoy it." Christian finally looked up, his mouth curving at whatever he saw on my face. "Rhys says it's my god complex. Knowing how important the lives at stake are and that they're in my hands."

I'd forgotten Rhys used to work for him. They were so different it was hard to picture them existing in the same sphere.

Rhys, for all his gruffness, stuck by the rules (unless Bridget was involved). Christian didn't seem like he had much use for rules at all unless they were his own.

"It's not." I may not know Christian that well despite living with him, but I knew he wouldn't do anything out of pure ego. He was too practical and calculating for that.

"No, it's not. Not entirely." He rubbed his thumb over the face of his watch. "If I only wanted money, I could obtain it any number of ways. Stocks, selling proprietary software...which I did, to raise capital for Harper Security. But once you reach a certain level of wealth, money is just money. It doesn't add any inherent value beyond that of ego. What's more important is your network. Access. The people you know and the things they're willing to do for you." A smile, equal parts sensual and dangerous. "One debt owed from a well-placed contact is worth more than all the cash in the world."

A shiver of trepidation crept up my spine. What he said made sense, but the *way* he said it made it sound more ominous than he'd probably intended.

"Speaking of business..." Christian switched topics so effortlessly it took my brain a minute to catch up. "How's the business plan going?"

"Good." I wanted to say more, but the brush of his knee against mine distracted me.

I hadn't realized how close we'd gotten during our conversation.

Masculine heat and decadent spice stole into my lungs and further distracted me before I grasped the rest of my near-forgotten words. "But I don't want to talk about that right now. Tell me more about you."

His mini-speech just now was my first insight into how his mind worked.

Christian wore his expensive suits and charm like armor, and I was desperate for a chink, for any glimpse into the man behind the mask.

What was his childhood like? What were his hobbies, his goals and fears? What made him into who he was?

I didn't know why I wanted answers to those questions, but I knew the tiny glimpse I'd gotten wasn't enough. It was too intoxicating, like a shot of fine tequila straight to the blood of an alcoholic.

"I'm not that interesting." It was the smooth, practiced

response of someone who'd spent a lifetime locking his private thoughts and feelings inside a vault.

"You're wrong." Our gazes locked like two pieces of a puzzle sliding into place. "I think you're one of the most fascinating men I've ever met."

It was a bold admission, one that had his eyes darkening into a rich, molten amber.

"One of?" The languid softness of his question stoked whatever wild alchemy burned between us. Dark flames devoured all the oxygen in the cabin, leaving next to nothing for my compressed lungs.

"Tell me more about yourself, and I might promote you to the top of the list."

His laugh stole into the remaining pockets of air in my chest. "Touché."

Christian's eyes dipped to my mouth, and the remnants of his laughter evaporated. Black swallowed amber, leaving nothing behind except promises of sin and dark pleasures.

Pinpricks of nervous energy buzzed beneath my skin. The memory of our almost kiss when I first moved in resurfaced, as it had a bad habit of doing since that night.

My nails sank into my knees, and I waited, not breathing, not moving, as Christian lowered his head—

"Mr. Harper, apologies for the interruption. But you wanted me to alert you fifteen minutes before landing."

The attendant's gentle voice sliced the moment into a thousand jagged pieces.

A cold wave of oxygen rushed back into my chest, followed by the acrid sting of disappointment when Christian drew back. Face blank, all traces of desire snuffed as if it'd never existed at all.

"Thank you, Portia." Perfectly even, perfectly calm, unlike the erratic heartbeat thundering behind my ribcage.

Portia nodded. Her eyes flitted between us before she disappeared to another part of the jet.

Christian returned his attention to his computer, and we didn't speak for the duration of the flight.

It was just as well.

I couldn't have formed proper words had I tried. I was too unsettled by the knowledge that Christian Harper had been about to kiss me again...and that I'd desperately wanted him to.

———

As nervous as I was about the Delamonte shoot, I was grateful for the distraction from my tangled feelings toward Christian.

I wanted him, but I didn't want to date him (or anyone else).

We lived together, but we barely knew each other.

The world thought we were dating, but we'd barely kissed.

The contradictions were enough to drive a girl mad.

Once I returned to D.C., I needed girl talk with Ava and Jules ASAP. I was too rusty in the boys department to sort through my mess on my own.

But, for now, I had something more urgent that required my attention: not screwing up the first Delamonte photoshoot of the most important brand deal of my life.

When Christian and I arrived at the studio, it was already bustling with activity. The photographer, makeup artist, hair-stylist, and various assistants and Delamonte staff rushed around, steaming garments, and fussing over lighting and props. A pop song played in the background, but all commotion halted when I walked in.

Spiders of anxiety crawled over my skin.

I had no problem doing solo photoshoots or being on

camera when I couldn't *see* people watching me. Being the center of attention at an in-person shoot was an entirely different matter.

"Stella!" Luisa broke the silence and greeted me with effusive kisses on both cheeks. "You look wonderful. And Christian." Her eyebrows climbed up her expertly Botoxed forehead. "*This* is a surprise."

"I'm in the city for business. Besides..." Christian rested a hand on my lower back. "I couldn't resist attending Stella's first photoshoot."

He looked and sounded so believable as a proud, doting boyfriend that I almost forgot we were pretending.

Almost.

"Huh." Luisa eyed him with fascination. "Indeed."

I was more surprised to see her on set than she was to see Christian. As the brand's CEO, supervising photoshoots was below her pay grade.

She must've read the confusion on my face because her eyes twinkled with knowing. "I couldn't resist dropping by as well. People say I'm micromanaging, but this campaign is my baby. I'm determined to make it the best one in Delamonte history, and you, my dear..." She patted my hand. "You're going to help make that happen."

The sandwich I ate for lunch churned in my stomach.

Right. No pressure at all.

Christian retreated to the back to take business calls while I sat through hair and makeup and met everyone on set, including Ricardo, the brand's in-house photographer. He was a handsome man in his forties, with tanned skin and a flirtatious smile that he bestowed upon me before it faded.

I followed his suddenly wary gaze to where Christian stood by the exit, his phone to his ear but his attention fixed on us.

"Your boyfriend is an intense one, huh?" Ricardo let out a

nervous chuckle before he cleared his throat. "No matter. Time to get started, darling. We have magic to make!"

He was charming enough to pull off such a cheesy line, and for the next hour, I tried my best to follow his guidance, posing and turning and contorting my body into strange, unnatural positions until sweat trickled down my spine.

The lights were insanely hot, and I pictured my makeup melting until I resembled a crazed clown.

Also, was it just me, or had Ricardo lost some of his enthusiasm? His encouraging shouts of "Gorgeous!" and "Beautiful!" had gradually tapered off into "Turn left" and "Too far left." Soon, only the clicks and whirs of his camera filled the studio.

No one spoke, but the weight of their stares pressed against me like a second layer of clothing.

Self-doubt crept into the vacuum left in the wake of their silence.

Pretend you're at home. Your camera is on a tripod facing you. You've perfected the settings and you're ready to shoot. You've done this a thousand times, Stella...

"Lift your chin higher." Ricardo's instruction interrupted the fantasy I'd concocted of being alone. "Drop your hand...a little more...relax those shoulders..."

It wasn't working.

He didn't say it, but I could *feel* it. The thick, sour sting of disappointment tainting the air. The one I was so used to tasting whenever I went home.

I was finally working with my dream brand, and I was screwing it all up.

Tears gathered behind my eyes, but I set my jaw and blinked them back. I would *not* cry on set. I could hold myself together until the shoot was over.

Besides, this was only the first session. There were three

more. I'll practice before the next one and improve...if they kept me on.

The unforgiving fist of anxiety strangled my lungs.

What if Delamonte terminated my contract? Were they allowed to do that?

My mind rifled through the contract's clauses, frantic in its search for one that allowed the brand to dump me if I didn't perform up to its standards.

Why hadn't I looked more closely at the language? I'd been so excited I'd signed after a quick check with Brady to ensure there were no major red flags. But what if—

"Stella, darling." Forced patience strained Ricardo's voice. "Let's take a break, shall we? Walk around, drink some water. We'll reconvene in ten minutes."

Translation: you have ten minutes to get your shit together.

Low murmurs broke out, and I spotted a frown on Luisa's face before she turned away.

The rush of tears pressed harder against the dam of my willpower.

Cool, calm, collected. Cool, calm, collected. Cool—

Warm, masculine spice filled my nostrils. A second later, the deep black of Christian's suit jacket came into view.

He handed me a glass of water. "Drink."

I did. It cooled some of the sweat inching my spine, but the air was still too hot, the lights too bright. I felt like a bug buzzing around in a fluorescent bulb, trying to escape before I burned to death.

"What are you doing?" I asked when Christian took my empty glass, set it on the nearest table, and returned to stand in front of me. Assessing me, the way he would a prospective investment or unsolved puzzle.

"Reminding you of why you're here." His tone was soft but authoritative enough to drown out the nasty taunts crowding my head. *Disappointment. Failure. Fraud.* "Why are you here, Stella?"

"For a photoshoot."

I couldn't summon the energy for a better, less inane answer.

"That's the *what*." Christian grasped my chin and tilted it until my eyes met his. "I'm asking you *why*. Why, of all the people who could be standing in your spot, are *you* here?"

"I..." Because I'd spent the past decade cultivating an image that had become a cage as much as it had a lifeline. Because I was deceiving my followers and almost everyone I knew to achieve some stupid, arbitrary measure of success. Because I was desperate to prove I *could* succeed to people who didn't even care.

Thickness clogged my throat.

"Because they chose you." Christian's cool voice sliced through my muddied thoughts. "Every blogger in the world would kill to be standing where you are, but Delamonte chose *you*. Not Raya. Not any of the other women at the dinner or in the pages of magazines. This is a multibillion-dollar brand, and they wouldn't have invested in you if they didn't think you can do it."

"But I can't." My whisper revealed the heartbreaking truth. I was an imposter, a little girl playing dress up in a grown up's clothes. "You see how it's going. I'm bombing."

"You are not bombing." The guided precision of his statement struck the shell of uncertainty in my chest. Dented, but not destroyed. "It's been an hour. *One* hour. Think about how much time you invested to get to where you are now. How much have you achieved? How many people have you outlasted? You downplay your accomplishments as ordinary when you would hail them as extraordinary on anyone else."

Christian kept his grasp on my chin as he brushed his

thumb over my cheek. He was close enough I could spot the gold flecks in his eyes, like fallen stars swimming in pools of molten amber.

"If you saw yourself the way other people see you," he said quietly. "You'd never doubt again."

Curiosity and something infinitely sweeter and more dangerous fluttered to life in my heart. "How do other people see me?"

Christian's eyes didn't leave mine.

"Like you're the most beautiful, most remarkable thing they've ever seen."

The words lit every molecule in my body and dissolved them into a pool of exquisite, unbearable warmth.

We weren't talking about other people, and we both knew it.

"This is one photoshoot, Butterfly." Another brush of his thumb, another gallop of my heart. "The first half was practice. The second half is yours. Do you understand?"

It was impossible not to get swept away by Christian's confidence.

Instead of adding a brick to my worries about not living up to expectations, his faith in me fortified me enough to lock those ugly, taunting voices in my head back in the box where they belonged.

"Yes," I said, my lungs tight but my breathing easier than it'd been all afternoon.

"Good." His lips dipped and touched mine in the softest of kisses.

It wasn't the first time we'd gotten this close, but it felt more effortless.

Less of a kiss, more of a promise.

My nerves settled while everything around me disappeared for one long moment.

Then the moment was gone, and so was he, but the warmth of his presence and the phantom brush of his mouth lingered.

Another flutter disrupted my heartbeat.

Cool, calm, collected.

I steeled my spine and faced Ricardo again with a smile.

"I'm ready."

If the first half of the shoot was a disaster, the second half was a revelation. Whatever had been blocking me unstuck, and Ricardo's rapid shutter clicks filled the studio with renewed enthusiasm.

Snap. Snap. Snap.

And we were done.

I hadn't moved more than a few inches the entire time, yet my heart thundered like I'd just ran the New York Marathon.

"Perfect! You are *stunning*, darling, despite the, ah, rocky start." Ricardo winked at me. "You were *made* for the camera. The final photos are going to be gorgeous!"

"Thank you," I murmured, but I barely heard the rest of his gushing.

My eyes searched the stark white room until they found Christian.

He stood in the back corner. Still on a business call, still gorgeous in his suit and tie, and still watching me with those eyes of whiskey over ice.

Despite the phone pressed to his ear and the hungry stares of every woman and several men in the room pinned on him, he didn't look away when I gave him a playful wink and smile.

It was an off-the-cuff, in-the-moment sort of thing, and not the type of action I'd usually take with a man I had barely even kissed.

But I was riding high after the shoot, and Christian was so composed all the time I wanted to knock him off-kilter.

Just once, just a little bit.

Nothing, however, could've prepared me for the devastation his lazy, answering smile wrought on my heart.

The butterflies lying dormant in my stomach went crazy, and I suddenly knew, with all the certainty in the world, that they were there to stay.

21

STELLA

THAT NIGHT, ABSENT OF ANY OTHER PLANS, I accompanied Christian to dinner at his friend Dante's house.

I'd met Dante before the night of the blizzard, but I'd forgotten how intimidating he was. Even in a simple black shirt and pants, he commanded authority in a way that was different from Christian but equally as powerful.

Christian was a finely honed assassin's blade sheathed in velvet; Dante was a hammer burning bright with deadly intent. Lethal and striking, with no ambiguity as to the damage he could inflict if crossed.

His fiancée Vivian, on the other hand, was open-faced and friendly, with beautiful dark eyes and a warm smile.

Strangely enough, she was quick to grace everyone with that smile *except* Dante. The engaged pair hadn't looked at each other once since Christian and I arrived.

"I didn't realize you were dating Christian when I met you." Dante's deep voice pulled me away from my curiosity and sent a pleasurable shiver down my spine. *Italian accents.* They did it for me every time. "Now it makes sense."

He bestowed a hard stare at Christian, who yawned.

For two people who claimed to be friends, they didn't act particularly friendly toward each other.

"What makes sense?" I asked.

"How distracted he's been lately." Dante swirled his wine in his glass. "Wouldn't you agree, Christian?"

"My record profits this quarter say otherwise," Christian drawled. He rested a hand on my thigh, the touch so casual yet possessive it sent heat arrowing to my core.

"It's not your business that's in trouble," Dante said dryly.

Christian stared back at him with as much interest as someone listening to an insurance sales pitch. He rubbed his thumb over my bare skin. Softly, just once, but it was enough to cloud my thoughts.

I was so focused on the warm pressure of his hand I couldn't focus on anything else, not even the delicious food.

What is wrong with me?

I'd never lost my head over a guy like this. It was disconcerting.

Vivian cut through the brewing tension with a well-timed interruption. "You and Stella make a beautiful couple." She shot him an amused glance. "I never thought I'd see the day when Christian Harper would get a girlfriend."

"Neither did I, but Stella took me by surprise." The reply was so warm and intimate, I almost believed it.

My heart rate kicked up as the butterflies in my stomach went wild again.

I took a big gulp of wine to calm them down.

It's just for show. It's not real.

Christian donned casual affection as easily as he did one of his suits. There was no reason to believe his actions were anything more than playing into our ruse.

Other than our almost but not really kiss two weeks ago, he'd never indicated he wanted us to be real.

Sure, he'd gone above and beyond when it came to the stalker, but that was literally a matter of life and death. It didn't mean he *liked* me.

Attracted to me? Possibly, but I didn't think he wanted anything more than sex.

My head spun. Everything felt too confusing after he kissed me today, even if it had just been to distract me from my nerves.

I firmly believed that if someone showed you who they were, believe them. And Christian had indicated time and time again that he wasn't interested in a real relationship.

The day people stopped thinking they could change someone who didn't want to be changed was the day fewer hearts got broken.

I wanted a real relationship one day, but I did not think for a second I could ever change Christian Harper.

It's just for show. It's not real.

Luckily, the tension blanketing the table gradually dissolved as dinner went on, drowned by good drinks and good food.

By the time the entrée rolled around, even Vivian and Dante were talking to each other, though their conversations consisted mainly of asking the other to pass the food.

But no matter who was speaking, half of my attention remained tuned into Christian. He sat inches to my right, his presence a living, breathing distraction that crowded my lungs and clouded my thoughts.

Easy smiles, teasing drawls, and skin gilded gold by the dim lighting and wine-fueled haze.

It was my first time seeing him in such a relaxed group setting, and I finally understood how people could get sucked into his charm and underestimate him.

For all his care and concern toward me, I'd never once doubted the ruthlessness that lay beneath his civilized veneer. But here, watching him laugh and joke with effortless grace, I almost believed he was nothing more than a wealthy playboy with only money and good times on his mind.

Christian turned to answer a question from Vivian, but his thumb made another slow sweep over my skin.

It's just for show. It's not real.

A tiny bead of sweat formed on my forehead. I was wearing a sleeveless dress, but I was burning up.

"How did you and Christian meet?" I asked Dante, both to distract from Christian's touch and because I was truly curious.

I hadn't met any of Christian's other friends (Brock and Kage didn't count since they worked for him), and I was dying to know their backstory.

"I was his first client." Dante leaned back in his chair. "He was a kid fresh out of college—"

"You're three years older than me," Christian cut in.

Our host ignored him. "I took a chance on him. Best and worst decision I ever made."

"Worst?" Christian scoffed. "Do you remember what happened in Rome?" He turned to me while Dante rolled his eyes. "We were transporting jewels to a new store in the city..."

A smile tugged on my lips as he told the story about how he prevented the Russo Group from losing millions of dollars worth of diamonds.

Not because the story was funny, but because Christian was the most unguarded I'd ever seen him.

He was so calculated and in control all the time that seeing him relax around friends was like getting a peek behind the curtain at the real *him*.

It was nice.

Better than nice.

If he acted this way all the time...

I took another gulp of wine before I finished my thought.

Don't go there.

"If there's one thing you should know about him, Stella," Dante said after he finished. "It's that he has an overinflated sense of self-importance. We could've handled the jewels situation without his help."

"Trust me, I know." A laugh rose in my throat when Christian slid a half-amused, half-exasperated glance in my direction.

"Whose side are you on?"

"Easy." I grinned. "Dante's."

The table broke into laughter while he squeezed my thigh and leaned closer until his mouth grazed my ear.

My pulse skipped.

"Not very girlfriend-like of you," he murmured.

"If you can't handle a little teasing, you're not ready for a girlfriend," I whispered back.

His laughter wound through me like a ribbon of dark velvet.

I relaxed into my seat with a lingering smile.

The teasing, the joking, the opening up about his past (even if it was work-related)...we almost felt like a real couple.

After dinner, Vivian took me on a tour of the penthouse while Dante and Christian discussed business.

Christian's house was all clean lines and modern minimalism, but the Russos' was a tasteful ode to decadence. Rich velvets, lush silks, and beautifully cut porcelain, all arranged in a manner that was extravagant but never tacky. The only thing that looked out of place was the hideous painting in their art gallery.

I had great respect for all creative works, but honestly, that piece looked like a cat had vomited all over the canvas.

"I don't know why Dante bought that." Vivian sounded embarrassed. "He usually has more discerning taste."

The compliment came out grudgingly, like she was reluctant to ascribe any positive qualities to her fiancé.

I suppressed the urge to ask what happened between them.

It was rude to pry into other people's business, especially when they were my hosts and I'd just met them.

We almost made it back to the dining room when we heard voices drifting from a crack in Dante's office door.

"...can't keep Magda forever," Dante said. "You should be glad I didn't throw it in the trash after the stunt you pulled with Vivian and Heath."

Vivian froze while my brow knit with confusion.

Who are Magda and Heath?

What stunt?

"It's a fucking painting, not a wild animal." Christian sounded bored. "As for Vivian, it's been months, and it worked out fine. Let it go. If you're still pissed, you shouldn't have invited me to dinner."

"Be glad things *worked out fine* with Vivian," Dante said coldly. "If—"

He stopped when Vivian coughed, her face inexplicably red.

A second later, the door flung open, revealing a surprised Dante and an impassive Christian.

"I see you've finished the tour early." Dante's dry tone cut through the ensuing silence. A faint blush colored his cheekbones as he flicked his gaze at a silent Vivian.

"Sorry." My own cheeks warmed at being caught eavesdropping. "We were on our way to the dining room and heard..." I trailed off, not wanting to confirm we'd been listening in on his conversation even though that was clearly what we'd been doing.

"We were just wrapping up," Christian said smoothly. There was no hint of the ire I'd heard earlier. "Dante, Vivian, it's been lovely."

I said my goodbyes as well, and we rode the elevator down to the lobby in silence. But when we reached the sidewalk, I couldn't hold back anymore.

"What's *Magda*?"

Now that we'd left the Russos, I didn't bother pretending I hadn't heard them.

Christian had said it was a painting, but I didn't understand why Dante was holding it for him. Christian didn't even *like* art.

"Nothing you need to worry about." His curt reply was chillier than the crisp evening air swirling around us.

The warm, easygoing Christian from dinner was gone, replaced by his aloof twin once more.

I tried again. "What stunt did you pull with Vivian and Heath?" *Also, who the hell is Heath?*

Normally, I wasn't this nosy, but tonight was my best shot at getting Christian to open up. He'd revealed a sliver of what he was like behind his perfect mask earlier; I just needed to dig deeper.

"Also nothing you need to worry about."

"That's not an answer."

We arrived at his building, which was only a few blocks from Dante's place.

"You know everything about me, and I know nothing about you," I added. "How is that fair?"

"You know plenty about me." Christian nodded at the door-man, who tipped his hat in greeting. "Where I live, where I work, how I take my coffee in the morning."

"Everyone can find those things out with a simple Google search. I just want—"

"Drop it, Stella." There was no guise of gentleness anymore, only the sharp slice of a blade shredding me into ribbons. "I don't want to talk about it."

My jaw tensed.

"Fine." Despite my cool reply, frustration bubbled hot and unchecked inside my veins.

I met Christian last year. We'd lived together and pretended we were a couple for weeks, yet I didn't know a single thing about him beyond the superficial.

Meanwhile, he knew things about me I'd never shared with anyone else. My history with my stalker. My anxiety. My dreams of starting a fashion line. The small but important bits of my life that I'd kept secret from even my closest friends.

I trusted him, but he clearly didn't feel the same way about me.

Something more bitter welled beneath the frustration.

Hurt.

Christian was nothing if not a master at making people believe in things that didn't exist.

It's just for show. It's not real.

We didn't speak again until we arrived at his apartment, where I bid him a stiff *good night* and retreated to the guest room before he could respond.

I couldn't sleep, so I lay there staring at the ceiling while the cool, dark silence peeled away my frustration to reveal the hurt underneath.

I was more attracted to Christian than I'd been to any man in years. Not only that, I was starting to *like* him. The way he comforted me after I found the note in my apartment, the way his smiles spilled butterflies in my stomach, and the unshake-able faith he'd shown in me during the photoshoot...they'd all eroded my resistance so slowly I didn't realize how much of myself I'd bared until I felt the sting of his rejection.

It burned like acid on raw skin, and it was my fault. I never should've let my guard down.

For all my aversion to relationships, I was a romantic in my most secret of hearts, and I was terrified that, like everything else I'd kept hidden, Christian would unravel that part of me until it was impossible to put back together.

He was dangerous, not just to his enemies but to those close to him.

And the only way to save myself was to make sure I stayed as far away from him as possible.

22

STELLA

ONE STEP FORWARD, TWO STEPS BACK.

That summed up my relationship with Christian.

I'd thought we were making real progress. Considering how easily he'd shut me out after dinner at Dante's, that wasn't the case.

I didn't hold a grudge often, but it'd been a week since we returned to D.C., and I still hadn't shaken off all my hurt.

There was nothing more upsetting than considering someone a friend only to realize they didn't feel the same way about you. The uneven balance in any relationship made my skin tight.

Drop it, Stella. I don't want to talk about it.

It wasn't like I'd asked him to spill his deepest, darkest secrets. Dante knew what happened with Magda and Vivian, so it couldn't be that bad.

Granted, I didn't have as long of a history with Christian as he did, but still.

I swiped my card at the self-checkout counter with more force than necessary.

I'd visited Maura that morning and stopped by the grocery store to pick up more wheatgrass powder for my smoothies on the way home.

Pro tip: Don't grocery shop when frustrated.

I came in for the powder and was leaving with two bags of popcorn, a pint of ice cream, a king-size chocolate bar, and a six-pack of Greek yogurt.

The air conditioning was on full blast, but a deeper, eerier chill swept over my skin when I turned to leave.

Every hair on my arms and the back of my neck stood on end.

The roar of blood in my ears drowned out every other noise as I scanned my surroundings with a white knuckle grip on my phone.

I didn't see anyone suspicious, but the ominous shift in the air was so tangible I tasted it in the back of my throat.

Someone's watching you. The soft, singsong warning drifted through my head.

And that someone wasn't Brock, whose presence was invisible but always warm and reassuring.

A shiver rattled down my spine.

I hadn't heard from my stalker since the break-in nor had I received any updates from Christian. I hadn't asked for them; part of me didn't want to know.

Out of sight, out of mind, except that obviously wasn't true.

Whoever the creep was, he was out there, probably waiting for another opportunity to pounce.

I hadn't mentioned my move on social media, but I was still living in the same building. If they could break into my apartment...

Stop it. He cannot *break into Christian's house.*

He couldn't hurt me when I was in public, either. Brock was there. I couldn't see him, but he was

It's fine. You're fine.

Still, I forced my legs to move and walked as quickly as I could back to the Mirage.

The chill evaporated beneath the blaze of the afternoon soon. By the time I locked the door of Christian's apartment behind me, I almost felt silly for how a mere sensation paralyzed me in the middle of a crowded grocery store in broad daylight.

It's fine. You're fine.

I twisted my necklace around my finger and dragged slow, deep breaths through my lungs until the vestiges of fear cleared.

Yes, my stalker was out there, but he couldn't get to me.

I may have been upset with Christian right now, but I trusted him to protect me.

He'd find the stalker soon. Then the whole situation would blow over and I could return to my normal life.

I was sure of it.

———

MY STREAK OF SUCCESSFULLY AVOIDING CHRISTIAN ENDED that night when he came home so early the sun still hung low in the sky and spilled golden washes of light across the light gray floors.

I'd just finished a pre-interview with Julian, the lifestyle columnist for *Washington Weekly*. He was doing an in-depth profile on me and my Delamonte ambassadorship, and we'd spent the past half hour discussing topics and logistics.

I was sketching in the living room when the front door opened and every hair on my body prickled with awareness.

I didn't have to see Christian to *feel* him. He consumed every room he walked into.

Don't look, don't look—

I looked.

Sure enough, there he was, striding across the room like a king to his throne.

Broad shoulders. Sharp cheekbones. Expensive suit.

"Slacking off?" I stood and tucked my sketching notebook beneath my arm. I didn't like sitting around Christian. It made me feel at even more of a disadvantage than I already was. "It's still business hours."

They were the first words I'd spoken to him since New York, and I would be lying if I said they didn't give me a heady rush.

His steps slowed until he came to a halt in front of me. "I figured you'd want to celebrate."

Confusion pulled my brows together. "Celebrate what?"

"You hit a million followers, Stella." Christian watched me, unsmiling, but his eyes glowed with a faint hint of amusement. "As of one hour ago."

One million followers.

There was *no way* I'd hit that milestone already. When I checked last night, I'd only been at...nine hundred ninety-six thousand, give or take a few hundred.

Oh my God.

Considering how fast I'd been growing since I started "dating" Christian, four thousand new followers overnight was fully within the realm of possibility.

"If you don't believe me, check for yourself." It was like he'd read my mind.

I dragged my eyes away from Christian's and took out my phone. A small tremble shook my hand as I tapped into my profile and zeroed in on the number at the top.

1M.

One million followers.

Oh. My. GOD.

The rush from seeing that number was so strong I grew dizzy.

I'd known it would happen eventually, but *actually* hitting that milestone was surreal.

A thrill sizzled down my spine.

I did it.

I did it!

A grin broke out, and it took all my willpower not to jump and scream like a twelve-year-old at their favorite pop singer's concert.

One million had been the goal since I started my account. It wasn't my *only* goal, but it'd been the big one. The golden ticket. The validation I was a success, that I hadn't made a mistake pursuing the path I was pursuing and that people liked my content and liked *me*.

After years of creating content, and thousands of posts, I'd finally hit it.

I stared down at my profile, waiting for the skies to open up, angels to sing, and confetti to rain down around me in congratulations.

At the very least, I expected the Instagram gods to pop up and slap a gold star on my hand for achieving such a huge milestone.

Nothing.

The exhilaration of joining the million-follower club was still there, but I'd also expected...*more*.

Some sense of achievement that would validate all the hard work I'd put into my account and the feeling that I'd made it, whatever *it* was.

But other than an excited, emoji-filled text from Brady and an inbox bursting with DMs, I was the same person I'd been an hour ago, with the same worries and insecurities.

Something jagged and morose punctured my thrill until I slowly floated back down to earth.

Somehow, it felt worse to achieve something and still feel dissatisfied than to not achieve it at all.

I had a million followers, yet I'd never felt emptier.

I tucked my phone into my pocket and tried to hide my disappointment.

"I didn't realize you were watching my follower count that closely," I said.

Christian didn't take the bait. Instead, he reached into his pocket and retrieved a distinctive red and gold box.

"For you," he said. "A congratulatory gift."

Curiosity and hesitation warred inside me.

Should I take it? I didn't feel right accepting a gift from him when we were little more than a business arrangement, but what could he have possibly gotten me? Considering the size and brand, it had to be jewelry.

In the end, curiosity won.

I took the box and slowly opened it, half expecting something to jump out at me, but my breath trapped in my throat when I saw what was nestled against the black velvet.

Holy hell.

It was a watch—the most gorgeous, extravagant watch I'd ever laid eyes on. Diamonds and emeralds formed delicate butterflies on the polished face, and smaller diamonds studded the platinum band.

"It's a limited-edition piece that hasn't hit the market yet," Christian said as casually as if it were a plastic toy he'd picked up from the mall. "There are only five in the world. One of them now belongs to you."

I ran my fingers over the jeweled face. The watch must be worth a fortune.

"How did you get it?" The question was a whisper in the dying sunlight.

I knew the answer before he responded.

What Christian Harper wanted, Christian Harper got.

"I have my ways."

The serotonin boost from holding a stunning piece of jewelry faded, replaced with wariness.

I couldn't hold on to any happy feelings these days.

I closed my hand around the watch until the jewels cut into my palm. "Why are you giving this to me?"

"I told you. It's a congratulatory gift."

"You said I didn't hit a million followers until an hour ago. You managed to get this watch *and* come home in that time?"

He responded with an elegant shrug. "I have good contacts."

My default was trust, but I tasted the bitterness of his lie on my tongue.

The diamonds dug deeper grooves into my skin before I loosened my grip.

"It's gorgeous, and I appreciate the sentiment, but I can't take this." I held out the watch.

I wished I could've kept it, but I'd always wished for things I couldn't have.

Love. Affection. Worthiness. Something deep and uncondi- tional that I could call my own.

In the grand scheme of things, a watch was nothing. It was beautiful, and I hated how much I wanted something that meant nothing, but it was only an accessory. If someone wanted it, they could buy it.

Those other things, no amount of money could buy.

Christian's expression flickered for the first time since he entered. "I gave it to you. It's yours."

"I'm giving it back. It's too much," I said firmly. "This is a *diamond* watch, Christian. It must be worth tens of thousands of dollars."

"Ninety-two thousand, six hundred."

I flinched at both the number and his cool tone.

"It's only money. I have plenty of it." Christian's brows dipped into a V. "I thought you'd like it. You said you needed a new watch."

I *had* said that. It'd been an off-the-cuff comment I made weeks ago.

I couldn't believe Christian remembered it.

"If I wear this, I'll get robbed the instant I step out of the house. Even if I don't..." I dragged a breath through my compressed lungs.

The oxygen stoked flames of old frustration until they incinerated my inhibitions and the rest of my words spilled out.

"It's not just the watch. It's everything. Our arrangement, my bodyguard, living here rent-free, taking your jet to New York. I feel like I'm your mistress, except we're not having sex. You're not my boyfriend. I'm not sure if we're even friends. So tell me, *why* are you doing all this? And don't tell me it's to congratulate me on my follower count or because you feel guilty someone broke into my apartment. I'm an optimist, not an idiot."

If it were anyone else, I would suspect Christian was trying to lure me into some weird sexual arrangement. But he was rich and gorgeous enough that he didn't need to lure anyone into anything. People lined up to do his bidding without him having to ask.

Why was he giving me special treatment when he barely knew me?

Tick. Tick. Tick.

The deafening march of the seconds passing by on the wall clock matched the muscle jumping in Christian's jaw.

Not a word, only silence.

He was a vault, brimming with se[...]
lock not even a master thief could pick. Da[...]
him, screaming at me to stop and turn back b[...]
late.

Like a reckless fool, I forged on.

"I don't expect you to answer. You never do. But, while [...]
grateful for your help with the stalker, I can't take anymore
from you than I already have."

I held the watch out further. His hands remained at his
sides, but the weight of his stare was a physical press against my
skin.

"We signed a contract, but the boundaries have blurred
since I moved in. It's time we revert to the original terms of our
agreement. We're together in public only, for mutually beneficial reasons, and we're housemates until we find my stalker and
put him behind bars. That's *all* we are. Nothing more, nothing
less."

The words stacked up like bricks in the wall I was building
between him and my misguided heart.

Tick. Tick. Tick.

Only my ragged breaths interrupted the agonizingly slow
pass of time.

My feet hadn't moved an inch since Christian came home,
but my chest heaved like I'd just climbed Mount Everest.

"Nothing more, nothing less." His lazy repetition of my
words sent a shiver of unease down my spine.

My throat was too tight to allow sufficient air through.
Everything around us buzzed with a ceaseless, dangerous hum,
like a warning before a storm.

He took a step toward me. I took an instinctive step back,
and another, and another, until my lower back hit the couch
and my heart beat hard enough to bruise.

nates who are seeing

_s?" The question was

edge of a freshly sharp-

shions on either side of

nk into myself so I didn't

ombust into flames. I was

atisfaction of hiding, so I

nk about the mere inches

separating my body ⌐

"That's all we're supposed to be."

"I didn't ask you what we're supposed to be. I asked you what we are."

"You never answer my questions," I said defiantly. "Why should I answer yours?"

The hum intensified, sweeping over us like a tidal wave over the shore. Christian's eyes darkened until the pupils nearly obscured the molten gold of his irises.

"Your questions." The cruel cut of his smile injected ice into my veins, and I suddenly regretted asking him anything at all. "You want to know *why*, Stella? Why I gave you the watch, why I moved you into my house, my *sanctuary*, when I've lived alone for over a decade and had planned to do so for the rest of my life?"

Every word spiked my blood with adrenaline until I was drowning in it. In him. In this wild vortex I'd sucked us into with no escape route in sight.

"It's because you haven't looked me in the eye since New York. Because you're all I can fucking think about no matter where I am or who I'm with, and the thought of you hurt or upset makes me want to raze this city to the ground." Soft, almost desperate viciousness coated his voice. "I've never wanted someone more, and I've never hated myself more for it."

The vortex dragged me deeper, submerging me beneath the waves of a thousand different emotions. Any words I might've spoken were too tangled up in my chest to escape.

A bitter smile slashed across that heartbreaking face. "*That's* fucking why."

In a cool brush of air, Christian was gone.

The door slammed shut behind him, and I collapsed against the couch, the watch dangling from my fingers and the ruins of the world as I knew it at my feet.

23

CHRISTIAN

Valhalla on a Friday night was pure debauchery, but instead of partaking in the high-stakes poker game at the casino or indulging at the gentleman's club in the basement, I threw back my sixth drink at the bar.

Scotch, self-loathing, and anger burned through my blood while the brunette next to me chattered on.

Three hours and twice as many drinks hadn't thawed the black ice coating my veins since I left Stella alone in the apartment. Neither had the women fluttering around me, all of them beautiful and accomplished in their own right.

A cosmetics tycoon. A candy heiress. A supermodel who seemed unconcerned about abandoning the media magnate she'd showed up with.

"I'm staying at a hotel nearby." The model leaned closer until her low, throaty voice percolated through the din and into my ears. "Perhaps you'd like to join me?"

I ran a thumb along the rim of my glass and observed her in silence.

Her skin flushed a faint red beneath my scrutiny.

Part of me was tempted to take her up on her offer and drown my frustrations with heat and sex. That had been my plan when I'd started flirting with her.

But that was the problem. No supermodels or sex could erase Stella from my mind for a single fucking second.

Aggravation tunneled through my veins.

"Not interested." My reply came out harsher than usual, and the aggravation deepened.

I needed to get the fuck out of here. I was too on edge. If I stayed, I was liable to do something I'd regret.

Before the model could respond, her date finally noticed she'd wandered off after he finished his conversation with another club member.

He barreled toward us, his face clouded with dark displeasure.

"Anya. I told you to stay by my side." He closed a proprietary hand around her wrist and glared at me.

I stared back, bored.

Victor Black, CEO of a media empire consisting of dozens of trashy but widely read newspapers and websites.

He was also one of the more annoying members of Valhalla.

"Sorry." Anya didn't sound sorry at all.

"Harper." Victor gave me a nasty grin. "Shouldn't you be spending your Friday night with your girlfriend instead of flirting with another man's date?"

My smile iced at the indirect mention of Stella.

If we weren't in public...

"You're right," I said amicably. "Have fun with your date."

Victor's grin wavered at my agreeable response. A hint of panic crept into his eyes as I stood and dropped a hundred-dollar bill in the tip jar.

"Where are you..."

I left without listening to the rest of his insipid question and made a pit stop at his prized sports car.

I may not have a gun on me since Valhalla didn't allow weapons inside the club, but that didn't mean I didn't have other, less obvious weapons at my disposal.

Two minutes and one planted device later, I got into my car and drove home.

When I pulled up to the Mirage, I watched the security footage from outside Victor's house on my phone. As expected, he'd left soon after me; his car pulled into his driveway less than ten minutes after I parked.

He and Anya exited the car and entered his house.

I waited until the door shut behind them before I activated the device.

I couldn't hear the footage, but I could hear the *boom* in my head as his car exploded into flames.

By the time Victor ran out, it was already a twisted, blackened hunk of metal beneath the raging fire.

For the first time that night, I smiled a genuine smile.

Much better.

I tucked my phone into my pocket and straightened my jacket as I stepped out of the car.

He could probably guess who was behind his car's untimely demise, but he wouldn't do a damn thing about it. He was lucky I didn't blow it up when he was *in* it.

Unfortunately, the relief I gained from fucking with Victor was short-lived.

Every step closer to my apartment reminded me of what happened with Stella.

We lived in the same house, yet I could feel her slipping away.

You're not my boyfriend. I'm not sure if we're even friends.

My jaw clenched.

I'd bought her the watch in hopes it would bridge the distance that'd sprung up since New York. That'd backfired.

I'd gone to Valhalla hoping to take my mind off her. That'd backfired as well.

I could've gone home with any woman I wanted, and I chose to come home to the one who didn't want me.

A caustic laugh singed my throat.

Fate was a fucking bitch.

———————

I LOOSENED THE KNOT ON MY TIE AS I ENTERED MY HOUSE. My earlier self-loathing flamed hotter in my chest.

I'd made a career out of not losing my cool, but I'd lost my cool when Stella attempted to return the watch.

That's all *we are. Nothing more, nothing less.*

Why are you doing any *of this?*

Because I've never wanted someone more, and I've never hated myself more for it. That's fucking why.

The echoes from our conversation swathed the air.

I'd intended to go straight to my room, but I stopped when I caught sight of curly dark hair peeking out from the top of the couch and the scent of Stella's favorite lavender-scented candle. It flickered on the coffee table, next to long, bare legs and a scatter of drawing pencils.

I dragged my gaze over the expanse of smooth skin and cotton shorts until I met a pair of wary green eyes.

"You're still up." Alcohol and desire roughened my observation.

Stella was usually in bed by now, or at least in her room. I didn't believe for a second that she went to sleep that early.

Why had she been avoiding me? It couldn't possibly be

because I'd refused to tell her about *Magda* and Vivian. That conversation had been trivial at best.

"I couldn't sleep, so I thought I'd get some drawing done." She returned her gaze to her sketchpad. "Where were you?"

Despite her casual tone, visible tension lined her shoulders.

Some of the ice finally melted. The trickles of warmth sluiced through my veins and pulled a dark smile out of me.

"Why do you ask?"

"You were gone for hours. Curiosity is natural."

She was good at bluffing; I was better at detecting bullshit.

I crossed the room until I stood behind her. Our reflections gleamed back at us in the window, so sharp I could trace every detail of her face—the long, thick sweep of her lashes, the slight tilt of her catlike green eyes, the delicateness of her chin and the elegant curve of her cheekbones.

"I went out for drinks." My casual drawl didn't match the beat of my pulse.

I wanted to wrap her hair in my hand and tug her head back until those eyes were on mine. To mark that perfect skin with my teeth and claim her mouth in a kiss so fucking deep it would erase the notion that we were *just housemates*.

My hands flexed before I forced them loose. *Not yet.*

I'd waited too long to waste all my hard work on one impetuous moment.

If Stella sensed the danger gathering behind her, she didn't show it beyond a further tightening of her shoulders. Her pencil flew over the page, sketching and shading in the details of a floor-length gown without pause.

"Yes. I can smell the alcohol." Tightness hampered her casual response. "Scotch...and perfume?"

"Jealous?" Silk wrapped around my soft, mocking tone.

"I have no reason to be." She continued sketching, but the strokes were faster, angrier. "We're just roommates."

"That's not an answer." I tucked a stray strand of hair behind her ear. My voice turned coaxing while her pencil slowed. "Ask me what you really want to know, Stella."

Her lashes dipped before they swept up and her eyes met mine in the window.

Stella could don a cold facade all she wanted, but she had a soft heart, and she wore that heart on her sleeve.

I could pick out the dozen different emotions swirling beneath those jade-colored depths—anger, frustration, desire, and something darker, more unknown.

"Who were you with?" Indifference clung to her words, but it was tattered enough for me to spot the underlying vulnerability.

She cared, and that hint of emotion slayed me more than any strike of a sword could.

"Three women."

I pressed my hand against her shoulder, forcing her to still when she jerked at my response.

"They were at the same bar as me," I said. "I could've fucked any of them. Made them do every filthy, debauched thing I could think of. Their mouth on my cock, my hands in their hair..."

Stella's lips pressed together. Pride lit a defiant spark in her eyes, but rawness stretched her features taut, and I detected a small tremble beneath my touch.

"Yet I didn't touch them. I didn't want to. Not one tiny fucking bit." I lowered my head, my chest on fire from how close she was. Every breath brought her deeper into my orbit, but I would've traded all of them if it meant I could have her, *all* of her, for just one moment. "Perhaps I should've. Perhaps then, you'd understand how I feel."

My breath grazed her cheek as I slid my palm over the curve of her shoulder and down her arm. "I'm not a jealous man, Stella. I have never envied someone for what they have or who they're with, and yet..." My fingers glided down to her wrist. "I'm jealous of every person you smile at..." A brush over her fingers. "Every laugh I don't hear..." My touch dipped to her knee and made a slow, languorous journey up her thigh. "Every breeze that touches your skin and every sound that pours through your lips. It. Is. *Maddening.*"

I paused at the hem of her shorts. My heart thundered, slipping into a primal rhythm that matched the roughness of my voice. The air swirled with uncaged desires so potent they threatened to consume us both.

Stella had stopped sketching altogether. Her pencil lay slack in her loosened grip, and she was still, so still, save for the frantic music of her pulse.

I heard it over the hot rush of blood in my veins. It was a siren's song beckoning me to my doom, and it was so beautiful I might've succumbed even knowing it would lead me to hell.

"Christian..."

Every muscle tightened at the whisper of my name. It sounded so sweet coming from her mouth, like it was the sound of salvation instead of ruin.

She was the only person who'd ever said my name like that.

My hand curled around her thigh. Roughness dug into soft flesh before I released her and straightened, hating myself more with every second.

"Go to your room, Stella." My harsh command shattered the raw intimacy of the moment. "And lock your door."

A beat of hesitation. A ragged exhale.

Then a rustle of papers and a loss of warmth as she fled the room.

I waited until I heard her door close before I released my own leashed breath.

My steps pounded in rhythm with my heart as I walked to

my bathroom, stripped off my clothes, and turned the shower as cold as it would go.

The icy blasts of water pummeled my skin but did nothing to quell the desire raging inside me and incinerating everything in its path until only visions of jade eyes and lush dark curls remained. The phantom scent of green florals swirled in the shower, as invisible yet tangible as the sensation of hot silk beneath my touch.

Stella had seared so deep into my consciousness that she was all I could smell. All I could feel. And, even when I closed my eyes, all I could see.

The need in my groin pulsed harder.

Goddammit.

I bit out a low curse before I caved and fisted my cock. It was hard and swollen and already dripping pre-cum, and my movements were rough, almost angry as I worked myself toward a much-needed release.

I could've kissed her. I could've fisted her hair and branded her with my mouth until I proved there was nothing *fake* about the dark fire that burned between us.

The only thing that'd held me back was a fine thread of self-control, woven from cold logic and the faintest shreds of my long-destroyed conscience.

I was well aware of the fact that, should either of us cave, I would be condemning not only myself but her to hell.

I would be touching her with bloodied hands and kissing her with a deceiver's mouth. She would be climbing into bed with a monster, and she didn't even know it.

Part of me wanted her so much I didn't care; the other part was protective enough that I'd have her sent away to a place where even I couldn't find her.

It was a paradox, as were all things in my life that related to her.

But if that thread had snapped...

I closed my eyes, my grip tight and my breath harshening.

She could be beneath me now, her nails clawing my back and my name a moan in her mouth...

My orgasm coiled at the base of my spine, slowly at first, then faster until it exploded in one blinding, deafening moment.

"Fuck!"

The force of my release drowned out my curse, but when I came down from my high, all that was left was cold water and the bright, mocking glare of the overhead light.

I rested my forehead against the icy tile and counted my deep inhales.

One. Two. Three.

Stella's room was down the hall from mine. Despite what I'd told her, a locked door wouldn't be much protection.

Four. Five. Six.

I kept counting until my heartbeat slowed to a normal pace and clarity chased away the scotch in my blood and the fog in my brain.

It wasn't the right night to make a move.

I'd waited this long. I could wait a while longer.

Because when I claimed Stella as mine, I would do it so fucking thoroughly there wouldn't be a shred of doubt in either of our minds as to who she belonged to...or who I belonged to in return.

24

STELLA

FOR THE RECORD, I WAS *NOT* JEALOUS OF THE WOMEN Christian saw last night. I was merely worried about him being gone for hours since he was my boyfriend—well, fake boyfriend—and it would create a lot of headaches for me if anything happened to him.

That was all.

My skin prickled with awareness as we waited for Josh or Jules to answer the door.

It was their belated housewarming, and Christian had finagled an invite since Rhys and Bridget were in town for both the party and some diplomatic event. Something about wanting to see Rhys and not being able to meet up with him separately.

I'd planned to avoid Christian until I sorted through my tangled feelings toward him, but now I had to spend an entire day with him while his confession and warning played like a broken record in my head.

I've never wanted anyone more, and I've never hated myself more for it.

Go to your room, Stella. And lock your door.

My imagination couldn't resist spinning fantasies of what would've happened had I not left after his warning...or if I hadn't locked my door like he'd told me to.

Rough hands. Whiskey kisses. Footsteps in the dark.

Heat arrowed down my torso and pooled between my thighs.

I clutched my housewarming gift closer to me as my breaths quickened.

Despite my love of crystals, tarot, and all things mystic, I didn't believe in magic. Not the spells and broomsticks kind, anyway. But in that moment, I was certain that Christian could crawl inside my mind and pick out every dirty, wicked fantasy I'd had of him.

His stare burned a hole in my cheek as the crisp April afternoon turned into a furnace. The sun blazed a ruthless path over my exposed skin and slowed my heartbeat while the silence wrapped tight hands around my throat.

I might've suffocated right there on the front steps had Jules not opened the front door and saved me.

"Stella! Christian! I *thought* I heard you guys," she bubbled. "I'm so glad you could make it!"

The tension collapsed, pulling Christian's gaze away from me and loosening the string holding me upright until I sagged against my boxed candle gift set with a mixture of relief and disappointment.

"We wouldn't miss it for the world." I thrust the box at her, hoping she couldn't pick up on my restlessness. Once Jules scented a whiff of gossip, she chased it down like a dog after a bone. "This is for you. Happy housewarming."

Her eyes lit up. She *lived* for presents. She once told me it was a shame Santa wasn't real because, as old as he was, she'd fuck him if it meant she'd wake up to a different gift every morning.

Granted, that had been after three eggnogs over the holidays, but still. Jules Ambrose's mind worked in fascinating ways.

"Thank you! Come in, come in. Everyone's already in the living room." She took the gift with one hand and opened the door wider with the other. "Just take off your shoes and leave them by the door. *I* personally don't care, but Josh is anal about that." She rolled her eyes in good-natured exasperation.

"That's because I don't want people tracking city dirt and grime all over our floors, you heathen." Josh came up behind her and kissed her cheek before greeting us with a dimpled smile.

"Hey, guys. Welcome to our humble abode." He swept a dramatic arm around the two-story townhouse.

I'd visited before, so I was familiar with the hardwood floors and charmingly mismatched décor—Jules's fluffy pink rugs next to Josh's black leather furniture, her red lip-shaped pillows offsetting the hideous paintings strewn on the walls.

Josh was easy on the eyes, but his taste in art was questionable at best.

"Nice art," Christian drawled.

"Thanks." The other man beamed. "I picked it out myself."

"I can tell."

I shot Christian a quick look, but his expression was impassive.

"I am *not* a heathen." Jules was still stuck on what Josh called her. "As for the grime and dirt, that's what cleaning is for."

"Yeah? And who does the cleaning?" he asked as we walked toward the living room. His lean frame moved easily around the skis propped haphazardly against the open door of the front hall closet and the empty Crumble & Bake box half-sliding off a side table.

He was an ER doctor at Thayer University Hospital, but with his tousled dark hair, tanned skin, and razor-sharp cheekbones, he could play one on TV as well.

"I do," Jules said primly. "When I have time."

"The last time you *had time*, you spent it giving yourself an at-home facial."

"My skin needs pampering. Being a lawyer is stressful." She tossed her hair over her shoulder. "Might I remind you that the last time *you* had time, you spent it getting your ass whooped at chess by Alex?"

Josh scowled. "I did not get my *ass whooped*. I was getting the lay of the land. Figuring out his weaknesses."

Jules patted his arm with a soothing hand. "There, there, babe. It's okay. I still love you even if you suck at strategy."

I swallowed a laugh at their bickering. Some things never changed.

We entered the living room, where the rest of the party sprawled across two leather couches.

Bridget jumped up and hugged me the instant she saw me. "Stella! It's so good to see you!"

"You too." I squeezed her tight. To the rest of the world, she was a queen, but to me, she'd always be the girl who I binge-watched *The Bachelor* and stayed up late drunkenly discussing the philosophy of life with when we were in college. "How's the royal life treating you? Behead anyone lately?" I teased.

She released an exaggerated sigh. "Unfortunately not, though I was tempted to sentence the minister of the interior to the guillotine. Rhys talked me out of it."

She cast a playful glance at her husband, whose muscled, six-foot-five frame made the couch he was sitting on look like a piece of doll furniture.

"Half me talking you out of it, half the fact no one uses guillotines anymore." Amusement softened his battle-hardened gray eyes.

"I could bring them back. I'm the queen. What I say goes." Bridget sank back onto the seat next to him with regal haughtiness, though her face glowed with mischief.

A grin split his face. "Of course you can, princess." He murmured something else too low for me to hear. Whatever it was, it made Bridget's cheeks flush pink with pleasure.

Jules nudged Josh in the ribs with a dreamy sigh. "Why don't *you* call me princess? It's so cute."

"Because you're not a princess. You're a hellion," he said, earning himself a deep glare. "And that's just the way I like it." He drew her to his chest and planted a dramatic kiss on her lips.

Jules made a half-hearted attempt to push him off, but laughter bubbled from her throat. "Nice save, Chen."

The lighthearted atmosphere eased my earlier tension as I leaned over to hug Ava.

She was curled up next to Alex, who eyed the other couples' sweet interactions with distaste while he wrapped a protective arm around her shoulders.

"If you want to engage in PDA too, now's the time," I joked.

She laughed. "Noted, but we're good for now." Her voice dropped to a stage whisper. "Alex is allergic to PDA."

"I am not *allergic*." He grimaced when Jules looped her arms around Josh's neck and said something that made his face soften. "Merely disturbed."

"Alex has performance anxiety," Josh said without looking away from Jules. "It's okay, dude. Happens to the best of us. Maybe you can invest in the development of a pill that'll help with your problem. It'll be like Viagra for kissers."

"If I were to invest in the development of anything, it would be a custom muzzle to keep you quiet."

A mischievous dimple creased Josh's cheek. "Alex Volkov spending all that R&D money on me? I'm honored."

Jules buried her face in his chest, her shoulders shaking with laughter.

Ava placed her hand on Alex's arm. "Don't kill them," she warned. "We can't lose a bridesmaid *and* best man this close to the wedding."

"The term *best man* is false advertising." Alex pinned Josh with a dark glare. "I should swap you out with someone else."

"You can try, but I'm your only friend, and who can throw a better bachelor party than me? That's right, no one." Josh answered his own question. "Besides, I already put down the deposit for the jumbo banana float and custom poker cards. They're illustrated with a drawing of Ava and a robot in a suit."

I turned my head away so Alex couldn't see my smile.

Besides Ava, Josh was the only person who could get away with provoking Alex like that.

Maybe.

"Christian, it's nice to see you again!" Ava chirped before her fiancé strangled her brother to death in the latter's living room. "I didn't realize you were coming."

They'd met once at Bridget's wedding, but meeting someone once had never deterred her from treating someone like they were an old friend.

"I wouldn't miss an opportunity to hang out with Stella's friends," Christian said easily.

He rested a hand on my lower back, and I almost stepped away from the sheer heat of him before I remembered we were supposed to be dating.

I'd caved and told my friends they could tell their significant others so everyone here knew we were pretending, even if they didn't say it.

Still, should I keep up the act for simplicity's sake or not?

Indecision tightened my muscles.

Christian must've picked up on my hesitation because his jaw flexed as his hand lingered for an extra second before he withdrew it.

Relief and disappointment battled for dominance in my chest.

Meanwhile, the room fell silent as six pairs of eyes ping-ponged between us. I wasn't the only one unsure about how to treat our relationship; I could see the confusion scrawled all over my friends' faces.

An awkward shadow darkened the room before Jules clapped her hands.

"Since everyone is here, let's start happy hour! I have a new margarita recipe I'm dying for you guys to try..."

No one questioned her, even though it was barely noon.

Several homemade margaritas and way too many chips later, I found myself on a couch with Ava, Jules, and Bridget while Christian, Alex, Josh, and Rhys sat across from us.

I'd stuck to my two drinks per party rule, but Josh had been so heavy handed with his pour that my head swam like I'd downed half a dozen tequila shots.

"We need a girls' trip soon." Bridget leaned her head back and yawned. "Something fun. I'm so tired of diplomatic trips. I fly thousands of miles to smile and shake hands with a bunch of old men. I could do the same thing in Parliament *without* the jet lag."

"Yes!" Jules brightened at the prospect of a wild weekend abroad. "Ava, your bachelorette is coming up. Let's make it big. Let's make it unforgettable. Let's make it—"

"Safe and legal," Ava said firmly. "I don't need to go to jail again."

Ava, Jules, and I had gotten arrested during Bridget's bachelorette after Jules punched some creep in the face for groping Ava. Thankfully, Bridget had left by then, but our stint in a cold Eldorran holding cell wasn't one of my fondest memories.

"Again?" Bridget's head popped up. "When were you in jail?"

"Uh..." Ava's cheeks pinked. "That was a figure of speech?"

We'd never told Bridget what happened because she would freak out. Besides, Alex had bailed us out and taken care of the aftermath—i.e. kept it out of the press—so no harm, no foul.

"You said *again*." Suspicion darkened Bridget's elegant features.

"She's talking about the time we broke into the clock tower in college and ran into campus security," Jules interjected. "Anyway, *of course* the bachelorette will be safe and legal. I like to live life on the edge, but I don't want Alex to murder me, thank you very much."

We looked over at Alex, who was listening to Josh detail the thirty-six different uses for a jumbo banana float with a pained expression.

On the other end of the couch, Rhys and Christian were engaged in conversation, their voices too low for me to hear. Rhys was scowling; Christian looked amused.

It should be illegal for that much gorgeousness to occupy such a small space. But while every man was devastating in his own right, my gaze was irresistibly drawn to the lean form lounging closest to the door.

Christian turned his head at the exact moment my attention landed on him. Our gazes locked, and an electric current of something primal singed my blood.

The fogginess clouding my head suddenly had nothing to do with the margaritas.

"Forget the trip for now." Jules's voice dragged my attention back to her, though Christian's eyes remained a hot brand on my skin. "What was that?"

"What was what?" My heart ricocheted in my chest.

The lingering aftertaste of strawberry and tequila dissolved into spice and whiskey on my tongue. It was how I imagined he would taste—like heat, sin, and pure, unfiltered masculinity.

"*That.*" Eyes like hazel blades punctured my feigned ignorance. She tilted her head a fraction of an inch toward Christian. "The sexual tension is so thick I can cut it with a butter knife."

"There's no sexual tension." Unless you counted the ache in my core and the awareness tightening my skin.

"There is. Even I feel it." Ava lifted her hair off her neck. "If it gets any hotter, I'll have to make Alex revisit his no PDA rule."

"Exactly." Jules stood abruptly, drawing the men's attention and interrupting Josh as he reached banana float use number twenty-five.

"Everything okay?" he asked.

"Yep. We just need to use the restroom." She grasped my wrist and pulled me up and toward the back of the house. Ava and Bridget followed us. "Don't eat all the chips while we're gone!"

"I'm a doctor, and I still can't find a medical reason for why girls always have to use the bathroom at the same time," I heard Josh muse as we left.

"You're an idiot," Alex said.

Their voices faded when Jules pulled us into the guest bath and shut the door behind us.

"Why do I feel like this is an FBI interrogation?" I leaned against the counter and eyed my friends warily.

"Because it is." Jules planted her hands on her hips and adopted her lawyer voice. "Now, tell us the truth. Are you, Stella Alonso, having or have ever had sexual intercourse with Christian Harper?"

"*No.*"

"Do you want to?"

Two seconds of hesitation was enough to elicit gasps all around.

"I knew it!" Triumph glowed in Jules's eyes. "I'm so happy for you! *Finally*, someone you're attracted to. Christian is crazy hot, and you're living in the same house. It's like the perfect setup for a sexy fling."

Bridget was less enthused. "I thought this was a fake relationship," she said gently. "What changed?"

"Like Jules said, he's pretty good-looking." I instinctively grasped my crystal necklace. The warm, clear stone was supposed to clear my mind and help my focus, but my thoughts tumbled in my head like laundry set on high. "Also..." After another moment's hesitation, I spilled everything that'd happened.

New York, Christian's weird aversion to art, the watch, his confession about wanting me.

By the time I finished, three eyes pinned me to the marble counter with varying degrees of shock (Ava), concern (Bridget), and delight (Jules).

"I had a feeling he was into you since the day we met him," Jules said sagely. "The way he looked at you when we signed the lease? *Whew.*" She fanned herself. "Listen, if you want to leave and bang his brains out, I won't be offended. It's a new season, babe. Time to clear out those cobwebs from your sex life. It'll be like spring cleaning for your vagina."

I winced at the mental visual.

"I wouldn't jump into anything that fast." A frown marred Bridget's forehead. "Christian is, well, you know my thoughts about him already. I'm forever grateful he helped me and Rhys with our photo leak problem, but he's not someone you turn to if you want a serious relationship."

"That's why I said bang, not date," Jules said. "I bet he's a beast in bed. He just has that look."

Heat stained my cheeks. "What would Josh say if he knew you were secretly assessing other men's sexual prowess?"

"He'd say he's still better than them, and he'd be right. Our sex life is fantastic." Jules cast an apologetic glance at Ava. "Sorry."

"I'm going to pretend I didn't hear that last part." Ava had accepted the relationship between Josh and Jules on the condition that they never discussed their sex life in front of her.

She turned to me, her dark eyes warm with concern and curiosity. "The question is, do you *want* just sex with him? Or do you want something more?"

"Don't be ridiculous," Jules said. "Stel isn't interested in dating. Right?"

The crystal flamed against my palm. I didn't answer, but my silence spoke volumes.

"Oh." Jules's smile slowly faded into realization. "*Oh.*"

Oh was right.

I didn't know if I wanted to date Christian, but I knew I wanted him.

And I knew it was only a matter of time before the dark chemistry between us exploded into something neither of us could come back from.

25

CHRISTIAN

"WHAT THE *HELL* DO YOU THINK YOU'RE DOING?"

"I'm drinking and enjoying your delightful company." I raised my glass. "It's nice to see you again, Larsen."

"I wish I could say the same."

Rhys had been grumbling and brooding since I arrived, which wasn't a huge departure from his usual demeanor, but now that the girls were out of the room, he turned the full force of his ire on me.

"One year of being Prince Consort and you've forgotten our history. Our friendship." I laced my tone with carefully crafted disappointment. "I thought you were different, but it's true what they say. Absolute power corrupts absolutely."

I used *friendship* in the loosest sense of the term. Our rocky, complicated relationship started with Rhys saving my life and him walking away from Harper Security to be with Bridget. The path between those points had been riddled with disagreements, barbs, and a strange mix of mutual respect and suspicion.

"Cut the bullshit, Harper." Rhys's glare crackled with irritation. Classic Larsen. If he brooded any harder, he'd require a plastic surgeon to carve the frown out of his face. "I told you to stay away from Stella. I don't care if it's fake. She's living with you, and I don't trust you under the same roof with her."

"You seem awfully concerned about her love life," I drawled. "Anything Bridget should know?"

The air dripped with silent danger, but no one seemed concerned except for the royal bodyguards shifting uneasily in the back of the room.

Josh watched our back and forth with fascination from Rhys's other side while Alex scrolled through his phone, looking bored.

"I'm concerned *because* of Bridget," Rhys growled. "Stella is her best friend. You fuck with her, Bridget's gonna be upset. Which means I'll be upset."

"Ah, I see." I swirled my drink in its glass before taking a thoughtful sip. "It must be tiring, having your emotions so intimately connected with another's. Does it work the other way around, or is it a one-way leash only she gets to yank?"

Josh snorted out a laugh.

"You act amused," Rhys said without looking at him. "Like Jules and Ava won't be riding your asses if anything happens to Stella."

Josh's smile disappeared. Alex looked up from his phone, those cold green eyes drilling into my skin for the first time since I arrived.

We hadn't acknowledged each other beyond an obligatory nod of greeting.

We didn'ts hide our quasi friendship, but we didn't announce it to the world either because there was nothing *to* announce. Other than our monthly chess matches and the occasional business interaction, we rarely saw each other.

"Obviously, I'm concerned," Josh said, doing a one-eighty

as he directed his next question at me. "What are your intentions with Stella?"

"I don't have to explain myself to you. I don't even know you."

A lie. *Magda* had inadvertently fallen into his hands before Dante bought it off him, which meant I knew every single thing about Josh Chen. His family background, his grades in med school, his favorite basketball team and how he took his coffee.

He was a golden boy with a dark streak, but not one I needed to concern myself with now that *Magda* was no longer in his possession.

"You're sitting in my house, dating one of my sister's *and* girlfriend's best friends, so you do, in fact, need to explain yourself," Josh said. "If you don't like it, feel free to leave."

I sighed, regretting my decision to attend this damned party.

If Stella hadn't been so adamant about attending, I could've spent the day doing something more productive, like hunting down her stalker, reorganizing my library, or finishing yesterday's crossword.

Anything was better than this insufferable conversation.

"You know..." Rhys's expression turned speculative. "Bridget told me about all the things you did for Stella. Lowering her rent, agreeing to the dating arrangement, moving her into your house when some creep spooked her." The speculation morphed into a knowing glint that set off a dozen warning bells. "Thought you didn't like people in your personal space. Any reason you're handing out special treatment like candy to her?"

"I have my reasons." I flicked a piece of lint off my sleeve, the picture of undisturbed calm, even as unease glided through my chest.

Rhys was a royal pain in my ass, not only because he was

one of the few people unafraid to stand up to me, but because he was observant as fuck and knew me better than anyone except Dante.

My annoyance ratcheted up another notch when he examined me with...amusement? What the fuck was so funny?

"I'm sure you do." Humor lengthened his drawl. "Catching feelings, Harper?"

"Only that of irritation at being interrogated." My back teeth clenched before I caught myself and relaxed. "What I do with my life and time is none of your business."

Rhys's grin widened. "Deflection. Which means I'm right." His low chuckle sharpened the edges of my displeasure. "Oh, this is rich. I never thought I'd see the day."

Beside him, Josh's fingers flew over his phone with alarming speed.

My eyes narrowed. "Are you texting Jules?"

"Of course not. But in case you're wondering, the girls will be in the bathroom for..." He checked his phone. "At least another half hour."

Jesus Christ.

Of all the people Stella could be friends with, she had to choose *these* people.

"Having feelings is nothing to be ashamed of." A tiny smile cracked the ice in Alex's expression. "You'll get used to it."

The Alex Volkov I knew three years ago would've never said such a thing, not even as a joke.

Yet another sign that love turned the most level-headed of people into fools. It was enough to make a man want to hunt Cupid down and string the bastard up using his own arrows.

Aggravation expanded in my chest. "Don't start with me. At least I didn't give up my company to follow a girl around for a year in hopes she would spare me a second glance."

"Yet I have the girl and you're sitting on a couch arguing

with her friends' significant others," Alex said mildly. "If you don't have feelings for Stella, you wouldn't be so worked up over it."

"Exactly." Josh nodded like he knew me even though we'd exchanged a total of five words prior to today.

My smile was pure ice. "I would spend more time improving your chess skills and less worrying about other people's business, Josh. I've beat Alex in chess. Have you?"

Josh's smile disappeared. "What do you mean, you've beat Alex in chess? When did you play chess together?" He whipped his head toward Alex. "You've been playing chess with *someone else*?"

Alex closed his eyes briefly before he opened them and glared at me, his expression filled with frost-tipped venom.

My smile widened. "We have a standing chess date every month." I swirled my drink in my glass. "Didn't he tell you?"

Josh looked stricken. "You have another, *secret best friend*? But...*I'm* your best friend! I bought you a banana float for your bachelor party!"

"I don't want a banana float, and he's *not* my best friend." Alex's glare intensified.

I shrugged, my meaning clear. *What can you do? C'est la vie.*

It wasn't my fault he was so antisocial that his best friend freaked out at him spending time with someone else.

"I can't believe it. Standing chess date," Josh muttered furiously. "Was *that* why you wouldn't watch the latest Marvel movie with me? Because you know I've been dying to see that movie for weeks..."

Rhys was too busy laughing to pay attention to the drama unfolding less than three feet away.

"Wait till I tell Bridget. She's going to *love* this."

My temporary good mood evaporated. "You won't tell her shit."

"Sure I won't." His big frame shook with mirth.

My back teeth clenched with aggravation.

If there was one thing I despised, besides incompetence and Valentine's Day, it was people digging into my personal business.

Once upon a time, Alex and Rhys would agree. Now, they were too whipped by their other halves to conduct themselves with a modicum of self-respect. Alex making a joke? Rhys giving up his privacy for a lifetime of paparazzi and ribbon cuttings?

It was nauseating.

Stella and I were different.

I didn't love her, but I wanted her with an intensity that left the flimsy, overused concept of love in the dust. It wasn't sweet or saccharine. There were no rainbows or unicorns, only desire edged with roughness and darkness.

Hot June days. Secret smiles. Turquoise.

I'd waited a long time.

Eventually, I would catch her, and once I did, I was never letting her go.

26

STELLA

I finished the first piece of my collection four days after Josh and Jules's housewarming.

It hung on the back of my door in a spill of silk and sinuous lines, its golden color a stark contrast to the dark wood background.

It wasn't perfect, and the fabric was expensive, which meant I needed a better wholesale option if I wanted to scale up production, but it was *done*. The first tangible evidence my dreams weren't just dreams and that I was finally taking concrete steps toward making them reality.

A complete draft, no matter how imperfect, was still better than no draft at all.

And this was my own pattern, own design. This wasn't just a quick Simplicity Pattern dress I'd made over Christmas break one year. This was mine.

Too much planning is a form of procrastination. Lilah's words from our coffee date echoed in my head as I ran my hand over the dress's bodice. The smooth glide of it against my skin sent a thrill darting through my blood. *If you want a brand, you need a product. Create a great product,* then *worry about everything else.*

The "everything else" encompassed pricing, sourcing, outreach to retail buyers, and a thousand other details that overwhelmed me every time I looked at my to-do list, but I had a product and a plan.

Everything else will flow from there.

A strange emotion welled in my throat, so unfamiliar it took me a minute to identify it: pride.

I hadn't felt it when I hit a million followers or when I woke up the next day to a flood of brand collab offers. But now, standing in front of a dress that'd taken me a day to sew and a lifetime to create, the warm glow of pride crested over me.

My entire life, I'd created for other people. My blog posts were for my audience, my photos were for my followers, my grades had been for my parents, and my ideas had been for *D.C. Style* when I worked there.

This was the first time in a long time that I'd done something for *me*, and honestly? It felt damn good.

Weightlessness expanded in my chest and pulled a huge smile out of me. I didn't even care that my monthly family dinner was that night. *Nothing* could bring me down—

My phone lit up with an incoming call from Natalia.

...except for a conversation with my sister.

My smile dimmed, but enough giddiness remained that my voice came out chirpier than usual when I picked up.

"Hey, Nat."

"This is a reminder that Mom and Dad are expecting you to bring your boyfriend tonight." Natalia dispensed with the niceties. "Remind him to come prepared with an accomplishment to share."

Yes, guests were expected to share their accomplishments

at an Alonso family dinner. How else would my family judge whether they were worthy of another invite?

"Christian can't make it." I put Natalia on speakerphone so I could finish getting ready. I'd lost track of time ogling my dress, and I was due at my parents' house in an hour. "He wants to be there, but he got sick last minute. Fever, chills, the whole thing."

It was scary how easily the lie spilled from my tongue.

It clattered to the ground with a soft *plink,* joining the dozens of other untruths I'd uttered over the past few months.

"Really." Natalia's tone went flat with suspicion. "How convenient."

I twisted my hair into a bun, hoping she couldn't hear the rapid pitter-patter of my heart. "It's unfortunate, but sickness doesn't conform to our personal schedules."

More lies. I could make a killing as a car salesperson if my clothing line didn't pan out.

Guilt speared my chest, but I held fast. There was no way in hell I'd subject even my worst enemy to dinner with the Alonsos. Plus, I required a clear mind and all my faculties to deal with my parents, and if there was one thing Christian was good at, it was clouding my judgment.

"Mom and Dad won't be happy," Natalia warned. "They were looking forward to meeting your boyfriend."

More like they were looking forward to grilling him. Jarvis and Mika Alonso had a strict list of requirements they expected from a future son-in-law, and while Christian ticked off almost every box—wealthy, well-educated, cultured—the interrogation process would be torture.

"You post about him so much. It must be serious."

My sister was so obvious about her fishing I would've laughed had I not been sick with nerves.

"We're taking things day by day." I dusted blush on my

cheeks. "I'm sure Mom and Dad will understand. Besides, you know how Mom is with germs. She wouldn't want a sick guest at dinner—"

"Actually, I'm feeling much better."

I spun around, my pulse skyrocketing at the sight of Christian leaning against the wooden frame, his suit jacket off and one hand in his pocket. A stray lock of dark hair fell in his eye, begging me to brush it back.

"I was out of commission yesterday, but I'm good as new today." He addressed Natalia over speakerphone, but his eyes didn't leave mine. "So Stella, darling, I'll be able to accompany you to dinner after all."

This wasn't happening.

Christian *would* overhear us the *one* time I put Natalia on speaker.

Someone in the high heavens must hate me. Perhaps I shouldn't have skipped church so much since I moved out of my family's house.

What are you doing? I mouthed, hoping my glare conveyed the full extent of my displeasure.

His only response was a smirk that made me reconsider my stance on non-violence.

Thou shalt do no harm...unless your fake boyfriend was trying to crash a dinner with your overbearing family.

Then again, dinner should be punishment enough. One meal with the Alonsos would send even the mighty Christian Harper running for the hills.

"Oh!" Rare surprise coasted through Natalia's voice before she recovered. "That's good to hear." The edges of her words softened now that she knew someone else was in the room. "We'll see you in an hour, then."

"Yes, you will. Looking forward to it," Christian drawled.

I hung up before I voiced the aggravation bubbling in my veins. "*What* was that?"

Cool, calm, collected. Cool, calm—

"That was me agreeing to dinner at my girlfriend's house." Christian straightened and ran a hand over his tie. "We've been dating for months. It's time I met your parents, don't you think?"

"*We're not actually dating.*"

"They don't know that." His calm rebuttal only infuriated me more. "I have to meet them eventually. There are only so many excuses you can make. This way, we get the meeting out of the way, and they'll stop badgering you."

He had a point. Still, I hated how he'd gone about it.

Dinner was in less than an hour, and I wasn't mentally prepared for a meal with Christian *and* my family.

How would my parents react to him? How would *he* react to *them*? I'd seen how Christian could charm a table in New York, but that had been with friends.

The last time I brought a boy home—Quentin Sullivan, high school prom—my parents had grilled him so relentlessly about his GPA, college acceptances, and five-year plan that he'd burst into tears during the limo ride to the dance. The minute we arrived, he mumbled something about making a mistake and spent the rest of the night dancing with some other girl.

Christian had no idea what he'd gotten himself into.

———

OUR RIDE TO MY PARENTS' HOUSE WAS AS SILENT AS THE one to Josh and Jules' over the weekend.

His confession about wanting me was the elephant in every room we were in together, but neither of us addressed it.

I didn't know *how* to address it. Maybe it'd be easier if I didn't want him too, but every time I tried to bring it up, my nerves got the better of me.

I snuck a peek at Christian. The air between us hummed with a hundred spoken words. They tightened my lungs and cut off the flow of oxygen until I grew lightheaded.

The air conditioning was on, but I cracked the window open and sucked in a small gasp of fresh air.

We stopped at a red light.

Christian didn't say a word about the window, but the heat of his stare was like a brand against my skin.

I kept my eyes out the window and away from him until we arrived at my parents' house, where bigger worries drowned out our tension.

As expected, my family greeted him the way they would any guest—polite and welcoming on the surface, but secretly sizing him up with every move he made and every word out of his mouth.

He'd brought a two-thousand-dollar vintage red from his extensive wine collection with us, which endeared him to my mother, but my dad was harder to impress.

"I've heard of you." Jarvis's tone suggested what he heard wasn't particularly flattering for Christian. "Harper Security, correct?"

"Yes, sir." Christian passed me the bowl of mashed potatoes. He'd donned a more casual outfit than his usual suits for dinner, but somehow, the button-down shirt and jeans made him look even more intimidating, like a wolf in sheep's clothing. A hint of challenge disguised as a smile flirted at the corners of his mouth. "I work with the government on occasion. I know Secretary Palmer well."

My dad's face settled into a mask of grim lines at the mention of his boss. "I'm sure you do."

The clink of plates and glasses replaced conversation until

the main course. The lull gave me a chance to rehearse my answer for our traditional sharing of accomplishments.

I finished the first piece of my fashion collection. Oh, did I forget to tell you? I'm starting a fashion brand. I have a—

"How's your job at *D.C. Style* going?" Natalia's question sliced through my inner musings.

I still hadn't told my family I'd gotten fired. Every time I tried, the words made it halfway up my throat before they withered and died.

"It's fine." I raised my water glass to my lips and hoped no one detected the slight shake in my hand.

"Hmm." The scrape of Natalia's fork against her plate sounded like nails against a chalkboard. "You know what's funny? I was in the neighborhood the other day. I had a meeting near your office, so I thought I'd drop by and say hi. But when I showed up, the receptionist said you don't work there anymore. She said you haven't worked there in almost two months."

All movement stopped like she'd pressed *pause* on the scene. We were no longer people but wax statues of ourselves, frozen into a grotesque tableau of shock and denial.

Christian was the only one who showed a hint of life. His concerned warmth caressed my suddenly icy skin, and the even rise and fall of his chest steadied some of my nerves.

I'd thought his presence at dinner would throw me off-kilter, but it was doing the exact opposite.

I couldn't say the same for my parents, though.

My father's skin had leached of color, and my mother's mouth formed a surprised red O. It took a lot to surprise Jarvis and Mika Alonso, and a crazy, inane part of me wanted to whip out my phone and record the moment for posterity.

"I told them it must be a mistake." Natalia's eyes pinned me like a bug to the ground. "There's no way you got fired and didn't tell us. Right, Stella?"

Regret coated the back of my tongue in the form of bile.

The urge to lie again was so great it almost dragged me under its spell, but I couldn't keep up the charade forever. Eventually, they'd discover the truth.

It was time to stop hiding and own up to what happened.

"It wasn't a mistake. I'm not working at *D.C. Style* anymore." Every syllable scraped my throat on its way out. "I got fired in mid-February."

Silence clung to the room for another beat before it exploded into curses and shouts.

"Mid-February! How could you keep this from us for so long?" my mother demanded in Japanese.

She grew up in Kyoto and reverted to her first language whenever she was upset.

"I was waiting for the right time to tell you," I answered in English.

I hadn't practiced Japanese in years, but its lilt was so familiar I felt like I was sitting in weekend school again. My parents had been too busy to teach me and Natalia the formalities, so they'd enrolled us in Spanish, German, and Japanese classes when we were children. They said it was to help us connect with our mixed heritage, but I suspected it had more to do with the fact foreign language proficiency looked good on college applications.

"And what have you been doing all this time?" The quiet rumble of my father's anger seeped into every corner of the room. "You haven't found a new job in two months?"

I twisted my necklace around my finger until it cut off my circulation.

Cool, calm, collected.

"I haven't applied for another office job. I earn a lot of

money from my blog, and I just signed a campaign deal with a big brand. Six figures. I'm earning a full-time income."

"Perhaps, but it's not a *stable* income." Jarvis pressed his lips so tightly together they were nothing but a slash of white against his brown skin. "What happens when the deals dry up? Or if you lose your account? What about an emergency fund? How much do you have in savings?"

He fired the questions like bullets.

"I…" I glanced at Christian, who tipped his chin in a silent show of support. His expression was placid, but something turbulent lurked beneath his eyes. A shiver scampered down my spine before I faced the firing squad again.

"I don't plan on becoming a full-time influencer. I actually…" *Just say it.* "I'm going to create my own designs. For a fashion line. And I have a bit of savings left, but I'll replenish it once I get my next payment for the Delamonte campaign."

A guillotine of silence hung suspended over the table before it sliced through the air and triggered another explosion.

"You cannot be serious!" Mika gripped her fork with a white-knuckled hand. "A *fashion designer*? Stella, you graduated from Thayer. You can be anything! Why in the world would you choose design?"

My father was stuck on the other part of my bombshell. "What do you mean, you have a bit of savings *left*? Where did the rest of it go?"

Sweat dampened the nape of my neck.

Go big or go home.

My parents were already pissed at me. I might as well rip the Band-Aid off my other secret and deal with the consequences all at once.

"I've been paying for Maura's care at an assisted living facility." I released my necklace and tucked my hands beneath my thighs to prevent them from shaking, but my right knee bounced with nerves.

It was a good thing my mom couldn't see, or she'd yell at me for that too. According to Japanese superstitions, shaking one's leg invited the ghosts of poverty or something like that. It was one of my mother's biggest pet peeves.

"She has Alzheimer's," I continued. My hand curled around the edge of the chair for support. "I've been paying her room and board for the past few years. That's where most of my money has gone."

This time, the silence wasn't a blade; it was a boa constrictor wrapping itself around my limbs and strangling me until my breaths puffed out in tiny bursts of air.

My mother paled until she resembled a paper cutout of herself. "Why would you do that?"

"Because she has no one else, Mom. She took care of me—"

"She is *not* family," Mika bit out. "We're grateful for the years she spent with you girls, and I understand why you have an attachment to her. But she hasn't been your nanny in more than a decade, and you aren't swimming in money, Stella. You're unemployed, for Christ's sake. Even when you worked at *D.C. Style,* your salary was pitiful. Spending tens of thousands of dollars a year caring for a former family employee when you're not financially stable is the most irresponsible, foolish—"

Anger lit a match in my stomach and eradicated every ounce of guilt over my lies.

I hated how my parents dismissed Maura as a mere *former family employee* when she'd been so much more. She'd sung me to sleep as a child, guided me through the turbulent years of puberty, and weathered the storm of my early high school angst with remarkable patience. She'd been there for every skinned knee and every teenage heartbreak, and she deserved more than a passing acknowledgment for all she'd done.

Without her, my parents wouldn't be where they are today. She'd kept the household together while they built their careers into legends.

"Maura *is* family. She was more of a mother to me than you ever were!" The words burst forth before I could stop them.

Natalia's gasp drowned out the clatter of her fork against her plate. She hadn't said a word since she outed my firing from *D.C. Style,* but her eyes were the size of saucers as she gaped at me.

Neither of us had talked back to our parents since our rebellious teenage years. Even then, our rebellion had been mild—a snarky comment here, a night of sneaking out to a friend's party there.

We weren't the poster children for bad behavior, but I...*oh God.* I'd basically told my mother she was a shitty mom. In front of a guest and the rest of our family. At dinner.

The pasta I ate earlier churned in my stomach, and I faced the very real possibility that I might throw up all over Mika's favorite Wedgwood set.

My mother reeled like I'd just backhanded her. If she'd been pale before, she was a ghost now, her cheeks completely blanched of color like someone had sucked the life out of her.

For once, Mika Alonso, one of the most feared attorneys in the city, the woman who had an answer for every question and a rebuttal for every argument, was speechless.

I wished I felt good about it, but all I felt was nausea. I didn't want to hurt her. I hadn't expected my words *to* hurt her because they'd been so obvious. My mother had never been around when I was a child. She'd once joked herself that Maura was our surrogate mother.

But there was no denying the hurt filling her eyes and twisting her face into an unrecognizable version of itself.

Beside her, my father's face was unrecognizable as well, except his was dark with barely leashed fury.

"You stepped over the line, Stella." His low voice sent another wave of nausea crashing against my insides. "Apologize to your mother. Right now."

The backs of my thighs pressed against the tops of my hands while my head swirled with a thousand responses.

I could apologize and smooth things over. Anything to erase my mother's hurt and my father's anger.

The little girl in me still cringed at the thought of making my parents mad, but anything less than full honesty would only be a temporary salve for a festering wound.

"I'm sorry if I hurt you, Mom." The crack in my voice matched the one splitting my chest. "But Maura practically raised me. We both know that's true, and she doesn't have anyone else to care for her. She spent the prime years of her life looking after me and treating me like I was her own daughter. I can't leave her alone now when she needs me."

I didn't look at Natalia, who'd liked Maura but didn't have the same bond with her. My parents' careers hadn't taken off until I was five and Natalia was ten. By then, she'd been too old to form the same attachment to our nanny that I had.

She wouldn't take my side. She never did.

Other than a small flinch, my mother didn't react to my words. My father, on the other hand, grew even angrier.

Jarvis Alonso did not take well to people disobeying his orders.

Thunder swallowed the usually warm brown of his eyes until they turned a hard, implacable black.

I'd never been scared of my father, at least not in the physical sense. But in that moment, I was terrified of him.

When he spoke again, it was in a rumbling growl he usually reserved for discussions about foreign dictators and terrorist cells.

"Stella Rosalie Alonso, if you do not apologize to your mother this instant, I will—"

"I suggest you don't finish that sentence."

Christian's quiet voice sliced through the toxic fumes of my father's anger like they didn't exist.

Like Natalia, he'd been silent since dinner went off the rails, but the tension pouring off him said a thousand words.

If my father's fury was a gathering storm, Christian's was a dark, silent tsunami. By the time those in its path scented danger, it was too late.

And as my eyes darted between my father's pulsating jaw and Christian's lethal stare, I had a sinking feeling that the bad evening was only going to get worse.

27

CHRISTIAN

"ARE YOU THREATENING ME IN MY OWN HOME?" A STEEL edge ran beneath Jarvis Alonso's voice.

"Not threatening, sir. *Suggesting.*"

The contrast between my polite tone and the tension crackling in the air drenched an otherwise deferential address with mockery.

I rested my hand on Stella's thigh beneath the table, stilling her. She'd done an admirable job of keeping her expression calm, but tiny shivers trembled under my touch.

I'd held off saying anything for as long as I could. It wasn't in my nature to sit quietly when faced with injustice done to me, and every fucking slight against Stella was a slight against me. But to her, this was a personal issue with her family. She needed to stand up to them and say her piece without anyone else stepping in.

I could deal with her parents getting angry, even though they'd been pissing me off all evening. But what I would not tolerate was anyone, even Stella's flesh and blood, guilt-tripping her into giving an apology they didn't deserve.

I fixed Jarvis with a pleasant smile that didn't match my icy tone.

"If you're wondering why your daughter would keep things from you, look in the mirror," I said. "Look at how you reacted. Instead of supporting her, you attacked her. Instead of being proud of her drive and passion, you force her into a box she doesn't belong in. Stella is one of the most selfless, creative, and brilliant people I know, yet you belittle her for not conforming to your limited definitions of success. Why? Because you're embarrassed to have a child who dared stray from the rigid path you yourself took? Your pride matters more to you than her happiness, yet you're surprised that she considers the *only* adult who was there for her growing up to be more of a parent than either of you were."

I addressed the last sentence to both her father and mother, who hadn't stirred since Stella's outburst.

The woman must be in shock.

Good. She deserved it.

Rage was a monster in my gut, aimed at both Stella's parents for jumping down her throat about her fucking finances without a single thought about how she was feeling and her sister for exposing her departure from *D.C. Style* in such a cruel, vindictive manner.

How many of Stella's insecurities had stemmed from growing up in such a judgmental household?

Most of them, I bet.

The only leash on my anger was Stella's presence and the fact this was her family. Despite her strained relationship with them, she probably wouldn't react well if I drained their bank accounts or targeted their devices with destructive viruses. There was one particularly nasty code I'd developed out of boredom last year that could collect and destroy all the data on an infected device until said device was nothing more than a useless lump of metal in less than ten minutes.

Jarvis glared at me, a vein throbbing so hard at his temple I expected it to burst at any second.

"This is a *family* matter," Jarvis growled. "I don't care how long you've been dating Stella. You are not, and never will be, family. I know your reputation, Christian Harper. You pretend you're an upstanding businessman, but you're a snake in the grass. You've got blood all over your hands, And if you think I'm letting you anywhere near my daughter after tonight, you're sorely mistaken."

I examined him with a faint smile.

Few things amused me more than people trying to threaten me.

He was Stella's father, which offered him some degree of protection.

But what secrets lurked in the cyber sewers of his digital life? Dig deep enough, and there was always something. Google search histories, photos, link clicks and emails and private chat rooms. People's online lives were rife with information, most of it tossed out so casually the owner didn't think twice about how it could incriminate them.

It was a goldmine for someone like me.

If Jarvis Alonso thought he could hold Stella over my head, he'd find out how quickly and easily I could expose the skeletons in his closet.

"Leave Christian out of this." Stella's soft, fierce voice interrupted my musings. "I don't care about unfounded rumors or what you *think* you know about him. Here's what I know from firsthand experience: he's been nothing except helpful since we've met. He encouraged me to follow my dreams and believed in me when I didn't believe in myself. He's been more supportive of me in the few months I've known him than you've been of me my entire life, and I won't let you insult him for standing up for me."

I was so startled I almost flinched before I caught myself.

Something warm and foreign moved in my chest, eating away at the steel barriers I'd erected.

No one had defended me before. Ever.

I didn't need or want them to, but Stella had always been the exception to my every rule, and seeing her so strong and clear-eyed with conviction lit a match of pride in my chest.

Her conviction was misplaced because I was exactly what her father accused me of—a snake in the grass, a monster with bloody hands and a bloodier past. But after seeing myself through her rose-tinted glasses, I wished, for the first time in my life, that I was the man she thought I was.

Ruthless, perhaps, but honorable at his core.

In reality, the only bits of honor I possessed these days were the ones reflected in her eyes.

"Get out." Jarvis didn't so much as blink at Stella's speech. His fury was a quiet thing, but it was all-encompassing in its intensity. There would be no reasoning with him tonight. "If you would rather side with an outsider you've known for a few months over your family, then you don't belong at this table."

Stella went rigid while her mother sucked in a sharp breath. "Jarvis—"

"Right now, Stella." He ignored his wife's broken protest. "*Leave* before I throw you out myself."

Natalia stirred, unease finally sliding over her face at the shitstorm she'd unleashed. "Daddy—"

"Perfect timing. We were just about to excuse ourselves." I folded my napkin into a neat square and placed it on the table before I pushed back my chair. "Stella."

I placed a gentle hand on her shoulder, rousing her from her stupor.

She stood and, after a last glance at her frozen family, followed me out the door.

Silence followed us into the car and onto the road like an unwanted interloper, but I let it sit until Stella broke it herself.

"He kicked me out." She stared out the window, sounding dazed. "My dad has never even yelled at me before."

"You hit a nerve. He wouldn't have reacted so strongly if a part of him didn't know you were right."

"Yeah, well." She let out a watery laugh. "Now you know why I didn't want you at dinner. My family puts the *dys* in dysfunction."

A grim smile touched my lips. If she thought her family was dysfunctional, wait till she learned about mine.

Not that she ever would.

"I've seen worse." I stopped at a red light and slanted a glance at Stella, my face softening. "You didn't have to defend me."

"I wanted to." The conviction in her voice sent a strange pang through my chest. "You didn't deserve to be attacked like that. You were standing up for me, and it's only right that I do the same." A hint of red colored her cheekbones. "Besides, what I said was true. Even though you piss me off sometimes"— my mouth curved at her uncharacteristic but adorable use of the term *piss me off*—"you're a good person beneath it all."

I would've laughed at her assessment had it not sharpened the pang into a blade that slotted neatly between my ribcage.

"You put too much faith in people. I'm not the knight you think I am," I said softly.

It was a warning as much as it was a compliment.

I usually scoffed at those who were naive enough to believe people were inherently good when there was so much evil in the world. One only had to turn on the news to witness the depths of depravity to which humanity could and would sink.

But for some reason, Stella's unwavering belief in the goodness of people struck a chord inside me I hadn't known existed.

She wasn't the only light of optimism around me, but she was the only one that mattered.

"Maybe not. But you're not the villain you think you are, either." The passing streetlights cast her face in a warm golden glow, highlighting her delicate features and the trust shining in those beautiful jade eyes.

If you only knew...

The light turned green. My eyes lingered on her for an extra second before I faced forward and stepped on the gas.

We didn't speak again during the ride, but at the next red light, I curled my hand over hers on the center console and kept it there until we arrived home.

28

STELLA

APRIL 27

There's a fifty-fifty chance my father disowned me tonight. I've never seen him that mad, not even when I scratched his brand-new Benz after I got my driver's license and secretly took it out for a joyride. (In my defense, that curb came out of nowhere).

But you know what the worst part is? It's not the hurt in my mother's eyes or the way my sister outed me. It's not even my father kicking me out of the house.

It's the fact that I wouldn't have changed what I did even knowing what the outcome would be.

I've always been the quiet, obedient daughter. The one who did everything my parents asked, who apologized even when I didn't need it to, and who bent over backward to make sure everyone was happy.

But every person has a limit, and I've reached mine.

I'm pretty sure nothing I do will be good enough for my family, so why even try? I might as well tell them the truth about how I feel. I should've done it a long time ago. But honestly, I *don't think I would've found the courage to do so tonight if Christian hadn't been there.*

It's ironic. I didn't want him to go, but he ended up being the best part of my night. There's something about him...I don't know how to explain it. But he makes me feel like I can be anyone I want to be.

Better yet, he makes me feel like I can be who I am.

Does that sound cheesy? Probably.

I cringed reading that line over just now, but it's okay. You're the only one who'll ever see this anyway, and I know you won't judge.

Actually, that describes how I feel about Christian perfectly, like he won't judge me no matter what I say or do. And in a world where I'm constantly being judged—online and in real life—that's the best feeling in the world.

DAILY GRATITUDE:

1. *Completing the first piece of my collection*
2. *The speakerphone function*
3. *~~Christian Early nights~~ Christian*

"ARE YOU PACKING FOR THREE DAYS OR THREE MONTHS?" Christian eyed my mountain of luggage with a raised brow.

"It's *Hawaii*, Christian." I wedged another swimsuit into my overstuffed suitcase. "My hair care alone takes up an entire bag. Do you know how much havoc the beach and humidity wreaks on curly hair?"

"No." His gaze was alight with amusement.

"Exactly." I stood to catch my breath.

My muscles ached from hours of packing. I'd put it off until the last minute, but I needed to get it done *today* since I left tomorrow for Delamonte's big photoshoot in Hawaii.

I didn't mind. Packing was a welcome distraction from the nerves swimming in my stomach and the specter of my family.

I hadn't heard a peep from them since our dinner two weeks ago, nor had I reached out to them.

Old Stella would've called them the next morning, apologizing profusely and wallowing in guilt over what had happened.

Granted, I *did* feel guilty, but not enough to back down from the silent battle raging in the Alonso family. While I regretted hurting my parents, I was stung that they weren't even attempting to understand where I was coming from. Plus, I was still stewing over my mother calling Maura a *former employee* and my father insulting Christian.

I was more surprised than anyone by how my protective instincts had surged during my father's rant. Christian didn't need help defending himself. I didn't even think he'd been offended; insults bounced off him like rubber bullets off titanium.

Still, I'd hated hearing how my father spoke to him. He hadn't deserved that.

"How are you feeling about Hawaii?" Christian asked.

He was working from home today, but he was still dressed in a suit and tie.

Typical.

"Great." My voice came out higher than usual. "Excited."

I wiped my palms on the outsides of my thighs and tried to calm the rapid *pitter patter* of my heart.

It was half true. I *was* excited. Hawaii was beautiful, and the photoshoot was the cornerstone of Delamonte's new campaign. The photos would be *everywhere*—online, in magazines, maybe even on billboards.

I didn't want to be a professional model, but the Hawaii campaign could do huge things for my career. I'd already made enough money from brand partnerships this past month to cover my expenses for the rest of the year; the Delamonte print campaign would skyrocket my profile even further.

But such an important shoot also came with a ton of pressure. It weighed on my shoulders and ate away at my excitement until my head spun with worst-case scenarios.

I'd gotten more comfortable posing in front of other people's cameras since my first Delamonte shoot in New York, but Hawaii was different. Hawaii was the big one.

What if I froze and didn't recover the way I had in New York?

What if all the photos came out horrible?

What if I got sick and *couldn't* shoot or broke my leg on my way to set or something?

The brand was spending a ton of the money on the trip, and we only had three days to get it right.

If I messed it up…

I dipped my head and focused on folding a sundress so Christian didn't see the panic in my eyes.

I should've known that wouldn't fool him.

"Nervous?" he asked, eerily astute as usual.

I swallowed past the lump in my throat. "A little." *A lot.*

Could Delamonte fire me for incompetence in the middle of the campaign? I have to talk to Brady and go over the contract again. Maybe they'll think they made a mistake and hire Raya instead or—

"Don't be. You'll do great."

"You have too much confidence in me."

"You have too little." His voice was closer this time, a velvet touch against the bare skin of my neck and shoulders.

I turned, my pulse skipping a beat at his proximity.

I've never wanted someone more, and I've never hated myself more for it.

The memory of his words sparked like electricity between us. His eyes flared with something bright and hot before they dimmed again, and my heart returned to its normal rhythm.

"We leave tomorrow morning at eight." Christian nodded at my luggage. "I'll hire a sherpa for you."

"You're exaggerating. I'm not taking *that* much stuff."

Two large suitcases, one duffel bag, and one tote seemed perfectly reasonable for three days in Hawaii.

"We'll agree to disagree. On a security-related note..." Christian's dry amusement faded into something more serious. "The Hawaii shoot isn't a secret, but I still want you to hold off on posting you're there until we're back in D.C."

My stomach swooped for a whole other reason.

Between Christian's confession, my family dinner, and preparing for the shoot, I'd pushed worries about my stalker to the back of my mind. Now they came roaring back in one giant wave.

"Do we have any leads yet?"

I hadn't asked him for regular updates. The more I focused on it, the more anxious I got, but I couldn't resist this time around.

"Nothing concrete, but we're getting there. He might not follow you to Hawaii, but it's better safe than sorry."

"Right." I rubbed a thumb over my crystal necklace. "Right."

Christian's face softened. "Everything will work out, with the shoot *and* the stalker. Trust me."

That was the scary part. I did.

"Get some rest. We have a long flight tomorrow," he said. "And Stella? Leave the unicorn."

"I wasn't planning on taking him," I grumbled at Christian's departing back.

After he left, I set Mr. Unicorn back on his perch near my bed. "We'll visit Hawaii together another time," I told him regretfully.

He was my trusty companion whenever I traveled solo, but since Christian was joining me, I didn't *need* to bring him. I just liked having a bit of familiarity when I visited new places.

I finished packing.

My emotions swung from excitement to dread to nervousness and back again, but I felt better knowing Christian would be with me.

The butterflies in my stomach fluttered again at the thought of three days in paradise with him.

It was a work trip, but still.

I had a strange sense whatever happened in Hawaii would change my life.

29

STELLA/CHRISTIAN

CHRISTIAN AND I ARRIVED IN KAUAI PAST DINNERTIME the next night.

Instead of venturing to the hotel's restaurant, which would take too much effort, we ordered room service and settled in the villa's living room.

True to form, Christian had taken one look at the room Delamonte booked for me and upgraded us to the last remaining villa.

I snuck a peek at him as we ate in companionable silence.

He lounged against his side of the couch, looking infuriatingly sexy with his rumpled shirt and tousled hair. Neither of us looked our best after traveling all day, but his dishevelment only made him hotter, not less.

"Like what you see?" he drawled.

"Yes." I made a point of looking around the gorgeous villa. It boasted stunning views of the Pacific, and the living room opened onto a furnished lanai, which in turn led directly to our private beach. "This place is stunning."

That wasn't what he was asking, but there was no need to

inflate his ego. He knew I knew he was hot, so what was the point of saying it?

Christian's knowing laugh warmed my stomach like decadent hot chocolate.

There was a certain magic in seeing him outside the confines of D.C. Like at Dante's dinner, he'd slipped into a more relaxed version of himself.

No suit, easy laughter.

"I like this version of you." I held my mug close to my mouth. "You're more..." I searched for the right word. "Approachable."

A smile played at the corners of his mouth. "Am I?"

"Let's put it this way. D.C. Christian looks like he would murder you if you cut him off in traffic. Hawaii Christian looks like he would give you a ride if he saw your car broken down on the side of the road."

The rich sound of his amusement filled the corners of the room once more. "We've been in Hawaii for less than two hours."

"Exactly. Imagine what three days in paradise would do to you." I took a thoughtful sip of tea. "Dancing in a Hawaiian-print shirt? Joining me for sunrise yoga? *Giving up red meat?* The possibilities are endless."

"Stella." He leaned forward, his face serious. "The day I wear a Hawaiian-print shirt is the day cows fucking fly."

"You never know at the rate technology is progressing. It could happen," I said, undeterred. "You know what your problem is?"

"Pray do tell. I'm on the edge of my seat."

I ignored his unhelpful sarcasm. "You take yourself too seriously, and you work too much. You should take more vacations, or at least connect with nature every once in a while. It's good for the soul."

"It's too late for my soul, Stella."

Despite his light tone, I sensed he wasn't joking.

My smile faded. "Spoken like a true pessimist."

"Realist."

"Cynic."

"Skeptic." Christian's lips tugged up at my frown. "Shall we continue playing thesaurus or move on to a more interesting topic?"

"We'll move on, but only because I want to spare you the indignity of losing," I said regally.

"That's very kind of you."

I didn't appreciate the knowing laughter threaded through his voice, but I let it slide. He was paying for this beautiful villa, after all, and he'd saved me from spending ten hours in a cramped airline seat, watching old movies and trying to prevent my legs from falling asleep.

There were few things more uncomfortable than being a tall person in economy.

I sank deeper into the couch and deliberated on a good topic before I said, "Tell me something about you I don't already know."

I'd forgiven Christian for shutting me out after Dante's dinner, but I hadn't given up trying to pry more personal tidbits out of him. I didn't care if they were as simple as his favorite superhero growing up; I just wanted *something*. Knowing things about Christian wouldn't do much to protect my heart, but we were stuck together for the foreseeable future and I wanted to make the best of it.

Part of me expected him to evade the request per usual, but to my surprise, he answered readily. "I don't like dessert."

A horrified gasp rose in my throat. "*All* dessert?"

"All dessert," he confirmed.

"*Why?*"

"I don't have a sweet tooth."

"There are non-sweet desserts."

"Yes, and I don't like them." He took a calm bite of his food while I stared at him in disbelief.

"I take back what I said. Your soul is definitely suspect. It's not normal for someone not to like dessert." I searched for a plausible explanation. "Maybe you haven't met the right dessert yet."

Who could hate baklava, cheesecake, and ice cream? The devil, that was who.

"Perhaps I'll meet it at the same time I meet my soulmate," Christian deadpanned.

"You joke, but it could happen. And when it does, I'll..." I faltered.

Threats weren't my forte.

"Yes?" He sounded like he was holding back another laugh.

"I'll never let you hear the end of it."

"Looking forward to it." Christian took pity on me after my lame response and switched subjects. "Time to reciprocate, Butterfly. Tell me something I don't know about you."

"Can't you look up everything you want to know on one of your fancy computers?" I was only half joking.

"I'd rather hear it from you."

For some reason, that sent a flutter through my chest.

I'd planned on sharing something silly and lighthearted, like how I watched YouTube tarot readings when I felt down because the readers always put such a positive spin on things or how I color-coded my closet for fun because the result was so aesthetically pleasing.

Instead, I said, "Sometimes, I fantasize about finding out I was adopted."

Shame curdled in my gut. I'd never, ever shared that sentiment with anyone, and hearing it aloud made my skin prickle with guilt.

I didn't come from a bad family. They were judgmental and had high expectations, but they weren't physically abusive. They'd paid for my college education in full, and I grew up in a nice house with nice clothes and nice vacations. Compared to a majority of people, I lived an incredibly privileged life.

But our lives were our own. There would always be people who were better and worse off than us. That didn't make our feelings any less valid. We could acknowledge how good we had it in some respects while criticizing other parts.

To his credit, Christian didn't condemn me for being an ungrateful brat. He didn't say anything at all.

Instead, he waited for me to finish with no judgment in his eyes.

"I would freak out if that actually happened, but it's the fantasy of having another family out there that's more...like a family, I guess. Less competition, more emotional support." I traced the rim of my mug with my finger. "Sometimes, I wonder if my sister and I would be closer if my parents hadn't pitted us against each other so much. They didn't spend a lot of time with us because they were so busy with work, and the time they *did* spend with us was focused on whichever child they could brag about the most. The one who had the best grades, the most impressive extracurriculars and college acceptances... Natalia and I were so busy trying to outshine each other growing up that we never connected with each other."

A sad smile touched my lips. "Now she's a vice president at the World Bank and I'm unemployed, so..." I shrugged, trying not to picture dozens more family dinners where I sat in shame while my parents gushed over my sister.

That was, if I was even invited to future dinners. After my fight with them, I wasn't so sure.

"I never fit in with my family even when I was employed, anyway. They're the practical ones. I'm the one who spent my childhood staring out the window daydreaming about fashion and travel instead of stacking my resume with college-boosting activities. When I was fifteen, I created a manifestation board for Parsons, my dream college, and covered it with photos of the campus and a mock acceptance letter I typed up."

My smile turned wistful at the memory of my optimistic teenage self. "It worked. I received an actual acceptance letter my senior year, but I had to turn them down because my parents refused to pay for such an 'impractical degree.' So I ended up at Thayer."

I didn't regret it. If I hadn't attended Thayer, I would've never met Ava, Bridget, and Jules.

Still, sometimes I wondered what would've happened had I attended Parsons. Would I have skipped the *D.C. Style* chapter of my life? Maybe. Would I already be a designer with multiple fashion shows under my belt? Less certain but probably.

"Take this from someone who's seen plenty of competitors come and go over the years," Christian said, pulling me out of my thoughts. "You can't measure your success based on someone else's progress. And I've met your family. Trust me, it's better that you don't fit in."

I let out a small laugh. "Perhaps."

It felt good to get all that off my chest, and it helped that Christian and I weren't as close as I was to my girlfriends. It made me less self-conscious about the things I was sharing.

Sleep tugged at the edges of my consciousness, but I didn't want to go to bed when Christian and I were finally having a real conversation.

The shoot didn't start until late morning tomorrow anyway. *Just half an hour more. Then I'll go to sleep.*

"What about your family?" I took another sip of tea. "What are they like?"

Christian never talked about his parents, and I hadn't spotted a single photo of them in his house.

"Dead."

The tea went down the wrong pipe. I spluttered out a series of coughs while Christian finished his dinner like he hadn't dropped a bombshell with the casualness of someone mentioning their family was out of town for the weekend.

"I'm so sorry," I said once I recovered. I blinked away the tears from my coughing fit. "I...I didn't know."

It was an inane thing to say because of *course* I hadn't known, or I wouldn't have asked, but I couldn't think of a better response.

I'd assumed Christian's parents lived in another city and/or he had a bad relationship with them. I never would have guessed he was an orphan.

"It happened when I was thirteen, so don't feel too bad for me. It was a long time ago." Despite his casual tone, his tight jaw and rigid shoulders told me he wasn't as unaffected as he pretended to be.

A deep ache blossomed in my chest. Thirteen was too young to lose one's parents. *Any* age was too young.

I might be upset and frustrated with my family, but if I lost any of them, I would be devastated.

"They were your parents. There's no time limit to grieving the loss of family," I said gently. I hesitated, then asked, "Who did you live with after they..."

"My aunt raised me until she died when I was in college." Christian answered my unfinished question. "I've been on my own since."

The ache spread until every part of me tingled with the need to comfort him.

He wouldn't respond well to a hug, but words could be just as, if not more, powerful.

"Don't pity me, Stella," he said, tone dry. "I prefer being alone."

"Maybe, but there's a difference between being alone and being *alone*." The former was the absence of physical company; the latter was the absence of emotional and interpersonal support.

I liked being alone too, but only in the first sense of the word.

"It's okay to feel sad," I added softly. "I promise I won't tell anyone."

I didn't ask how his parents died. I could tell we were already stretching the limits of his willingness to share, and I didn't want to destroy the fragile intimacy of the moment.

Christian stared at me with an imperceptible expression.

"I'll keep that in mind," he finally said, his voice a shade rougher than usual.

I expected him to end the conversation there, but to my surprise, he continued without me prompting him.

"My father was the reason I got into computers. He was a software engineer, and my mother was a school administrator. In many ways, they were the quintessential middle-class American family. We lived in a nice suburban house. I played Little League, and every Friday night, we ordered pizza and played board games."

I held my breath, so entranced by the rare glimpse into his childhood I was afraid to breathe in case it broke the spell.

"The only thing that didn't fit into this picture," Christian said, "was their relationship. My parents loved each other. Madly. Deeply. More than anyone else on the planet."

Of all the things I'd expected him to say, that didn't even

rank in the top thousand, but I swallowed my questions and let him continue.

"I grew up hearing the crazy tales of their courtship. How my father wrote my mother a letter every day while he was studying abroad and trekked two miles to the post office in the mornings because he didn't trust the university mailing system. How she ran away from home when her parents threatened to cut her off if she didn't break up with him because they'd wanted her to marry the son of a wealthy local businessman instead. She eventually made up with my grandparents, but instead of throwing a big wedding, my parents eloped and moved to a little town in Northern California. They had me less than a year later."

The haze of memories darkened Christian's eyes. "They settled into what outsiders might consider an ordinary life, but they never lost that fire for each other even after I was born."

Most people dreamed of the kind of love his parents had, but he spoke about it like it'd been a curse, not a blessing.

"Yet you don't believe in love," I said.

How was that possible? Most people's cynicism toward love came from seeing it stripped down to the barest skeleton of what it once was. Ugly divorces, broken promises, tearful fights. But it sounded like his parents had been a shining example of what it *could* be.

"No." The caustic cut of Christian's smile across his face raised goosebumps on my arms. "Because what my parents had wasn't love. It was ego and destruction disguised as affection. A drug they kept chasing because it gave them a high they couldn't get anywhere else. It clouded their judgment to the detriment of themselves and everyone around them, and it gave them cover to do all these irrational things because no one questioned them if it was for *love*."

He leaned back, his face hard. "It wasn't just my parents.

Look at the world around us. People kill, steal, and lie in the name of this abstract emotion we're told is supposed to be our ultimate goal. Love conquers all. Love heals all. Etcetera, etcetera." The curl of his lip told me how much respect he had for such platitudes. "Alex gave up a multibillion-dollar company. Bridget almost lost a country. And Rhys gave up his privacy, which mattered more to him than any amount of cash. It's completely illogical."

"Alex got his company back," I pointed out. "Bridget made it work, and Rhys didn't give up *all* his privacy. Sometimes, sacrifices are necessary for happiness."

"Why?"

I blinked, so startled by the bluntness of his question that it took me a minute to respond.

"Because it's the way the world works," I finally said. "We can't have everything we want without making some compromises. If humans were robots, I'd agree with your assessment, but we're not. We have feelings, and if it weren't for love, the human race wouldn't survive. Procreation, protection, motivation. It all hinges on that one emotion."

It was the least romantic and therefore the most effective answer I could've given.

"Perhaps." Christian's shrug expressed the depth of his skepticism more than words could. "But there's a second issue, which is that people use *love* so often it's lost all meaning. They love their dogs, cars, happy hours, and their friend's new haircut. They say love is this grand, wonderful thing when it's the opposite. It's useless at best and dangerous at worst."

"There are different types of love. The way I love fashion is different from the way I love my friends."

"Varying degrees of the same disease." Dark amusement filled his face when I winced at the word *disease*. "Is this where you'll try to change my mind? Convince me that love does, in fact, make the world go around?"

"No," I said truthfully. "You've already made up your mind. Nothing I say will change it. The only way you'll change your mind is through experience, not words."

Surprise coasted through his eyes before it submerged beneath something heavier, more slumberous.

"And do you think that will happen?" His low drawl condensed the air between us. "That I'll fall in love and eat my words?"

I shrugged, the casual movement at odds with the rapid beats of my heart. "Maybe. I'm not a fortune teller."

Secretly, I hoped he would. Not because I had delusions of being the one who could quote-unquote change him, but because everyone deserved to experience true love at least once in their lifetime.

"One of the clauses in our contract," Christian said, watching me with those all-knowing eyes, "is that I don't fall in love with you."

My mouth dried. "Yes."

"Why did you put in that condition, Stella?"

"Because I don't want you to fall in love with me."

He didn't smile at my quick quip. A long silence passed before he spoke again.

"You and I, we aren't so different," he said softly.

A spark ignited and burned up all the oxygen between us. The sound of my pulse faded into a distant whoosh.

Say something, Stella.

But his gaze held my voice captive, and before I could free it, his phone rang and shredded the moment to pieces.

Christian's eyes lingered on me for a fraction of a second longer before he took the call. He walked out to the lanai, where the distant roar of the waves drowned out his end of the conversation.

The weight on my chest eased, leaving me light-headed and dizzy. I felt like I'd been submerged beneath the ocean for the past hour and only just came up for air.

It was always hard to breathe around Christian.

One night in Hawaii down, two more to go.

I thought the trip would be a simple one. Arrive, do the shoots, leave.

But, as I was quickly realizing, nothing that involved Christian Harper was ever simple.

CHRISTIAN

"Someone hacked into the Mirage's security system," Kage said, sounding grim. "Our cyber team confirmed it was the result of a device similar to Scylla."

I bit back a colorful curse.

The last thing I wanted was to discuss work this late at night in fucking Hawaii. Granted, it was even later for him, but Kage worked all hours and his update was a mindfuck.

I'd developed Scylla two years ago. Named after the legendary Greek monster who devoured men off ships that sailed too close, the device didn't require a download or a USB port to hack into a system. It only needed to be within a few feet of the target for the owner to remote control into the device and fuck shit up as they saw fit.

No one knew Scylla existed except for the people at Harper Security and Jules, whom I'd lent the device to last year. She didn't know what it was when she used it, and even if she did, she didn't have the schematics for it, which meant one thing.

The traitor was still at Harper, and they were somehow connected to Stella's stalker.

Cold fury rippled through me.

I'd run a second round of checks on everyone I employed after the Mirage surveillance hack with a special focus on those closest to me, including Brock and Kage. They came back clean.

I'd let go of a few mildly suspicious employees, but they hadn't been high-level enough to know about Scylla.

Plus, unless Stella's stalker was a developer himself, it should've been damn near impossible for them to replicate Scylla's schematics...unless they got their hands on the blueprint hidden in my office.

My mind spun with a thousand possibilities, but when I spoke, my voice was calm. Rock solid.

"Pull all the security footage from the area around the building. I want video from every single corner and storefront that has a camera within a five-block radius of the Mirage. Unless the hacker can fucking teleport, he had to have gone somewhere after the break-in. Find him."

I hung up after Kage's grunt of affirmation.

The footage wasn't my top priority. My top priority was finding out who in my company was trying to sabotage me, but until I returned to D.C., gathering and screening the footage would give my men something to do while I hunted down the traitor.

Between the Scylla news and the stalled progress on Stella's stalker, May was shaping up to be a shitty fucking month.

Aggravation mounted in my chest while I calculated my next move.

If I were here for any reason other than Stella, I would fly back to D.C. first thing in the morning, but I couldn't leave her alone when there was a psycho on the loose targeting her.

I'd lied when I'd told her there was no news. I'd intercepted three more notes from him in her mailbox. They contained basic threats, nothing new, and they were still untraceable —for now.

The chances of him following her here were slim, but they weren't zero.

At least, that was what I told myself.

I returned to the living room and locked the sliding glass door behind me.

It was already midnight. I was wide awake thanks to the adrenaline from Kage's news, but Stella had passed out on the couch during my call.

I gently pried her empty mug from her hand and set it on the table before I picked her up and carried her to the bedroom. She was in such deep slumber she didn't even stir.

Moonlight cut a silvery swathe through the darkness as I laid her on the bed.

I tucked the comforter tighter around her, the gentleness of the action a sharp contrast to the roar in my blood. It seemed almost obscene to touch Stella while visions of blood and dismemberment crowded my brain, but I couldn't shut off the part of me that thirsted for vengeance.

The cold shower I took dampened my anger but didn't erase it completely. And, because I needed an outlet for my frustration that didn't involve physical release, the first thing I did when I emerged from the bathroom was open my laptop.

I skipped past the open window with an unfinished cross-word—I preferred physical puzzles, but I made do with digital versions when necessary—and opened the file I kept specifically for times like these.

I skimmed the list of names before settling on the president of a major multinational bank. He'd never been and would never be a Harper Security client. Contrary to popular belief, I did have fucking standards for the people I associated with, and this guy was a nasty piece of work. Embezzlement, tax fraud, three sexual harassment lawsuits from his former assistants that were settled out of court, and a penchant for slapping around both his wife and the women he cheated on her with. And that was just the tip of the iceberg.

"You're about to have a very bad day when you wake up," I told the photo of his red, beady-eyed face.

It took me less than five minutes to hack into his bank accounts and reroute the funds to various charities via anonymous donations and a network of proxy servers. It was almost embarrassing how easy it was. The man's password was his first car's model and his birthday, for fuck's sake.

I left a chunk of money for his wife along with the name of a good divorce lawyer before I forwarded some information to the IRS that the U.S. government would find highly interesting. As the cherry on top, I put his info up for sale on the dark web, sent several humiliating photos from his last visit with his mistress to all two hundred thousand of the bank's employees and, because the asshole once tried to steal a parking spot from me, I hacked into his car, killed the GPS, and wiped out all the vehicle's data.

By the time I finished, I felt calm enough to slide into bed next to Stella.

Contrary to what she said earlier about nature, nothing cleansed the soul like a good cyber rampage.

I stilled when Stella let out a mumble and draped her leg over mine. She must've liked the warmth because a few seconds later, she wrapped her arm around my waist and snuggled into my chest.

Even though she was already asleep, she released a small yawn that melted into a contented sigh and then...silence.

I stared down at her, waiting for her to wake up or at least shift again.

She didn't.

Judging from the steady rise and fall of her chest, she'd drifted back into sleep and had no intention of untangling herself from me anytime soon.

I hated cuddling after sex and cuddling *without* sex even more, but instead of pushing Stella away, I brushed a lock of hair out of her face and examined her in the moonlight peeking through the curtains.

The silvery glow caressed her skin in a way that made her look ethereal. An angel sleeping in the arms of a monster.

Few people trusted me enough to close their eyes when I was in the room, and here she was, cuddling against me like I was a damn teddy bear. Completely unaware of the violence brewing only inches away.

My hand drifted from her hair and onto the elegant curve of her cheekbone. I traced it down to her chin, keeping my touch featherlight so as not to wake her. I wanted to etch every detail of her into my mind until I could close my eyes and picture her as vividly as if she were standing in front of me.

Perhaps then I would understand the hold this woman had on me. How could someone so innocent and pure-hearted have branded herself so deep into my psyche I felt the agonizing burn of it this long after we met?

My touch lingered against Stella's face before I dropped it.

Invisible traces of the blood coating my hands streaked her cheeks. They were the same hands that fit easily around the metal of a gun and ended lives with the mere press of a button. A liar's hands at best, a killer's hands at worst.

I shouldn't be touching her and tainting her with my crimes, both past and future. She deserved to shine without darkness threatening to consume her, and if I were a better man, I would let her go.

But I wasn't.

My flickering conscience recoiled at the unseen smears of red against her skin while a twisted, possessive part of me thrilled at the sight.

But if there was one thing both sides agreed on, it was that she was mine.

And now that she was in my life, there was no letting her go.

30

STELLA/CHRISTIAN

STELLA

I woke up the next morning to rumpled sheets and a stomach full of butterflies, partly because of the shoot and partly because of the faint leather and spice scent in the air.

Christian was gone, but tiny prickles of heat consumed my skin at the sight of the rumpled sheets on his side of the bed.

I knew the villa had one bedroom. The front desk assistant told us so when he'd upgraded us. But the thought of sharing such an intimate space with Christian, even if I'd been passed out for all of it, electrified me in a way it hadn't the first night we'd shared a bed.

Stop it. It's just sleep.

I shared beds with my friends all the time when we traveled together. *That* wasn't a big deal, so this shouldn't be either.

Of course, I didn't want to have sex with my friends, but that was a minor distinction.

I forced my eyes away from the bed and got ready.

Since Delamonte would be providing the clothes and

makeup on set, it didn't take me long to throw on a simple linen dress and tame my hair into something manageable.

When I stepped into the living room, I saw Christian working on the lanai, looking far too stressed for his first morning in Hawaii.

"Good morning." I stopped next to his table. An empty coffee cup and a half-eaten slice of toast sat next to his laptop along with a a completed crossword puzzle. "You're up early."

"I'm working on East Coast time." He lifted his head, his brow smoothing when he saw me. "Are you ready for the shoot?"

"Yes." *Sort of. Maybe. Probably.*

My uncertainty must've bled through because his face softened further. "You'll do great."

"Thanks." I twisted my ring around my finger before his words sank in. *You'll do great.* "Are you not coming with me?"

"Not today. A work emergency came up."

"Oh." Disappointment bloomed in my stomach until I crushed it. Obviously, he wasn't going to stand around and watch me get my photos taken the entire trip. He had better things to do. "Nothing too bad, I hope."

"Nothing I can't handle." Christian nodded at the room service menu on the table. "Do you want something to eat beforehand? I can call the kitchen."

"No, I'm already running late." I also might throw up if I ate anything before the shoot, but I kept that to myself. "I guess, um, I'll see you later."

I left, feeling oddly like I was saying goodbye to my boyfriend before a long trip apart. Which was ridiculous, because he *wasn't* my boyfriend, and our hotel was only a fifteen-minute walk from the set.

When I arrived, I didn't recognize anyone except the

photographer Ricardo and Delamonte's fashion director Emmanuelle, who greeted me with a flurry of cheek kisses.

"Stella! How was your flight? You look lovely. We are so excited for the shoot...let's get you into hair and makeup though, yes? We're a *little* behind..."

The ensuing whirlwind of activity was so chaotic it drove all thoughts of Christian out of my head. They shuffled me from hair and makeup to my fitting to my test shots, and by the time the real photoshoot was ready to begin, I couldn't focus on anything except not screwing up so badly that Delamonte fired me on the spot.

I'm fine. I can do this.

We were shooting a different line every day—resort wear today, shoes and accessories tomorrow, and jewelry the day after that.

I was grateful for the breezy silhouettes because if I had to squeeze myself into anything more fitted, I might pass out right there on the beach.

"Angle your head toward the sun...yes, just like that!" Ricardo shouted. "Perfect!"

Maybe it was the sun and sea breeze or my high from being in Hawaii for the first time. Or maybe it was because I'd shot with Ricardo before and was more comfortable working with him.

Whatever it was, it melted my nerves until I finally relaxed enough to push the ugly, self-doubting voices out of my head.

For the rest of the morning and early afternoon, I turned and posed at Ricardo's direction. We stopped every now and then for an outfit change, but otherwise, the shoot was seamless.

Emmanuelle was ecstatic.

"You're doing wonderful!" she gushed during one of our breaks. "Wait till I show Luisa the proofs. She'll be *thrilled*..."

I smiled and nodded, but my eyes were busy searching the beach for a flash of dark hair and tanned skin.

Nothing.

Christian had said he couldn't make it, but I'd hoped...

It doesn't matter.

I'd see him later. We were sharing a room, for Pete's sake, and while I wanted him here, I didn't *need* him here.

I could do this on my own.

The realization struck me right as Emmanuelle finished talking.

"Don't you agree?" she stared at me expectantly.

"Yes." I had no idea what she talking about. "You're right."

"*Exactly*! Plaids for fall are overdone. I'm thinking brushed knitwear..."

I can do this on my own.

I repeated the words in my head.

I'd spent years building my brand by myself, but ever since the Delamonte deal and my stalker's reappearance, I'd been off balance. Unsure of myself.

I'd relied on Christian for confidence and a small part of me was convinced I would've bombed the New York shoot if it hadn't been for him.

But I'd completed the shoot this morning by myself, and I'd done a damn good job.

A smile bloomed on my lips.

"Stella, we need you back here!" Ricardo called from his position near the water. "Are you ready?"

I was still wearing my smile when I returned to my designated spot, my steps lighter than they'd been all day.

"I'm ready."

CHRISTIAN

Work kept me preoccupied for most of the Hawaii trip. As much as I wanted to accompany Stella to her photoshoots, I had contracts to negotiate, virtual meetings to attend, and a fucking traitor to catch.

But when our last day on the island dawned, I couldn't stay away any longer. I rescheduled my meetings and took the hotel's boat to the Nā Pali Coast, where her last shoot was taking place.

The silky white sand shifted beneath my bare feet as I walked toward the private beach where Delamonte had set up camp.

I'd visited hundreds of locations over the years, but the rugged coastline remained one of the most stunning places I'd ever seen.

Dramatic emerald cliffs towered thousands of feet above the Pacific, their steep ridges and narrow valleys curling around pristine beaches at their feet in a protective embrace. White-plumed waterfalls cascaded past sea caves carved into the cliffs, their soft roar mingling with the lap of waves against sandy shores.

The coast was a work of art forged by nature's most talented artisans, the closest to Shangri-La in the modern world, but it wasn't the most beautiful thing present.

Not by a long shot.

I stopped at the edge of the set.

Stella stood in the shallows, her arms covering her bare chest and her curls a wild cloud around her face. Her simple white bikini bottom offset the extravagant emerald necklace around her neck.

She was too focused on the camera to notice me yet, so I soaked her in at my leisure.

The late afternoon sun gilded her skin and formed a halo

around her gentle curves. Her face appeared almost naked of adornment. No obvious makeup, just huge green eyes, lush lips, and skin that had deepened into a warm brown after days in the sun.

She looked like Venus emerging from the deep blue sea, only a thousand times more spectacular.

My heart slowed to match the sensual ebb and flow of the water as she turned and posed according to the photographer's instructions.

Unlike at the first photoshoot, she appeared at ease here, with the wind rustling her hair and the waves lapping at her thighs.

A goddess in her natural element.

"And that's a wrap!" Ricardo shouted after a short while. "You are *gorgeous*, darling. Absolute perfection."

Stella responded with a shy smile. She dropped her arms an inch—not low enough to bare herself to the crew, but enough that the swells of her breasts peeked over her embrace.

A lethal spike of possessiveness surged through my blood.

I allowed my eyes to linger on her for a second longer before I dragged them away to assess Ricardo with a cold stare.

Half-naked models were de rigueur in the fashion world, but that didn't stop me from suddenly wanting to gouge out the eyes of the only male member of the crew—one who was staring a bit too appreciatively at Stella.

Ricardo Frenelli, age forty-six, twice divorced with one daughter who had a bad cocaine habit, employed at Delamonte for the past eight years. Well-respected in the fashion industry, but he had a secret gambling problem and owed a shit ton of money to people you didn't want to owe a penny to.

I'd done my research after the first photoshoot.

"Mr. Harper!" Emmanuelle finally noticed me.

Her greeting attracted the attention of everyone on the

beach, including Ricardo, whose head whipped around to me. His tan blanched white at my smile.

People scared so easily these days.

A flutter of movement shifted my attention back to the ocean. Stella hadn't moved from her spot in the water, but she'd turned to face me. Surprise, pleasure, and a hint of something unidentifiable passed through her eyes when they caught mine.

My ire toward Ricardo fell to the wayside, drowned out by the electric hum in the air.

I've met plenty of beautiful women in my life. Women with perfect hair, perfect skin, and perfect bodies. Supermodels and movie stars and heiresses molded by the best money could buy.

None of them held a candle to Stella. She glowed in a way that had nothing to do with her outer beauty.

Darkness was always drawn to light, but I wasn't just drawn to her; I was fucking obsessed. I would throw myself into her flame and let it burn me alive if it meant her warmth was the last thing I felt before I died.

Her lips parted on a sharp exhale, like the force of my need was so great it pulled a physical reaction out of her.

"...didn't realize you were coming." Emmanuelle's sycophantic voice buzzed like an irritating gnat in my ear. "You should've told us. We would've—"

"Leave." I didn't take my eyes off Stella, who stood so still she resembled a carved statue in the ocean.

Emmanuelle faltered. "Excuse me?"

"You and your crew have five minutes to vacate this beach. I'll take Stella back in my boat."

I'd chartered a private boat from the hotel and anchored it further down the beach, not far from Delamonte's own charter.

Emmanuelle's cheeks flushed crimson. I wasn't her boss, but like most people, she was susceptible to authority no matter what form it came in. Still, she put up a last-ditch effort to stand her ground.

"We can't pack that fast." Nervousness diluted the impact of her protest. "We also need to clean and store the necklace first. It's worth over seventy thou—"

"Bill it to me."

I couldn't give less fucks about how much the necklace cost. I wanted everyone except Stella gone.

When the director didn't move, I raised an eyebrow. "Do I need to repeat myself?" I asked pleasantly. I checked my watch. "Four minutes, Ms. Lange."

She finally picked up on the veiled warning in my tone and scurried off.

Two minutes later, the crew was gone, leaving nothing but footprints behind.

"Should I be worried?" The wind carried Stella's sweet, teasing voice to my ears. She was still in the ocean, but the crew's departure had broken the spell keeping her quiet. "You're not planning on murdering me here now that you've scared off the crew, are you?"

"They were annoying me." I walked closer to the shore until I reached the natural border demarcating dry sand from its damp, wave-tossed brethren. "And I didn't scare them off. I merely requested they leave."

"What would you have done if they hadn't complied?"

A strong breeze whipped a curl across her face. She brushed it away with one hand while keeping her other arm over her chest.

She looked different here. Without the nearby threat of the stalker hanging over her head and the proximity of her family dragging her down, she was brighter, more carefree, with a playful sparkle in her eyes that outshone the emeralds around her neck.

"I would've let it go like the gentleman I am." A smile worked its way onto my mouth at the way her brows formed twin arches of skepticism.

"You said you weren't a gentleman."

"I didn't. You did."

"And I was right."

My smile morphed into a soft laugh that promised all sorts of ways I could further prove her right.

"Come here, Stella."

CHRISTIAN/STELLA

340 ANA HUANG

Despite her dry c
slender frame ca
the water ca
behind

CHRISTIAN

Stella didn't move, though a hint of desire darkened her eyes at my velvet command.

"What'll you do if *I* don't comply?" Her tone remained light, but the electricity in the air intensified until it seeped beneath my skin and crackled in my veins.

My smile took on a more dangerous curve. "Stay in the water and find out."

I'd give her ten seconds before I went in after her.

It'd been forty-eight hours since our last real interaction, and I already craved her closeness like an addict hungering for his next hit.

I'd given up any concept of distance between us. I wasn't just fascinated with her—a puzzle to solve. Obsession felt simple to me now.

I *needed* her.

"You need to work on saying the word *please*. I promise it won't kill you."

...observation, Stella finally moved. Her tall, ...t through the shallows with fluid grace until ...scaded off her and left only tiny, glittering droplets

She stopped in front of me, so close I could smell the faint scent of coconut sunscreen and green florals mixed with the salty kiss of the ocean.

I didn't believe in paradise, nor did I believe I could reach it even if it existed, but she smelled exactly like how I imagined paradise would smell.

"Can't promise something that's yet to be tested, sweetheart." I brushed my fingers over the sun-warmed jewels draped around her neck.

Seventy thousand dollars for one moment alone with her.

It was worth it.

The rhythm of her breaths stuttered. "You're telling me you've never said the word *please*."

"Never needed to. People do what I want anyway." A chuckle vibrated in my chest at Stella's adorable grumble.

"I should've stayed in the water and made you say *please* before I got out. Teach you a lesson." She eyed me with curiosity. "What are you doing here, anyway? I thought you had work."

"I finished." Not all of it, but the rest could wait. "I couldn't leave without visiting the set at least once."

"I don't know if watching me stand and pout is exciting," she laughed. Her arms tightened over her chest, but neither of us made a move toward her clothes, which lay folded on a towel a few feet away.

"I could watch you count every grain of sand on the beach and it would be exciting."

I wasn't a patient man, nor was I one who dealt well with restlessness. That was why I enjoyed puzzles so much. They fed me the stimulation I required to stay sane, because God knew I couldn't rely on other people to keep me interested.

Stella was the only exception. Her mere presence fascinated me more than any rambling monologue on film, travel, or whatever the fuck people liked to talk about.

Her laugh faded into a hitched breath at the conviction in my voice.

"But if you want to know the truth..." My hand skimmed from her necklace onto the delicate slope of her shoulder. "I didn't come to watch the photoshoot."

A gentle shiver rippled through her body when my touch trailed down her forearm.

"Then why did you come?" Her question expanded between us like it was the most important thing on the beach.

"For you." I lingered on the soft, bare skin above her elbow. The sun blazed overhead, but it was nothing compared to the sparks igniting in the air. Thousands of embers peppered my skin and lit a trail of fire up my arm and into my chest. "Drop your arms for me, sweetheart. I want to see you."

It was the closest I ever came to begging.

Silence shrouded us and suffocated any remaining traces of lightheartedness. In its place was something dark and textured that weighed heavy on my shoulders while I waited for Stella's response.

The delicate column of her throat jumped as her eyes held mine.

Her eyes had always been her most expressive feature, like clear, jade-colored windows into her innermost thoughts. Every fear, every desire, every dream and insecurity.

For the first time, I couldn't decipher what she was thinking by looking at her, but I could *feel* the indecision twisting her inside.

We'd been inching toward this line in our relationship since we signed our agreement, but we both knew that if we crossed it, there would be no going back.

My pulse slowed to match the interminable wait.

Then slowly, ever so slowly, Stella lowered her arms, and my pulse shifted from slow motion into high gear as it throbbed to the frantic rhythm of my heart.

I didn't take my eyes off her face until she stood with her arms at her side and a ruddy flush beneath her tan. Only then did I allow my gaze to slide down and bask in the sight before me.

Firm, lush breasts tipped with sweet brown nipples that I ached to taste. Delicate curves and graceful limbs that dipped and rose beneath miles of luminous skin like a roadmap to a heaven I would never reach. And a tiny scrap of white fabric that covered her most intimate spot.

My cock turned to stone while a beast stirred in my chest, snarling at me to take her and mark her until it was clear to every single person who she belonged to.

Me.

Stella's breaths left her in shallow puffs as she shifted beneath my scrutiny. She was clearly unused to someone staring at her for so long, but when she moved to cover herself again, I stopped her with a grip on her wrist.

"Don't." Desire roughened the edges of my voice. "You don't need to cover yourself in front of me."

"I don't...I'm not..." Her throat moved again with a visible swallow. "It's been a while since someone saw me like this." Embarrassment coated her admission.

The fierce flame of possessiveness burned in my gut, a thousand times hotter than when I'd caught Ricardo staring at Stella after the shoot.

Of course, I knew she must've been naked in front of other

men before—just as I knew I wanted to peel the skin off said men's flesh and leave them to rot beneath the hot sun for daring to lay their eyes on her.

No one would ever be worthy of her.

"Define *a while*." My lazy request didn't hide the undercurrent of danger running beneath it.

Wariness flickered to life in her eyes. "Years."

The beast in my chest was fully awake now, and it wanted to press further. Demand the name of every fucking man who'd touched her so I could pay them a nice follow-up visit.

It took a good amount of willpower, but I caged those desires.

I was putting her on edge, and I didn't want to waste our last day in Hawaii focused on insignificant people.

I may not be her first, but I would damn well be her last.

Because once I took her, I would never let her go.

"I see." My voice softened into velvet again. "And when was the last time someone touched you like this, Stella?"

I stroked her breast, mapping out the soft swell with my palm before I grazed a thumb over her nipple. It hardened instantly, and a smile ghosted my mouth at her sharp inhale.

"I...I don't remember."

Beads of sweat bloomed high on Stella's forehead when my touch roughened, and I pinched her nipple hard enough to elicit another, even sharper gasp.

Her hand shot up to grasp my wrist. "*Christian.*"

My name fell off her lips in a sweet, breathless plea, but it might as well be the shot from a starting pistol.

One word, and the full force of my desire snapped from its leash.

I wanted to swallow the sound of my name from her mouth, see if she tasted as sweet as she made it sound or if it was dirty and wanton, like sin made verbal. More than that, I wanted to bury myself inside her, paint her with my cum, and ruin her so thoroughly it made the fall of the angels look like child's play.

I would never make it to heaven, but that didn't matter as long as she ruled beside me in hell.

Stella was made to be my queen.

Towering cliffs bracketed the beach, their steep walls worn smooth by the elements, and a gasp escaped Stella's throat when I pushed her against the nearby rockface.

My cock throbbed in sync with my pulse as I hooked a finger inside the string-tied waistband of Stella's bikini bottom and tore it off with one sharp tug.

A tortured groan rumbled in my chest at the sight of her already wet and glistening for me. She looked like a mythical goddess against the dark rock, all sinuous limbs and brown skin. Jewels encircled her neck where I wished my hands were, adorning her, caressing her, owning her.

The throbbing intensified until it was all I could see and hear.

I wanted to fall to my knees and worship her with my mouth. To touch her, taste her, fucking *drown* in her.

Every need and fantasy rushed through me at once, but there would be time for all of them later.

I finally had her in my hands, and I wasn't going to rush any stop along the way.

"You're fucking drenched, Butterfly." Lust rendered my voice unrecognizable as I dipped a hand between her legs. Her head fell back against the wall, and a moan scattered on the wind when I played lazily with her clit, circling and rubbing the swollen bud until her juices slicked my fingers. "Do you like this, hmm? Being spread wide and finger fucked where anyone can see you?"

No one would. And if they did, I would kill them before they could leave with memories of her naked form embedded in their brain.

Stella was mine and mine alone.

She was panting so loudly the sound almost drowned out the roar of my pulse.

I'd never lost control during sex. My previous encounters had been transactional, outlets for physical release and nothing more.

With her, I was undone before we'd even begun.

"I asked you a question, Stella." The silkiness of my statement betrayed the ruthless game I played with her arousal, pulling her to the edge and withdrawing just before she tipped over the edge. "Answer me."

"I..." Stella's pants reached a fever pitch when I pressed against a particularly sensitive spot. "I don't..."

"Wrong answer." I collared her throat with my other hand, pinning her against the rocky wall while I pushed her legs wider with my thigh. I kept the pressure of my thumb against her clit and slid a finger inside her tight, wet heat.

Desire flamed hotter with every inch deeper I went and every pant of her breath against my skin.

I wanted to swallow every gasp and feel every sigh against my lips until I consumed her and made her mine in every fucking way.

"I'll ask you again." I pushed my finger to the hilt and withdrew it slowly, wrangling the loudest moan from her yet. "Do you like being finger fucked out in the open like a good little slut?"

Stella squirmed, her body instinctively rebelling against the onslaught of sensation, but her struggles were futile against my iron grip.

"*Yes.*" Her admission spilled out as a choked sob. "Please...·oh God..."

Her head tipped back again as I dragged my fingers out and rubbed a lazy circle on her clit with my thumb before I slammed them back in.

Stella wasn't a screamer, but her little gasps and whimpers were the sexiest things I'd ever heard.

She writhed against the rock, her lids heavy and her mouth half-parted in a ceaseless moan. One hand splayed against the rock while the other fisted my hair hard enough to sting.

Lust soaked the air so thoroughly it would only take a graze to light the match on the gasoline of our desire.

Thin sheens of sweat that had nothing to do with the tropical heat misted our bodies, and the open nature of it all—the wind on my back, the ocean mere steps away—only heightened the eroticism.

There was nothing artificial about this moment. It was real and raw and so fucking perfect I wanted to keep us here forever, troubles in D.C. be damned.

"Scream for me, sweetheart." I pushed a second finger inside her, stretching her. My cock ached to replace my hands. I was close to losing it, and she hadn't even touched me. "Let me hear how much you love this."

The wet, filthy sounds of my fingers pumping in and out of her told me what I needed to know, but I wanted to *hear* her.

I wanted her to let go.

The volume of Stella's moans grew, but she still held back, her muscles visibly taut from the effort.

"Please," she whimpered. "I can't...I..."

"Let go, Stella." My mouth grazed her ear. "When I tell you to scream, I want you to fucking scream. Or I'll bend you over and spank your ass raw until you *beg* me to let you scream."

A surprised but wicked smile touched my lips when she clenched around my fingers at the threat.

I increased the pace of my pumps while I lowered my head and drew her nipple into my mouth.

I groaned.

She tasted just as good as I'd imagined. Sweet and perfect, made just for me.

I laved and sucked, teasing the tip until it hardened into a diamond peak. I moved on to her other breast, alternating back and forth and licking and suckling like I was a man starved.

I couldn't get enough.

The taste of her against my tongue was fucking heaven. Silky and addictive, like a shot of pure lust into my bloodstream.

I gently clamped my teeth around one of her nipples, flicked a firm tongue across its sensitive tip, and tugged at the same time I pressed against her clit.

After a breathless, suspended moment, she finally shattered.

Stella's cry of release drenched the air as she came in a shuddering, toe-curling orgasm that vibrated against my body.

I lifted my head, ignoring the insistent ache in my groin to soak in her dazed expression.

"Good girl," I murmured, withdrawing my hand.

We remained in our positions while Stella caught her breath—her back pressed against the rock, my body curved over hers in a protective shield.

She turned those slumberous green eyes on me, looking so innocent and content it formed an iron fist around my heart.

"Kiss me." Her whisper washed over my skin and tightened my muscles until every molecule of my body hummed with anticipation.

I shouldn't, for both our sakes.

Giving her release was one thing. Kissing was a whole other.

I could own every orgasm. I could stay buried inside her to feel her trembles as she gave in to me. But a kiss? It would touch a part of me I'd kept buried and hidden.

A kiss with her wouldn't be just a kiss. It would be my fucking end.

A shadow of uncertainty passed through Stella's eyes at my hesitation, and it was that split second of darkness that killed me.

She'd lived her whole life feeling unwanted by those closest to her.

I couldn't make her feel the same way.

Not when I needed her more than my next breath, and not when I would rather cut off my arm than deny her anything.

My resistance crumbled like a sandcastle at high tide.

I let out a low curse before I groaned, fisted her hair, and slammed my mouth down on hers.

Despite what I'd said about love being a drug, Stella was my greatest high.

A temptation with no escape.

An obsession with no end.

An addiction with no cure.

STELLA

Christian kissed the way I imagined he fucked: hot and commanding, with a whisper of sensuality that softened its ruthless edge.

It made every kiss I'd had before look like an imitation,

because Christian Harper's mouth on mine was nothing short of a revelation.

The defenses I'd constructed around my heart crumbled.

I was tumbling, dizzy with his taste and the way he gripped the back of my neck, every ragged inhale and sighed exhale an exchange of parts of me I didn't know I had to give.

He molded me against him and stripped away my layers, one by one, until there was only *me* left.

No walls, no masks.

For the first time, I felt free.

I tangled my hands in his hair right as he hooked his hands beneath my thighs and lifted me without breaking the kiss. I instinctively wrapped my legs around his waist and shivered when I felt the hardness of his arousal against my stomach.

I didn't care much for sex. My previous experiences with it had been lackluster, and I only did it because I held onto hope that *one day*, I would understand what all the fuss was about.

But at that moment, the only thing I could think about was whether Christian was as skilled in bed as he was with his fingers.

When I tell you to scream, I want you to fucking scream. Or I'll bend you over and spank your ass raw until you beg me to let you scream.

The memory of his words spread liquid fire through my veins.

He swept his tongue along the seam of my lips, demanding entry again, and I granted it. A sigh of pleasure drifted from my mouth to his when his thumb caressed my nape and he devoured me so thoroughly that I didn't know where I ended and he began.

He tasted like heat and spices, a combination so addictive I could easily spend the rest of my life consuming him and only him.

A sting of pain sharpened the pleasure when he nipped my bottom lip and smiled at my surprised gasp.

"You asked for a kiss, Stella." Christian's rough voice scattered tingles through my stomach. "This is how I kiss."

The words touched my skin like open flames.

I drew his bottom lip between my teeth. Gently tugged. And released.

"Just the way I like it," I said.

His resulting groan brought a smile to my face. I normally wasn't this bold, but I loved the idea that I could make Christian Harper lose control.

"You're going to be the death of me." He lifted one hand and rubbed a thumb over my cheek, his eyes darkening as the shadows rose to the surface. "You never should've let me kiss you, Stella. Because one taste isn't fucking enough."

His words and the touch of his gaze warmed me more than the tropical sun. "Who says it has to be one?"

He let out another groan before he kissed me again, hungrily and thoroughly, like a man starved.

The delicious slide of his tongue against mine renewed the ache between my legs, and everything fell away except for the heat of his skin, the race of my heart, and the firmness of his touch.

I'd never wanted someone as much as I did Christian, and the press of my bare breasts against his torso made me all too aware of the choice I'd made when I dropped my arms for him.

Risk over safety. Desire over comfort.

No regrets.

It wasn't the dirty words or sinful desires. It wasn't the way he'd fucked me with his fingers or wrapped his hand around my throat.

It was the kiss and the way it made me feel, like I could be the truest version of myself.

I sighed with pleasure at the skilled command of Christian's mouth.

I could've stayed there forever, wrapped up in his arms on a secluded beach, but the air eventually cooled and the setting sun cast long shadows over our bodies.

"What time is the wrap party?" he murmured.

The question penetrated the fog in my mind.

Shoot. I'd almost forgotten about the Delamonte wrap party that night. "Um..." I searched for the answer through the haze. "Eight."

"It's almost seven." Christian stroked his thumb over my hip. "We should head back soon."

"Right." I tried to hide my disappointment as he set me on my feet.

"You must love that dress," he said as I pulled on my swimsuit and threw the dress I'd worn to the shoot over it. The white lemon-print cotton piece was one of my favorites. "You've worn it five times since spring began."

My breath fluttered in my chest before it whooshed out in a surprised exhale. "I didn't realize you noticed what I was wearing."

"I notice everything about you."

There were no fluttering breaths this time. There were no breaths at all, only a smile that couldn't be contained and a light-headed giddiness that would've lifted me straight off the ground had Christian's presence not tethered me to his side.

I didn't respond, but the high followed me back to our hotel.

However, once I started getting ready for the wrap party, the giddiness gradually dissipated, leaving a void for my doubts to crawl in like scavenging insects.

I'd kissed Christian.

Christian, my fake boyfriend.

Christian, the man who'd told me straight out he didn't believe in love.

Christian, who set my heart on fire even as a voice in my head warned that the fire could destroy me from the inside out if I wasn't careful.

Not only had I kissed him, I'd *asked* him to kiss me after I let him bring me to orgasm on a beach during a work trip.

What have I done?

This was why I shouldn't be left alone with my thoughts. I ruined every good moment by overanalyzing it to death.

I put on my earrings.

It's fine. Everything will be fine.

"You look beautiful."

My heart skipped a beat. I turned my head, and my doubts retreated into the shadows once again when I saw Christian leaning against the doorframe, watching me get ready.

The slumberous heat in his eyes lit a trail of tiny fires across my skin while the memory of what we did earlier pulsed between us like a living thing.

If we hadn't needed to leave the beach...

"Thank you." My voice came out huskier than normal. I turned back to the mirror and lifted my hair off my neck. "Zip me up?"

The soft falls of his footsteps matched the thuds of my pulse.

"I love this dress on you." His gaze slid over my silk dress in an electric caress.

Breathe.

"I thought you don't believe in love," I teased.

"You're right. That was the wrong word." Christian touched the small of my back while his eyes met mine in the mirror.

"Because love is ordinary. Mundane. And you, Stella..."

The soft rasp of the zipper filled the air as he dragged it up my spine in one exquisitely, torturously slow glide.

My breath left my lungs at both the sensuality of the movement and the raw intimacy of his next words.

"You're extraordinary."

32

STELLA

DELAMONTE'S WRAP PARTY SHOULD'VE BEEN THE crowning highlight of my trip, a celebration of everything we'd accomplished over the past three days.

Instead, I spent the entirety of it replaying that afternoon in my head.

The memory of my kiss with Christian stayed with me through dessert, as did the phantom brush of his touch. With one zip of my dress, he'd awoken more heat in me than any of my previous partners had with actual sex.

I'd suppressed it during dinner, but the heat blossomed again as the bedroom door closed behind us.

We hadn't spoken since dinner ended, but the mere anticipation of what *could* happen rasped against my skin as surely as a calloused touch.

The air hummed with breathlessness as Christian walked to the dresser, his lean, powerful form slicing through the darkness like a freshly honed blade through silk.

Blood roared in my ears and drowned out everything except my heartbeats and the soft rustle of his movements.

"You don't have any other commitments tonight, I presume." His tone was relaxed, but when he turned, his eyes smoldered with so much heat I thought I would combust from the sheer intensity of it.

An electric current tied our gazes together as he removed his cufflinks with a slow, deliberate preciseness that made my mouth go dry.

Rough hands. Whiskey eyes. Control.

"No."

The whisper drifted down and tightened my nipples into hard, aching points.

My lungs barely expanded with my attempts to inhale and exhale.

"Good." *Clink. Clink.* The sounds of his cufflinks hitting the silver tray echoed in the dark and throbbed low in my belly. "Take off your dress, Stella."

His deceptively soft command burned up all the oxygen in the room and set every molecule of my body ablaze.

My breaths shallowed.

This was it.

The fork in the road.

I could stick with the safe path and tell him no, or I could throw caution to the wind and do what my heart and body were screaming at me to do.

I held Christian's gaze as I reached behind me.

A minute later, my dress pooled around my feet in a puddle of white silk.

No bra, no accessories, just a tiny scrap of underwear and a heart beating too fast.

Christian's expression didn't shift.

Standing there bared and open to him, I would've thought him unmoved had it not been for his eyes. Black pupils swallowed amber as he closed the distance between us, and the closer he got, the hotter I burned.

"Tell me." The tiny glide of his finger over my hip was enough to send my pulse into overdrive. "Do you want sex, or do you want to be *fucked*?"

My thighs involuntarily clenched at the way he said *fucked*. It was the dark purr of a predator toying with its prey, making them beg for their own destruction before it pounced.

The only difference was, I didn't feel like prey.

I had a choice, and I'd never felt more powerful.

Moisture gathered between my thighs. I was so wet I could feel it slicking my skin, but I was still half tempted to take the safe route. To have easy, ordinary sex where I didn't have to bare any part of myself except my body.

My mind warred with every other part of me for control.

Do you want sex, or do you want to be fucked?

I'd kept my desires caged for so long, but perhaps it was finally time I set them free.

I didn't want soft kisses and gentle caresses.

I wanted skin and blood. I wanted nails scratching down his back and bruises on my hips.

The commands. The release. The oblivion.

I wanted it all.

"I want to be fucked." My whisper was barely audible.

"I can't hear you." His fingers glided over the dampness of my panties, and I fought back a moan at the delicious friction.

Embarrassment and lust blazed through me in equal measure.

"I want to be fucked," I repeated.

Stronger this time, more confident, but it wasn't enough.

"Louder, Stella. Use your voice." His voice hardened, his words pitiless. "*Tell me what you want.*"

He pressed a firm thumb to my clit, his touch as brutal as

his command. White-hot sensation sparked through me and drowned out my embarrassment.

"I want to be fucked!" The words exploded out of me, raw and filtered, followed by a needy moan when Christian rubbed his thumb over me.

His smile was that of a dangerously seductive monster promising all sorts of filthy, debauched deeds. "That's what I thought."

He tore my underwear off with one sharp tug before his mouth crashed over mine, swallowing my gasp and ensuing moan when he fisted my hair hard enough to make my eyes water.

The hard tug arrowed to my core like there was an electric wire directly linking the two. My scalp throbbed in rhythm with my clit, and my mind was so clouded by desire I didn't notice we'd moved until my back hit the bed.

I watched as Christian shed his clothes, revealing broad, sculpted shoulders and a sexy V-cut that led down to his...

Oh my God.

My mouth dried at the sight of his cock. Long, thick, and hard, with a bead of pre-cum glistening at its tip. It was so big that I involuntarily clenched at the thought of it filling me.

The mattress dipped beneath his weight, and his thumb found my clit again, circling and stroking until it was swollen and needy and begging for *more*.

"How would you like to be fucked, Butterfly?" He kept his thumb on my clit and pushed a finger inside me, working it deeper with each movement. A whimper clawed up my throat as my body lit beneath his erotic manipulations. "On your back and spread wide, or on all fours taking every inch of my cock in that tight little pussy?"

Had I not been lost in a haze of lust, I might've been embarrassed by his filthy words. But I was too far gone, and Christian was the only man I'd ever truly fantasized about.

He was every dark thing that couldn't be whispered and dirty deed that I secretly craved.

"Both." More whimpers poured out when he worked another finger inside me and pumped both in and out—slowly at first, then faster and faster until he found a rhythm that made my head spin. "As hard as you can."

I heard a groan, followed by a harsh command.

"Get on your hands and knees."

I did as I was told. The cool air brushed my sensitized sex as I turned and positioned myself on all fours. I was drenched, dripping all down my thighs and probably ruining the sheets before we even started.

I heard the faint rip of foil before the heat of Christian's body enveloped me. He fisted my hair with one hand and gripped my hip with the other hard enough to bruise.

"Remember..." I let out a small cry when he yanked my head back until his mouth was next to my ear. The head of his cock slid against my slick entrance, until I practically panting with anticipation. "You wanted it hard."

He released my hair, pushed me face down on the pillow, and slammed inside me with a single powerful thrust.

I let out a small cry. I was wet enough that he slid in easily, but he was so big it was almost painful.

Pain warred with pleasure as my eyes watered and my inner muscles stretched to their max.

"*Fuck*, you're tight." Another, more guttural groan. "That's it, sweetheart. You can take it."

Christian held on tight to my hips and stroked his thumbs over the curve of my ass in soothing sweeps while I struggled to accommodate his size.

My breaths came out in soft pants. I was impossibly full,

but gradually, the pain subsided and gave way to delicious pressure.

My teeth unclenched enough for a low moan to slip out.

I pushed back at him, desperate for more.

More friction, more movement, more *anything*.

I heard a chuckle, followed by a soft "good girl".

Then Christian slammed into me again, this time with such viciousness it knocked the breath out of my lungs.

I squealed, my mind blanking at the sudden, forceful invasion. Dark pleasure burst through me, and I barely had time to catch my breath before he started moving again.

One hand stayed on my hip while the other pressed against the back of my neck, forcing my face deeper into the pillow.

Rough hands.

Savage strokes.

A punishing, carnal rhythm that coaxed moan after moan out of my mouth.

"You feel so fucking good," Christian grunted. "It's like your pussy was made for me. Every fucking inch."

He withdrew so just the tip remained inside me, paused, then plunged back in with one brutal thrust. Again and again, until the headboard banged against the wall and drowned out my muffled squeals and whimpers.

Tears and drool soaked my pillow as Christian pounded me mercilessly. I'd been reduced to a wreck, held together with nothing but mind-numbing pleasure and the softest pricks of pain.

It wasn't sex. It was pure, hard fucking...and it was exactly what I needed.

The guys I'd previously slept with had treated me like I was a porcelain doll in bed. Their intentions were good, but the sex had excited me as much as a game of golf.

I didn't want gentle. I wanted passion in its rawest form. I wanted the oblivion that came with pleasure and the knowledge that, no matter what form that pleasure came in, I could trust the person delivering it not to hurt me.

Because as rough as Christian was, I'd never felt safer.

Another cry fell from my lips when he wrapped his fist around my hair and yanked my head back again.

"You're dripping all over my cock, sweetheart. Look at you." He swept his thumb over my damp cheek. I was a mess, my face streaked with tears and my body trembling with lust. "An angel about to come from being fucked like a whore."

An electric shiver moved through my entire body at his words.

"Please," I sobbed. "I need—I can't—*please*..."

I didn't know what I was begging for. For release, for him to go harder, for this never to end.

All I knew was, he was the only one who could give it to me.

"Please what?" Christian kept one hand fisted in my hair while he reached his other around to my sensitized sex.

"Please, I need to..."

My reply devolved into a hoarse scream when he pinched my clit. My brain short circuited, and my body spiked with pleasure so intense I instinctively tried to scoot away.

I only made it a few inches before Christian dragged me back.

"Try that again, and I'll spank you so hard you won't be able to sit." I yelped when his palm landed on my ass with a warning slap. He lifted his hand and closed it around my throat. "I want to *feel* you coming on my cock, Stella." His fingers dug harder into my skin with each word.

I could only answer with a string of unintelligible moans. I'd lost my voice to the need coiled beneath my skin, threatening to split me apart at the seams and turn me into the ruins of the person I once was.

The one who'd played it safe her entire life, who'd been so afraid of going after what she wanted. she didn't dare voice her desires out loud.

She'd shattered beneath Christian's touch, and I never wanted her back.

I closed my eyes, picturing the obscene image we must've made. Me on all fours, my head pulled back and my back arched while Christian pounded me from behind. One hand around my throat, the other hand fisting my hair. A faint red mark from when his palm struck my ass...

Heat moved down my spine, building and building until I exploded into a thousand brilliant pinpoints of light. They raced through my veins and lit a match to every nerve ending until they consumed me whole.

Oh God. No wonder other people raved about sex. If that was what it was *supposed* to be like...

I was still clinging to the remnants of my orgasm when Christian flipped me over onto my back. His arms bracketed my body, and his mouth grazed mine as his thrusts slowed into...not something soft, but soft*er*. More sensual.

"I can still feel your pussy rippling around my cock." He cupped my breast and rubbed his thumb over the stiff peak. "As beautiful as I imagined."

He kissed me harder, his mouth claiming mine and his hands mapping my most erogenous zones as he fucked me toward another orgasm.

"Right there," I panted when he hit a spot inside me that made my toes curl. I clung to him, my legs spread wide to take him as deep as he could go. "Harder. Please, I...*oh God*..." My moans pitched higher when he increased his pace and the tremors of a second climax quaked through me.

Slowly at first, then all at once when Christian pinched my nipple and drove into me with as much force as the beginning of the night.

I cried out as wave after wave of pleasure washed through me.

I felt him shudder and jerk inside me before he, too, came with a groan, but I was swept up in euphoria so intense it drowned out everything else.

It went on for what felt like forever before I finally slumped into a sweaty, mindless heap.

For once, the voices inside my head were silent. I was floating on a cloud of post-orgasmic bliss, and I wanted to stay there forever.

No doubts, no insecurities, no overanalyzing. Just the soft, ragged sounds of my breaths and the press of Christian's mouth against my skin as he kissed his way down my neck and torso.

The gentleness of his touch was at complete odds with the savagery of his fucking, but it felt so right I didn't question it.

I nearly purred with contentment when he rolled me onto my side and smoothed a hand over my ass. His strong fingers kneaded the muscle until I melted into a boneless puddle.

"You did so well," he murmured. "Such a good girl."

His words wrapped around me like a soft blanket and sparked another ember of heat in my stomach.

I guess that was what happened when girls with a need for academic validation grew up. They developed a praise kink.

"We should do this every night," I said drowsily. It'd been a long day, and as much as I wanted a second round, I was so tired I could barely keep my eyes open. "It's better than yoga."

He laughed, a soft rumble of noise that was pure male satisfaction.

"I can't think of a higher compliment." He moved his body up until he lay next to me and dropped a kiss on top of my head. "No complaints from me if you want to make this your nightly routine instead."

"Hmm." I closed my eyes and snuggled closer to him.

As soft as this moment was, a part of me knew Christian and I had entered dangerous new territory in our relationship. And while my self-preservation instincts were doing their best to ring the alarm, I also knew there was no going back.

33

CHRISTIAN/STELLA

CHRISTIAN

She was dreaming. I could tell by the way her lips curved and the soft noises she made in her sleep.

I wondered what she was dreaming about and whether said dream included me.

If not, that was unacceptable.

I pressed a soft kiss to her shoulder and wrapped a possessive arm around her waist.

Whether in heaven or hell, in dreams or real life, Stella was mine.

And I didn't fucking share.

She stirred and let out a small, adorable yawn before her eyes fluttered open and met mine.

"Good morning."

A smile touched my lips at her shy tone.

"Morning, Butterfly. Sweet dreams?"

"Mmhmm." She stretched and snuggled closer to me.

"What were you dreaming about?"

"I don't really remember. Something involving a boat? I keep meaning to start a dream journal, but I always forget."

I chose not to ask what a dream journal was.

"Were you alone in the dream?" I asked casually.

"Hmm, now that you mention it, there *was* someone in the boat with me," she said. "Dark hair, tanned skin, a bit older than me but really good-looking..."

A smug grin crept over my lips.

Stella snapped her fingers. "I remember now. It was Ricardo!"

She let out a squeal of laughter when I rolled her over and pinned her arms above her head.

"You think that's funny," I growled, but a smile threatened to slip free at the sparkle in her eyes.

"I was only telling the truth," she teased. "Don't tell me you're jealous of a dream. I didn't think you'd be one of those guys who gets clingy after sex."

"I told you, Stella. I'm jealous of everything when it comes to you." Something dark and possessive moved through my chest. "And it wasn't just fucking sex."

Sex was a transaction, something people did to pass the time and find physical release. Anyone could have sex. But no one could rip me apart and put me back together the way she could.

"I was joking, Grumpypants." Stella lifted her head and pressed a light kiss on my mouth. "I don't remember the dream, but if I *did* remember, I'm sure it featured you."

"You're only saying that to make me feel better," I grumbled.

Her lips twitched. "Is it working?"

"No." But my shoulders relaxed and I released her wrists as her laugh wound its way through my chest.

I thought Stella would've lost her mystery by now. We'd

lived together for two months; I should've already gotten bored and moved on.

But the more I got to know her, the more she embedded herself into my being.

She was a study in contrasts, the most fascinating puzzle I'd ever come across—strength and vulnerability, calm and chaos, innocence and debauchery. The woman whose gentle smile soothed the savage beast inside me was the same one who unleashed it with her cries and pleas for *more*. For me to take her and mark her as mine.

Stella Alonso had consumed my world in a way that made it impossible to go back. There was only before her and after her.

We lay there for a while and soaked in the comfortable silence before she spoke again.

"I wish we could stay longer." Her wistful sigh tugged at my heart. "I don't want to go back to the city yet. I haven't even explored the island. It's just been Delamonte stuff the entire time."

"So let's stay."

I made the decision without thinking. It seemed my default setting was giving Stella anything she wanted.

I hoped no one ever discovered this weakness. It would be catastrophic for me and for her.

Her eyes widened with delight before she shook her head. "We can't. You have work, and you've already been gone for three days."

I had more than work. I had a fucking mess that required immediate handling.

The cold, rational part of me insisted I return to D.C. today as originally planned. Staying in Hawaii was the worst decision I could make, and I hadn't built an empire by making bad decisions.

But it was Stella's first time in Hawaii, and despite her protest, I could see the glimmer of hope in her eyes.

She really wanted to stay, and I would rather lose an empire than see her sad at my hands.

Whispers of the secrets I'd kept and the lies I'd told crept up before I smashed them.

"It's the weekend," I said. "We'll leave Monday. Two extra days won't hurt."

Hopefully.

Her face lit up. "Okay. I mean, if you insist."

My mouth curled into an indulgent smile as she rambled on about all the things she wanted to do.

Last night, our kiss on the beach...

I'd come to terms with my choice. I wouldn't hold myself back from what I wanted anymore.

And no matter how much I'd tried to deny it in the past, this was what I've wanted since I first saw her. Stella in my arms, happy and safe and *mine*.

But as perfect as everything was with us now, I knew that if she ever found out the truth, she would hate me.

Which was why she could never find out.

———

STELLA

Since we only had two days to explore Kauai, Christian and I packed as much into our itinerary as possible.

Hiking, sunset sails, helicopter tours, visits to local museums and secluded beaches...we did it all.

We woke up at sunrise and returned to our hotel past dinnertime, where we spent hours exploring each other as thoroughly as we did the island.

Whether it was slow and soft or rough and hard, sex with

Christian was as much an emotional release as it was a physical one.

However, on our last day, we stuck with something more low-key since Christian had a board meeting and we had to fly out early in the morning.

I didn't know the low-key thing *was* since he'd planned it as a surprise, but I was intrigued. He'd taken control of our itinerary since he'd been to Kauai before, and he'd yet to steer me wrong.

"Is *this* the surprise?" I eyed the Harley parked next to us as Christian fitted a helmet on me. "I never would've pegged you for a motorcycle kind of guy. It's kind of sexy."

More than sexy. In a simple white T-shirt and jeans, he was devastating. It was more than the clothes, though.

Two days of sun and relaxation had stripped away his carefully cultivated mask to reveal the playful, charming man underneath, and I wanted to hold on to him for as long as I could.

"Kind of?" He notched a dark brow as he straddled the motorbike. The engine roared to life and sent a thrill through my blood.

"I can't make a final determination until I see what your actual driving skills are like," I said solemnly. "So yes, for now, it's kind of."

"*You're* talking about driving skills?" His brow rose higher. "Butterfly, you almost rear ended our guide yesterday."

I *knew* he wouldn't let that go. "It wasn't my fault," I huffed. "He came out of nowhere!"

Christian pressed his lips together, and it took me a second to realize he was suppressing laughter.

"It's not funny." My cheeks flamed. Maybe I wasn't the *best* driver in the world, but I'd tried. "I felt bad about you driving us everywhere, so I offered...*stop laughing.*"

"I would never laugh at you," he said with a grin. "I will also never get in a car with you behind the wheel again."

"I take back what I said." I climbed onto the back of the bike and wrapped my arms around his waist with a disgruntled frown. "You're not sexy at all."

"It's okay." His shoulders shook with laughter as we pulled away from our hotel. "I'm sure I can change your mind."

"I doubt it," I muttered, but the wind swallowed my words as we sped down the island's tree-lined roads.

It took us twenty minutes to reach our destination. It was a secluded beach on the North Shore, and even though it was almost sunset, it was empty save for the gorgeous picnic set up on the sand.

Pillows, cushions, and blankets surrounded a low table draped in a silky white cloth. Tiny candles flickered next to a bottle of wine and a sumptuous dinner spread.

I sucked in a sharp breath. "How did you..."

"I had the hotel set something up." Christian's mouth curved. "Don't worry. They'll break everything down after we finish eating. Not a speck of litter will be left behind."

"It's beautiful."

A strange lump formed in my throat.

It was finally sinking in that this was our last night on the island. So much had happened since we'd arrived, and I'd tricked myself into thinking the fantasy could last forever.

Hawaii was a dream, but it wasn't something we could bring back with us.

What would happen when we returned to D.C.? Would we return to the status quo?

It was easy to act like a couple when it was just us in paradise, but we *weren't* a couple. We'd never had that conversation, and sex didn't necessarily mean anything in today's day and age.

Some people had sex with the same person for months and *still* didn't consider the relationship exclusive.

Christian and I settled at the table. Dinner was objectively delicious, but I barely tasted it because I was too busy imagining what would happen once we got off the plane tomorrow.

Finally, I couldn't hold it in any longer.

I hated breaking the spell, but if we didn't have *the* conversation, the uncertainty would eat me alive all night.

Are we dating? Is this a friends with benefits thing? Do you want to continue whatever "this" is in D.C.?

I ran through all the ways I could bring up the topic, but I was too terrified of his answer to use any of my initial options.

Instead, I took the coward's way out.

"Thank you for the past few days. They were just what I needed." I dug my toes into the cool sand and kept my eyes on the table. "We make a pretty good fake couple, don't we?"

The words burned like acid on their way out.

"Fake couple with benefits," I added, hoping to lighten the suddenly tense atmosphere.

I snuck a peek at Christian. His face looked like it was carved from granite, but his eyes burned dark and intimidating.

"Fake couple?" His silken voice wrapped ice around my throat.

A shiver rasped over my skin, but I forged on. "That was our agreement. A few kisses and sex don't change anything."

I wasn't naive enough to think that just because he slept with me, he wanted anything more than a good time. We'd given into something between us, but that didn't mean I had any commitment from him.

I'd seen too many people get their hearts broken because of such an assumption, and I refused to be one of them.

"They don't, do they?" Lower. More dangerous. "Then what, exactly, do those *few kisses and sex* mean to you?"

Something told me I shouldn't answer, but I did anyway. Self-preservation had never been my strong suit when it came to Christian.

"A fantasy. None of this is real." I gestured at the beach. "It's *never* been real. Hawaii is a dream, but it's ending tomorrow, and I want to set the right expectations before we return to D.C. You said it yourself." The lump in my throat grew. "You don't believe in love."

Despite my aversion to relationships, I was a romantic at heart.

When I found the right person, I *wanted* to get swept up in that grand, all-consuming love. The type of love that'd compelled Alex to move to another country for Ava, that gave Bridget and Rhys the courage to go against a country, and that transformed years of animosity between Josh and Jules into something beautiful.

That type of love existed. I'd witnessed it with my own eyes.

But it wasn't something Christian believed in, and while I knew he wanted me, he didn't want me enough to change such a deep-rooted belief.

Men like Christian Harper didn't change for anyone.

"Love has nothing to do with this." His hard reply proved my point.

The bitter taste of disappointment welled on my tongue. "Exactly."

"You were the one who told me not to fall in love with you, Stella. Do you remember that?" Those dark eyes pierced mine.

"Yes, and I meant it." I resisted the urge to twist my necklace around my finger like I always did when I was nervous. It was my tell, and I bet Christian had already picked up on it. "I still do."

Because if Christian ever fell in love with me, I didn't trust myself not to fall in love with him in return.

And I had a feeling love with him wouldn't be sweet or easy. It would be catastrophic.

"Things have gotten too complicated with me moving in, the stalker situation, and this trip," I said when Christian remained silent. "The original rules of our arrangement are getting blurred. Maybe we need to see other people so we don't—"

I didn't get a chance to finish before his mouth covered mine and he kissed me with a soft, desperate viciousness that I felt from my head to my toes.

"Tell me..." He curled a hand around the nape of my neck. "Does this feel *fake* to you?"

No. That was the problem. It felt too real, as did the possibility that he could break my heart.

"I want to make a few things clear." Christian's lips brushed mine with each word. "Touch another man, he dies. Let another man touch you, he dies. Tell me *I* can't touch you..." His grip tightened on the back of my neck as his voice dropped. "And I will fucking die."

An ache grabbed hold of my heart and twisted. "Christian..."

"*Love* is nothing but a word." The intensity of his words stole the remaining breath from my lungs. "This isn't about words. It's about us. Do you think I would disrupt my schedule and fly to Hawaii in the middle of a work week for anyone else?"

"It's a nice destination," I said weakly.

"I thought it was obvious, but in case it isn't, you're mine, Stella." His touch branded my skin with hot possessiveness. "I don't want to see other women, and I sure as fuck don't want you seeing other men." Ice frosted the word *men*. "You belong with me. Exclusively. There is not a world or lifetime where that's not true."

Emotion stung the backs of my eyes, but I managed to smile through the tightness in my chest.

"Christian Harper, are you asking me out?"

"Yes." Simple, unequivocal. *Real*.

It seemed almost comical that someone like him would do something as mundane as ask a girl out, but that didn't stop my stomach from fluttering or my mind from playing through the past two months.

On paper, our relationship had been fake, but there was nothing fake about the way he'd taken care of me, supported me, and believed in me. Nor was there anything fake about the way I felt when I was with him, like I could be *me* and he'd want me anyway, flaws and all.

"So..." Christian's mouth grazed mine. "What do you say, Butterfly? Want to give this dating thing a real shot?"

I shouldn't. There were so many ways this could go wrong, but wasn't that true of every risk people took?

No risk, no reward.

For once, I turned off the over-analytical part of my brain and went with what my heart told me to do.

"Yes." Simple. Unequivocal. *Real*.

I felt his smile against my lips before he kissed me again. Softer this time, more tender.

Tender wasn't a word I'd thought I would ever associate with Christian, but he constantly took me by surprise.

I melted into him and let his taste, touch, and the last few hours of our dream sweep me away to a place where my worries didn't exist.

I was used to being alone. Even when I was surrounded by people, a part of me isolated itself until I felt like I was watching a movie of my life instead of living it.

I had never belonged to someone, nor had someone ever belonged to me. The idea was equal parts thrilling and terrifying.

But what was even more terrifying was the realization that I didn't mind belonging with Christian.

Not even a little bit.

34

STELLA

CHRISTIAN AND I WERE OFFICIALLY DATING. IT FELT strange, not only because it wasn't something I'd ever thought would happen but also because to the outside world, nothing had changed. In their eyes, we'd been a couple this entire time.

I'd posted my Hawaii photos after we returned to D.C., and our couple shots did great, as expected. I was still keeping up with my Instagram, though my attention was now split between that and my fashion line.

The only people who knew our pre-Hawaii relationship *hadn't* been real were Christian, myself, and my friends, who'd greeted my announcement with considerably less surprise than they had the previous bombshell.

According to Jules, it'd been "inevitable" based on how we'd been eye fucking each other at her housewarming.

Christian and I went on our first real date a week after we returned from Hawaii. We took each other to our favorite places in D.C.—the U.S. Botanic Garden for me, Eastern Market for him.

Correction: a specific *vendor* at Eastern Market for him.

"Mr. C!" The vendor's face creased with a gummy smile when he saw Christian. "Good to see you again! And with a lovely lady by your side, too." He winked at me. "What are you doing with an ogre like him?"

He jerked his thumb at Christian, who shook his head.

"Beauty isn't everything." I patted Christian's hand. "He has other great qualities."

The vendor laughed while my new boyfriend sighed with exasperation, though a glint of humor surfaced in his eyes.

"Stella, meet Donnie. Wannabe comedian and woodworker extraordinaire." He tapped a puzzle on the table. "This is the only reason I put up with your old ass."

"My old ass has more wisdom than you do in your pinky," Donnie retorted.

A grin worked its way onto my face as I surveyed his wares. "These are *incredible*."

The table boasted the most intricate woodworks I'd ever seen, including model sailboats, miniature folding screens, and a selection of mind-boggling puzzles.

"Thank you." Pride glowed in Donnie's face. "Keeps me busy now that I'm retired."

Christian and I chatted with Donnie for a while until other customers pulled him away. We ended up buying two puzzles (Christian) and a set of gorgeous carved bangles (me).

"I'd say our first date was a success." I swung my shopping bag as we walked to a nearby restaurant for dinner.

"Of course it was. I planned it."

My mouth dropped. "Hello? Did you forget about the garden earlier? We *both* planned the date."

"Yes, but I drove us all day."

"That is not how planning works!"

Christian laughed as I lightly shoved his arm.

Other than his annoying habit of taking credit for dates we

both planned, Christian was a great boyfriend. Vague and moody at times, especially after a stressful day at work, but considerate and supportive almost all the time.

I'd all but moved into his bedroom and turned the guest room into an overflow closet. He worked from home twice a week so we could spend more time together, and even though we spent most of those days doing our own thing—him on his laptop, me on my fashion line plans—it was nice having him close.

All in all, I couldn't have asked for a more perfect real relationship.

Still, it took me another two weeks after our first date before I invited Christian to join me on a visit to Maura's.

I'd never brought anyone to see her before, and the prospect tore at my nerves. What if she didn't like him? What if *he* didn't like *her*? What if she got agitated and—

Stop. It'll be fine.

I took a deep breath and tried to calm my racing pulse as we stopped in front of her room.

"Here." I shoved the tembleque we brought into Christian's hands. "You hold it. I don't care if you don't like dessert. You need to butter her up."

"Here I thought my charm would be enough," he drawled, but he took the dessert without complaint.

"I doubt it." I twisted the doorknob. "She's not easily charmed by men."

But of course, he proved me wrong.

Maura *loved* him, and not just because of the tembleque, though that helped.

Christian swept into the room like Prince Charming, handing her the dessert and complimenting her on her necklace. Less than ten minutes later, they were laughing over a joke he made like they'd known each other forever.

I watched them, mouth agape.

It was one of Maura's better days, and she seemed in high spirits, but still. It was disconcerting to see them get so chummy so fast when even *I* had to warm her up a bit every time I visited.

I wasn't sure whether to be happy they got along so well or disgruntled that she got along with him better than she did me.

"Today's puzzle day," Maura said. "I like puzzles. Do *you* like puzzles?" She narrowed her eyes at Christian like his answer would determine whether they could continue their new friendship.

A smile spread across his face. "I love puzzles."

"What kind?"

"Every kind. Crosswords, jigsaws, cryptograms..."

"I like jigsaws the most." Maura interrupted him mid-sentence. "It's..." She hesitated, and I could see her wracking her brain for the right phrase.

I glanced at Christian as the minutes ticked by. He waited for her to continue without a hint of annoyance or impatience.

Something warm heated the pit of my stomach and expanded into my chest.

"It's satisfying," Maura finally said. The word came out slow and hesitant, like she was testing whether it was the right term. "When the pieces fit together and you see the whole picture."

Christian stared at her, his expression indecipherable. "Yes," he said quietly. "It is."

I'd seen many iterations of Christian Harper over the past three months, but the one sitting here today? He was the one I could most see myself falling for.

I blinked away my unwanted emotion and pasted on a bright smile.

"Maura, would you like to take a walk in the garden? It's a beautiful day."

Her face lit up. "Yes, please."

"Milady." Christian held out his arm.

He was laying it on thick, but Maura actually *giggled* as she took his arm. I had never, not once in all my years of knowing her, heard Maura giggle.

Unbelievable.

He must have the devil's magic on his side.

"How did you two meet?" she asked as we walked through the rose garden. It was her favorite, and we stopped every two feet so she could ooh and aah over the lush blooms.

"We..." I almost told her the story Christian and I had concocted, but I went with a semblance of the truth. It felt wrong to lie to her. "We live in the same building and have some mutual friends. I ran into a bit of trouble, and Christian helped me out."

"Oh. How nice of him," Maura said. She patted his hand. "You are such a gentleman. I can just tell."

He smiled and raised an eyebrow at me over her head.

I rolled my eyes, but I couldn't help smiling.

As insufferable as he would be after effortlessly charming Maura, I loved how well they got along. Nothing stressed me out more than people I cared about butting heads.

It was why my last family dinner had taken such a toll on me. Between Hawaii and my fashion line, I'd been busy enough to shove it to the back of my mind, but it haunted me still.

I refused to cave first, though. If my family wanted to talk to me, they knew where to find me.

Maura, Christian, and I wandered through the gardens for a while until Maura got tired and we returned to her room.

"I like him," she said when Christian went to the restroom. "Such a handsome young man. Charming too."

I stared at her. "Do you...have a *crush* on him?"

She snorted. "Of course not! I'm too old to have *crushes*. Besides, he only has eyes for you."

My face warmed. "I don't..."

"It is true." She coughed and picked up her teacup. "He doesn't...he..." Her hands shook as she brought the cup closer to her mouth. It almost touched her lips before she dropped it, and it shattered into a dozen jagged pieces.

Maura's mouth fell open. Her eyes widened and took on a familiar wild look.

"It's okay. It's okay," I said quickly. "It's just a cup. I'll get the nurses to—"

"It's *not just a cup*!" Her breathing quickened. "It's broken and it's...it's..." Her gaze darted around the room.

"Everything will be fine." I kept my voice calm despite the way my stomach dropped. She was growing visibly agitated, and once she got agitated, it was near impossible to calm her down without sedation. "I'll call a nurse and they'll clean it up. They're—"

"Already on their way." Christian's voice cut into the conversation. I hadn't heard him come in, but he moved quickly through the room and knelt in front of her. "There are new cups in the community room, along with puzzles. Would you like to do one together?"

Maura's eyes were still bright with panic, but her breaths slowed into something resembling normal. "Puzzle?"

"A jigsaw puzzle," he confirmed. "Their newest one. You'll be the first person to complete it."

"I...yes. I like puzzles." She released her stranglehold on her armrest. "I did a puzzle of a poodle once. I used to own a poodle. It's my favorite dog breed..."

She went off on a tangent about the best and worst dog breeds as Christian guided her to the community room.

I followed them, my throat tight.

"Thank you," I said once Maura was happily settled with her tea and puzzle. "For..." I gestured toward the hallway where her room was situated. "And for coming with me."

"There are worse ways to spend my day." Christian laced his fingers through mine and placed our hands on his thigh. "Thank you for inviting me."

I looked down at our entwined hands and couldn't stop my heart from expanding so much it made it hard to breathe.

I am in so much trouble.

———

THAT NIGHT, AFTER WE VISITED MAURA, CHRISTIAN AND I attended our first business event for him as a real couple.

The significance wasn't lost on me, though the actual event bored me to tears. It was some tech gathering, and I spent most of it smiling, nodding, and pretending I cared about what people were saying while Christian networked.

"The EU is killing us with its regulations," the man he was talking to grumbled. "It's untenable!"

I stifled a yawn while Christian answered him.

Tech regulation wasn't nearly as interesting as baby turtles.

While the other man droned on about some new law that just passed, I placed a hand on Christian's arm and whispered, "I'm going to the restroom. I'll be right back."

He nodded, and I slipped away before I had to listen to one more complaint about the EU.

There wasn't a line for the restroom, so I took the opportunity to fix my hair and makeup and check my notifications. My follower count was still growing, but it was slower now than in the beginning stages of our "relationship."

I didn't care as much as I used to. Joining the million-follower club made getting big partnerships easier, but it'd also made me realize how little the number meant on a personal level.

I slipped my phone into my clutch and exited the restroom.

I made it halfway back to Christian when the hairs on the back of my neck rose. I recognized that chill; it was what I felt when someone was watching me.

My head jerked up, and I scanned the room frantically for anything—or anyone—suspicious.

Nothing. Just a bunch of people in suits, grousing about the latest regulatory laws and bragging about their companies' market caps.

You're being paranoid. Your stalker is not here. This is a closed event—

A scream rose but stuck in my throat when someone grabbed my ass and squeezed. Hard.

I whipped around and stared in disbelief at the man leering at me.

He winked at me and moseyed on past like he hadn't full-on *groped* me in the middle of a professional event.

I was too stunned to say anything before he left.

The interaction had lasted less than a minute, but that was enough to make me feel like I was coated in a layer of grime I could never scrub off.

"What's wrong?" Christian picked up on my discomfort the instant I returned to his side.

He'd had his back turned, so he hadn't seen what happened. The man he'd been talking to had also wandered off, leaving us alone.

"Nothing." I shifted beneath his skeptical gaze before I admitted, "Someone groped me on my way back from the restroom."

Christian stilled.

"Who?" His tone was calm, almost pleasant, but it contained something that evoked an arctic chill beneath my skin.

My body betrayed the small voice warning me not to tell him.

I instinctively flicked my eyes toward the bar, where the man who'd groped me was hitting on an uninterested-looking woman.

Christian followed my gaze.

"I see." His inflection didn't change, but foreboding slithered down my spine like the cool, scaly skin of a snake.

Some people burned hot when they were angry, but Christian ran cold. The quieter he got, the more people needed to worry.

"It's not a big deal," I said anxiously. I didn't want him doing anything that might get him into trouble or that he might regret later. "It was only a passing grab. Not worth making a scene over."

"I won't make a scene." Christian set his empty champagne glass on a nearby table, his face unreadable. "In fact, I'm done here. Are you ready to leave?"

I nodded and breathed a silent sigh of relief. *Thank God.*

Between the mind-numbing conversations and the jerk who couldn't keep his hands to himself, I was ready to put the night behind me.

Still, when we exited the building and walked to Christian's car, I couldn't shake the sense that whoever had raised my inner alarms earlier hadn't been the man who groped me, but someone else entirely.

35

CHRISTIAN

THE DOOR CLOSED WITH A QUIET *SNICK* BEHIND ME.

In the hush of my satellite office, it sounded like a gunshot.

The man seated inside jumped, his knee banging against my desk as he swiveled to face me.

I recognized him from last night's tech event. Some low-level entrepreneur who'd weaseled his way into the gathering.

I'd let him wait in here alone because I wasn't worried about him stealing or snooping. I reserved my satellite office for more...unsavory conversations, and it didn't contain anything except basic office furniture.

"I've been waiting for half an hour." He stated the fucking obvious like I couldn't tell time.

"Have you?" I gave negative shits about how long he'd had to wait. Frank Rivers was a bottom feeder. He would wait two hours if I wanted him to. "Apologies."

I walked to my desk and took the seat opposite him.

Silence descended again as I studied him. My dispassionate gaze swept from his thinning brown hair to his tacky green shirt. His jacket stretched a little too tight across his shoulders, and a film of perspiration dotted his upper lip.

"Do you know why I asked for this meeting?" I asked conversationally.

"No. Your guy didn't say." Frank's eyes darted around. I'd had Kage bring him in, and I would've laughed at his obvious nervousness if I had an ounce of amusement left inside me. "I assume it has to do with my new business." His chest puffed up a little.

"Your new business."

He deflated. "Yes. I...I thought you wanted to talk business. Offer me security."

This time, I did laugh, though the sound lacked humor.

I wouldn't provide security for Frank Rivers even if he paid me a billion dollars and offered to wipe my ass every day for the rest of my life.

"No. That's not why I wanted to see you." I pulled open my desk drawer. "I heard you're a big fan of whisky."

Surprise flitted across his face, followed by confusion. "Yes..."

"I'm a fan myself." I retrieved a distinctive black box with gold lettering.

Judging by Frank's sharp inhale, he recognized it immediately.

"Yamakazi twenty-five-year-old whisky," I confirmed with a smile. "Cost me twenty grand."

I owned a bottle of fifty-five-year-old Yamakazi that cost forty times that, but I would never waste it on scum like Rivers.

"Would you like some?" I asked politely.

At Frank's eager nod—the man was practically salivating—I opened the bottle and filled the two crystal glasses sitting on my desk.

My lip curled with disdain when Frank pounced on his before I finished pouring the second.

No manners. Emily Post must be rolling in her grave.

"I did have one question," I said before the glass fully reached his fleshy lips. "When you groped my date at the event last night, which hand did you use?"

He froze. All the color blanched from his skin. "What—I—"

"My date." I leaned back, leaving my own drink untouched. "Tall, curly dark hair, black dress. The most beautiful woman at the event."

"I—I didn't know...I didn't know she was your date." Frank's stuttered excuse was almost as pathetic as his etiquette. "I'm sor—"

"I'm not interested in your apology. I'm interested in an answer." The finely honed edge of my rage sliced through my cordial mask. The thought of him even breathing in Stella's presence, much less fucking touching her, made acid burn in my blood. "Which. Hand?"

Sweat stains bloomed on Frank's shirt. "R-right."

"I see." My smile returned. "Put the drink down."

He was holding it with his right hand.

"I swear, I didn't know! I—I arrived late and—"

My eyes narrowed.

After a beat of hesitation, he set the drink down with a tremble. I could've sworn I heard an actual whimper.

My disdain deepened. *Pathetic.*

I waited until Frank's palm hit the wooden surface before I pulled the blade from my drawer and drove it through his hand. Flesh and bone yielded like butter to the cold, razor-sharp steel.

An inhuman howl ripped through the room while I frowned at the blood pooling on the vintage mahogany.

Perhaps I should've done this on a less expensive surface, but alas, it was too late.

I returned my attention to Frank. His eyes bulged with pain, and wheezing gasps left his throat as sweat trickled down the sides of his face.

"You made a mistake, Mr. Rivers." I kept my grip on the handle of the blade as I leaned forward.

"You touched what was mine. And if there's one thing I hate..." I pushed the knife deeper, letting the serrated edge tear through his flesh with agonizing slowness until his cries reached an inhuman pitch. "It's people touching what's mine."

"*Please.* I'm sorry. I—oh God." He let out a pained sob.

The sharp smell of urine filled the air.

Oh, for fuck's sake. That was a custom-made leather chair.

My back teeth clenched, but a glance at the clock told me I needed to wrap this up.

"I'm in a good mood, so I'll leave your hand intact." I could've stretched our session out for another hour, but it was taco night with Stella, and I needed to buy the ingredients on my way home.

"But if you ever touch, look at, or so much as *think* about Stella again..." I shoved the blade in all the way until the only remaining visible part was the handle. Frank had lost his voice from screaming and could only choke out a pained sob. "Your hand won't be the only thing I'll chop off."

I straightened, then paused.

"Ah, I forgot you wanted to try the whiskey." I picked up his glass and tilted it. The contents dripped onto his ravaged hand until the glass was empty and Frank's renewed screams bounced off the walls.

Hmm. Guess he has some voice left in him after all.

There was nothing like a bit of alcohol on an open wound to drive home the pain.

"Don't worry about reimbursing me for the wasted alcohol," I said. "I'll take it out of your account. Argent Bank, account number 904058891314, routing number 087945660, correct?"

He stared at me, his eyes swollen with tears and glassy with pain.

"I'll take that as a yes." I patted his cheek. "Let's keep this between us, shall we? I'd hate for us to have another chat."

I made it halfway to the door before I stopped. A mental image of the fucker grabbing Stella's ass flashed through my mind, and the rage resurfaced, churning like icy black waves beneath my skin.

"I changed my mind." I turned. "I'm not in a good mood after all."

The gunshot ripped through the air. Frank slumped onto the desk with a hole in the back of his head and open, lifeless eyes.

I tucked the gun back into my jacket and exited into the hall, where Kage lounged against the wall.

"Don't tell me you shot him," he said when he saw me. The office was soundproofed, but he correctly assessed my expression. "What a fucking mess."

"He pissed me off." I checked my watch. *Dammit.* The only grocery store that sold Stella's favorite salsa closed in fifteen minutes. "Clean that up for me, will you?"

"I always do," he said dryly.

Not everyone at Harper Security knew about the less legal side of the business, but Kage had seen enough shit in his life to keep his morals flexible. The world wasn't black and white; no one knew that better than someone who'd lived in the gray.

I washed my hands in the bathroom on my way out and inspected my clothes for any specks of blood before I gunned it to the grocery store.

36

STELLA

"THAT'S ALL I NEEDED. THANK YOU FOR YOUR TIME," Julian said.

We'd just finished our last interview for my *Washington Weekly* profile. We'd had a series of conversations themed around different aspects of my life over the past few weeks, and today, we'd discussed my fashion line for a good fifteen minutes after I mentioned it in passing.

It was off the record since Delamonte wouldn't appreciate me talking about my own brand in a story that was supposed to be about them, but I was excited to discuss it with someone who wasn't Christian or my friends. It made it more real.

"Of course. Let me know if you have any additional questions," I said warmly.

"I will, and I'll email you when the story is live. Congratulations again on everything."

I hung up and stretched with a yawn. It was late afternoon, but I felt like I'd been up for twenty-four hours straight. I'd finished all the samples for my collection last week and had spent the day taking photos of them for future marketing materials.

I was used to photoshoots, but I hadn't realized how much harder it was to take product photos for a website versus a blog.

Pieces from the shoot were scattered all over the room, including props, clothing, and camera equipment.

I forced myself off the couch so I could tidy up the mess before Christian came home.

Our dinners were my favorite part of the day. He always came home early enough to help with the cooking (though I suspected that was partly because he didn't trust me near the oven after the smoke alarm incident), and we spent the nights unwinding and talking.

I liked fancy dates and galas as much as the next girl, but nothing made me happier than simply spending time with someone I—

"Sorry I'm late."

I straightened and lit up when Christian walked in.

I finally understood why my friends gushed over their significant others. Every time I saw him or heard his voice, the butterflies went crazy.

"I had to get more salsa." He kissed me and placed his shopping bag on the coffee table.

I brightened further.

"Is that the brand that I like?" I recognized the name stamped on the bag. It was the only grocery store in the city that carried my favorite salsa.

"Yes." Christian's mouth tipped up when I squealed and peeked inside the bag. The grocery store was on the other side of the city, so I rarely made it out there even though it stocked some of my most loved, hard-to-find items.

The sight of the two glass jars made me inordinately happy.

It wasn't the salsa per se; it ~~~~~~~~~~~~~~~~~~~~~~
way to buy them for me.

"Congrats, you just wo~~~~~~~~~~~~~~~~

"Did I?" He placed hi~~~~~~~~~~~~~~~
arms around his neck. "W~~~~~~~~~~~~

"This." I gave him and~~~~~~~~~~~~~
groan.

It was only when I ~~~~~~~~~~~~~~~~
noticed the tension bunch~~~~~~~~~~~~~

I pulled back and e~~~~~~~~~~~~~~~~~
everything okay? You seem tense."

"Yes." Christian's expression didn't flicker. "Just a minor irritation at work."

"Hmm." I worried about him sometimes. He had an important job, but all that stress wasn't good for anyone.

Despite my best efforts to convince him, he also refused to take up yoga or meditation.

An idea sparked in my head. It was so out of character I almost dismissed it out of hand, but I was a new, bolder me. I could try new things.

Maybe.

"Sit on the couch." I tamped down the uprising of nerves in my stomach and kept my voice casual. "I can think of something that'll help you relax."

Christian did as I asked.

"Another massage?" he drawled, but his eyes darkened when I sank onto my knees before him.

"Sort of." I reached for his belt. His hand gripped my wrist before I made contact, and the air shifted into something heavier, more condensed.

"What," he said, his voice dropping to a rough pitch that made my thighs clench. "Are you doing?"

"I told you." I pulled my wrist free from his grasp and

unbuckled his belt, my
bird's. "I'm helping
Christian ar~
so bold abou~
Usua~
he got

heart fluttering like a nervous humming-
_____ you relax."

_____ I took turns initiating sex, but I'd never been

_____ ly, all it took was a certain look or smile from me and
_____ the hint. But this...this was way outside my comfort zone.

He didn't stop me again, but the heat of his gaze settled low
in my stomach.

My mouth dried when I finally worked him free of his
pants.

He was already hard, his arousal thick and dripping with
pre-cum. He let me set the pace as I slowly took him down my
throat, but he was so big I had to pause every few seconds to
adjust.

Eventually, however, I took him to the hilt and stayed there
for a minute with my lips stretched wide against the base of his
shaft.

I hummed with pride before I started moving. Slowly at
first, then faster as I got more comfortable with his size and the
angle.

Christian let out a low curse and tangled his hands in my
hair when I settled into a rhythm, licking and sucking until his
muscles tightened beneath my touch. I flattened my tongue and
ran it along the underside of his cock as I withdrew, then gently
sucked the head and slid him all the way down my throat again.

His grip tightened on my hair.

"*Fuck*, Stella." Christian's tortured groan sent another
arrow of lust to my core. "That feels so fucking good,
sweetheart."

I moaned with satisfaction and redoubled my efforts. Drool
leaked from the corners of my stuffed mouth and dripped down
my chin, but I didn't stop.

The blowjob was for him, but every groan and slide of his

heat against my tongue pulsed between my legs like it was for me.

I loved knowing that I could turn him on like this. That I could give and take pleasure at will.

I was on my knees, but I had the power to bring him to his.

"I knew you could take it. Every inch, just like that." His praise washed over me as I gagged around the base of his cock. "Good girl."

The ache deepened, and I couldn't take it anymore. I shifted positions so I could grind against his leg while I increased my pace and savored the hot, erotic taste of him.

It was easier for me to come when I was grinding on something versus using my fingers, and the firm pressure against my clit mixed with the filthy, sloppy sounds of the blowjob drove me higher toward release with each passing second.

I was drenched and probably making a mess of his pants, but I was too lost in a fog of lust to care.

"I can feel how wet your cunt is." Christian pulled my head back so I stared straight up at him, my eyes watering from taking him so deep for so long. "Does this turn you on, hmm? Grinding against my leg while you choke on my cock?"

"Mmmph." My muffled moan of affirmation cut off in a gasp when he abruptly pulled me off him, picked me up, and pushed me against the window in one fluid motion.

Desire pooled between my legs at the press of glass against my cheek and the heat of him at my back.

I loved when he was like this.

Rough. Demanding. A beast uncaged.

Christian yanked my dress straps off my shoulders and pulled the bodice down to bare my breasts.

"When you come..." He rucked the skirt up with his other hand and hooked his finger in the waistband of my underwear. "It'll be with my cock inside your pussy, not your throat."

I heard the tear of lace and the unmistakable rip of foil.

Then he was inside me, fucking me so deep and hard the living room echoed with the sounds of my cries.

My hands splayed against the window, which fogged with my gasping breaths.

It was made of tinted glass so people couldn't see inside, but there was still something so deliciously dirty about being taken against it while people went about their lives outside, oblivious to what was happening above their heads.

Christian pounded me savagely, with sharp, brutal thrusts that scrambled my thoughts into nothing.

There was no trace of the refined CEO. No suits, no polite charm, only his cock filling me up and his hand around my throat while he fucked me like an animal from behind.

His length stretched my inner muscles in a tight burn as I stood on tiptoes trying to take him deeper. Every scape of my rock-hard nipples against the cold glass sent another spark to the inferno building at the base of my spine.

Harsh breaths and needy whimpers mingled with the slap of flesh against flesh and the wet, slick sounds of his cock drilling into me.

The filthy symphony swirled around us, dragging me higher and higher until I crescendoed toward orgasm.

"Christian, *please*." His grip on my throat stole my screams and turned them into hoarse pleas. "I need...I'm going to..."

I lost the rest of my sentence to another wave of pleasure when he reached around to stroke my clit.

Once. Twice. Just enough to deepen the ache, but not enough to break the leash on my swelling release.

"I love when you beg so sweetly for me." He buried his face in my neck and nipped at the skin. "Do you need to come, hmm?"

"*Yes.*" My answer spilled out in a sob.

"Then be a good girl and push that pretty little cunt back on me."

I obeyed without thinking. I arched my back so I could fuck back at him while he gripped my hips with both hands and slammed me onto him. Broken squeals and whimpers fell out as my body shook like a rag doll's from the combined force of our efforts.

"Just like that," he groaned. "You look so beautiful like this, spread wide with my cock buried inside that tight pussy."

Electricity replaced the blood in my veins. I was lit up from the inside out, a live wire of sensation that he stoked hotter with every thrust.

Christian's hold on my throat tightened while he reached around and pinched my nipple with his other hand.

"Come for me, sweetheart."

That was all it took.

My orgasm finally broke free. It crashed through its restraints and consumed me whole, sending a wave of heat from the top of my head to the tips of my toes.

My body bowed from the intensity of the pleasure, and I would've collapsed onto the ground had Christian not been holding me up.

I was still floating on my high when he turned me around and lifted me up so my back was against the glass and my legs hooked around his waist.

He hadn't come yet, but his strokes slowed into a gentler rhythm.

"I love feeling you come around me." He kissed his way up my neck to my mouth. "You are fucking perfect."

The words hit me somewhere deep and vulnerable.

Emotion lodged in my throat, but I wrapped my arms around his neck and rode him faster, more comfortable with taking the lead than examining the feelings his statement brought to the surface.

Christian's breaths harshened. His muscles went taut, and I could feel him throbbing inside me before he finally came with a loud groan.

We held each other in the come down, our skin slick with sweat and our foreheads pressed against each while we caught our breath.

"So," I panted. "Do you feel more relaxed?"

His laugh rumbled against my skin and made me smile. I loved pulling a real laugh out of him. They were more common these days, but they were still sources of pride.

"Yes, Butterfly. I do."

"Good." I clung to him as he carried us to the shower.

If I were with anyone else, I never would've found the courage to do what I'd just done. The fear of rejection would've been too strong, even with someone I was dating.

But that was one of my favorite things about Christian. I could be who I was and who I aspired to be in equal measure.

I never had to worry when I was with him.

37

CHRISTIAN

My nights with Stella were the only peace I had.

My days were a tumult of work and chaos. I'd spent the past month weeding out suspects for the traitor, figuring out how the hell someone created a device similar to Scylla, what that someone's connection to Stella's stalker was, and tracking down the stalker bastard himself.

I already had a shortlist of suspects for the leak. Every name made my blood run cold, but I had to be careful how I handled the situation. I couldn't make a public move until I was certain who the traitor was. Loyalty ran both ways, and false accusations were the fastest way to seed resentment among the ranks.

I had the perfect trap in mind, but I needed to wait until Harper Security's annual poker tournament to set it. Until then, I couldn't trust anyone in the company with sensitive information.

As for Scylla, I could almost guarantee Sentinel was the one behind the knockoff device. They'd imitated everything else I'd done; copying proprietary hardware was the logical next step. I also wouldn't put it past them to bribe or blackmail whoever the traitor was.

I sat on that suspicion. First, I'll deal with the traitor. Then, I'll go after Sentinel.

The only remaining question mark was their ties to Stella's stalker and who the fucker was.

I'd combed through Stella's contacts, but she'd interacted with so many people over the years it was impossible to narrow them down to a decent suspect pool. The stalker could be anyone from an old colleague to the barista who made her drink every day.

Part of me admitted I could've gotten further in *all* my investigations had I not been distracted. I wanted to spend time with Stella, which meant no long hours or overtime at the office.

I took her on dates every weekend, ate dinner with her every evening, and fucked her into oblivion every night, all the while knowing I should spend that time doing something else.

Stella's ability to fuck with my rational decision-making crystallized a little over a week after Frank Rivers' timely demise.

I clicked and unclicked my pen as I stared at the note on my desk.

The stalker had gone underground since Hawaii. No new notes and no contact...until now.

Click. Click.

Two sentences, typed and delivered in a plain, unmarked envelope. It'd been tucked in with the rest of our mail even though it didn't contain an address.

You can't protect her, and you will NEVER have her. She's mine.

Whispers of rage brushed my senses.

The message itself wasn't concerning. It sounded like something a petulant child would write.

What *was* concerning were the three photographs that'd accompanied it: one of Stella getting breakfast at the cafe near the Mirage, one of her taking photos at the National Mall, and one of her exiting the grocery store.

All of them had been taken in the weeks since we returned from Hawaii.

The rage thickened and coated my skin with frost. I was tempted to give in and take it out on one of the many names I kept in my database for that very purpose, but I suppressed the urge in favor of calculating my next move.

I couldn't trust anyone except myself with Stella's safety, not even Brock. He wasn't one of my suspects, but he hadn't noticed the stalker getting close enough to take those photos of her, which was a big fucking oversight.

Granted, his job was protection, not surveillance, but it still pissed me off.

The stalker had resurfaced after weeks of radio silence, and I bet a forensic analysis of his note would return the same results as it always did.

Nothing.

Whoever he was, he was damn good at keeping his hands clean and sneaky enough to get that close to Stella without her or Brock noticing.

If anything happened to her...

My stomach clenched.

D.C. wasn't safe until I sorted out my internal mess. I couldn't focus on tracking down the stalker if I couldn't trust my men.

Click. Click.

I made up my mind on the second click.

I set my pen on my desk, tucked the note and photos inside my inside jacket pocket, and drove home.

Stella was in the kitchen when I arrived. She was so busy blending that atrocious wheatgrass smoothie she loved and humming along to the radio that she didn't notice my entrance until I wrapped my arms around her from behind and kissed her neck.

"Christian!" Surprised delight filled her voice. "You're home early."

"Slow day at work," I lied.

I breathed her in, reassuring myself that she was safe and in my arms. She smelled like sunshine and green florals, and I let the scent dissolve some of the tension in my muscles before I spoke again.

"I had an idea."

"Uh oh," she teased. "Should I be scared?"

"I doubt it. It's on your vision board."

I'd seen the list she'd pinned to the corkboard in our room. She said she'd created it in college and never threw it out.

The list consisted of three things: a brand partnership with Delamonte, an extended trip through Italy, and a walk-in closet. Two of those three were crossed off.

Stella turned to face me fully. Her eyes had widened with shock and a touch of hope.

"Italy," I confirmed. "Summer vacation. We can do a month-long trip through the country. Rome, Milan, the Amalfi Coast..."

Taking her out of town was the obvious answer until I sorted out the mess on my side, and her bucket list gave me perfect cover for the trip.

I didn't want to tell Stella about the stalker's latest note. It'd been directed at me, not her, and I didn't want to freak her out. Not when I didn't have a clear solution yet.

"*Another* trip?" Doubt colored her voice. "But we just got back from Hawaii."

She was right. We'd returned from Kauai only a month ago. It was too soon for another trip, especially with everything I had on my plate.

But the thought of that asshole possibly getting his hands on her...

It took only one slip up. One distraction, one mistake, and I could lose her forever.

I forced my lungs to expand past a rare bout of panic.

"The first half didn't count since it was for work," I said. "It was basically a long weekend."

Stella shook her head. "I'm beginning to suspect you don't actually work when you go into the office. I've never met a CEO with more vacation time than you."

My mouth tipped up despite myself. "It's a different type of work."

I earned a decent salary from Harper Security, but the bulk of my net worth came from the secret software and hardware I developed and sold to the highest bidder. There were certain groups I didn't do business with—terrorists, certain governments, and a few distasteful individuals.

Other than that, everyone else was fair game, and they paid a king's ransom for technology their competitors didn't have.

I spent fifty percent of my office time running Harper Security and the other half on development.

"Are you sure a month isn't too long?" Traces of doubt lingered. "We can't just up and leave for that long."

"I'm a billionaire. We can do whatever we want." I smiled at her playful eye roll. "Consider it my birthday present."

"We already celebrated your birthday," she pointed out.

I'd turned thirty-four last week. We'd celebrated with a

weekend of food, sex, and me eating her pussy out until she came on my face.

It'd been a good birthday.

"Besides, it doesn't make sense that you would take me on *my* dream trip for your birthday. We should go somewhere you want to go." Stella hooked her arms around my neck. "Spill it, Harper. What's your bucket list destination?"

"Don't have one, and spoiling you *is* for me." I dropped my forehead to hers. The note and photos burned a hole in my pocket. "Last chance, Butterfly. You in or you out?"

"When you put it *that* way..." A giddy smile spread across her face. "I'm in."

"Perfect." I kissed her again, this time on the mouth.

Fuck rationality.

When it came to Stella's safety, rational thought didn't exist.

38

STELLA

JUNE 16

I'M GOING TO ITALY!

Okay, I just had to get that off my chest because I still can't believe it. I've wanted to visit for so long, but I kept putting it off because I didn't want to go for just a week. I wanted to do the whole shebang like Christian said. Venice, Rome, Positano... I never found the time or money, but now, here I am, packing for a month-long trip.

I can't wait. I've already messaged Bridget for a list of her must-sees. I know Christian has visited Italy tons of times before too, but he's a guy. It's not the same. (Plus Bridget knows all the cutest cafes and best boutiques).

It does make me a bit uncomfortable that I'm spending so much of his money. I told Jules this the other day, and she told me not to worry about it because Christian has so much money that the amount he's spent on me is pennies to him. I guess that's true.

Every time I try to pay for something, he refuses and says I should invest that money into my brand instead. That's the one thing I drew a line at. I didn't want him throwing money at the line. If I do it, I want to do it on my own merits. I don't want to succeed just because I have a rich boyfriend who can bankroll me.

But, if I'm being 100% honest, it's hard for me to protest too much about the trip because I want it so much.

An all-expenses-paid trip to Italy? That's every girl's dream.

DAILY GRATITUDE:

1. *Bucket lists*
2. *Italy*
3. *The best boyfriend in the world <3*

ITALY WAS AS INCREDIBLE AS I'D IMAGINED. THE FOOD, THE beauty, the culture...everything lived up to my expectations and more.

Granted, part of that had to do with Christian getting us VIP access everywhere so we could avoid the crowds and explore at our leisure, but it wasn't just that. There was something magical in the air that melted my stress and turned my worries into distant memories.

Unlike Hawaii, which had a work element despite the dreamy second half of the trip, Italy was pure escapism.

I took videos and photos, but they were for memories more than for social media.

I couldn't share that I was currently in Italy, anyway, so I'd been posting old photos.

Other than that, there was no work, no cameras, just us.

In Italy, I wasn't a brand ambassador or a content creator

chasing the perfect photo. I was just a girl on vacation with her boyfriend.

It was liberating...*when* said boyfriend wasn't being a jerk about my driving skills.

"It's a Vespa. How hard can it be?" I planted my hands on my hips and leveled Christian with an insulted glare.

"I'm not saying it's hard. I'm saying there are a lot of pedestrians you can run over in the city." His mouth twitched at my gasp.

"I am *not* going to run over anyone. I have zero vehicular deaths on my watch, thank you very much."

"What about near deaths?"

I didn't dignify that with a response.

It was our first full day in Rome and our second week in Italy. We'd flown into Milan, made our way down to Florence, and arrived in Rome yesterday evening.

We had a full day of activities ahead of us, and I'd insisted on using Vespas to get around.

It might be cliche, but could one say they've visited Rome without riding a Vespa at least once?

Unfortunately, Christian and I had different opinions on how many we should rent. I thought it would be fun if we each had our own while he was convinced I would kill someone if left to my own devices.

Apparently, he wasn't over the ATV incident in Hawaii. It hadn't been my fault; I'd merely been rusty. I rarely needed to drive a car in D.C. when the Metro and buses were right there.

He sighed when he saw I wasn't backing down.

"Let's compromise. You let me teach you how to operate one, and if you pass the test, you can get your own."

"What is this, the DMV?" I grumbled, but I agreed.

Secretly, I was glad he'd offered to teach me because I had no clue how to operate a Vespa. It couldn't be that different from riding a bicycle, right? The only difference was it had an engine.

We'd rented our scooters from our hotel, and we stayed in the courtyard while Christian walked me through the proper procedure.

"Sit straighter and bend your elbows a little...a little more. Like this." Christian adjusted my position until I sat properly on the Vespa. "Now find your balance by shifting your body to the left and the right."

I followed his instructions until he declared me ready for the test.

"Don't look so nervous," I said as he tightened my helmet. "I'll be *fine*. I'm literally driving around the courtyard."

"Hmm."

I did not appreciate the amount of skepticism imbued in that one noise.

I switched on the bike and sped off.

See? This wasn't so bad. I was doing great. The cobblestones were a *little* hard to navigate, but I could—

"Shit!"

I'd turned too late and sideswiped one of the giant flower pots bordering the hotel's outdoor cafe.

I stuttered to a stop and cut off the engine while Christian came up beside me.

We stared at the giant crack in the terracotta urn. Luckily, it was so early the cafe hadn't opened yet, but the gardener working nearby saw the whole thing.

He shook his head. I thought I heard a faint *mio Dio* before he returned to his pruning duties.

I got off the Vespa and wordlessly handed Christian the keys.

My *tiny* little Vespa incident aside, our Rome stop went as smoothly as possible until our second to last day, when Christian and I visited one of the city's top art museums.

I'd been hesitant about putting so many museums on our itinerary since he wasn't an art fan at all, but he'd insisted we go to as many as I wanted.

We're in Italy, Butterfly. You can't visit Italy without visiting its museums.

To his credit, Christian hid his distaste well. If I hadn't known about his aversion to art beforehand, I would've thought he *enjoyed* the exhibitions.

"There's *no* way that is a person." I stopped in front of a painting that'd caught my eye and tried to parse out what, exactly, it depicted. "Did optical illusions exist in the eighteenth century?"

One second, it looked like a portrait of a nobleman. The next, it looked like a lurid table display of fruit.

It was unsettling but also kind of genius.

"Christian?" I turned at his odd lack of response and found him staring at something on the other end of the gallery.

I followed his gaze to where a young boy stood in the corner. He tugged insistently on what I assumed was his mother's sleeve, but the woman was too busy fawning over the paintings and taking pictures to pay him any attention.

The boy's chin wobbled, but instead of crying, he set his jaw and glared down the length of the gallery.

His eyes met Christian's, who stared back with what almost looked like a sympathetic expression.

I placed a hand on his arm. "Christian," I said, my voice softer. "Are you okay?"

He broke eye contact and turned his attention back to me. Tension poured off him in waves, and the set of his shoulders was visibly tighter than when we'd arrived.

"Yes." His smile didn't fool me for a second. "I'm fine."

"Do you know him?" I gestured subtly in the boy's direction, but when I looked again, he and his mother were gone.

"No. He..." Christian rubbed a hand over his jaw. "He reminded me of someone. That's all."

I had an inkling I knew who that *someone* was.

"Let's get a drink," I said. "I've seen all I wanted to see here."

He didn't argue.

We left the museum and made our way to a nearby cafe. Tucked on a quiet side street away from tourists, it was blessedly empty save for an older couple and a stunningly chic woman with a sleek black bob.

Christian and I took a seat in the corner of the outdoor dining area. The other customers were so far away we might as well be alone.

I waited until the server set our drinks on the table and disappeared into the kitchen before I spoke.

"The person that boy reminded you of. Was it you?" I kept my voice gentle. I didn't want Christian to feel like I was ambushing him, but we'd dated long enough that I wasn't as wary about broaching his past as I used to be.

He was naturally guarded, and I understood that. I didn't go around sharing details about my personal life with anyone who would listen either. But if we were going to make our relationship work, he needed to feel as comfortable opening up to me as I did with him.

I thought Christian might brush off my question the way he always did, but he surprised me with an eventual nod.

"Before you ask, I wasn't neglected as a child," he said. "Not in the way you think. My parents weren't abusive. Like I said, they were the quintessential American family, except..."

I waited, not wanting to push him.

"I told you my father was a software engineer. What I

didn't tell you was what he moonlighted as." Christian leaned back in his chair. "Have you ever heard of the art thief, The Ghost?"

My eyes widened with surprise at the seemingly sudden shift in topic, but I nodded.

I'd learned about him in my art crime and law class at Thayer. The Ghost, so named because he'd stolen dozens of priceless artworks without leaving a trace of evidence behind, was one of the most notorious art thieves of the late twentieth century. He'd operated for almost a decade before the police finally caught him and shot him when he tried to flee.

The details of his death were murky, and the stolen artworks were never recovered.

I told you my father was a software engineer. What I didn't tell you was what he moonlighted as.

Christian's words replayed in my head, and my breath caught in my throat.

"Your father. He was..."

"Yes."

The quiet word landed with the force of a nuclear bomb.

Oh my God.

The Ghost's identity had *never* been publicly revealed, not even after his death. No one knew why, but rumors abounded. Some said he had a powerful family who paid off the authorities, others said his real persona was so ordinary that the authorities were embarrassed they hadn't caught him before.

In the space of five seconds, Christian had just answered one of the biggest mysteries in the art world.

I was still wrapping my head around this explosive new piece of information when Christian continued.

"Ironically, he wasn't the big art lover in the family. My mother was. He claimed he stole the paintings as proof of his love for her. His willingness to risk everything just to make her happy. You'd think she would try to talk him out of it, but she encouraged it. Sometimes, she even joined him. She loved the thrill and the idea that he would go to such extremes for her. They tried to hide what they were doing from me when I was younger, but I eventually caught on. There were too many coincidences between my father's mysterious *business trips* and the dates the stolen art were reported on the news. When I confronted my father about it, he confessed."

Christian gave me a hard smile. "Even as a child, I wasn't the type to share the dirty details of my life with anyone. He knew he could trust me not to share his secret."

My chest clenched at the thought of a young Christian being burdened with such a big secret.

Maybe his parents hadn't been physically abusive, but it sounded like they hadn't cared about his emotional or mental well-being at all.

"When I was thirteen, he went on another heist. Instead of a museum, he tried to rob some wealthy businessman's house. The businessman had famously acquired a big art piece at auction, and my mom was desperate to have it. My father almost got away with it, but he tripped an alarm and got caught on his way out. He refused to surrender, and the police shot him when he tried to steal a gun off an officer and make another run for it. He died on the spot."

"My mom lost it when she heard the news. Two days after my father died, she decided she couldn't live without him and put a bullet in her own head. I'd been at school. My aunt came, called me into the principal's office, and told me." Another, more bitter smile cut across Christian's face. "It's like a fucked-up suburban version of Romeo and Juliet. Romantic, isn't it?"

A deep, painful ache unfurled behind my ribs.

I couldn't imagine what it was like to grow up in the family he'd grown up in, or to lose both parents at such a young age. I didn't have the best relationship with mine, but at least they were alive.

"My mother would rather die than live without my father, but she was perfectly fine leaving her only son behind." Christian's caustic laugh singed my lungs. "A mother's love is the greatest love of all, right? That's bullshit."

The ache spread burned behind my eyes.

I tentatively reached for his hand and curled mine over it.

"I'm so sorry," I said quietly. I didn't know what else to say.

I wished there were magic words I could utter that would make him feel better. But nothing could change the past, and people had to deal with their trauma in their own time.

Christian had been holding onto his for decades. It would take more than a few nice words to heal it.

The best thing I could do was be there for him when he was finally ready to confront it.

"I've never told anyone that before." The haunted expression lingered in his eyes for a moment longer before it disappeared.

"Now that I've ruined a beautiful Italian afternoon with my poor little sob story, we should go." Christian rose, his face an impassive mask once again. "We have lunch reservations in half an hour."

"You didn't ruin it." I squeezed his hand. "I care more about you than any fancy meal or museum outing."

Christian's jaw flexed. His gaze held mine for a brief, burning moment before he turned away.

"We should go," he repeated, his voice rough with emotion.

I let the moment pass. I sensed he'd reached his limit for personal introspection today.

We paid and left the cafe, but when we neared the main street, he paused. "Stella."

"Hmm?"

"Thank you for listening."

The ache returned in full force. "Thank you for telling me."

Christian thought he'd ruined our afternoon when, in fact, he'd made it. Not because I enjoyed hearing the heartbreaking details of his childhood, but because he'd finally let me in.

No more hiding behind his walls.

Despite all the luxury hotels we'd stayed at, the gourmet meals we'd eaten, and the extravagant activities we'd done, that was the best part of our trip so far.

As dreamy as our vacation was, I loved it not because I was in Italy but because I was in Italy with *him*.

And that made all the difference in the world.

39

CHRISTIAN/STELLA

CHRISTIAN

Italy was a strange dichotomy of calm and chaos. I spent my days visiting local landmarks and shopping with Stella and my nights monitoring the situation in D.C. after she fell asleep.

I'd called in a favor and asked Alex to keep an eye on things for me while I was gone. He didn't have any unusual updates for me, but I remained on edge. My gut told me something was brewing on the horizon and that I damn well wouldn't like what it was.

Until I had a clearer picture of what I was up against, however, there was nothing I could do.

I pushed thoughts of D.C. out of my mind as Stella and I walked down a winding street in Positano. It was nearing sunset, and pastels painted the sky in a soft palette of pinks, purples, and oranges.

We were in week three of our Italy trip, and we'd left the cities behind for the seaside charm of the Amalfi Coast. We'd wound our way through Salerno and Ravello and arrived in

Positano yesterday. Next was Sorrento, followed by our last stop in Capri.

A smile played on my mouth as Stella tipped her head back with a dreamy expression.

She was always beautiful, but in Italy, freed from the pressures of the city and the lurking threat of her stalker, she was a different person. Happier, more playful and carefree, even compared to Hawaii.

I twined my fingers through hers when we resumed walking toward a viewpoint for sunset. I normally hated hand-holding, but I could make the occasional exception. We were on vacation, after all.

"So, does Italy live up to your expectations?" I asked.

"Nope." An impish smile appeared at my raised brow. "It's exceeded them. This place is..." She sighed. "*Incredible*. I mean, look at it."

My smile blossomed into a grin when she released my hand and twirled. Her white dress flared around her thighs, and the setting sun gilded her skin with gold.

She looked so content and at peace I wished I could keep us here forever, ensconced in a bubble and untouched by the dangers that lurked back home.

"I'd rather look at you," I said.

Stella stopped in front of me, breathless from her spin. Her gaze locked onto mine, and the summer air grew heavier between us, sweet with the scents of lemon verbena and sunshine.

"For someone who claims he's not a romantic, you say the most romantic things." She plucked a petal from a nearby flowering tree and tucked it into the pocket of my linen shirt. "I'm onto you, Christian Harper. Beneath that hard, cynical exterior..." She pressed her hand flat against my chest. "You're a softie at heart."

I would've laughed had she not been half right.

Only for you.

I lifted her hand and curled mine protectively around it.

"If you tell anyone, I'll have to kill them." I smiled to soften the statement, even though I wasn't joking.

In my world, weakness was unacceptable, and she was the greatest weakness I had.

Stella gave me an exasperated look. "You always have to bring death into it."

I laughed.

We continued walking until we reached the viewpoint. Nestled high in the hills and hidden from tourist traffic, it offered a perfect view of the pastel buildings and deep blue sea below.

Stella rested her head on my shoulder and stared dreamily at the landscape. "I'm in love with this place."

I wrapped an arm around her waist and drew her closer. My eyes lingered on the delicate lines of her profile, tracing a path from the stray dark curls billowing around her face to the sparkle in her eyes and the curve of her lips.

I didn't care much for art, but if I could immortalize her in that moment as a painting, I would.

The setting sun cast a gorgeous glow over the island, but I didn't bother looking at the view. I kept my gaze on Stella.

"Me too."

STELLA

My relationship with Christian could be measured in incremental shifts. It started with my move into the Mirage and inched forward milestone by milestone—our almost kiss, his confession, dinner with my family, Hawaii, our real kiss, and a million other moments that transformed us from strangers to something so much more.

But our time in Italy, especially after what he shared about his family, felt like more than an incremental shift.

It felt like a turning point.

Perhaps the turning point should've been our first time having sex or when we'd agreed to officially date, but Christian had never shared as much about himself as he had in Rome. And it hadn't been just anything; it'd been a fundamental part of his upbringing, something that'd shaped him into who he was today.

He'd finally opened up. His past was ugly and messy, but it was real, and that was all I could ask for.

I turned my head and watched Christian adjust something on the boat's instrument panel.

I'd seen him captain a boat before in Hawaii, but that'd been in the dark. In the sunlight, wearing nothing but black Tom Ford swim shorts and miles of bronzed skin, he looked like a Greek god come down from Mount Olympus.

"You should captain a boat more often." I stretched, luxuriating in the sunshine. "It's sexy."

It was something I would've cringed at saying to anyone else, but I didn't have to worry when I was with Christian. I could say anything and he wouldn't judge or laugh at me.

His eyes glowed with amusement. "Good to know." The rich, slightly husky timbre of his voice sent a delicious thrill down my spine.

We were currently anchored off the coast of Capri, our last stop in Italy.

There was no one around except us, a gentle breeze, and the faint scent of coconut sunscreen and salt-tinged sea air. The island's famous Faraglioni rocks loomed in the distance like mountainous sentries emerging from the deep blue depths of the Tyrrhenian Sea, and the gentle rock[...] dream-like quality to the scene.

In fact, the entire past month had been a dr[...] scared I would wake up and find out it'd all been a[...] my imagination.

There was magic in reality, no matter how temporary.

"You're overthinking again." Christian could always tell when I spiraled down the dark paths of my mind.

"I can't help it," I admitted. "It's my default setting."

He settled beside me and wrapped a muscular arm around my waist. "What are you thinking about?"

"About how this doesn't feel real," I said softly. "It's too good to be true."

Every time something good happened to me, something terrible lurked in the wings, waiting to drag me down from my high.

My relationship with Christian had been perfect so far, but a part of me was waiting for that inevitable crash.

"It *is* real." He pressed his mouth to the base of my throat. "And if it isn't, I'll find a way to make it real." His kisses burned a path up my neck to my mouth. "There's nothing I wouldn't do for you, Stella."

My heart expanded so fast and full I thought it might explode.

"I know," I whispered.

Christian pressed a light kiss on my mouth before he slid a hand over my hip. "Good. Now..." He hooked a finger in the string of my bikini. "Let's quiet that overactive mind of yours, shall we?"

The air shifted. Heat drowned the soft emotion from a moment ago, and suddenly, my flushed skin had nothing to do with the sun blazing overhead.

...pt to play it cool. "How do

...ensual wisp of smoke in my ...the boat, Butterfly."

...painful insistence between ...ed up, but...

...ea. There was no one else ...long at any moment.

..ise." Christian watched me carefully, his eyes like pools of golden-dipped amber in the sunlight. "Do you trust me?"

My pulse fluttered with nerves, but after a long, hesitant second, I nodded.

If he said no one would see us, no one would see us.

I would never tell him because I didn't want to inflate his ego to Jupiter-size proportions, but I was convinced Christian could bring down the stars if he wanted.

My reservations melted when I felt the first bite of the rope around my wrists. I'd taken my bikini off at his orders, and I lay face up on the cushioned seat at the end of the boat while he bound my wrists together above my head.

The tighter the ties, the wetter I got.

I used to feel ashamed or embarrassed about my sexual proclivities, but being with Christian had put most of my worries to rest. He never made me feel bad about what I wanted in bed. He pushed me out of my comfort zone and embraced my fantasies so thoroughly they felt normal—which they *were*, according to my online research, but there was a difference between knowing something and feeling it.

Still, my body tightened with surprise when I saw the silk scarf in his hands.

"If you want me to take it off, tell me," Christian said.

"Okay." My voice pitched higher than usual.

I'd never been blindfolded during sex. The thought of not seeing the world around me made my stomach flip, but my tension eased when he tied the scarf around my eyes.

The hint of sunlight filtering through the thin silk was enough to help me relax.

I waited.

And waited.

I heard Christian moving around the boat, but he didn't touch me.

In the absence of visual stimulation, all my thoughts turned to how vulnerable I was at that moment. My hands tied, my eyes covered, my body naked and bared to his gaze.

He could do anything he wanted to me.

Anticipation shivered over my skin.

I heard a soft *clink* and the nearing of footsteps.

My muscles pulled taut, waiting for—

A soft noise of surprise escaped when something cold pressed between my breasts.

An ice cube.

It didn't touch my nipples, but they immediately hardened from the proximate chill. They poked against my bikini top, so sensitive the friction sent a tingle straight to my core.

"It's a hot day," Christian said lazily. "We need to cool you off before we get started."

My breaths turned into pants when he dragged the ice cube down to my stomach, then up again, over and over until it melted against my skin.

I heard another *clink,* followed by the glide of another ice cube over my nipple.

Shivers erupted all over.

My nipples weren't just hard anymore; they were almost

painful with need as he circled them with the cube and rubbed it over the firm peaks.

Just when I couldn't take it anymore, when the pleasure and pain formed an unbearable burn, the wet warmth of Christian's mouth replaced the cold.

The sudden change in temperature sent shockwaves through my body.

"*Christian*," I gasped. "Oh God."

It wasn't just the ice, the tight bindings on my wrists, or the way I tugged and twisted that made everything feel impossibly erotic. It was the play between hot and cold, the heightening of my senses due to the blindfold, and the way he took his time pleasuring every inch of my body.

My neck, my breasts, my stomach...by the time he moved between my legs, I was already a wet, slick mess from both my arousal and melted ice.

A noise between a gasp and a yelp climbed up my throat when he rubbed a warmed cube over my swollen clit.

"You have the prettiest cunt I've ever seen." Christian groaned. "Open wider for me, sweetheart."

I spread my legs farther, and he pushed the ice inside me at the same time he sucked my clit into my mouth.

One ice cube. One flick of his tongue. One reach of his hand up to pinch my nipple.

That was all it took.

My mouth parted in a silent cry as my orgasm exploded behind my eyes and traveled down my body in electric waves. It was like the sensations were so intense they snatched away my ability to scream, gasp, or do anything else except burn in a fire so hot I disintegrated right then and there on the deck of the boat.

No thoughts, no words, just a boneless heap of pleasure.

The orgasm went on seemingly forever, but when it finally subsided, sound rushed back in a deafening wave.

I sank deeper into the cushion, my chest heaving with ragged breaths.

I was so dazed I didn't hear Christian switching positions until he hiked my legs up onto his shoulders.

"You look so beautiful tied up and blindfolded." The tip of his cock brushed against my still sensitive sex as his voice roughened. "There's no one around, Stella. I can make you scream as loud as I want. Fuck you as hard as your pussy can take it until you come all over my cock."

A needy whimper left me.

I'd just come, but I *needed* him inside me.

I loved when he used his fingers and mouth, but there was nothing better than the sensation of Christian stretching and filling me.

The most intimate part of him in the deepest part of me.

Nothing else compared.

"You like that, don't you?" he taunted. "The idea of me wrecking that tight little cunt while you're helpless and bound?"

"*Yes*. Please," I begged. "Fuck me."

Another groan.

A pause.

And then a slam of his cock inside me as he fucked me like I'd asked.

No, not fucked—he ravaged me, turning me inside out with his touch and his words.

My body was bent practically double with my ankles by my ears and my hands tied together above my head while Christian pounded into me.

Brutally. Mercilessly. Perfectly.

Every thrust sent me sliding toward the edge of the seat, and my world devolved into a haze of sex, sweat, and heat.

The blindfold made everything twice as intense—the sensitivity of my skin, the feeling of his cock inside me, the sounds of squeals and broken whimpers mixed with his grunts and the obscene slap of flesh against flesh.

I craved release yet never wanted it to end.

Christian's hands tightened around my ankles as he bent over me and forced my legs further back.

I was flexible enough that the angle didn't hurt. However, it allowed him to slide deeper than he'd ever gone before, and I couldn't hold back a gasp at the new sensation.

The ache in my center built to an excruciating level.

"So tight. So wet. So *mine*." A thrill went through me at the dark possessiveness in his voice. "Come for me, Stella."

He stayed buried inside me while he reached one hand down to pinch my clit.

This time, my screams echoed in the sultry air as my body shook from the force of my climax. I came so hard tears sprung to my eyes and leaked down my cheeks from behind the blindfold.

"Good girl."

Christian kissed the tears away and slowed his thrusts, drawing out my release until he wrung every drop of pleasure from me.

It was only when I went limp with pleasure that he, too, came with a loud groan.

We lay there for a while, panting and blissed out. When our breaths finally slowed, he eased off me and removed the blindfold.

The world burst into color again, and I blinked a few times to adjust to the light.

"I hope that helped with your overthinking." Christian

untied my hands, his casual statement at odds with the savagery with which he'd just fucked me.

He smoothed gentle fingers over where the rope had bitten into my wrists until the faint burn subsided.

"Yes." I let out a breathless laugh. "Best kind of cure."

Christian came into view, his skin flushed from our most recent session. Somehow, he looked even more gorgeous than before.

His brows rose beneath my scrutiny. "What's wrong?"

"Nothing." My smile grew. "Absolutely nothing."

I didn't want to move, but I forced myself to sit up and put on my swimsuit in case we ran into other boats later.

Christian sank into the seat next to me and wrapped an arm around my shoulders while I snuggled closer to his side.

The gentle rocking of the boat, the soft lap of the waves, the quiet, drowsy contentment in the air...

I couldn't have asked for a more beautiful afternoon.

I ran a lazy hand over Christian's abs and chest. I rarely had the chance to soak him in like this. He was always the one taking care of me, not the other way around.

I rested my hand on his chest and kissed my way along the curve of his shoulder, up his neck, and along his jaw.

Christian lazed still, letting me explore him at my leisure.

The world saw him as a rich, handsome CEO, which he was. But there was another layer of Christian Harper beneath his carefully cultivated exterior.

I saw it in the way he looked at me like I was the most beautiful thing he'd ever seen.

I heard it in the way he encouraged me and stood up for me.

And I felt it in the way he held me like he never wanted to let go.

I pressed my lips to the corner of his mouth, my heart aching for a reason I couldn't name.

Rich, handsome men were a dime a dozen, but men with hearts like his were a rare breed.

He wasn't perfect, but he was perfect for me.

My lips brushed his once. Twice.

Maybe it was the sun, the dreamy lull after a month in Italy, or my lingering post-orgasmic high.

Whatever it was, it uncorked a hidden bottle of courage that poured onto my tongue and pushed three little words out.

"I love you," I whispered.

I knew he didn't believe in love.

I knew there was a strong chance he wouldn't say it back.

But I had to tell him anyway.

It was time I stopped holding myself back from doing things I wanted because of how people *might* react.

Christian's entire body went statue still. Even his breaths seemed to have ceased.

I lifted my head. A dark, tumultuous storm brewed in his eyes and charged the air with electricity.

"Stella..." His raw voice wrapped around my heart like a vine. "I don't deserve your love."

"You deserve it more than anyone." His heartbeat thundered beneath my hand. "I'm not expecting you to say it back right now. But I wanted you to know."

Christian's chest rose and fell with ragged breaths. He curled his hand around the back of my neck and pressed his forehead to mine.

"The day I met you," he said. "Was the luckiest day of my life. You've always been the brightest part of my world, Butterfly. And you always will be."

The depth of emotion in his words stung my eyes. "You don't strike me as a guy who believes in luck."

"I believe in everything when it comes to you."

Including love.

The implication resonated in the timbre of his voice and the way he kissed me again, like he was drowning and I was his only source of oxygen. Vital. Precious. Loved.

I melted into his embrace and let it sweep me away the way it always did.

Christian had his hang-ups about the L word, so I understood why it was difficult for him to say it out loud.

But I didn't need to hear it when I *felt* it. And my conviction in our love was so strong, my high from my confession so great, that they drowned out the small, insidious voices whispering that the greatest falls always came after the greatest highs.

40

STELLA

SADLY, ALL DREAMS HAD TO END.

Our boat trip in Capri was our last full day in Italy before Christian and I returned to D.C. with two new suit-cases of gifts and souvenirs and my love confession trailing behind us.

Old me would've felt embarrassed about saying those words and not hearing them back, but new-ish me (because there were still parts of the old me in there) was more comfort-able letting things play out in their own time.

That being said, our return to the city was more jarring after Italy than after Hawaii. After a month away, Christian was immediately swept up in the chaos of work, and I spent a good week digging myself out of the emails, mail, and tasks that'd piled up while we were gone.

I visited Maura, worked on my marketing plan, had drinks with Ava and Jules, and ran a million errands.

The adjustment to my normal daily life was harder, partly because I'd been gone for longer and partly because there was *so much more* to do this time around.

By the time the week ended, I was tired, cranky, and in desperate need of an extra-long restorative yoga session.

I decided to take that Monday slow and was making my usual morning smoothie when my phone lit with an incoming call.

"Hello?"

"Hi Stella, this is Norma."

My hand froze over the blender.

Norma was one of my favorite nurses at Greenfield, but she wouldn't call out of the blue unless something was wrong.

I set the half cup of ice back on the counter and twisted my necklace around my finger.

"Is Maura okay?"

She'd seemed fine when I visited her yesterday, but anything could've happened since then. She could've had a seizure, a fall, hit her head...

Worse case scenarios ran rampant through my head.

"She's physically okay." Norma's soothing voice eased some of my nerves. "But she, ah, remembered what happened to Phoebe and Harold this morning."

Just like that, the nerves came rushing back. "Oh no."

It didn't happen often, but whenever Maura remembered her husband and daughter, she got extremely agitated. The last time that happened, she threw a vase at a nurse. If she'd been at full strength, the nurse would be in a coma right now.

"Like I said, she's fine now," Norma reassured me. "Unfortunately, we had to sedate her."

My stomach clenched. I'd asked Greenfield to call me whenever they sedated Maura. It wasn't something they did lightly. Sedation meant she'd had a *really* bad day.

"I'll come over right now." I was already halfway to the door when Norma stopped me.

"No need. I know you want to see her, but she's already

sleeping, and you just visited yesterday." Her voice gentled. "I only called to give you a heads up. Don't stress too much about it, hun. These things happen, and we have it under control. I promise."

She was right. As much as I hated the thought of leaving Maura alone after she'd been so upset, the staff at Greenfield were professionals. They were trained to handle such situations, and they could do it far more effectively than I could.

"Right." I forced a smile even though Norma couldn't see me. "Thank you for calling. Please let me know if there are any updates."

"I will."

I hung up and went through the motions of finishing breakfast, but I was too distracted to taste anything.

Maybe I should swing by Greenfield later just in case...

My phone buzzed again, this time with a new text that proved the day could, in fact, get worse.

Natalia: STELLA

Natalia: What the hell is this?

A photo from my Hawaii shoot accompanied her text. The Delamonte print campaign had finally gone live along with my *Washington Weekly* profile. Julian had done a great job writing it up, and Luisa was thrilled. She'd emailed me yesterday gushing over the piece.

Apparently, my family was less thrilled.

I could see why they might be shocked. My back was turned to the camera in the photo Natalia sent, but I was obviously topless. My bikini bottom covered the necessary bits and not an inch more.

The composition was artistic, not sleazy, but it was still probably the most scandalous thing an Alonso had ever been involved in.

Stella: A photo

I wasn't in the mood to indulge Natalia's demand for answers.

I'd known my family would freak out over the Hawaii photos, but I didn't care. We hadn't spoken since our dinner almost three months ago. Perhaps it was pride and stubbornness keeping us apart, or maybe I'd been right all along. They couldn't care less if I was part of the family or not.

The only time they cared about what I was doing was if I embarrassed them. I wasn't the least bit surprised that Natalia's first message to me in months involved criticism.

Natalia: You're NAKED

Natalia: Mom and Dad are freaking out!

Stella: I'm HALF naked. And if Mom and Dad are freaking out, they can tell me themselves. They're adults. They don't need you acting as their mouthpiece all the time.

We were texting, but I could practically hear her stunned silence.

I'd spent my life doing whatever my sister wanted and letting her push me around. I was sick of it.

If my parents had a problem with me, they could say it to my face.

And if Natalia had a problem with *that*, she could shove it up her you know what.

The three dots that indicated she was typing popped up, disappeared, then popped up again.

Natalia: I don't know what's gotten into you lately, but it's not cute. YOU'RE an adult, Stella. Act like one.

Natalia: Also, half naked isn't much better than fully naked

Natalia: Dad is the chief of staff to a cabinet

secretary. How do you think this will reflect on him?

Aggravation sunk its claws into my skin.

Arguing with Natalia was like arguing with a brick wall. She never backed down or tried to see the other person's side. She was always right, and everyone else was always wrong.

Instead of texting back, I called her.

When she picked up, I didn't give her a chance to speak.

"I. Don't. Care." I hung up and switched my phone to silent.

Was I acting like a brat? Maybe.

Would I regret my mini tantrum later? Probably.

But I'd deal with that when the time came. For now, shocking my sister into silence was the brightest spot of my morning.

Still, I couldn't focus on work, so I changed into an old T-shirt and shorts and turned to the only thing that made me feel better when I was super stressed: deep cleaning.

I started in the kitchen and worked my way through the penthouse, dusting and wiping every corner and crevice. Nina cleaned once a week, but her last visit had been five days ago, so there was plenty for me to do.

My friends thought it was a weird stress relief tactic, but it was the perfect mindlessly productive task. Plus, every swipe of a damp cloth through dust felt like I was clearing out stagnant energy, which was a bonus.

Eventually, I made it to Christian's office.

I hesitated outside the closed doors.

I only entered his inner sanctum to water his poor plants, which I'd continued taking care of even after I moved in. He'd offered to hire someone else to do it, but I'd grown attached to them.

Christian wouldn't care if I went in when he wasn't there,

right? He was fine with me going in to water the plants. If he *didn't* want me in there, he would've told me.

After another beat of hesitation, I opened the doors.

I spent longer in Christian's office than anywhere else since I was so careful about putting everything back exactly where it was.

The room was a study in monochrome with its light gray walls, black leather chair, and massive glass and metal desk. Even the globe in the corner was black and gray.

Apparently, he was as allergic to color as he was to art.

"Christian doesn't know it yet, but we're going to add a bit of life to you," I told his desk. It was empty save for his laptop, two extra monitors, a paperweight, and a matte gray holder containing four identical Montblanc pens. "Eventually."

I wiped down the desk and was so busy trying to figure out what the paperweight was—a jaguar? A boar? A deformed cat? —that I accidentally knocked over his pen holder.

I knelt and retrieved the pens, but I miscalculated the distance from the floor to the desk and accidentally banged my head against the underside on my way up.

"Ow!" I winced at the sharp burst of pain.

Maybe the planets were out of alignment because today was *not* my day.

I waited until the bout of dizziness passed before I rose again. This time, I slid my hand against the side of the desk on my way up so I didn't make the same mistake.

This is why I can't have a glass desk. They blended a little *too* well into their surroundings.

My fingers brushed against a small bump, but I didn't pay much attention to it until I stood and noticed one of the drawers had popped up.

It looked different than the others. Smaller, made of black

instead of gray metal, and nestled within a larger drawer filled with office supplies.

A secret compartment.

"Oh my God." I stared at it in disbelief.

I knew Christian had all sorts of gadgets and devices at his disposal, but a *secret drawer*? Seriously? I thought those only existed in movies.

I should close it and move on. It probably contained confidential information that was none of my business, but curiosity got the better of me.

A *little* peek couldn't hurt, right? Besides, the contents looked innocuous. They were just a bunch of plain black binders.

I picked up the top binder and flipped it open.

It looked like a bunch of boring text until my eyes zeroed in on the name at the top.

Stella Alonso.

I blinked twice to make sure I read that clearly, but no matter how long I stared, the words didn't budge.

I skimmed over the rest of the page quickly and realized it wasn't just random text about schools and birthdays and hobbies. It was about *me*.

Everything about my life—my birthday, my friends, my hobbies and where I went to school starting with pre-K going all the way up to college—was laid out in black and white.

Why would Christian have a file on me? To look into my past so he could weed out my stalker?

I'd already told him everything I knew, but maybe he was worried I'd missed something.

However, when I flipped through the rest of the binder, that clearly wasn't the case.

My entire life was distilled into these pages. Everything from basic information like my parents' occupations to my favorite foods, school extracurriculars, and my favorite freaking professor in college. He even had a list of every person I'd ever dated.

I'm going to be sick.

Bile coated my throat, but I set the binder down and picked up the second one with shaking hands.

It was worse than the first. It contained full dossiers on not only me but everyone closest to me, including my family, friends, Maura, and previous boyfriends.

The third folder housed a collection of media—my college graduation photos, a *Thayer Chronicle* article about the holiday food drive I'd organized, and a shot of me attending my first fashion show that'd made it onto some influencer gossip site years ago, to name a few.

The photos and articles were all public domain. There were no private or candid shots, but seeing them together along with the rest of my files made me want to throw up.

For a second, I thought he might be my stalker, but it didn't make sense logistically. I also knew Christian well enough to know he wouldn't terrorize me the way my stalker had.

Not well enough that you anticipated him having a dossier on your entire life, an insidious voice in my head sang.

Perhaps Christian had a good reason for the files, but it was still a huge invasion of privacy. He hadn't dug into just my life; he'd dug into everyone I knew.

He'd done it without my consent, and he'd kept it from me.

How long had he had those files? Days? Weeks? *Months?*

My stomach rebelled, and I barely made it to the nearest bathroom before my breakfast made a messy reappearance.

Tears stung my eyes as I heaved.

This time last week, we'd been on a boat in Italy. I'd told him I'd loved him, and he'd kissed me like he loved me back.

Seven days felt like a lifetime ago—long enough for a dream to twist into a nightmare.

Maybe he needed that information to track down my stalker. Maybe he wanted to make sure no one in my life was a serial killer. Maybe...maybe...

I was grasping at straws, but all I could think about was Christian sitting at his desk, picking through my life with the ease of someone typing in a Google search.

Even if he wasn't my stalker, he'd crossed many of the same boundaries. Stepped over many of the same lines.

The urge to vomit rose again. I'd already thrown up all the contents in my stomach, so I could only dry heave into the toilet.

I have to get out of here.

He wouldn't be home for another few hours, but I couldn't risk him leaving the office early and finding me like this.

I couldn't pretend everything was okay when it felt like nothing would be okay ever again.

I forced myself off the floor and quickly cleaned up before I entered our bedroom. Although I had a ton of stuff stored in the guest room, I'd all but moved into Christian's room after Hawaii.

He'd cleared out a section of his closet for me, and the sight of my clothes hanging next to his familiar dark suits twisted my heart into an excruciating knot.

"It wouldn't hurt you to wear something other than black, gray, and navy, you know." I lay in bed, wrapped up in the comforter and watching Christian get dressed.

Suit. Tie. Watch. Cufflinks.

I never thought watching a guy put on cufflinks would be sexy, but he made everything look sexy.

"Other colors hurt my eyes."

"I wear other colors all the time."

"That's different. I love everything you wear."

My stomach flipped, and I flopped back on my pillow with a sigh. "It's not fair that you can end every argument by saying things like that."

Christian's laugh lingered in the room long after he left.

The memory pulled a smile out of me, but it faded when my current reality sank in again.

The binders. The secrets. The need to get the hell out of here before he came home.

I couldn't face him right now, not when my emotions were so raw and all over the place.

I needed time to think and space to process *away* from him.

I forced my eyes away from his section of the closet and threw the essentials into a duffel bag. A few changes of clothes, toiletries, and Mr. Unicorn, who I grabbed on my way out.

At the last minute, I scribbled a quick note to Christian and left it on his office desk. That and the files should be self-explanatory.

I wasn't ready to talk to him, but I worried what he might do if he came home and found me gone without a trace.

I hugged Mr. Unicorn tight to my chest as I took the elevator down to the lobby. I didn't care that I was an adult walking through public with a stuffed animal. He was the only male who'd never let me down.

I knew Brock was keeping an eye on me and that he'd alert Christian to where I'd gone, but I'd deal with that later.

For now, there was only one place I could go that was almost as safe as Christian's used to be.

"Ava?" I called her on my way out of the building. My voice wobbled, but I refused to cry. *Not now, not here.* "Can I come over? Something...something happened."

41

CHRISTIAN

THE STALKER WENT UNDERGROUND AGAIN DURING OUR trip to Italy, as expected. That was what I wanted; I needed him out of the way while I sorted out the mess in my company.

Alex hadn't reported anything suspicious while I'd been gone, but instinct told me the stalker was planning something bigger than a few measly notes and wanted to fly under the radar until he could bring it to fruition.

His note to me had likely been a slip-up. An ego-induced mistake that'd compelled him to prove he wasn't scared of me and that he wasn't going away.

However, I needed to flush out the traitor first before I could deal with him effectively.

Harper Security's annual poker tournament was coming up in a few weeks. It was the one time of year when almost every employee could gather in one place for a night of fun and relaxation. The only people who couldn't make it were those on long-term jobs, but my suspects would be there. I'd made sure of it.

I loosened my tie as I took the elevator up to my apartment.

Work was a goddamn shitshow these days, and my nights with Stella were the only things keeping me sane.

I love you.

My heart thrummed at the memory.

It'd been a week since Stella turned my world upside down, and I was still reeling from the impact.

I'd kept telling myself I didn't believe in love, that what I felt for her *wasn't* love, but she'd shattered that illusion with one simple phrase.

The minute she'd said those words and looked at me with those beautiful green eyes, I'd known the truth.

I was in love with her.

It'd happened slowly. Bit by bit, piece by piece, like a puzzle becoming whole, until I couldn't deny or ignore it any longer.

I believe in everything when it comes to you.

That'd been the closest I could bring myself to admitting the truth out loud. One of my fundamental life beliefs had fractured, and I hadn't had time to process.

When I eventually said the words, I wanted them to be real. Heartfelt.

The elevator doors slid open.

I stepped into the hall and entered my penthouse, but I paused two steps in. The hairs on the back of my neck prickled in warning.

A strange stillness hung in the air. Usually, Stella was in the living room taking photos or working on her collection. Even if she was elsewhere, I *felt* her when I came home. Her warm, calming presence filled whatever space she was in.

That presence was gone, replaced with the lemony scent of disinfectant.

Nina wasn't scheduled to come in today, so Stella must've

been the one who cleaned. She only did that when she was particularly stressed.

I quickened my steps and checked her favorite rooms. She wasn't in the library, bedroom, or kitchen either, nor was she on the rooftop where she usually did yoga. I didn't have any missed messages from her, and she didn't pick up when I called.

"Stella?" I called out. My voice sounded calm despite my rising panic.

No answer.

She's fine.

She probably stepped out for fresh air or a snack. If something was wrong, Brock would've contacted me.

Christ, why is it so fucking hot in here?

I pushed the sleeves of my shirt up. The air conditioning was on full blast, yet I was burning up.

I doubled back to the living room but saw something that gave me pause along the way.

My office door was open.

I *always* closed it before I left for work, and Stella never went in there except to take care of the plants. Even then, she closed the door on her way out.

I pulled my gun from my waistband and kept it in hand as I stepped into the office.

Cold foreboding splashed the back of my neck.

The first thing I noticed was the spill of papers on my desk, along with three plain but distinctive black binders.

The second thing I noticed was the note penned in her delicate, sprawling script.

We need to talk about the files, but I'm not ready. I'll be back when I am.

I let out a string of curses.

I shouldn't have left the files somewhere where she could

stumble on them, but I'd wanted to keep them close and couldn't bring myself to throw them out after all these years.

What if she saw them and thought...

"Stella!" This time, my panic was audible.

I knew she wasn't there, but that didn't stop my stomach from hollowing at the silence.

Goddammit, sweetheart, where the hell are you?

I held onto the hope that she'd stepped out to gather her thoughts and would be back that night until I reentered our bedroom and took closer stock of what was missing.

Her favorite clothes. Her toiletries. That fucking unicorn.

My blood roared in my ears.

Stella wasn't gone for the afternoon.

Stella was gone, period.

———

AFTER MY INITIAL BOUT OF BLIND PANIC, I'D PULLED myself together and called Brock. Unless Stella gave him the slip, which I doubted, he had to know where she was.

It took me less than a minute to get the location out of him. She was safe, and he'd simply thought she was visiting a friend.

I would've torn him a new one for such an idiotic assumption—who the fuck visited their friend with a fucking stuffed unicorn?—if I hadn't been so focused on getting to Stella as soon as possible.

Of course, she had to choose the one place where I couldn't easily waltz in and demand to see her.

"Volkov!" I banged on the door. "Open the fucking door!"

I'd been knocking and ringing the doorbell for the past five minutes, and I'd used up all my patience.

I'd done plenty of Alex's unsavory tech work over the years.

I had enough dirt on him to bury him alive, and if he didn't answer within the next thirty seconds—

The door finally swung open.

Instead of Alex's cold green eyes, I found myself staring at five feet five inches of thinly veiled suspicion.

"Oh. It's you." A frown marred Ava's normally friendly face when she saw me. "You're interrupting our lunch."

"I want to talk to her."

"I don't know who you're talking about."

My back teeth clenched. "*Stella*."

Ava's hand tightened around the doorknob. She stood squarely in the entrance, barring me from entering. "She's not here."

"That's fucking bullshit. I know she's here." I ditched the softer approach. "Step aside, Ava, or I'll—"

"Careful how you finish that sentence, Harper." Alex appeared beside his fiancée, his eyes like chips of jade-colored ice as they roved over my disheveled appearance.

Loosened tie, no jacket, hair rumpled from the number of times I'd raked my fingers through it in frustration.

It was the most unkempt I'd looked since I hit damn puberty, but I didn't care.

I only cared about one thing, and that was seeing Stella.

My jaw flexed. "I'm not leaving until I see her."

I glared at Alex, who stared back with a bored expression. He didn't give two shits about other people's drama unless it directly involved Ava, but he knew how stubborn I was.

I meant what I said. I'd camp out in the damn hallway until I could talk to Stella.

I just needed to explain.

She'll understand. She had to.

Alex flicked a glance at Ava, who shook her head. "No way.

You heard what he did! He—" She stopped, obviously realizing she messed up.

The confirmation that Stella was inside renewed my fire.

"Stella!" I shouted.

Desperation and something heavier, more foreign settled in my chest.

Fear.

Not fear that Stella was in physical danger, but fear that I might not see her and that I'd lose her forever.

"Just let me talk to you." I didn't even know if she could hear me, but I had to try. "I—"

"Go. Away." Ava pushed against my chest. For someone so small, she was surprisingly strong. "*She doesn't want to see you.*"

"Guys, it's fine."

We all froze at the sound of Stella's voice.

My eyes searched over Alex's shoulder until they found her.

She stood in the middle of the living room, her face pale. She didn't look at me as she spoke to Ava. "Let him in."

"But Stel, what if he—"

"I just want to get this over with," Stella said. "He won't do anything when you guys are right there."

A lance of pain speared through my heart. "I would never hurt you."

She didn't acknowledge me.

Ava released the doorknob and stepped aside with obvious reluctance.

I immediately pushed past her and ignored her and Alex's warning stares as I followed Stella deeper into the apartment.

She'd started walking before I fully entered, but I kept up with her easily until we reached what must've been her room.

Her overnight bag sat on the floor next to the unicorn, and her clothes covered the bed.

My stomach tightened at the sight.

They shouldn't be here. She belonged with *me*, in my house, not in her friend's fucking guest room.

Stella closed the door and finally faced me.

Now that I was closer, I could see the red rimming her eyes and coloring her nose. The thought that I was responsible for her tears made my heart ache in the most painful way.

"Stella..."

"Don't." She hugged her arms around her waist. "I just want to know one thing. Are you the stalker?" Her voice wavered on the last word.

I blanched. "*No.*"

I'd done plenty of morally questionable and downright awful things in my life, but I would never terrify her like that.

"Then why do you have those files on me?" Her chin wobbled. "We met last year, but those pictures are from *years* ago. The information on me, my friends, my family...what possible reason could you have to dig that deep?"

The turquoise ring weighed heavy in my pocket. A symbol of the secrets I'd kept and the lies I'd told.

"Because the first time I saw you wasn't the day you signed the lease at the Mirage," I said. "It was five years ago."

Stella's mouth parted in shock.

The truth emerged in bits and pieces after years of being hidden.

"I was sitting outside a cafe in Hazelburg. You were walking past when someone grabbed your purse and ran."

I hadn't cared about such a minor theft, but I'd been intrigued enough to stay and watch the scene unfold.

"I remember that day," Stella said quietly. "It was my senior year of college. I was on my way home from class."

I nodded. "A passerby caught the kid, the police came, and that should've been it. But when you found out he stole your purse because he needed the money for food, you *gave* him all the cash you'd had on hand instead of pressing charges."

"ARE YOU SURE?" THE POLICE OFFICER LOOKED AT THE brunette like he couldn't believe what he was hearing. "You want to give him the money?"

"Yes." She glanced at the surly teen. He glared back at her, but I spotted the tiniest glint of hope in his eyes. "The cash means more to him than to me."

"He tried to steal *from you*." The officer sounded as baffled as I felt.

I leaned against a nearby building and scrolled through my phone, but all of my attention was focused on the interaction playing out less than ten feet away.

I didn't know what'd compelled me to stick around after the kid had been caught, but I was glad I had.

I'd been bored all day, but this...this was interesting.

Why the fuck would someone give money to the person who'd tried to rob them?

"Yes, I know," the brunette said patiently. "But he's just a kid, and he needs the cash. Charges aren't necessary."

The officer shook his head. "It's your money."

I tuned him out as he closed out the case and examined the brunette, fascinated.

I'd heard her give her name when the police first arrived.

Stella Alonso.

She looked like she was in her early twenties, with curly dark hair, green eyes, and a quick, warm smile. She was gorgeous, but that wasn't what enthralled me.

It was the gentleness with which she spoke. The absurdity of *her action. The unwavering optimism in her eyes even when an attempted robbery in broad daylight should've shaken her faith in humanity.*

The way she'd reacted hadn't been at all what I'd expected. If there was one thing that never failed to spark my interest, it was people who subverted my expectations.

A smile curved my lips for the first time that day.

Eventually, the officer left after giving the teen a stern warning. The kid lingered like he wanted to say something. He must've thought better of it because he soon scampered off without a word, not even a thank you.

Stella didn't appear perturbed.

She simply hiked her bag higher on her shoulder and walked away like nothing had happened.

As she did, something slipped off her hand.

I didn't call after her to alert her to the missing item. Instead, I waited until she disappeared around the corner before I walked over and retrieved the turquoise ring from the ground.

I PULLED THE RING OUT OF MY POCKET. THE USUALLY warm stone felt ice cold in my palm.

Stella stared at it for a second before she sucked in a sharp breath.

"My ring. It was always falling off because it was too loose. I thought I..." Her eyes met mine again. "You've had it this whole time?"

I swallowed hard. "It reminded me of you."

I'd kept it as a token of her goodness. A reminder that, amidst all the death and chaos, a light existed somewhere in the world.

Some days, that light had been the only thing that'd kept my soul intact.

"I was fascinated," I said. "You were an enigma, a puzzle I couldn't solve. I didn't understand how anyone could be...*good* enough to do what you did. So I looked into your background."

I couldn't read Stella's expression, but she didn't say anything, so I forged on.

"It started with basic background information, but it spiraled until it turned into what you saw. The more I learned about you, the more I wanted to know."

Not wanted. *Needed.*

She was a living contradiction, and she'd consumed my thoughts in a way no one and nothing had before or since.

The fashion blogger who spent hours putting together the perfect outfit and the volunteer who spent her free time cleaning up trash from the parks.

The social media star who was glued to her phone but was always there for her friends.

The introvert who lived her life in the public eye online.

The calm and the chaos, the silence and the storm.

The calm to my chaos, the silence to my storm.

I'd been obsessed with Stella Alonso for five years, and I couldn't bring myself to regret it.

"How long did this go on?" Stella finally asked, her voice dull.

My hand closed around the ring. "Almost a year."

"A year." She paled further. "You were stalking me for *a year?*"

"I wasn't stalking you. I..." Guilt and frustration knotted in my chest. "Other than the background info, everything I knew was public knowledge."

It was a flimsy excuse.

I hadn't followed her physically, but I'd used all the tools at my disposal to dig through her life. Nothing and no one around her had been off-limits.

It wasn't stalking in the traditional sense, but I'd crossed massive boundaries, nonetheless.

"I stopped when I..." *Realized how attached I was getting.* Even then, I'd known that Stella was a dangerous distraction, and I'd resented the hold she had on me. It had been equal parts fascinating and frustrating.

"I stopped after that," I finished. "I didn't dig any deeper, and I only knew what you posted online. I had no idea about your stalker, Greenfield, or anything that happened that you didn't talk about publicly."

It had taken all my willpower to stay away physically, but no matter how hard I tried to forget her, I couldn't.

I hadn't spoken a word to her, and she'd remained at the forefront of my mind for years.

Then, in a stroke of luck, her best friend fell in love with Rhys, who referred Stella to my building, and the rest was history.

"That doesn't change the fact that you lied to me this entire time." Stella wrapped her arms tighter around her waist. "You let me believe we'd never met before."

"Because we *hadn't*." "I shouldn't have deceived you, but I can't change the past. If I'd told you what I did, you would've left."

After wanting her for so long, I'd finally had Stella close, and I hadn't risked driving her away.

"I'll destroy the files," I said desperately when Stella remained silent. "I'll never look at them again, and we can move on from this." Every word scraped through my chest.

Her humorless laugh singed my lungs. "We can't move on from this."

My frustration mounted. I wasn't used to being this out of sorts, and it was harder than usual to find the right words.

"Why the hell not?"

Why didn't she understand? Why couldn't I make her see that I'd changed in the months we'd been together? That I wasn't the same person I'd been when I made that file.

"Because it was an *invasion of privacy!*" she yelled. Tears leaked down her cheeks. "You did *not* have my permission to dig into my life like that. But that's always been our story, hasn't it? You know *everything* about me, and I know nothing about you. You want other people to be an open book while you keep yours closed. I thought you were so thoughtful and perceptive because you knew all these things about me. My favorite foods, my favorite flowers...but you had that stupid dossier the whole time. Was it that easy? Just pull up the file and see what scrap you can throw my way to make me fall for you?"

A strange sensation burned behind my eyes. "I haven't looked at that file in years. I swear—"

"You're the same as my stalker." Stella's breaths shallowed. "No, you're *worse,* because at least they didn't make me fall in love with a lie."

Her words pierced me like a knife through my heart.

"I would never hurt you," I repeated.

"You already have."

The knife twisted harder.

"I trusted you," she whispered. "I trusted you when I barely knew you. I guess that was my fault." Her bitter laugh made me flinch. "You told me about your family, but I don't even know if the story is true. Was that also a lie? I have no idea who you are or what you're capable of. Your dreams, your fears—"

"My dream is to be with you. And my biggest fear," I said, my voice low and ragged with emotion. "Is losing you."

A small sob wracked her body.

My heart cracked at the sound. It fucking killed me that I was the one causing her tears.

Deep down, I knew I didn't deserve her forgiveness, but

that didn't stop me from instinctively reaching for her and wanting to comfort her.

She shrank away before I made contact. "Don't touch me."

If she brought me to life with three words—*I love you*—she slayed me with an equal number. *Don't touch me.*

Every syllable dragged through my already destroyed heart like a freshly honed razor blade, leaving nothing but ruins behind.

"I can't do this.," she said, her eyes glossy with tears. "I'll move the rest of my stuff out of your apartment tomorrow."

Raw panic scraped at my veins.

I couldn't lose her. Not like this.

I grasped onto the only straw I had left. "It's not safe. Your stalker is still out there."

Stella set her jaw. "Brock can stay, but that's it. I need space. I can't think right now. I just need..." She drew in a shuddering breath. "I need you to go. "

I'd broken bones. Been shot at. Got lost in the desert for fucking days with the sun blistering my skin.

None of that had hurt as much as this.

"Don't do this." My voice cracked. "Butterfly, please."

I had never begged anyone for anything. Not when my parents died, not when I'd needed startup money for my company, and not when I'd faced imminent death at the hands of a pissed-off warlord.

But I would gladly get on my fucking knees and beg if it meant Stella would stay with me.

"I don't want you keeping tabs on me anymore." She continued like I hadn't spoken. "Not through Brock, Alex, Ava, or anyone else. Not through my blog or social media. I know you could if you wanted to, but I'm asking you..." The last word broke with unshed tears. "To leave me alone, Christian."

The air went silent save for the painful sounds of our breaths.

I was drowning. Drowning in emotions I'd never felt before, in dark waters that saturated my lungs and made reaching for the surface impossible.

Panic. Shame. Regret.

"Do you want to know another secret, Stella?" My voice was unrecognizable in its rawness. "I can't say no to you." Not when it came to the things that mattered. "But I will always be here if you need me, no matter how far in distance or time. I don't care if we're on different continents or if it's five, fifty years in the future. I never want you to wake up and feel like you're alone because you're not. You'll always have me."

My eyes burned as my final, greatest truth scraped up my throat. "I love you. So fucking much."

I thought saying those words for the first time would feel strange.

They didn't.

They felt like they'd been waiting to find their home all these years and found it in her.

Stella squeezed her eyes shut. A broken sob bled through her lips, but otherwise, she didn't respond to my confession.

It was what I'd expected, but agony twisted my gut nonetheless.

I allowed myself to look at her one last time before I walked out and closed the door behind me.

There was nothing else to say.

I ignored Alex and Ava's curious stares as I left the apartment, my body numb. Pieces of my heart were scattered all over her room, and my mind had devolved into an endless loop of her tears. Even the blood seemed to have vanished from my veins, leaving nothing but cold emptiness behind.

There was nothing left of me when I took out all the parts that belonged to her.

I'm asking you to leave me alone, Christian.

Leaving went against my every instinct. Every molecule of my body demanded I stay and fight for her, to beg and plead until she forgave me.

But I had already crossed too many boundaries with her, and I couldn't cross another one. Not when she'd explicitly asked me not to.

I'd meant what I said.

I would give Stella anything she wanted, even if it killed me in the process.

42

STELLA

I waited until the door shut behind him before I collapsed.

Sobs wracked my body as I sank onto the floor and finally let the full flood of my tears flow.

I love you. So fucking much.

The words echoed in my head like a taunt, as did the image of Christian's face before he left.

The agony in his eyes. The torment in his voice. The brokenness that I felt as surely as if it were my own because it *was*.

My heart had splintered into a thousand jagged pieces, and they cut and cut until I couldn't stop bleeding.

It was very possible I might die right there, with my knees drawn to my chest and my trust in shambles.

I believed he was sorry, and I believed he loved me in whatever way he knew how.

But they didn't change the fact that our relationship had been built on a lie. He *knew* how much the stalker had traumatized me. How much I hated the invasion of privacy and loss of control over my own life.

Christian did what he did before the stalker showed up, but he'd sat on those files for years and never told me.

He'd held all the cards while I held only the scraps he gave me.

Our power imbalance wasn't about money or security; it was about trust. I'd always given more than I received from him.

The thought of him sitting at his desk and poking through the most intimate parts of my life with a mere press of a button sent another shiver down my spine.

I pulled my legs tighter to my chest and buried my face in my knees.

I'm so, so stupid.

I'd seen all the warning signs and ignored them because I'd been too caught up in the excitement of falling in love for the first time.

I will always be here if you need me.

I should've been happy Christian was gone. Instead, my heart hollowed in my chest while a barrage of memories played in my head.

Get in the car, Stella.

I've never wanted anyone more, and I've never hated myself more for it.

Because love is ordinary. Mundane. And you, Stella...you're extraordinary.

I believe in everything when it comes to you.

One week ago, we'd been in Italy, and we'd been happy.

Part of me wished I'd never stumbled across that secret compartment or looked through those files. Then we'd still be happy, and I wouldn't be sitting in the ruins of what we used to be.

Christian was the only safe space I had, and now he was gone.

My gasping sobs filled the cocoon of my arms and legs. I'd been crying so hard and for so long that my ribs hurt and I couldn't draw enough oxygen into my lungs.

I couldn't breathe. I couldn't—I needed...

"Stella?"

I heard Ava's voice followed by a knock, but the sounds were muted, like they were traveling to me underwater.

I was drowning in grief, and I didn't know how to pull myself out.

"It's okay." Ava's voice was closer. She must've entered when I didn't answer. "Oh, sweetie, it'll be all right. I promise."

She wrapped her arms around me and rubbed soothing circles on my back while I leaned my head against her chest and cried until I ran out of tears.

Part of me had anticipated this crash from the beginning. My relationship with Christian had been too perfect, and nothing that good could last forever.

What I hadn't anticipated was how much the crash would break me.

But the most terrifying part wasn't my broken heart. It was the possibility that I might never be able to glue the pieces back together again.

43

CHRISTIAN

"You've had seven drinks in two hours, bud." The bartender stared at me with a dubious expression.

"And I'm ordering an eighth." I enunciated each word with cold precision. I didn't slur or sway. I could be blackout drunk and no one would be the wiser. "You got a problem with that?"

He held up his hands and shook his head.

"It's your liver."

Goddamn right.

It was my liver and my money. I could do whatever the hell I wanted with them.

I tossed back the glass he slid in my direction and drained it in a minute flat.

The alcohol had stopped burning four drinks back, and it tasted like water going down.

It pissed me off. What was the point of alcohol if it didn't numb the way it was supposed to?

"Is this seat taken?" A blonde slid onto the stool next to mine before I could answer.

Tiny dress. Long legs. Lips that would make Angelina Jolie

cry with envy.

I didn't spare her a second glance. "Not interested."

It was the same fucking thing every time. Couldn't a guy drink in peace without getting hounded?

I could've saved myself the trouble and drank at home, but the apartment was too depressing these days. I also didn't want to go to the Valhalla Club since everyone there was nosy as fuck. No one liked seeing a member down more than the other members.

So here I was, holed up in some shitty dive bar near the office, drowning my sorrows in equally shitty scotch.

If my liver rebelled, it wouldn't be from the quantity of drinks. It would be from the quality of them.

The offended blonde left in a huff, clearly unused to being rejected.

Tough shit.

It'd been two weeks since Stella and I broke up.

Two weeks of unrelenting hell where *everything* reminded me of her. The blender she made her smoothies in, the tub where she'd bathed, the cafe where she bought her pastries. Even the fucking trees and plants outside reminded me of her.

It was enough to make me want to lock myself in a dark concrete box and never come out.

The jangle of bells above the entrance pulled me out of my pathetic self-pity and drew my attention to the door.

My heart stopped.

Dark curls. Green eyes. Warm smile.

Stella.

For a second, I thought I was hallucinating and had conjured her from my thoughts.

Then her voice wound toward me, as real and tangible as the cracked vinyl cushion of my stool and the muted baseball game playing on TV.

I straightened, my spirits lifting until I saw the guy standing next to her. He looked vaguely familiar, and he said something that made her smile.

My hand tightened around my glass as an icy black wave of possessiveness rippled through me.

Whoever the guy was, I wanted to fucking kill him.

My eyes tracked them as they sat at a table across the room.

Stella hadn't noticed me yet. She said something else to the soon-to-be dead fucker, but she must've felt the weight of my stare because she finally looked up.

Our gazes collided like sparks in the air.

Our relationship had turned to ashes, but the fire between us was still there, burning up space and oxygen until we were the only people left.

My blood roared at the sweet relief of seeing her again.

She asked me to leave her alone, and I had. Us showing up at the same bar on the same night would've been a coincidence, but nothing was a coincidence when it came to her.

It was fate.

Stella's smile faded. She turned away, and the sounds of the bar rushed back in a painful whoosh.

I wasn't sure what was worse—seeing her and not being able to touch or talk to her, or knowing that seeing me had caused her light to dim.

Restlessness and the urge to rip out the throat of the man she was talking to churned beneath my skin.

Instead of ordering another drink, I slid off my stool and pushed my way through the crowd to the bathroom.

The sting of cold water against my face cleared the haze from my vision.

Giving her up was the hardest thing and the biggest sacrifice she could've asked for. It went against my every instinct.

She would never know if I checked her social media or

blog. But every time I went to pick up the phone or pull up Stella's profile, something held me back.

I'm asking you to leave me alone, Christian.

I yanked a paper towel from the dispenser and wiped my hands dry before I stepped into the hall.

I made it two steps before I stopped.

Stella stood at the end of the hall, her tall, slim frame silhouetted against the bar lights. Still, I could make out the way her lips parted in surprise.

We stared at each other.

Music pulsed a few feet away, but here, in this hall, there was only silence and the hum of things I wanted to but couldn't say.

I'm sorry.

I miss you.

I love you.

A burst of laughter from the main room shattered the spell. My face darkened when I looked over her shoulder and I saw the guy she'd arrived with joking with the server.

Violence pulsed through me at the thought of him touching Stella. Holding her, making her laugh.

I had never hated anyone more.

Stella must've picked up on the glint in my eyes because she followed my gaze and paled.

I walked down the hall, intent on leaving before I gave in to the urge to touch her. She stopped me with a low warning on my way past.

"If anything happens to him, I'll never forgive you."

The only words she'd spoken to me after our breakup, and they were to save another man.

A muscle in my jaw flexed before I walked past her and out the door.

Coldness invaded my chest.

Just when I thought I'd experienced all the ways a heart could break, she proved me wrong.

———————

STELLA

I sagged with equal parts relief and disappointment after Christian left.

I told myself I'd gone into the hall to return a call, but I could've done that outside the bar. The truth was, I'd *wanted* that passing interaction with him, and I hated myself for it.

After two weeks, my bright burst of anger had faded into a deep, ceaseless ache.

I hadn't forgiven him, but I missed him so much it was hard to breathe.

Ironically, the rest of my life was on an upswing after our breakup. It was like now that my love life was in shambles, the universe was working overtime to make it up to me in other areas.

The Delamonte print campaign and *Washington Weekly* profile had opened a new flood of opportunities, as expected. Luisa was ecstatic about how the partnership was going. Maura hadn't had any issues since her sedation, the stalker hadn't made a reappearance, and my blog and social media were thriving. I hadn't publicly announced my breakup with Christian, but I wasn't posting about him anymore. That hadn't hurt my engagement as much as I'd thought, though I didn't care much either way.

I'd also started reaching out to local boutiques about my collection. In fact, I was here celebrating with Brady because one of them finally agreed to carry a few test pieces.

Overall, my life was going great...except for Christian and my family.

Speaking of which...

I took a deep breath and refocused on the reason I'd excused myself from Brady. A quick glance told me he was still talking to the server and that Christian was nowhere in sight.

Maybe I was being paranoid, but I could've sworn there'd been a moment when Christian had looked at him like he was capable of murdering him.

I dialed the number from my latest missed call and tried to unknot my nerves while the phone rang.

She picked up on the third ring.

"Hi, Stella."

"Hi, Mom."

It was the first time we'd spoken since our family dinner in April.

Four months.

It was the longest we'd gone without contact, and hearing her voice again caused a lump to form in my throat.

I'd had my reasons for lashing out the way I had during the dinner, but she was still my mom.

"How are you?" A rare thread of hesitation ran beneath her voice.

"I'm okay." I twisted my necklace around my finger. "Sorry I missed your call. I'm out with a friend and I didn't see it earlier."

"That's okay. It's nothing important." She cleared her throat. "I read your *Washington Weekly* profile. It's a great piece, and your Delamonte photos are beautiful."

All the air left my lungs. Of all the things I'd expected her to say, that hadn't even been in the realm of possibility.

"Really?" I asked in a small voice.

My confidence had grown over the past few months, but there would always be a little girl inside me that wanted nothing more than her parents' approval.

"Natalia said you and Dad were upset about the photos."

My last conversation with my sister still left a bitter taste in my mouth.

"Well, we would've preferred it if you'd worn more clothes," my mother said dryly. "But we were more shocked than upset. The profile, however...I had no idea you'd accomplished so much with your blog, or that you felt so strongly about fashion starting at such a young age."

I didn't point out that was something I'd been trying to tell her since I was in middle school. I didn't want to start another argument.

"Is the profile the only reason you called?" I wouldn't be surprised. My parents loved anything that made the family look good. "We haven't talked in months."

My mother was quiet for a minute. "Everyone's emotions were running high after the dinner," she finally said. "After things calmed, I wasn't sure you wanted to hear from us. You always call, and when you didn't...you were so upset..."

You always call.

Translation: I always apologized first.

My hand curled tighter around my phone. "Dad told me to get out, and I didn't know if you even cared that I wasn't around."

My mother let out a sharp exhale. "Of *course* we care. You're our daughter."

I twisted the necklace harder. "Sometimes, it doesn't feel like it," I said, my words barely audible.

"Oh, Stella." She sounded more distressed than I'd ever heard her. "We didn't..."

Raucous cheers from the bar drowned out the rest of her sentence. The Nationals must've scored a run; their game against the Rangers was playing on all the TVs.

When the noise died down, my mother spoke again.

"You're out with a friend, so this isn't the best time to talk. Perhaps we can all meet as a family soon? Not a dinner. Something more casual where we can just talk."

"I'd like that," I said softly.

I didn't want to hold onto grudges, especially not against my family.

I hadn't seen them in so long, and I wasn't angry anymore. I was just sad.

After I hung up, I stayed in the hall and tried to wrap my head around the events of the day.

My call with the boutique, seeing Christian, talking to my mom...

It was too much at once, but the only thing I could focus on was how much I wanted to share what'd happened with Christian.

Not just the boutique and my mom, but *everything*.

How I accidentally used the wrong milk for my smoothie that morning and nearly gagged at the taste.

How Ava and Jules offered to be fit models for my collection.

How proud I was of all the local outreach I'd done.

How much I missed him.

I was so used to sharing the details of my life with Christian that even journaling didn't fill the void.

In fact, I hadn't touched my journal since we broke up; it was filled with too many memories of us.

I was upset with him, and I wished he were here. Both things could be true at once.

Light and dark. Flame and ice. Dreams and logic.

Our relationship had always been a dichotomy. It made sense that its death would be as well.

44

CHRISTIAN

Harper Security's annual poker tournament took place in the company's multipurpose room, which had been transformed into a mini-casino with an open bar and half a dozen poker tables.

It was usually restricted to staff only. This year, I broke my own rule and invited Rhys, who was in town without Bridget for once for some diplomatic event, and Alex, as a thank you for keeping an eye on things for me while I was in Italy. Josh was invited by default since he'd insisted on tagging along when he found out Alex would be attending.

I let him. I had too much other shit to worry about than his delusion that I was trying to steal his best friend.

The four of us sat at a table by the bar. The air was alive with the sounds of laughter, clinking glasses, and shuffling decks, but the merriment did nothing to lighten my black mood.

"How many poker tournaments have you attended in the past?" Josh asked Alex suspiciously.

Exasperation filled Alex's face. "I told you, this is my first one."

"Just making sure." Josh plucked a card from his deck and tossed it on the table. King of hearts. "Since you'd played *dozens of chess matches* with *him*"—he jerked a thumb at me— "and I didn't know about it for literally *years*."

Alex sighed.

"If you keep asking the same question over and over again, you can leave," I said icily. I didn't have time for Josh's bullshit.

"Someone's moody." He raised an eyebrow. "Is it because Stella broke up with you?"

My jaw flexed while Alex and Rhys hid their smirks behind their cards.

I'd done a decent job of not thinking about Stella tonight until Josh fucking Chen brought her up.

You can't kill a guest, a voice in my head reminded me.

Actually, I could do whatever the fuck I wanted, but then I'd have to deal with Alex. I also assumed Stella wouldn't be too happy about me murdering her best friend's brother.

"I am not moody. *You* are simply annoying."

I didn't know what Stella told her friends about us, but since she'd moved into Alex and Ava's house, it was obvious we weren't together anymore.

Josh shrugged. "Perhaps, but at least I'm not single."

My hand twitched toward my gun.

"Keep provoking him, and he'll kill you." Rhys knew me too well. He'd been quiet most of the night, but humor lit his eyes when he looked at me.

"Is something funny?" I tossed out a card without looking at it.

"As a matter of fact, yes. Christian Harper moping over a girl," he drawled. "Never thought I'd see the day."

A migraine gathered behind my temple.

"I'm not *moping*." It took all my willpower not to punch the shit-eating grin off his face. "I don't *mope*."

What I'd been doing the past few weeks wasn't moping. It was...processing.

"That's not what Alex said." As usual, Josh piped up even though the conversation had nothing to do with him. "He said you showed up to his house in tears the day Stella moved in."

"I wasn't in fucking tears!"

The room quieted as every head swiveled in my direction.

I saw Brock's mouth drop and Kage's eyebrows fly up out of the corner of my eye.

I never yelled.

Not when I'd found out about *Magda*'s theft, and not when shit went sideways at work. But it'd been a hellish two weeks, and I'd bled the database of people to fuck with when I had a bad day dry.

There were only so many computers I could hack into before it lost its luster.

I would've put more effort into creating a new list of names if I thought it would help, but it wouldn't.

I didn't need more people to fuck with.

I needed Stella.

"Oh. I must've remembered wrong," Alex said mildly.

If I didn't know better, I could've sworn that was laughter in his eyes.

"Remember when you gave me shit after the Bridget situation?" Rhys was practically in schadenfreude, that bastard. "You said love is, and I quote, *tedious, boring, and utterly unnecessary. People in love are the most insufferable on the planet.*" His grin widened. "Want to take that back?"

My teeth ground in irritation.

"It's deeply concerning that you can quote me word for word. Find a new hobby, Larsen. Obsessing over me isn't healthy." I pushed back my chair, too aggravated to sit any longer.

"Where are you going? It's your turn!" Josh protested. "We're in the middle of a game!"

I ignored him and walked off with Rhys's laughter at my back and irritation flickering through my veins.

I *had* said those things he'd quoted. Now I was one of those insufferable idiots, pining after the only woman who'd ever broken my heart.

Karma was an even bigger bitch than fate.

I entered the kitchen and poured myself another drink. It was only my second of the night. I'd set the trap for the traitor earlier, but I needed to keep my head clear just in case.

Four suspects. Four different pieces of information I'd casually slipped into a conversation about how I'd developed a new device that made Scylla look like child's play.

The traitor wouldn't be able to resist leaking that information to Sentinel. Once they did, I only had to look at the details of what was leaked to pinpoint the rat.

It was a simple trap, but it worked every time. I'd just needed to get all the suspects in one room so I could have the conversations without raising suspicion. My men all knew I didn't discuss these things over the phone.

And if the traitor was who I thought it was...

I drained my glass.

My life was going to shit, and alcohol was the only thing that made me feel better these days.

That and the letters.

My mind flashed to my desk drawer.

"Hey." Rhys's gruff voice dragged me back to the kitchen. "You good?"

"Never been better." The acerbic bite of my words strained the air.

He leaned against the counter and crossed his arms. His

eyes moved from the tight set of my jaw to my empty glass and back again.

His earlier laughter faded, replaced with sympathy. "You've got it bad."

I didn't answer.

"How much did you fuck up?" His eyebrows rose when I remained silent. "That much, huh?"

"It's complicated."

"These things always are." Rhys sighed. "Whatever you did, it's probably not as bad as you think. Stella is one of the nicest people I know. She'll forgive you. She just needs time."

Perhaps. But privacy was one of the most important things to Stella, and I'd crossed so far over that line I couldn't see it.

Her stalker had terrorized her for months, and the fact that I reminded her even a little of the bastard...

The alcohol churned in my stomach.

"Rhys Larsen giving relationship advice. Hell must've frozen over." I brushed over his statement for a safer topic.

Rhys snorted. "It froze the day you uttered the word *love* in a non-demeaning way." He straightened and clapped his hand on my back. "If Volkov can get his girl back after a year, there's hope for you. Just don't fuck it up again."

I poured myself another drink after he left and drank it alone in the company kitchen.

My life really had gone to shit.

45

CHRISTIAN

I DIDN'T RETURN HOME UNTIL TWO IN THE MORNING.

My footsteps echoed against the marble floors on my way to my office. I'd grown to hate the walk from the front door. I passed by too many quiet rooms and too many ghosts of our memories.

Stella had lived with me for only a few months. I'd lived alone for years without her and been fine.

But now that she was gone, the penthouse felt empty, like all the heart and soul had been sucked out of it, leaving nothing but a hollow shell behind.

My office door opened soundlessly, and I sank into my seat without turning on the lights.

I'd shredded all the files I'd had on Stella the day after she found them, but their phantom presence tainted what used to be a sanctuary.

Still, I preferred the office to my bedroom, where her soft scent lingered in the sheets and pillows weeks later. Sometimes, I heard her laugh. Other times, I rolled over and could've sworn she was next to me, teasing me like she always did.

I tipped my head back.

Scotch and adrenaline from the poker tournament lingered in my blood.

Brock had been the big winner. He was off duty since Stella was home for the night, but I hadn't congratulated him. It was hard for me to look at him when he reminded me of her.

It was even harder not to ask about her.

I'd instructed him to alert me immediately if she was in danger, but otherwise, her present-day life remained a mystery.

I'd been tempted to call Jules for information as well. She owed me for getting her out of a tight spot last year, and she was one of Stella's best friends. If anyone knew what Stella was thinking and feeling, it was her.

Stella's last request to me was the only thing holding me back. It was a leash I could easily break, yet it shackled me more effectively than iron restraints.

I felt so fucking stupid for missing her so much and even stupider for the coping mechanism I'd developed since she left.

I lifted my head and opened the secret drawer that used to hold her files. Now, it was filled with letters I'd never sent.

One for every day we'd been apart.

It was the type of sappy, pathetic behavior I'd derided in the past. If Past Christian could see me now, he'd shoot me and put me out of my misery.

I didn't care. The letters were the only way I could talk to her these days, and writing them was almost therapeutic.

They covered a span of topics, from snippets of my life growing up to my favorite books to how much I despised clowns (I was convinced they were the devil in human form, except less fun). The letters were like chapters from separate books, tossed together in the chaos that made up my life.

The only thing they had in common was that they were all for her.

Stella said she knew nothing about me, so I poured all of myself out to her.

I picked up a pen and started writing that night's letter. When I finished, exhaustion blurred my vision, but I tucked the note carefully into the drawer along with its brethren.

Instead of retiring to my bedroom, I stayed in my office and stared out the window at the dark night sky.

My collection of plants lined the sill, silhouetted against the moonlight.

They just need a little love and attention to thrive.

I'd been watering and taking care of them religiously since Stella left. She loved those plants.

But no matter how much care I gave them, they still looked sad and droopy, like they knew their usual caregiver was gone and was never coming back.

"I know," I said. I couldn't believe I'd sunk to conversing with plants, but here we were. "I miss her too."

JULY 30

Stella,

I have a confession: I never wanted a pet, not even when I was a kid.

My parents asked me once if I wanted a puppy, and I told them in no uncertain terms that I did not.

It's not because I hate animals. I just always thought they were too much work for too little reward. I didn't understand why someone would bring a dog or cat into their home, treat it like their child, and love it for years when they knew that animal's lifespan was so much shorter than their own.

It was like they were asking for their heart to be broken.

Now, I understand.

It's because the time they spent together was worth the heartbreak.

Before you get angry, I'm not comparing you to an animal. But if I had the chance to go back in time and leave the cafe a minute before you passed or stay in my office instead of dropping by the apartment the day you signed the lease, I wouldn't.

Even knowing what the outcome would be.

Even knowing that I would eventually get my heart broken.

Because all the most beautiful days of my life have been with you, and I wouldn't trade that for anything in the world.

I would rather be miserable now after having been loved by you than be happy without having ever known you.

August 6

Stella,

Remember when you ran into me in the lobby the night we signed our agreement? You mentioned a date should include dinner, drinks, and hand holding. Or, as an alternative, cuddling on a bench overlooking the river, followed by whispered sweet nothings and a goodnight kiss.

At the time, it was the most atrocious thing I'd ever heard, but if you ever come back to me...I have it all planned out.

We'll have dinner at my favorite Italian restaurant in Columbia Heights. It's a tiny place, barely large enough to seat a dozen people at one time, but they make the second-best gnocchi in the world (after my grandmother's).

She's not here anymore, but when I was a kid, I went to her house after school and she spent hours teaching me how to cook. Besides my time with you, those days were my happiest. Laughing with her in the kitchen, rolling the dough and getting flour all over ourselves while the old sixties music she loved played in the background.

Her gnocchi was my favorite dish. Unfortunately, her recipe was lost after she died, but when I tried it at this restaurant...it was the closest I'd found to how she used to make it.

I know I went off on a tangent, but I wanted to share that story with you. I've never told anyone about how I learned to cook before.

Anyway, I think you would love the restaurant. After that, we'll have drinks at a bar nearby, then go to the Georgetown waterfront and sit on a bench by the river. We can kiss and hold hands and whisper however many sweet nothings you want.

Because if this date does happen, it means you've forgiven me. And if I have you back, I'll never give you a reason to leave again.

AUGUST 12

Stella,

It's two-thirty in the morning as I write this.

I haven't slept in almost twenty-four hours.

But I couldn't go to sleep without telling you this...

I'm trying, Butterfly. I'm trying so fucking hard.

To stay away from you. To not think about you. To not love you.

My life would be so much easier if I could move on, but I know I can't.

Even if you never forgive me.

Even if you never talk to me again.

Even if you move on.

I'll still love you.

You will always be my first, last, and only love.

46

STELLA

THAT WEEKEND, MY FAMILY AND I MET AT A CAFE IN Virginia.

We sat in a booth near the exit. It was the quietest corner of the restaurant, which bustled with the Sunday brunch rush.

My father wore his favorite blue polo shirt, my mother wore her signature pearls, and my sister wore lethal heels and a mildly annoyed expression, the way they always did during our monthly meals.

It was like our family dinner had transplanted itself into a green leather booth instead of my parents' prized mahogany dining table.

The only differences were the sunny windows and the awkward silence blanketing the table after we ran out of small talk.

"So." My mother cleared her throat. "How's Maura doing?"

I blinked at her choice of topic, but I answered readily. "She's doing well. She has her garden and puzzles at Greenfield, so she's happy."

My mother nodded. "Good."

Another silence fell.

We'd been dodging the elephant in the room all afternoon. At this rate, we'd be here until closing time.

I closed my hands around my mug and took courage from the warmth seeping into my palms.

"About what happened at the dinner..." Everyone visibly stiffened. "I'm sorry if I hurt your feelings, Mom," I said softly. "That wasn't my intention. But you have to understand why I've been paying for Maura's care. She's always been there when I needed her. Now she's the one who needs me, and I can't leave her to fend for herself. She has no one else."

"I do understand." My mother gave a small smile when I startled in surprise. "I've had time to think about it over the past few months. The truth is, I've always been a little jealous of your relationship with Maura. It's my own fault, of course. I was too busy with my career to spend much time with you girls. By the time I realized how much I'd missed, you were all grown up. You didn't want to spend time with us anymore. We practically have to force you to come to our family dinners."

"It's not that I don't want to spend time with you. It's..." My cheeks warmed. "It's the accomplishments game."

It sounded stupid when I said it out loud, but every time I thought about that "fun game," anxiety crawled beneath my skin and ate away at my nerves.

"It makes everything into a competition," I said. "You, Dad, and Natalia all have these high-powered jobs, and I'm...well, you know. I love fashion, and I'm not ashamed of it. But every time we play that game, I feel like I'm the biggest disappointment at the table."

"Stella." My mother sounded pained. "You're not a disappointment. I admit, we don't always understand your choices, and yes, we wished you'd chosen a more financially stable career than fashion. But you could never disappoint us. You're our daughter."

"We want what's best for you," my father added gruffly. "We weren't trying to keep you from doing what you loved, Stella. We just didn't want you waking up one day realizing you've made a mistake when it's too late."

"I know." I didn't doubt that my parents wanted what was best for me. It was the way they went about it that was the problem. "But I'm not a child anymore. You have to let me make my own decisions and mistakes. If my fashion line takes off, great. If it doesn't, I've learned some important lessons and I'll do better next time. I just know that's what I want to do. I can't go back to working for someone else."

My parents exchanged glances while Natalia shifted next to me.

"I have a decent amount of money from some big brand deals I signed, and I..." I hesitated before I finished. "I completed my first collection. A local boutique agreed to stock it, so I'm hoping that'll bring in more money as well."

I also planned to do an official launch online, but I wanted to test the waters first.

My mother's eyes widened. "Really? Oh, Stella, that's amazing!"

"Thank you," I said shyly. I traced the handle of my mug with my thumb. "So, you're not mad that I'm not looking for an office job?"

Another exchange of glances.

"Obviously, you're doing well with your partnerships, and the fashion line is off to a good start." My father coughed. "There's no reason why you should get an office job if that's not what you want. *But*," he said when a smile blossomed on my face. "If you ever run into trouble, you need to tell us. No hiding it like you did the *D.C. Style* debacle."

"I won't," I promised.

"Good. Now, where's that smart-mouthed boyfriend of yours?" he grumbled. "It was disrespectful, the way he spoke to me in my own home, but I suppose he wasn't entirely wrong."

My smile dimmed. "We, um..." I swallowed past the sudden lump in my throat. "We broke up."

Three pairs of surprised eyes turned to me.

Considering the way Christian and I had defended each other at the dinner, they'd probably thought we would last longer than a few months.

So had I.

"I'm sorry," my mother said sympathetically. "How are you doing?"

I forced a smile. "I'll be okay."

"You'll find someone better." My father's tone turned brisk. "Never liked him. If you knew some of the rumors"—he broke off when my mother elbowed him sharply in the ribs—"But I guess they don't matter now," he finished with another grumble.

I switched topics, and the conversation lightened until my father went outside to take a call and my mom went to use the restroom.

Natalia had been noticeably quiet all afternoon, but she turned to me when they were out of earshot.

I stiffened, bracing myself for another critical or snarky comment.

Instead, she looked almost sheepish as she glanced at me. "I didn't want to bring it up again in front of Mom and Dad," she said. "But I'm sorry for the way I outed you about *D.C. Style*. I didn't mean to be malicious."

"Didn't you?"

Her eyes widened before a flush stole over her cheeks.

"Maybe a little," she said quietly. "You were right when you said everything feels like a competition."

"It doesn't have to be."

"No." Natalia examined me with a curious expression. "You've changed. You're..."

"Bolder?" I said with a small smile.

Her smile matched mine. "Yes."

That was one of Christian's greatest gifts to me. Not expensive jewelry or fancy trips, but the courage to speak up for myself.

My sister and I lapsed into silence again when our parents returned.

I felt strangely tired all of a sudden, but maybe that was the emotion draining me.

"We have to leave for an event, but family dinner soon?" my mom asked hopefully. "Though perhaps we should skip the achievements portion and simply enjoy the meal."

I let out a choked laugh. "That's probably a good idea."

I breathed in her familiar perfume when she hugged me.

My family hugged all the time in public, but that was mostly for show. We had to play our part as the perfect family.

This time, it felt real.

Brock waited until my family left before he ventured over.

He'd given up trying to melt into the shadows since my breakup with Christian. I wasn't sure whether it was on his boss's orders or if he was more worried now that I was no longer living in Christian's house.

Either way, I appreciated and resented it.

Appreciated it because I liked the sense of security.

Resented it because he reminded me of Christian, and every reminder was a knife through the heart.

"Are you ready to leave, or do you want to stay longer?"

Brock asked. Maybe it was the lighting, but he looked several shades paler than when he'd entered. "We can..."

He swayed on his feet.

A sharp stab of concern pulled my brows together. "Do you need to sit down? You don't look so good."

Actually, I didn't feel great either. My earlier lethargy intensified and tugged at my limbs and eyelids. Brock's face swam before me until I blinked the blurriness away.

"Yes, I"—he gripped the edge of the table. "I"— his face turned ghostly white before flushing crimson. "Stay here. I'll be right back."

He bolted toward the bathroom. The door slammed shut. A second later, I heard the faint but unmistakable sound of vomiting.

My own stomach twisted at the noise.

I hoped we hadn't gotten food poisoning, but something was clearly wrong.

My vision blurred again. This time, blinking didn't help.

I stood, hoping the change in altitude would clear my head, but an instant wave of dizziness forced me back into my seat.

What is going on?

I'd only had tea and a pastry. Could you even *get* food poisoning from tea and pastries?

Black dots danced in front of my eyes, and panic tightened my lungs.

Air. I need air.

I stumbled out of the booth toward the entrance.

Booth had said to stay and wait for him, but the noise around me had coalesced into a concrete weight in my chest. No matter how many deep breaths I took, I couldn't push it off.

But...

I made it halfway to the door when something hit me. What if someone had drugged me and Booth and was *waiting* for me to leave? It seemed far-fetched, but stranger things had happened.

I paused at the exit and tried to sort through my increasingly muddled thoughts.

If I stayed, I might suffocate. If I left, I could be playing right into a hypothetical attacker's hands.

Think, Stella.

Was I being paranoid? It wouldn't hurt to sneak a quick breath of fresh air, right? I could stay right by the—

Someone came up behind me close enough to touch, and I realized I was blocking the door.

"I'm sorry," I mumbled. The words came out slurred. "I'll move out of your way."

"Don't be sorry," the figure said. "You just made things a *lot* easier for me."

Something cold and hard pressed against my back.

I was so out of it, my brain took several moments to register what it was.

A gun.

My panic exploded into a trapped scream that never made it out of my throat.

Not so paranoid after all. I was so stunned about being right that I couldn't process what was happening. I felt like I'd been dropped into the middle of an action thriller with no warning.

"Don't scream." The gun pressed harder. "Or this will be very messy for everyone involved."

How was he able to do this in public? Did no one notice what was happening?

But it was the lunch rush, and my body was shielding his, and...

My thoughts jumbled further.

I didn't have the energy to sort through what was happening, nor did I have a choice.

I followed the figure outside and would've tripped and fell had he not held me up.

The world was a kaleidoscopic haze of concrete and distant car horns.

Eventually, the sounds faded, and there was only the crunch of gravel beneath our feet.

"Apologies in advance." Now that we were somewhere quiet, the voice sounded clearer. More familiar. I'd heard it before. *Where?* "This is going to hurt."

I didn't get a chance to process his words before something hard hit me over the head and full darkness engulfed me.

47

CHRISTIAN

SENTINEL CEO'S TO HIS TOP CYBER DEVELOPER FILLED MY computer screen.

It was a role Kurtz had copied from—who else?—me, since most security companies didn't develop software or hardware, but that wasn't the issue.

The issue was what was in the email.

As expected, the traitor had run straight to Sentinel with the information I'd fed him at the poker tournament.

He worked faster than I thought; it'd only been two days.

I read and reread the last line of the email, which included the details I'd changed for each suspect to parse out who the leak was.

Now I knew.

Ice sluiced through my veins as I exited the email app and pulled up surveillance footage from the front of his building.

I waited until he got in his car before I stood, slipped on my jacket, and walked calmly to the Mirage's garage.

Instead of my McLaren, I selected the gray sedan I used

when I tailed someone. It was utterly unremarkable and blended in with every other vehicle on the road.

I'd put a tracker on all the suspects' cars weeks ago, so it didn't take me long to tail the traitor to an abandoned junkyard on the outskirts of the city.

Kurtz was already waiting there with a smarmy smile.

I wanted to rip out every tooth and shove them down his fucking throat, but I forced myself to breathe through my crimson haze.

Patience. I would deal with him later.

I parked in a spot that was out of their eyeshot but gave me an indirect view of them via one of the old junk cars' rearview mirrors.

It was there that I watched Kage exit his car and greet Kurtz.

My hand tightened around the steering wheel.

Of the four suspects, Kage had been the most and least likely.

Most, because he was the one who'd been best positioned to access the high-level leaked information.

Least, because he'd been the closest thing I'd had to a brother at Harper Security since Rhys left.

Rage rolled through my blood in an icy, unforgiving wave. It begged me to release it, to destroy not only the people in the junkyard but everything they loved.

Kurtz's company. Kage's reputation. Their money, their families...

I forced the urge at bay. *Later.*

"Do you have the blueprint?" Kurtz asked.

"Not yet. It's a brand-new device." Kage ran a hand over his buzz cut. "I don't have the details yet, and I can't leak it too soon or he'll get suspicious. He's already on alert because of Scylla."

"Then why the fuck did you tell him about the copy?" Kurtz's smile collapsed into a scowl. "Now he knows he has a problem."

"I had to get him off my ass," Kage growled. "Keep his trust. He was getting suspicious about why it was taking me so long to figure out what happened. It's that damn woman he's dating." His tone darkened further.

I hadn't told anyone except Brock that Stella and I had broken up. It was none of their goddamned business.

"Don't worry about him tracing the copy back to you. He's so distracted by pussy he's lucky the company is still running properly. He took a month off to play tour guide for her around Italy, for fuck's sake."

"Ah, yes. Stella. I met her. At least it's fine pussy." Kurtz laughed, and my rage deepened into a crimson-tinted cloud. "You know Harper. He's so blinded by hubris he thinks he can handle anything and that no one would dare betray him. I would've loved to see his face when he found out about Axel."

Kage snorted. "That fucker was getting on my nerves. Always trying to kiss ass and one-up me. Thank fuck we made him the fall guy and Harper fell for it. One less problem on my plate."

I'd suspected Axel might not have been responsible for *Magda*'s theft when I discovered another leak months ago.

The confirmation elicited a rare twinge of regret, but I couldn't change the past, so there was no use agonizing over what happened.

The best thing I could do was exact proper justice on the *real* traitor.

"Yes, well, that had to be done. Too bad we never figured out what was so special about that hideous painting. Went through all that trouble to get it only to have to sell it before Harper traced it back to us," Kurtz grumbled.

"That's one thing he never told anyone, not even me." Kage shrugged. "If I find out, I'll let you know."

"You do that." Kurtz's smile was not unlike that of a shark grinning at prey. "In the meantime..." He retrieved a briefcase from the trunk of his car. "Your second half of the cut for the Scylla information. Cash only, as requested."

A briefcase? Really?

I couldn't decide what pissed me off more—Kurtz's face, Kage's betrayal, or the fact that they were acting like villains in a bad TV cop drama.

"You must really hate him to fuck him over like this," Kurtz said as Kage counted the cash. "Thought you and Harper were brothers in arms till you reached out a couple of years ago."

"We were," Kage said coldly. He snapped the briefcase closed. "Things change. No one wants to live in another's shadow forever."

"Ambition. Love to see it." Kurtz clapped him on the shoulder. Kage grimaced, but the Sentinel CEO didn't seem to notice. "You know, when you first contacted us, I thought you were setting me up, but you've proven to be a useful ally. I've been dying to see Harper taken down a peg or two for years." He got in his car and winked. "Nice doing business with you, as always."

Kurtz drove off.

I would deal with him later. Now that I'd confirmed Sentinel was behind the Scylla knockoff, I knew they were also the ones who'd supplied the device to Stella's stalker. That fact alone earned them more than a little system crash.

Kage tossed the briefcase in his trunk and walked around to the driver's seat while I got out of my car, my footsteps silent against the soft earth.

"Whatever he paid you, it wasn't enough." My casual

observation bounced off the twisted metal heaps surrounding us.

I stopped a few feet from where he'd parked.

To his credit, Kage only froze for two seconds before he recovered.

He straightened and faced me, his mouth relaxing into an easy smile. "Christian. What are you doing here?"

Despite his casual tone, I saw the emotions play out in his eyes.

Surprise. Panic. Fear.

"I had some free time. Decided to check in on my best employee." My smile matched his.

His eye twitched at the word *employee*.

We stared at each other, the air taut with the scents of rusted iron and brewing violence.

Now that we were face to face, I allowed my emotions free reign for the first time since I saw Kurtz's email.

Kage was my oldest employee. My right-hand man.

Once upon a time, he'd saved my life, and he was one of the few people I'd trusted.

His betrayal twisted around my insides like barbed wire and squeezed out drops of blood.

One drop for every meal we'd shared, every conversation we'd had, every problem we'd tackled together and every tough situation we'd pulled each other through.

The crimson pool filled my stomach with acid and ate away at my armor until grief and another twinge of regret over what I had to do peeked through.

I eased a breath through my lungs.

The armor rebuilt itself and trapped my floating emotions back in their cage.

Five seconds. That was the longest I allowed sentimentality to stay.

"What was it?" I broke the silence. "You wanted a higher salary? More recognition? A fucking thrill because you're so goddamned bored?"

Kage dropped the playing dumb act.

"It's not about the money. It's about *you*." Resentment leaked into his words. "If it weren't for me, the company wouldn't be where it is today. *I'm* the one who runs the day-to-day operations while you jet set around the world with your fucking private plane and fancy hotels. Yours is the name on the door. You're the one everyone fawns over. You're the CEO, and I'm a fucking employee. I'm not your partner. I'm just a soldier in your command. Every time I go somewhere, people only ask me about *you*. I'm *sick* of it."

Oh, for fuck's sake. I was almost disappointed the reason for his betrayal was so pedestrian. Envy and resentment were as mundane as I used to think love was.

But that was the thing about humans. Their most basic emotions were the most dangerous.

"More recognition, then," I said mildly. "Enough that you would run to our biggest competitor and fuck over your friend and what you said you helped build. You could've talked to me, but you fucking didn't. That doesn't make you a hero, Kage. That makes you a goddamn coward."

Kage *had* helped me in the company's infancy, and he played an integral role in the company's operations. I'd compensated him extremely well for both those things over the years.

However, Harper Security flourished not because of its operations but my contacts and the cyber arm I'd built. Kage had little interest in networking and even less knowledge of cyber development. His reasoning was flawed.

The only thing he was right about was my distraction. I would've caught onto him sooner had it not been for Stella.

I'd had a tiny inkling since the Deacon and Beatrix accounts, which he worked closely on, but I'd brushed it off in lieu of more important matters.

"At least Sentinel appreciates what I'm doing for them, and I got to see *you* brought down a notch. It's been fun playing spy. Sabotaging you from the inside and you didn't even know it because you were so caught up with your fucking girlfriend while I kept the company running." Kage's smile iced over. "You haven't treated me like a friend in a long time, Christian. You treat me like a dumb lackey you can just order around. Like you wouldn't be lying dead with a bullet in your head if I hadn't saved your ass."

The memory flickered in front of my eyes.

Colombia, ten years ago. Things got messy with an arms dealer and I'd found myself in the middle of a shootout.

I still remembered the sweltering heat, the rapid-fire gunshots peppered with shouts, and the force of Kage yanking me out of the way milliseconds before a bullet pierced the back of my head.

He'd been guarding a corrupt local businessman, and we'd shot our way out of an impossible situation.

Now here we were, a decade later, on the brink of another shootout.

My eyes were on Kage's, but my attention was lasered in on the bulge in his waistband and the press of my gun between my hip and the small of my back.

"Personal is personal, business is business," I said coolly. "When we're working, you are an *employee*."

Kage's eye twitched again.

"I assume the Deacon and Beatrix accounts were also your doing."

"I did what had to be done. Sentinel was getting antsy after *Magda* turned out to be a dud." He raised an eyebrow. "Don't suppose you'll tell me what's so special about that painting after all?"

"Keep it a mystery. Makes life more interesting. The question now, of course..." My voice softened. "Is what to do with you."

I did not tolerate traitors. I didn't care if they were friends, family, or someone who saved my life.

Once they crossed that line, they had to be dealt with.

Silence pulsed for an extra beat before Kage and I pulled our guns and fired at the same time.

Gunshots exploded, followed by the clang of metal striking metal.

I ducked behind the rusted skeleton of a car, my heart drumming, my pulse alive with adrenaline.

I could easily end him with one shot. His aim was good; mine was better.

One shot, however, was too easy for such a big betrayal.

I wanted it to hurt.

"You're not going to kill me," Kage called out. I saw his reflection in the windows of the car opposite me. He'd taken cover behind a truck near where'd been standing, but his gun and a sliver of his jeans peeked out from behind the old metal frame. "Not here. I know you. You're probably thinking up ways you can torture me right now."

I didn't take the bait. I wasn't going to shout across a junkyard like some B-list actor in an action movie.

My phone buzzed with a new text.

I would've ignored it given my current...distraction, but a warning instinct tugged at my senses.

Something's wrong.

I flicked my eyes down at the screen for a millisecond.

Brock: 23, District Cafe

My brain automatically translated the company code into a full message given the context.

Incapacitated, need eyes on Stella ASAP. We're at District Cafe.

Panic like I'd never known coiled my spine and spiked in my blood.

Something happened to Stella.

He didn't say it, but I *felt* it. The same warning instinct that'd compelled me to check my texts in the middle of a goddamned gunfight rang the alarms so loud they nearly drowned out Kage's voice.

"It's not going to happen," he continued. His voice was harsh with excitement and a tinge of regret. "Only one of us is making it out of here alive, and it's not going to be you."

I made my decision in an instant.

"That's where you're wrong." I stepped out from behind the car frame.

Kage left his hiding place and aimed his gun at me, but I pulled the trigger before he could fire.

The gunshot echoed in the empty junkyard, followed by three others.

One to his chest, one to his head, and one to each kneecap in case he survived and foolishly decided to continue the fight.

He staggered, then toppled to the ground.

I kept my gun aimed at him as I walked over. The soft rustle of grass gave way to the crunch of gravel until I stood over him.

Eyes blank and wide open, mouth agape. Blood pooled beneath him in a growing puddle and stained the ground with dark crimson.

I didn't have to check his pulse to know he was dead.

A decade together gone in minutes, all because he'd resented me for his choices.

I stepped over Kage's dead body and returned to my car.

I didn't have the time or capacity for more sentimentality. Anyone who betrayed me was dead to me, literally and figuratively.

By the time someone, if anyone, found Kage, his body would've been picked apart by wild animals.

Kurtz was the only person who might be a problem, but he wouldn't say a damn thing. A dead Kage was useless to him, and he wouldn't risk his own neck to point police in the right direction.

Since I was Kage's employer, I would have to figure out a good story to tell the authorities and the rest of the company, but that wouldn't take long. I'd figure out the details later.

23.

Brock's message replayed in my head as I gunned it out of the junkyard. My panic spiked again, mixed with a healthy dose of fear.

When I hit the main road, I'd already forgotten all about Kage.

The only thing that mattered was Stella.

48

CHRISTIAN

My warning instincts from earlier clanged louder the closer I got to the cafe, and they curdled into dread when I arrived to find Brock puking his guts out in the bathroom.

There was no Stella in sight.

He managed to outline the basics of what happened before he went back to heaving over the toilet.

I didn't bother interrogating him further. Every second counted, and he was in no shape to stand, much less speak.

Instead, I went straight to the counter, my blood like ice water in my veins, and demanded to see the security footage from the past two hours.

Five minutes of splutters and tedious protests later, the cafe manager pulled up said footage in his cramped back office.

My heart thrummed as I watched the grainy scenes play out onscreen.

Stella and Brock entered. They placed an order at the counter and sat at separate tables before her family arrived.

Despite the gravity of the situation, I felt a pinprick of pride at the way she took control of the conversation. I couldn't hear what they were saying, but I could read their body language.

After her family left, Brock approached her again, but his steps were shakier than when he'd entered. He and Stella had a quick exchange before he rushed off to the bathroom. A minute later, she stood and swayed then sat back down. Her face was pale, and she looked like she was having trouble breathing.

My knuckles turned white against the back of the manager's chair.

Someone had to have drugged her. That was the simplest, most plausible explanation.

The urge to step inside the screen and comfort her, then pulverize the bastard who'd done that to her, overwhelmed me.

Stella stood again and stumbled toward the door. She was right by the exit, and she only made it a few feet before someone came up behind her.

My senses went on high alert.

I stared at the figure. Tall, baseball cap, dark jacket.

They paused by the exit, then left at the same time.

I couldn't see the full scope of what happened due to the angle, but the way the figure's shoulders shifted, the jacket in the middle of summer, the careful way he kept his face turned away from the camera...

He had a gun. I was sure of it.

I was also sure I'd seen that jacket before.

My pulse roared with lethal certainty.

"Rewind the tape," I ordered. "Stop."

The video paused where Stella and Brock placed their orders. The same figure stood next to them at the counter. He paid for his drink in cash and drummed his fingers until Brock turned his back to say something to Stella.

What happened next took only a few seconds.

A casual reach inside his jacket, a quick tap of what looked like two tiny packets into Stella's and Brock's mugs, and a return to drinking his coffee.

He was fast.

He'd also slipped up.

When he turned his head to face forward again, I caught a glimpse of his profile. I'd seen it before during two separate background checks.

Motherfucker.

All the pieces clicked into place.

How he got into the Mirage. Why there had been no evidence of him leaving the building. His connection to Stella.

I didn't bother thanking the manager or getting Brock, who was still incapacitated in the bathroom.

Instead, I sent out a code black to the company along with the stalker's name and instructions to find him and Stella as soon as possible.

Reserved for extreme emergencies, the code black alert recalled all agents in the area for a new assignment.

I had never once used it until now.

If the stalker had been smart enough to evade detection this long, he was smart enough not to turn on his cell phone or use his personal car.

Still, we had the information necessary to track him down.

I only hoped that, when we did, it wasn't too late.

49

STELLA

A PRICKLE OF SENSATION DRAGGED ME FROM THE DARK, murky wells of unconsciousness.

It started as a tingle in my fingers and toes. Then it was the hard press of wood beneath my thighs. Finally, it was the rough abrasion of ropes around my wrists and a pounding pain behind my eyes.

The only times I'd been tied up were with Christian, but that'd been consensual. This...I didn't know *what* this was.

All I knew was, it hurt, and my throat was dry, and my head throbbed like someone had shoved a jackhammer or ten in there.

Concrete anchors dragged down my lids. The darkness wasn't soft and gentle like the gradual drift to sleep. It was endless and menacing, like the weight of the earth after being buried alive.

I forced my lungs to expand past my rising panic.

Breathe. Think. What happened?

I struggled to sort through the day's events.

I remembered meeting my family at the cafe. Brock

running to the restroom. Nausea, dizziness, stumbling out for air...and the cold press of a gun against my ribcage. A voice, then blackness.

Oh God.

I'd been kidnapped.

The realization sank in with cold, sharp claws.

The desire to sink into panic consumed me, but I gritted my teeth and forced myself to stay in the present.

I was *not* dying like this. I wasn't dying at all. Not for a very, very long time.

I pried my eyes open through sheer force of will. Dizziness warped my vision before my surroundings took shape.

I was in some sort of ramshackle cabin made of corrugated metal and wood. A thick film of grime coated the windows and muted the sunlight scattered on the floor. There was no furniture other than the chair I was bound to and a lopsided table that held a length of rope and, almost laughably, a takeout container of food.

Bile coated my throat.

Where was I? Judging by the light, it hadn't been long since I was knocked out, which meant we couldn't have gone too far.

"You're awake."

My head whipped toward the familiar voice, and a second bout of dizziness washed over me.

When it cleared, the bile thickened.

I knew why the voice was so familiar.

"No." The croak sounded pathetically weak.

Julian smiled. "Surprised?"

D.C.'s most celebrated lifestyle journalist looked different outside the glossy confines of his *Washington Weekly* headshot and the one time we'd met in person.

It'd been for my profile photoshoot, and he'd been nice. Unassuming.

He'd been even nicer during the dozen or so times we spoke on the phone.

But now that I looked closer, I spotted the mad glint in his eyes and the unnaturalness of his smile.

It was the smile of a psychopath.

My pulse jackknifed.

"I thought you might be." Julian smoothed a hand over the front of his shirt. "You don't remember me, do you?"

"You're a writer for *Washington Weekly*." My tongue felt thick in my mouth.

He must've slipped something in my drink at the cafe. Whatever it was, its effects lingered and clouded the edges of my consciousness.

"Obviously." I could've sworn he rolled his eyes. "*Before that*, Stella. We had a class together at Thayer. Communications Theory with Professor Pittman. You sat two seats in front of me and to my right." A smile of reminiscence appeared. "I liked that class. It was where I first saw you."

Thayer. Communications Theory.

Quick flashes of a quiet blond boy sitting in the back of the class filtered through my mind's eye, but I'd taken that class *years* ago. I barely remembered what the professor looked like, much less my classmates.

"I didn't tell you during our many lovely chats. I wanted to see if you remembered." His smile collapsed into a frown. "You didn't, but that's okay. I was a different person back then. Less successful, less worthy of you. I told you how I felt with my letters, but I had to make something of myself before I knew you'd accept me. It's why I didn't contact you earlier. But now..." He spread his arms. "We can finally be together."

"Be together? You *kidnapped me!*"

I couldn't wrap my head around what he was saying. The situation was too surreal.

"Yes, about that. I'm sorry I had to knock you out, but it made things easier." Apology entered his voice. "I would untie you too, but I can't do that until we fix you."

The scene was growing more surreal by the second. "What are you talking about?"

"Christian Harper." The name dripped with so much acid it burned in the back of my throat. "You think you're still in love with him. I can see it in your eyes."

Oh God. Christian.

The full import of what was happening hit me.

Julian was clearly off his rocker, and he had me tied up in the middle of God knows where. I could try to escape, but I had no car, and I was still woozy from being hit over the head.

There was a strong possibility I would never see Christian, my friends, or my family again.

Panic climbed higher in my chest, but I forced it back down.

I'll figure out a plan. I had to.

Until then, I needed to keep Julian talking instead of doing...whatever else he had planned for me.

My stomach lurched. "I'm not dating Christian anymore."

God, I wish I were.

I wished I was in his apartment right now, making tacos while he teased me about putting too much cheese on mine and grumbled when I answered my social media messages instead of paying attention to him.

Hot tears pooled on my lower lids.

"I didn't say you were still dating him," Julian snapped. "I said you're still *under the delusion that you love him!*"

His voice escalated before he took a deep breath and smoothed a hand over his shirt again.

"It's okay. It's not your fault," he said soothingly. "He deceived you. Tricked you into falling for the looks and money.

But *we're* the ones who are supposed to be together. I've known that since I first saw you. I dreamed about you after that first day of class, you know."

Another smile took over his face. "I dreamed we were married and living in a little cabin in the woods. We had two kids. I worked all day, and when I came home, you were waiting for me. It was beautiful. I'd never dreamed about a girl before. If that's not a sign from God, what is?"

A *dream?* I'd gone through hell because of a freaking *dream?*

Breathe.

Stale air scraped against my lungs.

"There's no one more beautiful than you are, Stella. You were always so quiet and nice to me, even when everyone else ignored or made fun of me. You have the qualities I'm looking for in a wife. You're perfect for me."

I wasn't the same person I'd been in college, but it was clear he didn't see me as my own person. He only saw me as a trophy, something he could own.

"How did you get all those pictures of me?" I moved my hands behind me as much as I dared, searching for something, *anything,* I could use to break the rope. "How did you break into my apartment?"

My breath hiked when I hit what felt a hard, sharp protrusion on the back of the chair. It felt like a nail.

The chair was so old I wouldn't be surprised. Honestly, I didn't care *what* it was. I only cared whether it could fray the ropes enough for me to free myself.

I kept my eyes on Julian as I worked my binding over the nail as discreetly as possible.

"I've always been good at digging into people. Journalism major, you know. Plus, I blend in with the crowd. Makes it easy to follow someone without them knowing. As for your apart-

ment..." Julian grinned. "That's the best part! I have an apartment in the Mirage as well. My grandmother passed it on to me
after she died. I don't live there full time, but I have the keys.
We're practically neighbors. I was so upset when you didn't
notice me the one time we shared an elevator, but you were too
busy looking at your phone." He let out a snort.

I kept quiet. I was too focused on my task.

Luckily, Julian liked to make a production of his story,
pacing and gesticulating as he told me what he did.

Every time he turned his back, I worked faster, then slowed
when he faced me again.

Sweat beaded from my efforts, but the rope had loosened
enough that it no longer dug into my skin.

Just a little more...

"It was harder to hack into the surveillance system, but I
had help for that. I hired Sentinel Security. They're Harper's
biggest competitor, and I figured they'd take any opportunity to
take him down a peg. I was right. They gave me some fancy
device I could use, and the rest is history."

He stopped in front of me.

I froze, praying he didn't look over my head and behind my
back.

"I did all that for *you*, Stella. Because I love you. I only wish
I hadn't left you for two years. Unfortunately, I had to go back
home and take care of my grandmother." He sounded annoyed.
"She was the one who left me the apartment and all the money
we could need. She was big on real estate, and since my parents
died, I got everything."

"You started dating Harper while I was gone, which wasn't
very nice." Disapproval formed a deep crease in his brow. "But
I'm back, and you're out of that asshole's house. I had to lay low
for a while after I returned, you know. Couldn't risk Harper

tracking me down. The good part is, I had time to plan all this out."

Julian knelt and smoothed my hair out of my face. "We can finally be together *after* we fix you. I don't think it'll take long, though. A few weeks with me and you'll see. We're meant to be together."

He beamed.

A sick feeling ballooned in my stomach.

He was delusional. *Beyond* delusional.

He said he loved me, but what he was doing wasn't love.

Love was accepting me for who I was, flaws and all.

Love was believing in me even when I didn't believe in myself.

Love was quiet moments and soft kisses, breathless exhilaration and rough hands all rolled into one.

Love was what Christian gave me.

He'd crossed boundaries and kept secrets, but he would never do *this*. He would never drug me or intentionally hurt me.

I knew I should play along until I could escape, but even the thought of pretending to want to be with Julian made me want to vomit.

"Julian..." I looked him in the eye.

He smiled, his face bright with sick anticipation.

"I would rather *die* than be with you."

I headbutted him as hard as I could.

His howl of pain ricocheted through the cabin.

Lights washed across my vision at the force of the impact, but I didn't have time to waste. I slammed my wrists down as hard as I could behind me until the frayed rope snapped against the protrusion.

Luckily, Julian hadn't tied my legs, and I stumbled to the door. I almost made it before strong hands yanked me back.

I hit the floor with a *thud*.

Julian pinned me to the ground and manacled my wrists above my head.

"Let go of me!" I struggled against his hold.

"You're mine," he said calmly, like we were at a picnic in the park and he wasn't holding me hostage. "It'll be so much easier if you give in, Stella. I don't want to hurt you."

I couldn't keep struggling forever. My energy was already fading, my muscles sore and my thoughts jumbled with panic.

I turned my head a fraction to the right, and my breath hitched when I saw my purse lying a few feet away.

My taser.

I always kept it on me. If I could only reach it...

Julian followed my gaze and chuckled. "Oh, don't worry about your taser. I took the batteries out. I—" His sentence cut off with another, more animalistic howl when I took advantage of his distraction, sank my teeth into his neck, and tore.

The wet, sickening sound of flesh tearing ripped through the air.

His grip slackened. I shoved him off to crawl toward the entrance.

I didn't look behind me. My stomach turned at the metallic blood in my mouth, but I didn't have time to dwell on my disgust.

I reached for the doorknob and used it to pull myself up...

A scream of frustration scraped up my throat when Julian dragged me back again. He slammed me face-first into the wall next to the door.

Pain exploded in my head. My vision crackled and fizzed like the static on an old TV.

"You disappoint me, Stella." Menace twisted Julian's grunt into something dark and sinister. The blood from his neck wound dripped onto my skin and burned like acid. "I was trying to be nice. I thought you understood. If I can't have you..." The press of his gun against the underside of my chin sent an icy splash of fear down my spine. "No one can."

I let out a small cry when he wrenched my head back. The gun was cold, but his breaths were hot and sinister against my neck.

"Maybe you're beyond saving. You've been ruined. But that's okay. We can be together in our next life." He kissed my neck. A shiver of disgust rippled down my spine. "We're soulmates. Soulmates always find their way back to each other."

He cocked the gun.

Pain and terror dissolved into numbness. I closed my eyes, not wanting this cabin to be the last thing I saw before I died.

My breaths slowed as I mentally retreated to my safest place.

Whiskey eyes. Warm murmurs. Leather and spice.

Silent tears dripped my cheeks.

Time slowed as snippets of my life passed through my mind. Dressing up as Bratz dolls with my friends for Halloween, assembling puzzles with Maura, family vacations to the beach, posting my first blog post, calls with Brady and afternoons in cafes and photoshoots by the water...and Christian.

Of all the people I'd miss most, he took the top spot.

I love you.

A loud gunshot rattled my eardrums.

I flinched and waited for the burst of pain, but it never came.

Instead, I heard the slam of a door, followed by shouts and a violent rush of air as Julian's body was yanked off mine.

My eyes flew open, and I watched, stunned, as half a dozen men poured into the cabin with guns in hand.

One of them subdued Julian easily while the others swept the space.

Everything happened so quickly I was still standing by the door when a warm, familiar presence touched the side of my neck.

It can't be.

But when I turned, there he was.

Dark hair. Bright eyes. Face carved with cold, pitiless rage.

Christian.

My trapped sob finally broke free.

As angry as I'd been when I'd found the files, and as much as he'd betrayed my trust in the past, there was no one I'd rather see at that moment than him.

"Stella." Relief softened the razor edges of his fury.

He said my name like a prayer, a whisper so raw and heart-felt it obliterated any resistance I might've had.

I didn't think. I didn't speak.

I just crossed the room and crumpled into his arms.

50

CHRISTIAN

She's here. She's safe.

I repeated the words in my head as I held Stella tight.

Tiny shivers rippled through her body, and even though she was almost as tall as me, she felt fragile. Breakable.

Fierce protectiveness burned in my chest.

"It's all right, sweetheart," I murmured. "You're okay. You're safe."

She buried her face deeper in my neck, her soft sobs twisting my heart like a wrung-out rag.

I was holding her again for the first time in weeks, but this wasn't how I'd wanted it to be.

Not with her bruised, hurt, and terrified.

The relief I'd felt at seeing her alive gave way to renewed rage.

My cold gaze found Julian over Stella's shoulder.

He glared back at me, his eyes filled with hatred, but he didn't say a word as Steele and Mason secured him with restraints.

I'd recognized Julian's face from his *Washington Weekly* bio. I also recognized it from the background check I'd run on his grandmother when she first bought her apartment at the Mirage. After she died, the property passed to him.

I didn't involve myself in the mundane details of tenant turnover, so I hadn't connected that detail.

No wonder there'd been no evidence of him leaving the Mirage after he broke into Stella's apartment. He'd been inside it the whole time.

"Keep him alive," I said. "I'll deal with him personally."

I wanted the pleasure of tearing the bastard apart myself.

However, a glimmer of pride sparked in my chest when I saw the nasty wound on his neck. Stella must've taken a chunk out of him before we arrived.

That's my girl.

Steele nodded. "You got it."

We'd tracked Julian down via the credit card he'd used for his car rental, then tracked the car to this shittastic cabin in the Virginia woods. The car's built-in GPS made that easy.

I hadn't wanted to take any chances, so I'd called in a handful of men to accompany me and dispatched another to get Brock.

Julian must've drugged him and Stella with different substances—one to incapacitate Brock and get him out of the room, the other to disorient her.

I wanted nothing more than to flay him alive, but Stella took priority.

I rubbed a hand over her back. "We'll check into a hotel and get you cleaned up," I murmured. "I have a doctor who can meet us there and take a look at your wounds."

I hated hospitals. All that fucking paperwork and lax security. It was easier to take care of her myself.

When she gave a tiny, silent nod, I left my men to deal with the mess in the cabin and gently guided her into my car.

My anger flared again at the sight of her cuts and bruises in bright daylight, but I tamped it down.

Later. Once I made sure she was okay, I could take all the time I wanted dismantling Julian.

Stella didn't speak as I pulled away from the cabin.

I wanted to take her back to my apartment, but I didn't want to violate the boundaries she'd established during our breakup.

However, when we arrived at the nearest decent hotel, she didn't budge from the car.

She stared at the entrance, her knuckles white around her knees.

"Can we go to your house instead?" she asked quietly. "I want to be somewhere safe."

My heart roared to life, but I kept my voice even. "Of course."

Dr. Abelson was already waiting for us when we arrived at the Mirage. He was technically retired, but one of my clients had referred me to him years ago when I'd mentioned needing a private, discreet doctor.

Apparently, Abelson needed something other than golf and television to pass the time during retirement.

I didn't need the other residents asking questions, so I took us through the back entrance up to my penthouse.

I had a special room set aside for medical treatment, and I watched impatiently as Abelson introduced himself to Stella and checked her injuries.

"Is she okay?" I demanded after an interminable length of time that was in reality less than thirty minutes.

"She has a few cuts and bruises, plus a mild concussion, but she'll be fine," he said. "Nothing time and rest won't heal."

The diagnosis should've placated me, but all I focused on was the word *concussion*.

I mentally added another fifteen minutes to my time with Julian.

"I'll do it," I said when he moved to bandage one of her cuts. "You can leave. Thank you."

Other than a small lift of his eyebrows, Abelson didn't react to my request.

"Do I want to know what happened?" he asked as he packed his bag. He kept his voice low

Stella sat on the far side of the room. She'd been silent during her examination, but that didn't mean she couldn't hear us.

"No." He was on call to handle medical issues, but I kept him out of the loop on how, exactly, those issues arose.

"That's what I figured." He shook his head. "Call me if any complications arise. I don't anticipate they will, but you have my number."

That was why I liked Abelson. He was discreet, competent, and didn't ask unnecessary questions.

After he left, I finished bandaging Stella's cuts.

The tips of my fingers skimmed her skin as I gently pressed the bandages over her wounds. The steady hum of the air conditioner mingled with our soft breaths, and an electric current wound my muscles tight until I finished my ministrations.

"If you're hungry, I can make us food," I said.

She shook her head. "I just want to shower and sleep."

I didn't argue. Instead, I guided her to the hallway and stopped between the guest room and my bedroom.

I shouldn't ask. I knew it might cross boundaries again, and that she might not be ready. But I had to try.

"Stay with me." I softened the words into a request, not an order. "Just for tonight. Please."

We were in the safety of my penthouse, but it wasn't enough.

I'd almost lost her, and I needed her close.

I needed to see her, touch her, comfort her. Reassure myself she was actually there and not a figment of my imagination.

Only then could I breathe.

An eternity of a second passed, followed by a small nod, sweet relief, and the *click* of my bedroom door closing behind us.

Stella and I took turns showering.

She'd moved all her belongings into Ava's house, so I gave her one of my old shirts to wear.

The sight of her in my clothing tugged at my heart.

It didn't mean she forgave me or that we were back together. She'd gone through a traumatizing experience, and her actions now weren't indicative of her regular behavior.

But it was progress, and I'd take anything I could get.

"How did you find me?" she asked as I slid into bed next to her.

She'd regained some of her color after the shower, and she was making conversation again.

More progress.

Another tingle of relief eased my tension.

"Brock texted me, and I saw him on the cafe's security footage." I gave her a quick rundown of what happened, leaving out the part about Kage and the junkyard.

"Will he be okay?"

Stella *would* be worried about someone else when she was the one who'd been abducted.

The corner of my mouth kicked up. "Yes. He'll be fine with some rest."

"Good." She half faced me with one hand tucked beneath her cheek.

Despite what she'd said about wanting to sleep, she seemed reluctant to do so.

"Talk to me, Butterfly. What's on your mind?"

"Well, I've had an exciting day."

Another smile crossed my lips. Jokes, no matter how dry, were always a good sign.

"But I don't want to talk about what happened right now." She shifted so she faced me fully. "Tell me a story."

"A fairytale?" I teased.

She shook her head. "Something real."

I thought about it before my smile gradually faded. "How real do you want, Stella?"

"As real as it gets." Her voice softened. "Tell me a story about you."

I was quiet for a moment before I spoke again.

"I told you about my father and how my parents died. What I didn't tell you was what my mom left behind." The words came out faded, like furniture webbed with dust after being hidden for so long. "It was a goodbye note."

The police found it on the scene. My aunt hadn't wanted me to see it, but I'd insisted.

I still remembered how it smelled, like ink and my mom's favorite perfume. My skin had still been warm from the afternoon sun, but I hadn't been able to stop shivering when I read the note.

"She told me how much she loved me and didn't want to leave me, but that she had no choice. That she couldn't live without my father and that her sister would take care of me."

A bitter smile touched my lips. "Imagine telling your child you *loved* them before you left them all alone in the world.

Knowing they'd lose the only parent they had left because you couldn't stick around long enough to even *try*? It'd been two days. That was it. I wasn't sad when I read that letter, Stella. I was *angry,* and I was glad about that, because anger is easier than abandonment."

"But my mom also left something else behind. Her one attempt at painting. She loved art, but she was a terrible artist, and even my father couldn't lie and tell her it was good. We put it in the basement, but after she died, I dug it up and held onto it. I didn't know why. Maybe because I resented what art had done to my family, and I liked seeing its ugliness and chaos immortalized on canvas. I had her note as well, and when I was older, I reworked the frame and placed it inside the painting. The most fucked up part was, I named it after her. *Magda*."

"Yes," I said when Stella's eyes widened. "The same *Magda* you heard me talking about with Dante. I should've tossed both the painting and the note out long ago, but I couldn't bring myself to do it. It wasn't the items themselves. It was what they symbolized—what my parents did and how they abandoned me. I hated *Magda*, yet she was the most important thing in my life. Enough so that I had it under guard. I even forged documents saying it's this priceless piece of art so no one would question why I was expending so many resources on it."

A rough laugh left my throat. "It seems like a stupidly elaborate ruse for something so simple, but that painting has always fucked me up. I could never let it go. That hideous piece of art symbolized everything she loved more than me. Whenever I see it, I see *her*. I see her sitting down, writing that note, then blowing her brains out."

Stella flinched at the visual imagery, but I was too far gone to stop.

"I see myself sitting in my classroom when the principal

called me into his office. I see my aunt's face and the funeral and the pitying looks everyone gave me after she died. The town didn't know the truth about my father; the businessman he was stealing from didn't want any extra publicity about the case, and he paid off the authorities to keep the whole thing quiet."

I swallowed past a strange lump in my throat. "A mother's love for her child is supposed to be the greatest love of all. Yet it wasn't enough for her to stay with me."

Stella had been quiet throughout my story, but now she looked at me with a thousand words in her eyes.

"Christian..." she breathed, her voice thick with unshed tears.

I tucked a stray strand of hair behind her ear. "This isn't a sob story, Butterfly," I said gruffly. "Don't feel bad for me. I got over it a long time ago."

It was a heavy story to tell given the day she'd had, but she wanted real. And my history with *Magda* was as real as it got.

"I don't think you've gotten over it," she said softly. "Not if you're still holding onto it."

"Technically, Dante is holding onto it." I sidestepped her observation.

"How did he get it?"

"The painting got stolen, then sold in a bunch of estate sales." I didn't get into the dirty details about Kage, Sentinel, and how, in the mother of all coincidences, it landed in Josh's hands. I'd found it before Josh bought it and retrieved the note, but I'd let the painting's sales run their course in order to track down who stole it. I'd been right about Sentinel and wrong about Axel. "Dante acted as my proxy and bought it back since I didn't want more people knowing about my connection to it. He's holding it at his place while I figure out what to do with it."

"Have you?" Stella asked. "Figured out what to do with it?"

"Not yet. But I will."

We lay there, our breaths intertwining in the compressed space between us.

Stella was right. I hadn't gotten over *Magda*. I'd pushed it to the back of my mind because of everything that had happened the past few months, but I could still feel its skeletal grasp on me.

I could destroy it, or I could live in its stranglehold forever.

But that was a decision for another day.

"Can I tell you a secret?" Stella whispered. "When I was in the cabin, and I thought I was about to die...the person I thought about most was you."

Her words sliced me open and dug into my heart—both the part about her almost dying, and the part where she thought about me.

"I'm not saying I'm one hundred percent over what you did because I'm not," she said. "But I also understand keeping things secret and not knowing how to tell the truth. I also realized I was wrong when I compared you to Julian. You would never hurt me the way he did. And, to be honest, I..." Stella visibly swallowed. "I missed you."

The compression in my chest loosened, and my mouth softened in a genuine smile. "I can work with that."

"Also..." A ruddy flush spread across her cheeks. "I *might* be able to up the percentage if you give me a goodnight kiss."

Laughter rumbled in my chest. "I can *definitely* work with that."

I drew her closer. "I missed you too," I added softly before pressing a gentle kiss to her mouth. I could kiss her forever, but I forced myself to pull back after the count of three. Now wasn't the time for a hot and heavy makeup session. "That's all you're getting for now. You need rest."

Stella sighed. "Tease."

Despite her grumbling, she was out like a light minutes later.

I tucked her closer to my chest and, after weeks of restless nights, let the soothing rhythm of her breaths finally lull me to sleep.

51

STELLA

I SLEPT IN UNTIL NOON THE NEXT DAY. IT WAS THE LATEST I'd ever woken up, but the previous day's events had taken their toll. Even after a solid sixteen hours of rest, fogginess clouded my brain as I walked to the kitchen.

Being drugged and kidnapped. Finding out my old classmate slash the reporter who'd written that amazing profile on me was my stalker. Nearly dying, then getting rescued by Christian, staying the night at his house, and sort of/kind of making up with him.

I'd had time to process, so it was easier to wrap my head around what happened, but yesterday was so surreal I still felt like I was walking on the edge of a dream.

It was Monday, so I'd expected Christian to be at work. But when I entered the sun-splashed kitchen, I found him standing by the espresso machine, dressed in a black shirt and pants instead of his usual suit.

I blinked with surprise. "You're here."

"It *is* my house," he said dryly. He nodded at the array of covered plates on the kitchen island. "Nina's here and made breakfast. Lemon ricotta pancakes, your favorite."

My stomach growled at the mention of breakfast. I'd had a pastry for lunch and skipped dinner yesterday, so I would be happy with *any* kind of food.

"How are you feeling?" he asked, watching as I dug into the pancakes.

God, these were good. Possibly the best pancakes I'd ever had.

"I'll survive." My muscles ached and my head still hurt a bit, but it wasn't anything critical. "Aren't you supposed to be at work?"

"I'm leaving soon." Christian set his coffee mug in the sink. "I had to tell Ava what happened since she was worried when you didn't come home last night. She correctly guessed you were with me."

I winced. I'd totally forgotten to let Ava know I was okay.

"She told Jules." His tone dried further. "They should be here soon. They can keep you company while I deal with Julian."

"You're letting them into your house? I thought you didn't like guests."

"I figured you wouldn't want to be alone." Christian's frown deepened. "If that's not the case, I'll tell them not to come."

"No. It's fine. It'll be good to see them." He was right about me not wanting to be alone.

Seeing my friends would give me a sense of normalcy, though I knew they must be freaking out.

"What are you going to do with Julian?" I asked, sure I didn't want to know the answer but was too curious not to ask.

If it were anyone else, I'd insist they let the police handle it.

However, trying to convince Christian to turn a case over to the cops would be futile, and I didn't have the best experience with the police.

With my luck, Julian would weasel his way out of a heavy sentence and be back on the streets in a few months.

Christian's eyes darkened. "Nothing he doesn't deserve."

A chill skated down my spine at the calm lethalness of his response. I suddenly wondered, on a more visceral level, why he was wearing all-black, casual attire instead of a suit.

Christian had proved he was a better man than I'd expected.

But I knew with sudden, blinding clarity that he was also capable of worse things than I could imagine.

Our gazes locked. My heartbeat slowed beneath the weight of his appraisal.

He knew I knew, or at least I had an inkling. And he wanted to see if I would condemn him. Try to stop him.

My fork grew cold in my hand. But I didn't say a word.

The chime of the doorbell broke the spell, and I instinctively glanced toward the living room.

Nina must've answered the door because I heard the faint sounds of my friends' voices followed by the patter of footsteps.

"If you have time today..." Christian's quiet voice drew my attention back to him. "Look in the drawer where you found the files. There's something there for you."

The uncharacteristic uncertainty in his tone sparked a seed of curiosity and something warmer that slid through me like molten honey.

My friends' voices grew louder.

Christian moved to leave, but I stopped him before he reached the doorway.

"Christian."

He turned to look back at me.

"Don't give him any pieces of your soul," I said softly.

Julian made his bed, and it was time to lie in it. But Christian...I didn't want him doing anything that would haunt him, especially if it was for me.

Especially if it would break any part of him.

"One of my favorite things about you," he said, his voice like the darkest of velvets. "Is that you think I have any pieces left."

I was still standing in the kitchen after he left, his presence a cool, lingering draft in his wake.

I only had a few seconds to breathe in the silence before my friends spilled into the room and wrapped me in a cocoon of hugs and concern.

"I'm sorry I didn't call yesterday," I said, hugging Ava. "So much happened, and it completely slipped my mind."

"I understand," she reassured me. "I'm just glad you're okay."

"What I *don't* understand," Jules said. "Is why you're at Christian's house. I thought you broke up. What the hell happened?"

What didn't *happen?*

"It's a long story," I said. "You might want to sit down first..."

TWO HOURS AND ONE EXHAUSTIVE RECOUNT OF MY kidnapping and the aftermath later, I found myself staring at three slack-jawed statues. Two in person, and one on Face-Time, since Bridget was in Eldorra but would murder me if I left her out of the loop on this.

Apparently, Christian had merely told Ava I'd had a "run-in" with my stalker, so ninety-five percent of my story came as a complete shock to them.

Jules recovered first.

"First of all, Julian deserves *jail*." She shook with fury. "Second of all, I'm *going* to jail for what I'll do if I ever come across him. I will cut his balls off, do you hear me? I'll slice them open with a machete and shove them down his throat so he chokes—"

"*Okay*, I think we've had enough violence for the week," Ava cut in. Worry creased her forehead. "Stel, are you sure he's taken care of? He's not going to escape or anything?"

I shook my head. "I doubt it. Harper Security has him."

"What about Christian?" Bridget asked. She was in what looked like her office, and a giant portrait of some old Eldorran monarch glared at me from behind her. "Does this mean you're back together?"

"We're..." I hesitated. "Working things out."

"That's great!" Of all my friends, Jules was the most enthusiastic about Christian. Probably because he'd lowered our rent so much when we moved into the Mirage. "He's not that bad of a guy. I mean, sometimes he does bad *things*. Those files were totally not okay, and you had every right to break up with him. *But...*" Her voice softened. "He really loves you."

I swallowed past the knot of emotion in my throat. "I know."

Luckily, the conversation soon moved back to safer ground with Jules detailing all the creative ways she'd murder Julian (much to Ava's chagrin).

My friends' company grounded me back in reality.

When lunchtime passed, however, I gently but firmly insisted that they go about the rest of their day and that I didn't need babysitting.

I appreciated their company and concern, but I'd

exhausted my social battery for the day. I needed alone time to recharge.

The door closed behind them, and I sucked in a breath of silence.

Nina was also gone for the day, so it was just me and the empty penthouse.

When I first moved in, I thought it was cold and impersonal, like a model showroom. Now, being here felt like returning home.

That was the couch where I'd created my collection, those were the plants I'd lovingly tended to for months...

And that was the office where I'd found the files that shattered it all.

I stopped in front of the entrance. For once, Christian had left the door open.

If you have time today, look in the drawer where you found the files. There's something there for you.

Staying away was impossible.

My heartbeats collided with each other as I walked to his desk and triggered the secret drawer mechanism.

The compartment slid out soundlessly.

I experienced a twinge of surprise when I saw its contents.

Instead of black binders, the drawer was filled with letters. There were at least a dozen of them, handwritten on simple cream stationery.

I recognized Christian's bold, elegant scrawl immediately.

I flipped through them, my heart rate climbing with every sheet that came into view.

They were all addressed to me and dated from the day we broke up.

One letter for every day we'd been apart.

Emotion swelled in my throat at the thought of Christian

sitting here night after night, writing me notes I might never see.

Except I was here now, at his request, and I couldn't have stopped myself if I wanted to.

I sank into his chair, picked up the first letter, and started reading.

52

CHRISTIAN/STELLA

CHRISTIAN

"Hello, Julian."

I examined Stella's stalker, who was strung up with heavy cuffs locking his wrists and ankles into a vertical spread-eagle position. Nails pinned his palms to the wall behind them, while black and blue bruises mottled his body like an obscene piece of abstract art.

We were in the warehouse I'd bought for this specific purpose. Remote, soundproofed, and guarded enough that an ant couldn't crawl across the floor without me knowing.

Not all of my guys were okay with dirty work, which was fine.

I only needed a few who were, and they'd done their job prepping the bastard for me. I couldn't have him waiting *too* comfortably while I tended to Stella.

My gaze flicked to the floor.

A small pool of blood stained the smooth gray concrete.

That was also fine.

It would grow soon enough.

Julian's face was so beaten up it was unrecognizable, but the heat of his glare made me smile.

He had a bit of fight left in him. *Good.*

That would make our session so much more fun.

"I'm sorry to tell you this, but you might have trouble writing any more notes in the future." I snapped on a pair of gloves, my voice casual as I examined the array of tools available to me on a nearby table.

A different dozen blades. Brass knuckles. Screwdrivers, whips, nails, hooks...

Hmm. Choices, choices.

"Fuck you," Julian spat.

My men had been relatively soft with him. It must've given him a false sense of security that what he'd gone through was as bad as it got.

I smiled. *If you only knew.*

"*Language,* Mr. Kensler. Honestly. Did your grandmother not teach you manners?" I selected one of the blades. I had a soft spot for knives.

They were lethal, precise, versatile. Everything I liked in a weapon.

"Here's the thing." I pressed the tip of the knife into his sternum. "I don't like getting my hands dirty. Blood doesn't go well with any of my clothes. But sometimes..." I dragged the knife down his torso. Blood welled and snaked down his body like thin rivulets of red. "Someone pisses me off enough that I make an exception."

I paused at the soft flesh of his belly, then rammed the blade in so hard he would've collapsed had he not been strung up.

An inhuman scream ripped from his throat, followed by a second scream when I yanked the knife out.

"Here's the thing, Julian." I continued like nothing

happened. "She'll *never* be yours. She was always mine. And your biggest mistake..." I dropped the bloodied knife on the table and selected a meat cleaver. "Was hurting someone who was mine."

I didn't say Stella's name. It didn't deserve to live in a place where pain and death reigned, but we both knew who I was talking about.

Blood stains. Bruised skin. Terrified eyes.

My pulse pounded at the memory.

I usually stayed in control during these sessions. Cool, calm, even conversational as I worked on the subject.

But whenever I pictured the haunted look in her eyes, or the purple and black marring her gorgeous skin, something dark and icy rooted in my lungs.

Rage, and the primal need to tear anyone who even *thought* about hurting her apart from limb to limb.

If I'd been one minute late, she would've died. Her light snuffed out, just like that.

The rage coiled tight and exploded through the sharp blade of the cleaver, which smashed through flesh and bone until an animalistic howl of agony split the air.

"See?" My chest heaved from the force of my swing as Julian's right hand hit the floor with a *thud*. "Hard to write again. Or type."

That was all it took for his fight to melt like ice cream on hot concrete, which was disappointing.

Breaking them down was so much more satisfying when they didn't bend so quickly.

"Please," Julian gasped. Tears ran down his cheeks and dripped down his chin. "I'm sorry. I..."

"What would you have done had I not showed up? Raped her? Killed her?"

"No," he blubbered. He trembled as I swapped blades again. "I...I didn't want to hurt her. I..."

It was too late.

An image of Stella pinned beneath him, crying and bloodied, flashed through my head.

I punctured his chest and ignored his cries.

The mere fact that he'd put his hands on her and caused her even a second of pain...

When I was in the cabin, and I thought I was about to die...

Thought I was about to die...

About to die...

My vision tunneled.

A snarl broke free as I peeled off a square of her stalker's flesh with a vicious tear.

Another howl rattled the bare bulb illuminating the space.

I didn't indulge in these warehouse sessions often. The people who crossed me had to have committed sins great enough to warrant such treatment, and like I'd said, I didn't like getting blood on my clothes.

But hurting Stella? There was no crime greater than that in my book.

The sounds of Julian's screams and pleas drowned beneath the tidal wave of my anger. My world shrank to one that consisted solely of metal, blood, and agony. The snap of bone, the wet sound of tearing flesh, the barest elements of a man spilling from the seams of his gutted torso like stuffing from an old doll.

I could've spent the entire day working on Julian. Twenty-four hours was nothing compared to the months of hell he'd put Stella through.

Perhaps I would've, had I not returned to the table to swap my dull, overworked knife for a fresh one and saw the message waiting for me.

I'd left my phone next to the blades. The text onscreen was comically out of place, a jarring reminder that life existed outside these walls.

Stella: *Come home to me.*

My breathing slowed.

I was drenched with sweat and splattered with blood. My usual restraint had snapped beneath the weight of Stella's hurt, but her words tethered me back to earth.

An image of Stella looking at me with those soft, knowing green eyes that morning replaced the warehouse.

Don't give him any pieces of your soul.

I'd thought I didn't have any left, but I was wrong. There was one remaining piece, and it belonged to her.

Crimson gradually retreated from my vision.

I dropped the knife and stared at the broken down, barely conscious man hanging on the wall.

The urge to make him suffer longer was still there, coiled like a vicious snake in my gut.

But the desire to return to Stella was stronger.

Come home to me.

"You got lucky," I said.

I picked up my gun.

Three strategically placed shots later, Stella's stalker was nothing more than a lifeless, bloodied heap of flesh.

For her, I'd given him the greatest mercy I was capable of giving: a quicker death.

I left the basement while Steele and Mason swooped in to clean up the mess.

The torture didn't faze them; they were even more comfortable with the warehouse sessions than I was.

Unlike Kage, they also had no ambition other than to excel in the roles they already held. It was why I'd selected them to oversee Julian's detainment.

Still, I would have to overhaul the company processes after I returned to the office. Change access codes, restructure teams. I didn't want to risk another Kage situation.

But until then...

I entered the warehouse's bathroom, washed off the blood, changed my clothes, and went home to Stella.

STELLA

"You're home."

My heart tripped when the door opened and Christian entered.

At first glance, he looked the same as when he'd left—black shirt, black pants, hauntingly beautiful face—but a closer look revealed the quiet storm brewing in his eyes.

"You asked me to come home." He watched, body still but gaze burning like an open flame, as I closed the distance between us. "So here I am."

His rough velvet voice held a note of caution.

It'd been five hours since he left, and we both knew he hadn't been at the office.

"Is..." I trailed off, not wanting to say Julian's name.

"You don't have to worry about him anymore."

"Right." I swallowed the hundred questions crowding my throat and went with a safer route. "I read the letters."

All twenty of them. Each one wrung my heart like a knot pulled taut, because I knew how hard it was for Christian to share anything about his personal life.

Those letters weren't just letters—they were pieces of him, poured from his soul and inked in black.

And I loved every piece, no matter how flawed or broken he thought it was.

The storm in Christian's eyes threatened to suck me into its vortex.

"I meant what I wrote," he said quietly. "Every word."

"I know." I pressed my lips to his jaw. He went still, his muscles taut and his breaths quickening as I kissed my way up his jaw to the corner of his mouth.

"Welcome home," I whispered.

A small shudder went through him before he turned his head and our mouths met. Static filled me as he cupped my face with one hand and curled his other hand around the back of my neck.

Last night's kiss had been soft, gentle. An easing into the waters after our separation and a comfort after a hellish day.

This one was passion and desperation, a thorough reclaiming of what we were and the birth of what we could be.

No lies, no secrets, just us.

I sank into the familiar glide of Christian's tongue against mine and the warmth of his hand against the back of my neck.

I didn't ask questions about what he did in the five hours he was gone.

The world wasn't black and white, no matter how much I wished it were.

And sometimes, we found our happiness in the shades of gray.

53

STELLA/CHRISTIAN

STELLA

"So? What do you think?" Christian watched with boyish anticipation as I lifted a forkful of gnocchi to my mouth.

I pretended to mull it over before I proclaimed, "Best I've ever had."

His grin made the butterflies in my stomach reel. "Told you," he said, oozing playful self-satisfaction.

We were eating dinner at a tiny Italian restaurant tucked in the heart of Columbia Heights. It was the one Christian mentioned in his letters, and it was just as charming as I'd envisioned.

Instead of individual tables, one rustic wooden table stretched down the middle, just large enough to seat a dozen people. A candlelit chandelier bathed the room in a flickering amber glow, and a display of copper pots and pans hung on the exposed brick wall.

It felt like we were eating in someone's home, especially since Christian had booked out the restaurant so it was just us and the server.

"Don't be too smug." I pointed my fork at him. "The date is only half done. I've yet to grade you on your hand-holding, cuddling, and sweet nothing skills."

"Of course. Apologies," he drawled. "Didn't mean to jump the gun."

"Apology accepted." I tucked into the rest of my meal primly and barely suppressed a smile at his laughing expression.

It'd been a month since we got back together, and we'd spent that time exploring the contours of our new relationship.

No fake dating, no stalker scare forcing us together, no hiding behind flashy gestures and expensive gifts.

Just us, flaws and all, going on normal dates and living normal lives.

Well, as normal as life could get with Christian, anyway.

In a perverse way, my kidnapping had reset our relationship for the better. Nothing provided clarity like almost dying.

I'd mostly put the ordeal behind me, though sometimes I was still plagued with nightmares of surprise notes and a ramshackle cabin in the woods. But I would work my way through it. It just took time.

I'd also moved back into Christian's house two weeks ago. I didn't want to impose on Alex and Ava anymore, especially with their wedding coming up in a few weeks. I could've moved back to my old apartment now that I didn't have a stalker threat hanging over my head, but honestly, I didn't want to live anywhere else.

His apartment was home.

"By the way, did you hear what happened with Sentinel's CEO?" I asked. "It's wild."

I was sure he had, but I had to bring it up.

Sentinel's demise had dominated the past month's headlines. Apparently, they'd been working on a new piece of code

that somehow self-destructed and
infrastructure so thoroughly it was impossible to
sified information about their clients had also
caused a massive uproar, given how high profile some o
clients were and how sensitive some of that data was.

If that wasn't enough, the authorities had arrested
Sentinel's CEO Mike Kurtz that morning for embezzlement
and tax fraud. The whole thing was a mess.

"Yes. I'm not surprised it's played out the way it has,"
Christian said mildly. "Companies should stick to their lane.
Sentinel is a security corporation. They had no business
venturing into cyber development when that's not their area of
expertise."

"While you, Mr. Security CEO, are also a cyber expert," I
teased.

His smile spread through me like sun-warmed honey.
"Exactly."

"I don't suppose you know anything about the code they
were working on," I added casually.

An uninterested shrug. "Not a thing."

I let it go. He was vengeful and I'd accepted that about him.

Plus, Sentinel's destruction came from the inside out. No
one could blame Christian for a mistake on their part.

The conversation moved on to Stella Alonso the brand,
which officially launched last week. It wasn't an original name,
but eponymous labels were de rigueur. I'd double-checked with
Delamonte first, but they were okay with the launch as long as
it didn't interfere with my ambassador duties. We had different
target audiences, anyway. Theirs was ultra-high-end while
mine tipped toward the mid-range of the luxury spectrum.

By the time dinner ended, I was flush with wine and
giddiness.

It was the perfect date night. Simple, casual, *real*.

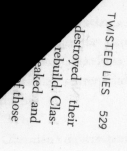

...en I moved to leave. He leaned ... sensual masculinity and lazy ..."

...ugh the air and settled between

...as an arch of his dark brows.

...he table, unsure whether I owed my steadiness to the wine or the wetness slicking my thighs.

The mere anticipation of what might happen turned me on as much as an actual touch.

When I reached Christian, he stood, pushed his plate aside, and lifted me onto the table in one smooth movement.

My pulse spiked, but rationality clung to the edges of blooming arousal.

"Christian," I hissed. "We'll get in trouble!"

The curtains were drawn, and drapes covered the front door, shielding us from passersby. Our server was MIA, but that didn't mean he couldn't show up at any minute.

"No one is here, Butterfly," Christian drawled. "I paid the server to leave until I give him the green light. Cooks are gone. It's just us."

He pushed my dress up around my waist and hooked his fingers into the elastic band of my underwear.

The air condensed into something thin and infinitely flammable.

"What are you doing?"

"Eating dessert." Christian eased my hips up so he could pull my underwear down before he returned to his seat.

"You don't like dessert." My voice had gone to smoke, as insubstantial as the remnants of my resistance.

Christian's slow, answering smile throbbed in my blood.

"I changed my mind."

CHRISTIAN

"*Oh God.*" Stella's breathless moan sparked in my blood like a flame against gasoline.

Her hands tangled in my hair as I hiked her legs higher on my shoulders and gave her clit another long, languorous lick.

"We just got started, sweetheart," I drawled. "This is going to be a long course."

I drew her swollen bud into my mouth and sucked, reveling in the way she shivered and panted around me.

I fucking loved eating Stella's pussy. The taste, the smell, the way she clenched around my fingers when I pumped them inside her and hit *that* spot.

It was the world's most intoxicating feast.

Her cries of pleasure spurred me on as I licked, sucked, and tongued that sweet little cunt until she was dripping all over me, her pretty clit swollen from my attention and her juices slick on my tongue.

After a while, I pulled back, my chest heaving as I admired the sight before me. So wet and perfectly prepared for the main event.

"*Now,*" I said. "I'm ready for dessert."

I spread her thighs wider, dipped my head, and devoured her.

Stella's squeals and whimpers escalated into inelegant screams as I alternated between fingering her and worshiping her clit and fucking her with my tongue. Harder, more intense than the first time, like I was dying of thirst in the desert and she was my only source of salvation.

"*Christian.*" My name broke into a sob. She fisted my hair, her muscles taut with desire.

"You taste so good." I buried my nose in her and breathed her in. Her pussy was like the world's sweetest nectar, and I was ravenous for it.

I wanted to drink up every fucking drop and come back for seconds. Thirds. Fourths. For the rest of fucking time.

I would never be able to get enough of her.

"Do you want to know what you taste like?" I slid two fingers inside her and lifted my head so I could see her.

Stella gazed down at me, her eyes half-lidded with desire and bright with clear, pure trust.

It undid me.

My cock was so hard it felt like it would split open from the pressure, but the walls around my heart had crumbled, baring the soft, beating organ to her every whim and desire.

"Like honey and spices." I pushed my fingers deeper. She was so tight I could *feel* her stretching around me, inch by inch, until I was knuckles deep inside her.

"Like sweetness and sin." In. Out. Slowly and thoroughly, letting her feel every glide of friction.

A full-body shudder rolled through her.

"You taste..." I removed my fingers and lowered my head. "Like *mine.*"

A keening cry echoed through the room as Stella's body bowed off the table. Her muscles went taut, vibrating with the force of her orgasm as she came on my tongue.

Desire burned up the fuel in my veins, but I took my time, leisurely savoring every drop while wave after wave rolled through her.

Finally, her cries subsided into a dazed whimper, and she sprawled, loose-limbed and sated, on the table.

"My favorite part of the meal," I said lazily. "You were right." I gave her clit one final, languid lick. "I just needed to find the right dessert."

54

STELLA

ALEX AND AVA'S WEDDING TOOK PLACE IN EARLY October, at a gorgeous vineyard in Vermont. Stunning red, orange, and yellow foliage transformed the setting into an autumnal fairytale, and the beautiful sky draped over us like a sheet of azure, sun-warmed silk.

Bridget, Jules, and I stood on one side of the extravagant floral wedding arch in matching bridesmaid dresses while Alex, Josh, Rhys, and Christian stood on the other.

Originally, Alex had wanted no groomsmen other than a best man, but Ava had convinced him otherwise.

A rustle of leaves kicked up before the familiar strains of the wedding march filled the air and Ava appeared.

I didn't cry in public often, but moisture prickled my eyes when she walked down the aisle on Ralph's arm.

Ralph was Alex's old Krav Maga instructor and the closest Alex and Ava had to a parent these days. They visited him every Thanksgiving, and his face glowed with emotion as if she were his real daughter.

"Am I crying?" Jules whispered next to me. "Can't tell if it's the wind or not."

"No," I said through my smile. I didn't look at her, afraid any movement would break the well containing my tears. "Am I?"

"No...well, a little. But our mascara is waterproof, so it's okay."

"*Shh,*" Bridget hissed. "*No one* is crying." She discreetly wiped a tear from her cheek.

Ava drew closer.

The skirt of her gorgeous mermaid-shaped gown trailed behind her in a cloud of soft tulle, lace, and silk, adorned with ripple-like textures that resembled the crests of ocean waves.

Her face was radiant, her eyes bright and her smile brighter still.

She looked so beautiful and happy my chest warmed until I no longer felt the fall chill.

Bridget had been the first of my friends to get married, but Ava's wedding hit on a different level. She and Alex had perhaps the darkest pasts and the rockiest path toward their happily ever after. Seeing them overcome all of that to finally be together was incredible.

Across from us, Alex resembled a statue in his stillness. He was always attuned to Ava, but in that moment, he looked at her like the world was the night sky and she was the only star in existence.

For once, his eyes weren't hidden beneath a layer of ice. Love shone through, so clear and bright it eclipsed the sun.

It intensified when Ava reached the altar, and he murmured something that made her cheeks pink with pleasure.

Their eyes lingered on each other before they faced the pastor, who began the official ceremony.

"Dearly Beloved, we are gathered here today to celebrate Alex Volkov and Ava Chen in holy matrimony..."

While his speech continued, my eyes connected with Christian's.

Our lips curved and our gazes lingered before we turned our attention back to the wedding.

The old, insecure me would've kept checking to confirm he was still there and that he wasn't a fantasy I'd concocted.

The present me knew he wasn't.

He was real, and no matter what happened, he would always be there.

———

THAT NIGHT'S RECEPTION TOOK PLACE IN THE VINEYARD'S restaurant, which had been cleared out to make room for a dance floor, two long banquet tables, and a live music stage. Exposed wooden beams crisscrossed the space, lending it an air of rustic charm, but there was nothing rustic about the custom engraved china plates, the fifty thousand dollars worth of luxury floral arrangements, or the world-famous singer crooning onstage.

As expected, Alex had spared no expense.

"You should've asked him for a bathtub of diamonds," Jules told Ava. "He would've made it happen."

Ava had needed a breather from all the mingling required of the bride, so Bridget, Jules, and I had ushered her off to a corner while the rest of the guests drank and danced.

"Jules," Ava said patiently. "What would I do with a bathtub of diamonds at my wedding?"

"Roll around it like the rich bitch you are. And I mean that in the most affectionate way." Jules's eyes glinted with mischief. "*Or* you could pass them out to your guests, specifically your wonderful bridesmaids, who very much did not get you into trouble in Barcelona."

I spluttered at the mention of Ava's bachelorette trip. "*Jules.*"

"What? It was harmless fun. Who knew Alex would get so upset about male strippers? It was a *bachelorette party.*"

"I think it was less the strippers and more the *waking up in a strange hotel in Ibiza* part," Bridget said dryly.

"I think it was both," I decided.

We'd been fine, but the guys had been less than pleased when they found out about, well, everything.

Honestly, they shouldn't talk after what happened to *them* and the banana float.

"Guys, please." Ava held up her hand, looking pained. "No diamonds, no Barcelona talk."

"Fine," Jules grumbled. "But *I* thought the trip was fun. It was like college again."

"What was like college again?" Alex walked over with Josh, Rhys, and Christian in tow. He kissed Ava's forehead, and she snuggled into his side, her smile blossoming so wide it made *me* smile.

"Last night," Bridget said smoothly before Jules could rupture Alex's artery by mentioning. "Girls' night in. Just like in college."

"You were talking about Spain, weren't you?" Christian murmured when the conversation topic switched

He wrapped his arms around me from behind, enveloping me with warmth and spice.

"I'm convinced you can read minds."

His laugh vibrated down my spine. "Your guilty expressions give it away every time." He kissed my neck. "You look gorgeous, Butterfly."

Tingles raced from where his lips touched my neck to the rest of my body.

"So do you. Being a groomsman suits you," I teased.

"Don't get used to it. I only did this because I owe Volkov a favor," he said dryly. Apparently, Alex had looked out for his business or something during our Italy trip. "Do you know what dealing with Josh so often is like? You should've seen him and that damn banana float at the bachelor party."

I stifled a laugh.

"You better take care of Ava," Josh was now saying. "If anything happens to her, if she gets eaten by a wild animal or anything like that, I will hunt you down and use a scalpel in ways that are *not* approved by the medical board."

Rhys snorted out a laugh while Alex gave his best man a wry stare. "What exactly do you think we'll be doing on our honeymoon?"

"Watching lions and other *things* I'd rather not think about my best friend and sister doing." Josh shuddered with disgust. "Maybe I should join your safari to keep an eye on things, just in case."

Alex and Ava left for their safari/beach honeymoon in Kenya and the Seychelles tomorrow.

There was a time when Ava's aquaphobia prevented her from even going near the water, but she'd overcome it over the years with Alex's help.

Jules rolled her eyes. "Leave them alone. You are *not* going on their honeymoon with them."

"That would be disturbing in so many ways," Bridget added.

"*No one* appreciates my good ideas," Josh muttered. He looked at Rhys hopefully. "Larsen?"

"Let me put it this way," Rhys said. "If you'd tried to tag

along with me and Bridget on our honeymoon, I would've tossed you out of the plane after takeoff. *Without* a parachute."

A laugh rose in my throat, but I tuned out the rest of my friends' bickering when Christian turned me around and rested his hands on my hips.

"Your friends are something else." He sounded half amused, half appalled, even though Alex and Rhys were his friends too.

"They're...unique," I acknowledged with a laugh. "But I love them."

Somehow, four strangers that'd been randomly assigned to the same dorm room their freshman year of college had evolved into what we were now—a beautifully messy, perfectly imperfect family that'd gone through our share of ups and downs but made it through to the other side.

There'd been a time after graduation when I worried our friendship would fray outside the confines of campus and the structure of our college lives. The years had proven that wasn't true. In fact, our friendship had strengthened after being tested by real life.

Natalia was my sister by blood, but Ava, Bridget, and Jules would always be my sisters by choice.

"If you're up to it, want to take you somewhere after the reception," Christian said, drawing me out my thoughts. "It'll be a quick trip. Two days max."

My eyebrows rose. "Where?"

"It's a surprise." He kissed me. "Trust me."

I did.

"I should take a photo of this moment," Rhys drawled as he and Bridget passed us. My friends had paired up to dance after the music shifted to a slow song and Ava's cousin Farrah and her husband Blake pulled her and Alex away. "A besotted

Christian Harper. What a sight. I should blast it out to the Harper Security alumni network. The guys would love it."

Christian narrowed his eyes. "You're one to talk, Larsen. Didn't I see pictures of you attending a royal tea party the other week? With a cat in your lap, no less."

Color rose on Rhys's cheekbones. "It was not a *tea party*," he growled. "It was a *lunch ceremony,* and Meadows gets upset when we leave her alone for too long. At least I didn't buy up all the fucking *wheatgrass* in the grocery store..."

Bridget caught my eye and shook her head.

Men, she mouthed, her expression one of exasperated affection.

I stifled a laugh.

The guys would never admit it, but their insults and arguments were how they showed affection for each other.

And as I swayed to the music in Christian's arms, listened to the comforting rumble of his voice and the familiar warmth of my friends' laughter, I felt something that'd eluded me for so much of my life.

Happiness, in its purest and most complete form.

55

CHRISTIAN

THE NIGHT AFTER THE VOLKOVS' WEDDING, I FLEW STELLA and me to my hometown.

I hadn't stepped foot in Santa Luisa, California since my parents died. It'd been two decades, yet the tiny seaside town along the northern coast remained the same.

Quiet streets, a quaint downtown, colorful stucco buildings.

Returning here was like stepping back in time. I had changed, but everything else remained the same.

Stella was quiet as we stopped in front of a warehouse in the town's desolate industrial quarter. Our car was the only one on the street, and many of the warehouses' metal doors had rusted with disuse, including the one before us.

I hadn't told Stella the purpose of our visit, but she knew I grew up here and therefore, the visit must have something to do with my parents.

She was right.

I pressed a button, and the warehouse door clanked open

with a groan. A cloud of stale must billowed out before it dissolved in the long-forgotten sunshine.

"Oh my God." Stella's stunned whisper echoed through the room when we walked inside and she saw what it contained.

Dozens of art pieces filled the small space, from priceless oil paintings to small modern sculptures. Many of the paintings had withered after twenty years of neglect, but a few resilient pieces remained intact.

"Welcome to my inheritance, my father's stolen treasure trove," I said, the words both hollow and self-deprecating. "My mother gave me the location in her note."

It'd been coded—she knew how much I loved puzzles even as a kid—but I hadn't tried cracking it until a few weeks ago. It'd taken me less than a minute.

"Have you visited before?" Stella asked softly.

"No."

I'd made virtual arrangements before we arrived, but it was my first time seeing it in person.

I thought the sight of my father's legacy would make me angry. This was what he'd dedicated his time and energy to instead of his only son. This was what killed him and, by extension, my mother and our family.

I should've felt the same rage I'd felt when I first read my mother's goodbye note.

Instead, I felt nothing except the overwhelming desire to burn it to the ground—not out of spite, but out of exhaustion.

I was tired of whispers from the ghosts of my past.

Stella brushed her fingers over a nearby sculpture. They came away with a thin film of dust.

"What are you going to do with it all?"

"If they're not savable, destroy them. If they are, donate them or return them to their original owners."

All done anonymously, of course.

"Except..." I stopped in front of a familiar painting. "This one."

Its gold frame gleamed in the weak light, and brown and green splashed across it a hideous approximation of art.

"*Magda*," Stella surmised. "I recognize it from Dante's gallery."

"Yes."

I'd tucked my mother's note back inside its frame, then finally had Dante send her back where she belonged.

I stared at the swirls of color until they blurred into a dark kaleidoscope.

In hindsight, she was so inconsequential. A complicated problem of my own design, fabricated to shield me from my past.

Everyone thought she was important because she contained some big business secret or shocking revelation when the truth was so much simpler.

She represented the part of my past I'd never been able to let go of. A wound I'd covered with temporary bandaids to hide the festering disease that'd been eating me alive from the inside out for decades.

We didn't speak again until I took the painting out to an empty lot near the warehouses.

Other than the buildings, there was nothing around except for metal and concrete. A bird circled overhead, its squawk echoing in the wide-open space, and the hot sun beat down with unusual intensity.

It was the last time I would ever step foot in Santa Luisa. I might as well go out with a bang.

I retrieved a lighter from my pocket and flicked it open.

"Afraid of fire, Butterfly?"

Stella shook her head and slid her hand into mine again. "No."

"Good."

I held the lighter to the painting. The oils were so combustible flames erupted almost immediately, swallowing the painting and the letter it contained whole.

I watched dispassionately as the fire twisted my mother's legacy into a blackened, unrecognizable heap, but when Stella squeezed my hand, I gave it a small squeeze back.

I could've done this on my own, but I wanted her with me. If it hadn't been for her, I'd still be holding onto that painting, hating it but unable to leave it at the same time.

But now that I finally had a future worth living for, it was time to let go of the past, once and for all.

56

STELLA

ONE YEAR LATER

I watched from backstage as Ayana, the hottest supermodel of the moment, strutted down the sidewalk. Her flawless dark skin glowed beneath the lights and provided the perfect contrast to the crowning piece of my collection: a striking purple dress that could be worn day or night depending on how it was accessorized.

The rest of the models followed behind her for the closing walk until they all exited the runway.

"Stella, *go*." My new assistant Christy nudged me. "This is your time to shine!"

Right. I can do this.

I took a deep breath and walked out, tentatively at first, then more confidently as the applause intensified.

I took a bow, my skin warming with pleasure.

My first fashion show in Milan.

After dozens of sleepless nights, panic attacks, and fits of self-doubt, it was finally over and, based on the roar around me, a resounding success.

I couldn't believe it.

I did it. A grin spread across my face. *I did it!*

It was hard to imagine that it'd only been a year since the official launch of Stella Alonso the brand. Its profile had skyrocketed in an astonishingly short time thanks to Bridget's support, who wore at least one item by me at every public event, if possible. From her, whispers of the brand trickled into the other corners of Europe and then Hollywood where, in the most surreal of moments, I'd watched Kris Carrera-Reynolds walk down the red carpet wearing one of my designs.

Her husband, action movie star Nate Reynolds, won his first Oscar that night.

Since then, it'd been a steady upward climb.

Brady wasn't my manager anymore since I'd stepped back from my personal accounts to focus on the brand, but I still talked to him often. I'd also become good friends with Lilah. She couldn't make it tonight because of her own show, but she'd been instrumental in helping me get started.

I wasn't naive enough to think my big wave would last forever, but I was going to ride the hell out of it while it did.

"Go, Stella!" A familiar voice rose above the din. "You kicked ass, babe!"

I searched through the crowd until my eyes landed on a cluster of familiar faces in the front row. My smile grew.

The room was packed with fashion insiders and celebrities, but the people I cared about most were right there in front of me.

Alex and Ava, who glowed with pregnancy. She was three months along, and her baby bump had just started showing.

Rhys and Bridget, who was regal as always in the blue Stella Alonso dress she'd made a cult hit.

Josh and Jules, who had shouted the *kicked ass* statement

and looked like she was about to run onstage u̶
her back.

And my family, whose beams of pride curled thr̶
chest and settled there like a warm blanket. My mothe̶
father, my sister...they were all there.

Our relationship had come a long way over the past year. It
wasn't perfect, but what family was?

What mattered was that they'd showed up.

Finally, my gaze made it to the most important person in
the room.

He draped across his chair in a spill of Italian wool and silk,
so beautiful he could've modeled onstage himself had I
designed menswear.

Christian didn't holler and cheer like everyone else, but the
curve of his lips and the warmth in his eyes said more than
words could.

My heart ballooned in my chest.

I love you, I mouthed.

Those whiskey pools sparkled and danced beneath the dim
lights.

He didn't need to say it for me to hear him.

I love you too.

AFTER MY SHOW, CHRISTIAN AND I STAYED AN EXTRA TWO
nights in Milan before he whisked me off to Positano.

I'd protested half-heartedly, saying I had too much work to
go on vacation, but honestly, it didn't take much to convince
me.

I fell in love with the Amalfi Coast before I ever visited it,
and I fell even more in love after visiting.

The scent of salt and water filled my nose as we walked

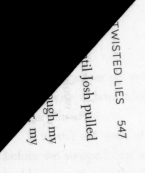

...ow beautiful this place was. Not ..., but because of what it meant to

... love. That'd been planted long ... y. But it was the place where it ... ath the Mediterranean skies like ...world's most beautiful canvas.

"Penny for your thoughts." Christian walked alongside me, his suits traded for a casual linen shirt and pants.

"Just a penny? I thought you were a billionaire."

"A quarter then. Final offer," he said with the seriousness of someone negotiating a multimillion-dollar contract.

I laughed. "Fine, I'll take it, but my thoughts might be too sappy for you." I looked out at the ocean, my words soft with reminiscence. "I'm thinking about our first trip here and how much I love this place. We've visited a lot of places together, but Italy...Italy will always be special."

"I'm glad you think so." Christian's velvet murmur brushed my skin, along with an odd roughness I'd never heard before. "I couldn't decide whether to do this in Hawaii or Italy, but it seems I made the right choice."

"Do what?" I turned, and the breath disappeared from my lungs.

Because before me, framed by pastel-covered hills and the golden hues of sunset, was a sight I'd never anticipated.

Christian Harper on one knee, velvet box open in hand to reveal a dazzling diamond ring set with emeralds.

Tears blurred my vision as I pressed a hand to my mouth.

When he spoke again, the odd roughness was still there, but it was braided with so much love and hope they narrowed my world to this one moment with this one man.

"Stella, will you marry me?"

EPILOGUE

STELLA

Four years later

"Take your summer Friday off," I told my assistant. Christy and I stopped in front of my office. "I can survive an afternoon by myself."

"Are you sure? I can—"

"*Yes*. Go." I shooed her away. "Enjoy the weather. It's gorgeous outside."

"Okay," she said reluctantly. "Text or call if you need anything. Which reminds me, I forgot one thing." A sly smile replaced her anxiousness at leaving work early, even if it was part of the company's vacation policy. "You have a visitor."

My brow furrowed at both the unexpected addition to my schedule and the mischievous twinkle in her eyes. "Who..."

My question cut off with a sharp inhale when I opened the door and saw who was standing inside.

Dark suit. Whiskey eyes. And a bouquet of the most gorgeous roses I'd ever seen.

A slow, devastating smile spread across his face when he saw me.

Beside me, Christy sighed and visibly swooned.

She wasn't the only one.

Even after three years of marriage, that smile never failed to make my heart flutter.

"Morning, Butterfly." The lazy timbre of his voice sent a whoosh of warmth through my stomach.

"What are you doing here?" I breathed. "I thought you were on a business trip."

He'd left for London two days ago and wasn't scheduled to return until Sunday.

"Flew back early." He gave a casual shrug. "I missed you."

It was a good thing I was still holding onto the doorknob. Otherwise, I might have melted straight to the floor.

"Ahem." Christy cleared her throat. "I'm taking that summer Friday now. Have a good weekend."

She winked at me before she left.

I would've been mortified by the insinuation in her voice had I not been so distracted by the gorgeous male specimen standing less than five feet away.

"It's been five minutes, Mrs. Harper," Christian drawled. "Are you going to make your husband wait even longer for a kiss?"

"You," I said. "Are unbelievable."

Then I ran and threw my arms around his neck, my heart swelling as the rumble of his laughter filled the room.

I kissed him, drinking in his taste and smell like we'd been apart for months, not days.

"I can't pass up the opportunity to visit my talented wife at her office," he said when we finally broke apart. He wrapped his arms around my waist while I buried my face in his chest and breathed in the rich, familiar scent of him. It was the scent of love and comfort and safety. My favorite smell in the entire world. "Offices in Soho. You've officially made it, Stella Alonso Harper."

The Stella Alonso brand had expanded rapidly over the past few years to include clothes, accessories, and fragrances. Its office had expanded accordingly.

I smiled at Christian's teasing, but a sudden pang of melancholy hit me.

We'd moved to New York after we got married, and both our businesses were now headquartered in Manhattan.

Jules and Ava remained in D.C., but the three of us plus Bridget saw each other in person at least twice a year: once for our annual girls' trip and once for the holidays.

My family visited a few times a year and vice versa.

It was a wonderful life, but there was one person I missed greatly.

"I wish Maura were here to see it," I said softly. "She would've loved it."

Maura had made it to our wedding, where she'd been the most lucid I'd seen her in years.

A month later, right after Christian and I returned from our honeymoon, she'd passed away in her sleep.

I'd been devastated, but I knew she'd been ready to go and that she was in a happier place now. Even though she hadn't remembered me in the last years of her life, a part of me wondered whether she'd been waiting for me to find my home before she moved on.

"She knows." Christian sounded so confident I believed him.

"Since when did you become the optimist out of the two of us?"

"Since I married you." He ran a hand down my back. "I

blame it on those wheatgrass smoothies you make me drink every morning. They must be laced with something."

My burst of laughter shattered my remaining melancholy. "They'll extend your lifespan, Mr. Harper. I want many, many years with you."

"Not years, sweetheart. Forever." Christian tipped my chin up, and my heart tingled all over again. "But just in case, we should make the most of what we have."

A half gasp, half laugh poured from my throat when he swept the papers off my desk and set me on top of it.

"*Christian*," I admonished with no fire. "That was a week's worth of work!"

"I'll clean it up later," he said lazily. "But in the meantime, I can think of some ways to make it up to you."

Then he knelt before me and spread my legs, and suddenly, work was the last thing on my mind.

CHRISTIAN

One thing no one told me about being married was how often I had to interact with my wife's friends.

Holidays, birthdays, dinner parties when they were in town...my once business-oriented calendar was now bursting with things like fucking Broadway nights and Christmas at the von Aschebergs.

We alternated hosting the holidays, so this year, we were at Rhys and Bridget's getaway villa in Costa Rica.

Specifically, we were in their living room for the annual Christmas Eve board game night.

I finished my wine and waited for the inevitable complaints. It happened every damn year.

"There's no way you're not cheating." Josh stared at the

Monopoly board with disbeli

you win *every time*?"

"What can I say? I work i

haps if we play a medical

chance."

"I refuse to believe it."

"*Every* Christmas..."

"There, there." Jules pa

game."

Meanwhile, Jo

laughter when

"Can't

growled

be a

Her diamond ring flashed beneath the lights with every movement. She and Josh had finally gotten engaged last summer, though they hadn't set a wedding date yet.

"It's not just a board game, Red. It's my pride. My dignity. My—"

"Fake money?" Ava raised an eyebrow. "You say the same thing *every* year."

"Yes, well, it doesn't make it any less true," Josh grumbled. He leaned down until he was eye level with his three-and-a-half-year-old niece and nephew. "Your dad is a cheat."

Neither child seemed impressed by his accusation.

"Daddy won!" Sofia insisted.

"That's right, Little Sunshine." Alex cast a smug look in Josh's direction before he swept her up and kissed her cheek. She giggled with delight. "Your Uncle Josh is a sore loser."

Her twin brother Niko sat back on his haunches and pounded the board with tiny fists. "Uncle loser! Daddy winner!"

The Monopoly pieces went flying from the force of his pounding.

I silently cursed as one of them landed in my wine. There was no fucking way I'd drink the rest when it'd been tainted by a dirty game piece.

sh playfully tackled Niko, who shrieked with
e started tickling him.

believe you betrayed me like that, bud," Josh
his voice thick with amusement. "We're supposed to
eam."

Next to them, Bridget and Rhys's daughter watched their
roughhousing with a mystified expression that was far too
mature for her years.

With her blond hair and gray eyes, little Camilla von
Ascheberg was a miniature clone of her parents. She also
looked surprisingly regal for a two-year-old in her blue dress
and matching hair bow.

Her brow scrunched when Josh and Niko accidentally
knocked over a glass of water.

"Daddy." She tugged on her father's sleeve and pointed at
the spill.

I could've sworn I heard a note of disapproval.

"Don't worry about it, sweetheart." Rhys sighed. "Happens
every year."

"I never thought I'd say this, but Rhys's kid is the only one
who isn't a little terror," I muttered to Stella. At least Camilla
had the decency to sit still.

I watched, appalled, as Sofia played with Alex's hair.

"Daddy! Braids!" She twisted the strands into something
that did not resemble a braid in any way, shape, or form.
"Look!"

"They look great," he said indulgently while she continued
to massacre his perfectly styled hair.

I was convinced an imposter had swapped bodies with the
normally ice-cold Alex the day he became a father. It didn't
make sense.

Stella laughed. "The twins are adorable, and you know it."

"I know no such thing," I said, even though, as far as children went, Sofia and Niko *were* pretty cute.

I glanced back at Rhys.

"I thought seeing you whipped for one girl was bad," I drawled as he and Bridget cooed over a now giggling Camilla. "Two is even worse."

Now that the game had ended, the rest of the group had broken off to do their own thing until dinner.

Josh was still trying (and failing) to get Niko to say *Uncle Josh is a winner.*

Ava was taking pictures of Alex and Sofia, who had moved on to climbing over her father like he was a jungle gym.

Stella sat next to me, watching our conversation with amusement. She was used to my strange friendship with Rhys. Once, she tried to call it a bromance, which I shut down immediately.

Ab-so-fuckinglutely not. I was not a *bromance* kind of guy, and neither was Rhys, who appeared unfazed by my last comment.

"You talk a lot of sh—*fudge* for someone who's already eaten words once," he amended when Bridget gave him a warning look.

"Come on, sweetie. Let's go look at the pretty flowers while your father, uh has a chat with Uncle Christian." She scooped up Camilla and took her out to the gardens, no doubt worried we would slip into profanity at any second.

"I'll also be back," Stella said quickly. "I'm going to get some water."

I waited until she left before I arched an eyebrow at Rhys. "No idea what you're talking about."

"Sure you don't, Mr. I Don't Believe in Love."

Aggravation lit in my chest. "Are you *still* going on about that? It's been five..." I lowered my voice so Sofia and Niko couldn't hear. "Five *fucking* years."

"Oh, I'm going to give you shit about it for the rest of our lives, so get used to it," Rhys said. "And when you have children, you'll eat your words again." He leaned back and laced his hands behind his head with a smug smile. "Good track record of that happening."

I couldn't stand his ass.

Before I could respond, Stella poked her head out from the kitchen. "Christian? Can you come here? I need your help with something."

"Be right there." I rose and pinned a laughing Rhys with a cool stare. "While I help my *wife*, you think about when Camilla grows up and starts dating," I said, wiping the smile off his face. "Have fun."

Satisfaction filled me when I heard his low growl.

When I walked into the kitchen, I found Stella downing what must've been her fifth glass of water that night.

"Are you sure you don't want any wine?" She wasn't a big drinker, but she usually had a glass or two. "It's a great vintage."

"Yes, I'm sure." She set her glass down and looked at me with an oddly nervous expression. "I can't drink alcohol right now."

She said it with meaning, like I was supposed to know what that meant.

Why would it matter that she wasn't drinking alcohol? Granted, it was a bit odd that she...

I can't drink alcohol right now.

I replayed her words.

Can't. Not *don't want to.*

She *couldn't* drink alcohol, which likely meant...

My pulse slowed into one long, disbelieving beat.

"I didn't want to tell you in front of the others, but I also couldn't wait anymore." Stella's voice lowered. "Christian, I'm pregnant."

"You're pregnant," I repeated.

The words echoed in my head, too gilded with shock to sink in fully.

Stella confirmed with a nod, her face glowing with equal parts excitement and nervousness.

Pregnant. Babies. *Our* baby.

The breath left my lungs in one fell swoop.

I closed the distance between us with two long strides and kissed her fiercely, my heart thudding hard enough to bruise.

Forget every uncharitable thought I'd had about children.

We were going to be parents. I was going to be a father, and I was going to see Stella swell with our child. A little boy, perhaps, with curls and brown skin. Or a little girl with her mother's green eyes and sweet smile.

A fierce protectiveness gripped my chest.

The baby hadn't even been born, and I already wanted to guard them with my life.

A boy or a girl, it didn't matter. All that mattered was that they were ours.

"Does that mean you're happy?" Stella asked hopefully when we broke apart.

My laugh was rough with emotion. "Of course I'm happy, sweetheart. How could I not be?"

I needed to find the best obstetrician in the country ASAP, plus redo the penthouse (which was currently as non-child-proof as it could get), take Stella shopping for maternity clothes, book a babymoon...

"Well, you just called our friends' children little terrors, so..." Her voice held a teasing note.

"Yes, but that won't be *our* child."

Our child would never do to my hair what Alex's did to his.

Stella gave me a wry look. "As much as I'd like to believe our baby will be the first baby in the world that doesn't scream or cry, there's a chance that won't happen. I want you to be prepared."

"I don't care. They could scream and cry all they want, and they'd still be like their mother." I brushed her lips with mine. "Perfect."

A small shudder of pleasure rippled through her body.

"I was right all those years ago," she murmured. "You, Christian Harper, are a softie at heart."

I laughed softly. "Only for you, Butterfly."

I kissed my wife again, and I let her warmth wrap around me while our friends' laughter drifted over from the living room.

The scene was so cheesy and cozy that the old, pre-Stella me would've despised it on principle. But that was the difference between then and now.

Once upon a time, I hadn't believed in love.

Now, I realize that love was the last piece that'd been missing in the puzzle of my life.

With it, I was finally whole.

THE END

Thank you for reading *Twisted Lies!* If you enjoyed this book, I would be grateful if you could leave a review on the platform(s) of your choice.

Reviews are like tips for author, and every one helps!

Much love,
Ana

For bonus Christian/Stella and Twisted series content, visit this link: BookHip.com/STFFHMM

Keep in touch with Ana Huang

Join my Facebook reader group, Ana's Star Squad, to get the latest updates and talk about books, Netflix, and more!

facebook.com/groups/anasstarsquad

You can also find Ana at these places:

Website:
anahuang.com

Bookbub:
bookbub.com/profile/ana-huang

Instagram:
@authoranahuang

Goodreads
goodreads.com/anahuang

ACKNOWLEDGMENTS

To my readers—Thank you for the love you've shown Christian, Stella, and the entire Twisted family. You are the best part of my life as an author, and your kind messages, reviews, posts, and edits always make my day. I adore you.

To Becca—Thank you for being my rock and cheerleader during this entire process. It took many late nights, long calls, and frantic messages, but *we did it*!

To Amy and Britt—Thank you for your keen eyes and for putting up with my tight deadlines. You are rockstars!

To Brittney, Sarah, and Rebecca—We started with Rhys and Bridget and now we're here. Thank you for being my ride and die alphas. You make my stories shine, and I couldn't have done this without you.

To Salma—Your videos and reactions are everything! Your feedback has been so helpful, and you are truly a gem in the book world.

To Aishah—You've been there since the very beginning, and I am so grateful to have you as not only a reader but a friend. From your song suggestions and Twisted cookbook agenda (I swear I would if I could) to your deep affection for Leather the parrot, you always make my day brighter.

To Amber and Michelle—Thank you for keeping me sane and taking the random questions I drop into our group chat with no warning in stride. This indecisive Pisces wouldn't know what to do without you.

To Trinity—Thank you for dealing with all my last minute requests. You are the best!

To Amanda—Thank you as always for the beautiful cover.

To Eleanor Russell and the Piatkus team—Thank you for being such a joy to work with! I couldn't have left my babies in better hands.

To Kimberly Brower—Thank you for all you do. I am endlessly grateful to have you as my agent.

Finally, to the wonderful ladies at Valentine PR—Thank you for your hard work and for making this release possible. I appreciate you!

xo, Ana